# A Triumphal Procession

A Story of Byzantine Valor and Adventure

Basheer Abu-Eid

Cover portrait is from a mosaic of Emperor John Komnenos in Hagia Sophia

Map by Florin Safner

# DEDICATION

To the memory of a great empire that still lives in so many people, in so many ways.

# ACKNOWLEDGEMENT

With a full time job, a loving wife and three wonderful children, finding the time and the atmosphere to write has been a challenge. My wife Amira provided both, making the challenge achievable.

The passion for story and history were first kindled in me by my father whose fascinating bedtime stories I can still remember to this day. My candle is shedding light because he ignited it.

For many of the details, I am grateful to the podcast *The History of Byzantium*. Mr. Robin Pierson's engaging podcast has been my companion throughout my writing period.

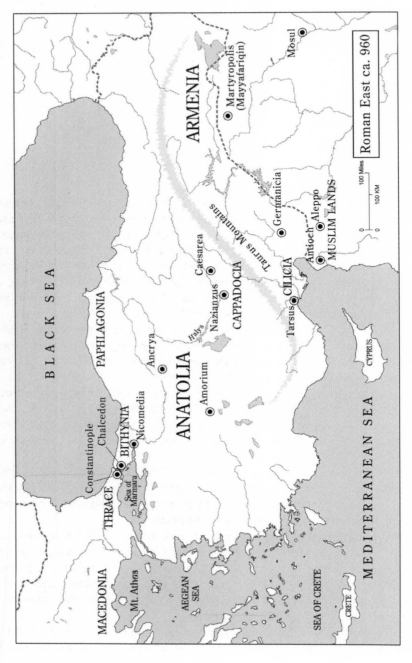

# Chapter One

- ∞∞ -

## Constantinople, Spring 961

It was a little after sunrise when Theodore Sgouros began his daily walk along the main street. Rays of sunlight penetrated the misty air of that early spring morning and slowly spread warmth to the buildings and streets of the Imperial city. Theodore had followed the same route for the past twenty-eight years. By now it almost felt like his feet had a mind of their own, advancing involuntarily towards their destination. In any case, it wasn't a very long walk to the Great Palace, barely half an hour, but it had become part of a morning ritual he wouldn't have traded for anything.

He was once offered, by one of the high officials, residential accommodation within the palace premises, just like the other craftsmen and bureaucrats who populated that city-within-the-city. But he rejected that offer, preferring to live with his family outside the palace walls.

The high porticos on both sides of Mese Street protected him from the summer sun and the winter rain alike. It was delightful to walk through the open-air museum. There was something worth admiring on every corner; and as years passed by, he appreciated the beauty and grandeur of his surroundings even more.

The Mese penetrated the Forum of Constantine, and Theodore followed it through that circular monument which bore the name of the city's founder, the first Christian emperor who six and a half centuries before founded the new capital of the Romans.

Every morning, as Constantinople shook off the darkness of night, he would walk from there down the wide and famous Mese Street. Carriages of all shapes and sizes passed over the well-paved roadway; men and women of all ages and backgrounds pursuing their business and affairs brought the city back to life like blood rushing through the veins of a mighty creature.

Shop owners unlocking their doors always exchanged morning greetings with Theodore. They knew and admired him as an honorable

1

figure in that part of the city.

Refreshing aromas of Indian spices and Arabian incense wafted from the open shops. In fact, one could find practically anything one wanted on Mese Street. It was as if the whole world had pooled all its resources, pouring them into that one particular location, in an unrelenting stream of goods. Hundreds of shops lined both sides and were bursting with exquisite as well as not-so-exquisite goods. Merchant ships and caravans brought linen from Egypt, silk from Syria and China, fur and amber from the northern lands, and sandalwood from India; but also peaches from Thrace, honey from Macedonia and dates from Mesopotamia.

Even though there was great hostility between the Romans and the Saracen Arabs – who more than three centuries before had occupied the empire's wealthy eastern provinces- but the state of war seldom interrupted trade. The desire for profit proved stronger than to be hindered by conflict, Theodore often witnessed the Syrian and Egyptian caravans emptying their cargos in his home city.

But he hardly ever saw any goods arrive from the west. Old Rome along with what was once the empire's western provinces had been lost a long time ago. The barbarians - whose embrace of Christianity had changed very little of their crudeness – founded their kingdoms in the western lands. The ruined city of the popes had little to offer the world anymore. The center of the world had since the time of the Great Constantine shifted to New Rome, the breathtaking capital of the Romans.

As he approached the Great Palace, something captured his interest. He caught a glimpse of a garment of patterned Chinese silk from one of the shops. It attracted his eye so much that he couldn't resist the urge to go straight in.

"Good morning, Cyril," he cordially greeted the shop owner who was then examining a piece of blue silk.

"Aha! I was almost sure you would come in! It was that red patterned piece that lured you inside, wasn't it? The moment I displayed that piece, I knew you wouldn't be able to ignore it. I just purchased thirty identical pieces from a Syrian merchant yesterday. Marvelous, isn't it?"

"Well, yes," Theodore said with a smile that diminished in comparison to Cyril's exuberance, inspecting the piece gently with his fingers. "The patterns are beautiful, and the color is vivid; but honestly, the quality of the thread is no match for the products of the Imperial Workshops."

"And have I ever claimed otherwise?" Cyril protested, shifting in a blink of an eye from jubilation to surprise "Everyone knows that the

Imperial Workshops produce the finest silk, but who can afford that? Not too many, trust me! Yet, this piece is so beautiful. These Syrian craftsmen have golden fingers! Even you couldn't resist its beauty."

"You will make good money selling these pieces. Have a nice day my friend. I can't be late."

"The Lord be with you. Come by in the afternoon for a cup of tea!" Cyril almost shouted, following his friend out to the busy street.

Theodore was back on his way and in few minutes was standing in front of the main palace gate, called the Chalkis – Bronze – Gate. It was a majestic entrance, befitting the compound that lay beyond it. A large icon of Jesus Christ the King stood above the gate, gazing with piercing eyes at all who entered.

The Great Palace was where Theodore had spent most of his adult life. He was the private tailor to the Imperial household; a position he never dreamed of when his career began over three decades before. From childhood, he had developed a love for fabrics. He was amazed by the fact that changing one's clothes could totally change the way a person saw the world, as well as the way the world saw him. By the time he was twelve, he could tell the difference between a twill silk and a damask silk. His father had sent him to be trained by one of the finest tailors in Constantinople, and that tailor soon discovered in his new pupil a latent talent and creativity combined with unique dexterity and a love for learning. It wasn't long until the Imperial recruiters discovered his talent and lucky Theodore was enrolled among the army of craftsmen and artisans that served the First Family.

In his long career at the Palace, Theodore had seen emperors come and go, but it wasn't until the late emperor Constantine Porphyrogenitus that he was elevated to his present status. The current Emperor, Romanos II, and his wife, the Empress Theophano, were exceptional individuals. Both were very young, kind, and outstandingly good-looking. Their two little boys, Basil and Constantine, made them the ideal royal family, capturing the hearts of their subjects.

When it came to dressing the royal family, the Emperor was content with simple clothes, a long flowing tunic, trousers and the royal red boots. The Empress's taste, however, appeared to be more revolutionary. In fact, a connection could easily be made between the Empress's wild taste and her upbringing. Every emperor, when choosing a bride would inevitably marry beneath him, for anyone and everyone is inferior to Roman royalty. In the case of Emperor Romanos, that phrase couldn't have been truer. The gorgeous Theophano was but an innkeeper's daughter whose beauty completely captivated the young Emperor; so

3

much so as to inspire Romanos to obtain a promise from his father, Constantine Porphyrogenitus, allowing him to marry any woman of his choosing. The unsuspecting father didn't know that his son and heir to the Roman throne had had his eyes on a common girl. But a promise is a promise, let alone a royal one, and soon enough, the sixteen-year-old beauty became the beloved wife of the twenty-year-old crown prince. The dying emperor didn't have the energy to stand in the way of his son and successor.

Back then, news of the prince's wedding to the innkeeper's daughter had stirred much gossip in the city, from the porters down at the harbor, right up to court officials. Some were happy for the stability the new family might bring to the empire, but the aristocrats were resentful of this scandal, as each of them had hoped his daughter would be the next empress. Unlike most of those in the court, Theodore truly liked the new Empress, and when her father-in-law Constantine died at the young age of forty-six, he refused to believe rumors that she had poisoned him.

Theophano's strong personality, superior intelligence, and perfect figure made serving her much easier than her predecessors. She knew exactly what she wanted; choosing the designs, fabrics, and colors with ease, wasting no time, completely consistent with the reputation she had developed as a determined and knowledgeable woman. But in spite of her less-than-modest upbringing and her young age, she never overcompensated for any feelings of inferiority that one would expect. When it came to Theodore, he believed she deserved the crown she married into a thousand times more than the innkeeper's apron she was born into. During the short sessions when she would discuss her family's attire with him, she would speak and act in a gracious and natural way, uncommon to the predominant affectation of most inhabitants of the palace. He felt the empress could sense his genuine faithfulness, and she rewarded it with her trust.

At the gate, the guards saw before them a figure they knew all too well. The fifty-five-year-old man was of medium build and upright posture. He had small brown eyes, a thin dark beard, and a cheerful face.

There were about a dozen of the Varangian guards stationed at the gate. To someone who wasn't familiar with these Norsemen, their appearance was indeed frightful. Tall, robust, and armed with the traditional Scandinavian axes which they wielded with great skill, these warriors were extremely loyal, well-disciplined, and very well paid. They had only recently been recruited as the emperor's bodyguard, arriving from their gloomy northern lands. They proved worthy of every nomisma they received. Two of them greeted Theodore as they opened the gate into that walled compound of marvelous buildings and lush gardens that comprised the beating heart of the empire.

Theodore walked on a wide path of white marble surrounded on both sides by flowerbeds and large birch trees that were beginning to sprout in springtime. A few workers could be seen affectionately taking care of the gardens.

The tailor's workshop occupied a part of a building entirely reserved for the people who managed the daily works and necessary maintenance of the palace. It had a spacious hall on the ground floor with large windows overlooking the green area outside. There in that workshop, Theodore oversaw the royal family's clothing, assisted by weavers, dyers, and tailors, supervised by his assistant, Paul.

A tall, thin man in his mid-thirties, Paul had come to Theodore's workshop as a teenager and owed all that he knew to his master and tutor.

"Good day," he said, entering the workshop with his familiar deep voice.

"Good day, master!" came a unanimous reply from his industrious employees After all, Easter was less than a month away, and the ceremonial clothing of the royal family was only half-completed. Paul came to meet his master and receive Theodore's instructions for the day's work.

"The weather is finally getting warmer, sir!" said Paul hurriedly, smiling.

"Yes indeed, Paul," Theodore replied, taking off his coat. "Have the weavers started yet with the new silk thread we received for her majesty's cloak?"

"They have, sir, and its beauty is beginning to show. Today, we should also be receiving the order of shellfish purple from the Royal Warehouses."

"Excellent. Now, Paul, please bring me his majesty's lorum and the pearl box."

Theodore had been working for the past few weeks on a lorum for the Emperor. It was a silken scarf draped around the body, heavily jeweled with pearls and sewn with gold threads; the centerpiece of the emperor's festive clothing for the coming great feast. It was a work that required talent and experience that very few possessed.

To his staff, Theodore wasn't just their boss. He was the man they spent more time with than their own families, a man who looked after them and did all he could to help in times of need. They all remembered when Lambros, the old weaver, lost his house to a fire, five years before, and ended up on the street with his wife. As soon as he heard about it,

Theodore went and spoke with the palace chamberlain, and the old man and his family were granted one hundred nomismata in compensation; more than enough to buy a new house. They also remembered when one of their own, Martha, got terribly sick and was closer to death than to life. Everyone felt very sorry for her five children, the youngest of whom was barely two years old at the time, but Theodore had to do more than feel sorry. Upon Theodore's intercession, the Emperor sent his private physician to Martha's humble home, and after a couple of weeks of therapy and care, the poor woman regained her strength. She always said afterward that she owed her life to Theodore.

Theodore sat behind his working desk, and resumed from where he had left it the day before. His face was unusually somber as his needle pierced the beautiful red silk, dotting it with little white pearls. Paul sat at an opposite table, cutting a piece of linen with a pair of large metal scissors. Suddenly, Theodore lifted his head, looked at Paul and said, "When is your wife due to give birth, Paul?"

"In about two months, sir!" he replied, excited that his boss had shown an interest in his private life. Encouraged, he asked, "What is it like being a father?"

"A father!" Theodore said with pride, his eyes glowing. "Once you become a father, you should first accept the great gift that life gives you, and then say farewell to a thousand other things. You magically stop worrying about yourself and start worrying about how to shelter these new little creatures from the troubles life continually sends you. While they are still small, you do all you can to protect them and keep them under your wing; but once they have grown and become independent men and women, there isn't much you can do but watch and pray.

"You know, Paul, I still can't believe how quickly time passes. It seems just like yesterday when they were so little, filling the house with noise and giggles. Mark my words. Once a day is done, it will never come back again and with every passing year, they will grow a bit older. Cherish every moment with them knowing that it is a unique gift.".

Paul, who had listened attentively to his master's words, looked back down on his work and said as he cut another piece of the cloth:

"I've always had the impression that your two sons Alexander and John are the kind of children any father could ever ask for."

"Indeed, they are, I couldn't complain." He took a deep breath and slowly exhaled. "I want you to go and check on the weavers now, Paul."

"Yes, sir. Right away"

Paul walked to the far end of the workshop where half a dozen weavers worked on a couple of wooden weaving machines that produced just as much noise as they did the fascinating cloth. He left his superior deep in thought.

*Paul's words are the truth. Both my sons are good men.* He nodded twice then cut the silk thread with a small pair of scissors. *Alexander is doing fine at his fur shop, he has gotten married and will soon make me a grandfather, I hope, but John ... if only John had listened and stayed home.*

*But then again, how could he have resisted such a temptation when the only thing anyone his age wanted was to sail on that campaign? I should stop blaming him. The whole city talked of only one thing: the Cretan expedition, retrieving Crete from the Arabs. Soldiers were being enlisted by the thousands, supplies amassed at the harbor, and ships ... oh, the scene of those hundreds of dromons gathered at the harbor certainly was something the young generation had not seen before, and it made quite an impression. Those imperial recruiters, too, who were touring the city, calling upon the able-bodied men to join the campaign, promising good pay, spoils, and honor. Then it was the Patriarch's turn with his fiery sermons in Hagia Sophia, calling upon Christians to save their captive brothers and sisters from the tyrannical rule of the infidel. Put all of that together with the spirit of a nineteen-year-old so eager for adventure, and there we have a warrior ready to board the first ship leaving for the front, completely ignoring the fact that he had never wielded a sword in his life!*

He shook his head then glanced at his staff. They all appeared to be working just fine so he just dipped his chin again and let his mind wander.

*He worked with his brother in the fur shop, and fared quite well, or so I wanted to believe. Was I that naïve to think he would continue in that job for the rest of his life?*

*After all, he is my youngest, he never really felt the weight of family responsibility upon his shoulders. He is a free soul that cannot be tied to one place.*

When John was ten, Theodore had gotten him a tutor to teach him reading, writing, and mathematics. The tutor had said that he was a clever boy and he learned to read and write fairly quickly, but it soon became apparent that books were not going to be his passion. By the age of fourteen, he was going with his brother to the shop. Every day, he opened the shop with Alexander, and would meet all sorts of customers and merchants coming from lands far away and would ask them endless questions about their countries and their language. His father would watch him sometimes as he listened to their replies with eyes wide open, and he would marvel at such a curious soul. Then came the time when that curiosity and the love of adventure pulled him to where, as he described it, 'history is to be made'.

Ever since his son left with the army, such memories visited Theodore more often.

*Only one letter in nine months? If only you knew how desperate your mother is for learning your whereabouts.*

Theodore remembered the day they received that solitary letter, which did include some quite surprising news. Two months before, a ship had arrived from Crete carrying letters from the front. A messenger had dropped a letter from John. Theodore's wife couldn't believe it and begged him not to open the letter until she had done something of the utmost importance. She put her scarf on her head and ran with his daughter-in-law, Zoe, to the Church of the Holy Apostles, where she lit a candle in front of the icon of Our Lady and prayed fervently for his safety. When she returned home, they sat down and opened his letter together. They had never imagined the kind of news contained in that piece of paper.

They learned that the army had been laying siege around Chandax for half a year and engaging in skirmishes with the Saracen forces both on land and sea. The Romans had more men, and were better equipped. The Saracen Emir of Crete, however, had vowed not to surrender but to fight till victory or death. John made sure to praise the wisdom and bravery of general Nicephorus and, though he did not relay the details, he wrote that he had been serving in the general's own bodyguard unit.

*Young John in the domestic's bodyguard! And I wanted him to stay behind and sell fur. But at least you don't get killed selling fur! Oh God, if he doesn't return soon, I will probably end up losing my mind. His mother hasn't had a good night's sleep ever since he left.*

He picked up a few shiny pearls and threaded them, one by one, with a golden thread.

*Gold and jewels … there must be heaps of them inside Chandax. That pirate Emir of Crete has been amassing wealth in his capital, seized from countless ships by the pirates under his command every year.*

Theodore was so absorbed in his work and thoughts, he did not notice the man who had entered into the workshop. The hush his presence produced finally caught his attention. He raised his head and saw a messenger walking towards him.

"Her majesty wants to see you."

It was one of those days.

Theodore got up off his chair and walked with the man in military uniform, only pausing for a moment to place the precious lorum in its ornamented mahogany box, then carrying it with him to the royal chambers.

# Chapter Two

## - ဆၢၳ -

Theodore left with the messenger around noon. They walked through the palace gardens for about a hundred paces until they reached a wide stairway of polished white marble. Carrying his precious work, he slowly ascended the stairs leading to a huge open terrace lined on both sides with the same tough specimens of Varangians. From there they entered the spacious reception hall called *Nineteen Couches,* for the obvious reason that it contained that exact number of couches, and continued their walk to the *Boukoleon Palace*, housing the throne hall and the royal family's residence. A tall gilded door was thrown open, leading to a great hall lavishly decorated with mosaics and charming artifacts.

Theodore had been to this part of the palace countless times, yet every time he walked through that door, he could not help being overcome with awe, viewing the most impressive spectacle.

The empress was sitting on the slightly lower of two thrones set in the middle of the hall. The throne next to her was empty. Her stunning beauty and imperial garb gave her the appearance of a Greek goddess. As Theodore approached and prostrated himself in front of her, she stepped down the two small steps that elevated the throne above the rest of the hall.

"Rise up, Theodore, and show us what you have prepared."

Theodore stood up straight and proudly presented the empress with the lorum.

She examined it with apparent satisfaction. "You have done an excellent job as usual, Theodore. But you still need to complete the embroidery down to the waist line as we agreed before … and the collar needs more gold threads."

"Yes, Your Majesty," answered Theodore, as the artisan continued to record the empress' instructions and answer her queries.

A few minutes later, quick footsteps were heard approaching, and a group of three men entered the hall. Two court servants hurriedly followed their master; a slight beardless man in a black robe and with piercing blue eyes.

The moment Theodore saw them, he realized that his conversation with the empress had come to an end. He bowed respectfully and withdrew to one side of the hall. The little man in black was none other than the chamberlain Bringas.

If Theodore's opinion were sought, he would have declared without doubt that for a castrate of little stature, Joseph Bringas had more 'balls' than most of the palace officials put together. Although an illegal operation, he had been castrated by his parents while still a child in hope of holding a high position in the future, in the service of some aristocrat, or possibly the royal palace. The little boy survived the dangerous procedure, carried out in his home province of Paphlagonia, far away from the eyes of the authorities. A few years later, a series of lucky coincidences led him to the royal palace. He quickly ascended the hierarchy until appointed chamberlain by the young emperor Romanus.

The little man bowed with respect in front of the empress while the two servants prostrated themselves on the marble floor.

From his abrupt entrance and hasty walk, the empress could see that his arrival was a matter of some importance. It was midday, and for two hours a day the Royal family normally enjoyed a private life away from the burdens of public responsibility and palace bureaucracy. The only thing that crossed her mind at that moment was the safety of her husband. He had been away for the past two days on one of his frequent hunting trips. Romanus adored this sport of royalty, but hunting was an activity that involved more accidents and conspiracies against the life of a monarch than any other, she thought. Could something bad have happened to him?

In her eagerness to know what the matter was, Theophano quickly said: "Speak up, Joseph! What brings you here at this hour?" she demanded from a man for whom she never felt a genuine liking.

His next words, though, were the last thing she had expected to hear. "I have great news, Your Majesty! A commander of one of our naval squadrons has just arrived with tidings of a decisive victory in Crete and the complete recovery of the island!"

"Oh, thank God! Our efforts have not gone in vain! Nicephorus has proven to be worthy of the mission entrusted to him!"

The empress' praise appeared to dampen the chamberlain's initial enthusiasm. "Indeed, Your Majesty," he said in a less exited yet still eloquent tone. "What more than a great victory like this to befit the inauguration of his majesty's prosperous reign?"

"Make sure you deliver this news to the emperor immediately!"

"Yes, Your Majesty. He needs to be called back at once so as to be present in the capital when the great news is announced to the people. It should take no more than two days for his majesty to return, at my best guess."

"My thoughts, as well," she said. "But how can we be sure that the news isn't already spreading in the capital as we speak? This squadron commander and his mariners could be easily boasting in the city now."

"I took care of that, Your Majesty"

"Good work. Now, hasten to call the emperor back!"

The chamberlain gestured to one of the two assistants who quickly grasped the visual instruction. He quickly but respectfully left the throne room to initiate the chain of communications that would reach the emperor at his hunting retreat.

Just as the servant was leaving, both the empress and the chamberlain suddenly noticed Theodore, whose presence had been completely forgotten. He had been standing like a statue next to a marble column at one side of the hall with the jeweled cloth in his hands.

Bringas gave Theodore a menacing look, and, crooking his index finger, called him to come closer.

Theodore approached slowly, and when he was close enough, the man in black whispered,    "Listen to me well, tailor, if one word of what you have just heard comes out prematurely, you shall only have yourself to blame. Am I clear?"

"Yes, lord. My lips are sealed," Theodore said, struggling to find the right words, then bowed a deep bow.

"You have a son with that campaign, don't you, Theodore?" asked Theophano.

"Yes, Your Majesty."

"Alright, Theodore, you may be excused now. We shall continue our talk some other time."

"Yes, Your Majesty."

As the tailor left the throne hall and descended the stairs back to his workshop, he couldn't remember the last time when he felt so happy. The safe return of his son was now guaranteed. The war was over, and a great victory had been achieved. The boys were finally coming home. He knew, though, that he had to keep the news to himself. Not even his beloved wife Anastasia could hear of this. The chamberlain's orders were a serious business.

# Chapter Three

- ೞೞೞ -

That Saturday evening, Theodore was on his way back home as night spread its wings over New Rome. Anastasia was almost done preparing the evening meal. Helping her was her daughter-in-law, Zoe. Both Zoe and her husband Alexander, the elder son of the Sgouros family, lived together with the parents as all happy extended families did.

"Oh, you are finally here, dear Theodore," Anastasia said from inside the kitchen. "At least one of you two has arrived on time. I wish Alexander would come before the soup gets cold."

"He will not be long, I'm sure," Theodore confirmed. "It's cold and windy outside and there is scarcely anyone in the streets."

Alexander owned a shop down by the harbor that sold a popular commodity: fur. After peace had been established with the northern Rus tribes some fifteen years before, these pagans stopped their frequent naval raids against Constantinople and, instead of warships, merchant boats arrived at the capital bringing to its markets fur and other commodities. The treaty signed with their Prince Igor gave them advantageous trading privileges and safer, more reliable access to the riches of Constantinople.

Thus, five years before, Alexander took his father's advice and opened a shop that sold these Nordic products. It had since grown in reputation and revenue, becoming one of the more famous shops of its kind.

Anastasia left Zoe in the kitchen and came to greet her husband who had washed up, changed into more comfortable clothes and was sitting at the round wooden table in the middle room.

She came with a cup of warm chamomile tea, sweetened with honey, placed it in front of him and said with a smile, "This should warm you up after your walk from the palace."

He clasped her hands in his and, looking into her eyes, he saw the person he had married thirty years before. Though she was in her late forties, Anastasia was still as beautiful as when he first knew her. Her long golden hair, now mixed with a few gray strands, was tied back in a thick knot. Her cheerful round face shone with the inner peace and great faith she possessed and lived by. She was a real angel, and he adored her.

"Thank you, my dear. How was your day?"

"Glory to God!" she said, smiling. "Zoe and I went to the Church of St. Euphemia. We attended the morning liturgy. The church was packed. As always, we poured out our hearts before Our Lady to give John her protection and return him safe to us. So many other families were there praying for their own, even little children standing next to their mothers and repeating the prayers they were taught at home. Oh, Theodore, if you only knew how eager everyone is for this campaign to end."

"I know dear Anastasia, I know."

"We then passed by the market and bought some lentil for the soup. I'm sure you are going to like it. How about you? Still working on that lorum, aren't you?"

"Yes, still working on the final touches. God willing, I will be done with it by Monday."

Not wishing to go into detail about the day's events, Theodore took a sip from the warm chamomile. Zoe finally emerged from the kitchen to greet her father-in law, a young woman in her early twenties, with light brown hair and a slightly elongated face. She greeted the family patriarch and had just sat at the table when the door opened, and Alexander finally entered. He was tall, with broad shoulders and of muscular build. One would wonder how the average-built Theodore and the tiny Anastasia could have produced such a sturdy man as him. He wore a thick fur coat and was rubbing his hands for warmth.

"Good evening," he said, smiling. "I see you all gathered here waiting for me. I hope I didn't keep you waiting for long."

"Not at all. We just sat down. The soup is still warm," the mother quickly responded as Alexander took off his coat and proceeded to kiss the hands of both his parents, then planted a kiss on his wife's cheek.

He took his place at the table while the two women brought in the food from the kitchen. Lentil soup, black bread, a plate of green olives and some spring onions. It was a typical Lenten meal.

"Today, the strangest thing happened at the harbor," Alexander said, dipping a piece of bread in the soup.

The other three faces around the table looked at him curiously.

"I was bargaining with a woman over a coat and a pair of boots, the difference between us had already been reduced to merely two miliaresions, when clamor from the outside pulled my attention. I looked and saw people calling on one another and pointing through the gate towards the sea. Eager to learn what was going on, I let the woman have the merchandise with the price she wanted and stepped out of the shop to have a look myself. A dromon appeared on the horizon and was sailing fast toward the harbor. Suspecting it to be one of our fighting ships from Crete, a small crowd gathered at the harbor, awaiting it to drop anchor. Shop owners, porters and mariners. I too went to see in hope of hearing any news the ship might be carrying from the front. But just as it drew closer to the berth, everyone heard a sudden uproar coming from behind. I looked over my shoulder and saw the carriage of the chamberlain Bringas, accompanied by the usual guard, riding swiftly toward us. The soldiers manning the sea walls must have seen the vessel long before we did and sent word of it to the Palace. The guards pushed us away and cleared the way for the carriage which came to a stop by the sea gate.

"A few minutes later, the ship was in its berth. The chamberlain disembarked from his carriage, all dressed in black, and waited on the pier for the ship commander to cross the gangway. We all looked from afar and saw the commander descend to the pier. He bowed to the chamberlain and handed him something, probably a letter, then after a short conversation the droungarios – the ship's captain – set sail again, leaving as quickly as it had come. The chamberlain, having made sure of the ship's departure, went back to his carriage and dashed off."

"What a strange occurrence," Zoe said. "Didn't they even resupply with food and fresh water?"

"I'm telling you, I've never seen anything like it. We stood for a while looking stunned before speculations about the truth of the matter began to spring. They spanned from suggesting a crushing defeat in Crete to an Arab attack in the east," he took a short pause to have another bite.

Theodore looked at his wife and saw worry suddenly drawn upon her face. "That ship could have come for any of a multitude of reasons," he said trying to tone down the impact his son's words had left.

As they went on eating their soup silently, the fact that Theodore could not comfort his family with the information in his possession tormented him. He only hoped that the emperor would return soon from his hunting trip and news of the victory be announced to the populace.

# Chapter Four

- ∽◌◌◌◌∾ -

"What is it that you want, Joseph?" complained the youthful monarch who hated being bothered with matters of state while still in bed, or at any time for that matter.

"This is really important, Your Majesty. He will be arriving soon, and you haven't yet decided how to deal with him," said the only man in the empire who was allowed to intrude upon the emperor's privacy and wake him up.

"Do we have to discuss this now? What time is it anyway?" He yawned, projecting forth a strong smell of wine.

"It is almost noon, Your Majesty," he replied mechanically and signaled for a servant to open the drapes, emitting a burst of bright light into the royal bedroom.

"Fine, fine, say what you want but be quick, I haven't recovered from yesterday. Those accursed Thracian deer can be quite elusive," he said, sitting up and rubbing his eyes with his palm. "We chased a couple of them deep into the forest for hours. I really don't know how that messenger of yours was able to find us. But it was really fantastic, you must come with us one day."

"I'm sure it was, Your Majesty. Now about our issue …"

"What issue? We have just recovered Crete. It is a time for celebration! Your nomination of Nicephorus to lead the campaign could not have been more successful. What are you complaining about now?"

"Well, Your Majesty, that is the root of the problem. Nominating a renowned general to lead a campaign is one thing; but having him complete his mission successfully and return in triumph is another. He is becoming a threat; a danger worse than the Arabs."

"This is ludicrous. I know Nicephorus, he's not like that!"

"One can know people only so much, Your Majesty. Power and popularity are an intoxicating mixture."

"He has been Domestic of the Schools for more than five years, the supreme commander of the eastern armies, and he has shown us nothing but loyalty."

"*Shown* is the keyword here, Your Majesty. We can only see what he shows us. Who knows what he is thinking about right now? He has great victories to his credit, the entire fleet and a vast army at his command, all arriving here very soon. It is better to be safe than sorry."

"The man has won every battle against the infidel," continued the Emperor in an attempt to describe the Nicephorus he knew.

"And that troubles me most, Your Majesty. I would rather have a domestic that wins every other battle than one who amasses fame and power incessantly."

"This is insane, Bringas, and you know it. You would rather have us lose against the Arabs? It sounds like treason to me."

"On the contrary, Your Majesty, treason would be for me to allow someone else than you to capture the hearts and minds of the people. Please consider the measures I outlined, Your Majesty."

"You just never give up, do you? I shall think about what you suggested and let you know later." he said, slipping back under the sheets.

"Do we announce the news of victory today, perhaps in the afternoon?" the chamberlain asked in his constant effort to remind his sovereign of his duties.

"No!" Romanus replied through the fluffy pillow, with closed eyes. "Leave it till tomorrow morning!"

"Fine, Your Majesty. One last thing before I go, though."

"What now? What other thing? Will you not let me have any rest?"

"Polyeuctus, the patriarch, came to me this morning with a complaint," he said, undeterred by the monarch's complaints.

"What does that grumpy old fool want?"

"Word has spread that you have been hunting during lent."

"So?"

"It is considered a sin by the Church, Your Majesty."

"Tell Polyeuctus he can go to hell. I am emperor and I shall do as I please."

"I do not disagree, Your Majesty, but for the sake of image, your image in front of your subjects as a just and pious ruler, I believe it would be beneficial if you abstained from hunting these coming days, as well as the other activities that go along with it. You know what I mean."

"Alright, alright. Now close those damn curtains and leave, and don't let anyone disturb me, not even Theophano. Am I clear?"

"Clear as crystal, Your Majesty."

# Chapter Five

- ℰℛℂℬ -

Two days had passed since the news of the victory became known to Theodore. They were two especially hard days for him. He watched his wife helplessly, her heart plagued by uncertainty, knowing that he couldn't provide her with the information in his possession that would ease her suffering.

It was Monday morning, and Theodore was getting dressed for work when a half-opened window conveyed the distant ringing of bells from the Hagia Sophia. It was not unusual to hear the morning bells echoing in the greatest city in Christendom. But a moment later a second set of bells began chiming and a third and a fourth until a thousand belfries filled the air with a jubilant symphony. It didn't take Theodore long to guess the reason. Finally, he could get this burden off his chest.

Though it was cold and damp, the people opened their windows and doors and ventured out onto the streets full of curiosity.

"Put your shoes on and run to the church of St. Euphemia. Find out what this is about," Theodore ordered his son.

On his way, Alexander was met by a couple of young lads running back in the opposite direction. "We have won! Crete is ours!"

"What else do you know?" Alexander stopped them to inquire, and one shouted: "We won, we won! They say the army will be arriving back in a few days; just after Easter!"

It was the piece of news everyone had waited for eagerly.

\*\*\*

It took but a few minutes for the good news to spread over the entire metropolis. Services of thanksgiving were announced for that afternoon with the main event taking place in Hagia Sophia where a sublime service was to be held by the patriarch Polyeuctus in the presence of the emperor himself.

The recapture of Crete from the Arabs was reason enough for the entire empire to celebrate. The Saracen piratical emirate which had established itself on that island a century and a half before had been

17

ravaging Roman shores, plundering coastal cities and capturing ships at sea; something which made trade and travel in the eastern Mediterranean almost impossible. Campaign after campaign had miserably failed to regain the island to Roman sovereignty, but this one was obviously different. The large and rich island was back in the fold and the victory was indeed intoxicating. It was an unmistakable sign of God's favor to his people.

The preparations to receive the victorious army and its outstanding commander, the domestic Nicephorus Phocas, were already underway. The usual parade route of celebrations was being decorated with banners, flags and other symbols of victory.

"Did you hear that, my dear?" Theodore looked at his wife whose tears of joy rolled down her cheeks. "Your prayers have been answered and John will be among us in but a few days."

"Glory to God!" she said, and wiped her face with the back of her palm as if ashamed of her tears.. Theodore could sense his wife's immense happiness. He was simply feeling the same.

"I shall leave now," he said to her, putting his coat on. "I might return early today."

"May the Virgin shield you under her protection." She crossed herself.

In spite of the thrilling news, Theodore made it to the palace for the last time before Easter, but he noticed on his way that the city was not the same. The news of victory and the fact that Pascha was less than a week away made that Monday morning exceptionally busy, adding stir to the usually bustling streets.

On his way, he came across a religious procession headed by a dozen clergy, penetrating the crowded Mese Street, all wearing their colorful vestments. A young deacon holding high a tall wooden cross marched a few steps ahead of them and on both sides were two more deacons swaying silver censers, filling the air with a scent of devotion.

A multitude of pious-looking people chanted, "O Lord, Save Thy People and Bless Thine Inheritance," temporarily transforming the street into an open place of worship with additional participants joining the procession on its way to Hagia Sophia.

***

Holy Week had begun, and the Sgouros family's daily activities revolved around the church services. There were morning services and evening services. Fasting took a most austere form. On Great Friday, the family did not consume any food or drink except for a little bread and some water in the evening. It was unthinkable to indulge in the pleasures of the body when the Lord himself was nailed to the cross. From morning till afternoon, all the capital's church bells sounded slow monotonous rings, commemorating the death of the Nazarene.

That awesome afternoon, the view of black-clad women making their way to attend the service of lamentation conjured up the image of the few grieving women who long ago stood by the cross on a barren hill in Palestine.

It was a dramatic change from the atmosphere of jubilation that prevailed just a few days before. Yet, amid all the devotional melancholy, a flame of joy burnt in the hearts of the people.

On the evening of the Great and Holy Saturday, the churches were beginning to fill. The Cathedral of Hagia Sophia was where the royal family celebrated Pascha along with the state elite, the aristocracy, dignitaries and about ten thousand other citizens. The largest church in Christendom had been built five centuries before by the magnificent Justinian in enormous proportions and decorated with the finest marbles, mosaics and icons brought from all over the empire. Its towering dome extended a permanent invitation to God to descend to earth and be present with a people who had done an outstanding job reaching out to him.

On evening services like this, the edifice was lit by a great number of exquisite brass chandeliers hanging from the floating dome, as if suspended from Heaven.

The emperor arrived. Surrounded by his entourage, he cut through the loyal crowds with majesty and grandeur, heading towards the sanctuary where his presence would initiate the service. He walked right beside Theodore and Anastasia wearing his ecclesiastical vestments.

Anastasia took a good look at the lavishly decorated lorum draped from his shoulders.

*This is what Theodore has been working on for the past months. It is absolutely wonderful! Never seen such giant gems in my life.*

The Empress Theophano and her two little boys walked behind Romanus and ascended the *loge of the empress* accompanied by the countless servants and members of the entourage who followed the royal family like their shadows.

The reverent silence that accompanied the entrance of the royal family finally came to an end when the service began. Dozens of clerics and psalters celebrated the Divine Liturgy with unique discipline and diligence. Long hours passed in prayer with the standing multitude of worshippers seeming not the least fatigued.

A little after midnight came the long-awaited moment when the Patriarch emerged from the sanctuary and announced loudly and jubilantly the famous phrase, "Christ is risen!"

All those in the cathedral responded with a unanimous, "Indeed He is risen!" and the bells began to chime joyously.

The exultation and triumph in the faces of the men and women was obvious and prevalent. It was as if they had learnt of the Lord's resurrection for the first time; as if Christ had just left his tomb that moment; as if each one of them had been Peter or Maria Magdalena. Some had tears rolling down their faces, others were fervently crossing themselves and the entire multitude appeared to be going through a state of spiritual ecstasy.

Theodore glanced at Anastasia. She was in deep prayer, her face serene, her eyes closed. He could almost tell for sure what was on her mind at that moment: the resurrected Lord, and her home-coming son. The liturgy continued for another three hours and was concluded at dawn with the blessings of the Patriarch and the Emperor.

***

In the morning, it was easy for Theodore, standing on his roof terrace, to notice how Easter of this year was special. Not only did this day of spiritual triumph coincide with a distinguished military triumph, but the weather, too, played its part in making it truly ideal. A long period of damp and cold weather had ended. The sun was brightly shining again over the rain-washed red rooftops and glittering church domes. The Sea of Marmara was calm and clear as if announcing its preparedness to host the armada of ships that would soon sail through its blue waters.

With the longest fast in the ecclesiastical year finally coming to an end, the smell of roast meat wafted around the city. Banquets were being prepared in every house and palace. Both old and young, poor and rich, foreign and native, celebrated the most important day of the year with food, drink and dance. In the city squares, makeshift kitchens were temporarily built with donations from the wealthy to feed the less fortunate. No person was to remain hungry on the *feast of feasts*.

In the Sgouros's home, the table was being set. The family had been away in the morning, exchanging greetings with extended family and friends, but now they were back home for the yearly meal.

Anastasia said with a twinge of sadness as she carried a round metal tray full of roast lamb chops, "I hoped a miracle would happen and John would be home for Easter. He loves this food so much. It would have been just perfect to have all of us here together on this day. But what am I complaining about? Thanks be to God for his great mercy. The war is over and a few days delay is nothing!"

"Yes, mother," said Alexander, chuckling. "Only a few days and your beloved boy will be sitting next to you at this table, and then we get to eat roast lamb for a *second* time in a fortnight!"

Theodore came from the bedroom wearing his comfortable home clothes and said as he took his place around the table, "The weather, my dear, has been as unfavorable for sailing as you have ever witnessed, but now with this shining sun outside and the gentle breeze, I have no doubt of their imminent arrival!"

"From your mouth to God's ears!" she said with a shining face.

"But I have this feeling that we will not see in John that same young lad who left us nine months ago." Zoe speculated. "This period of hard military life away from home must have transformed him one way or another."

"It shall not be long until we find out," Theodore replied, raising his glass of wine and adding, "To John's safe return!"

"To John's safe return!" replied the others, their glasses held high.

# Chapter Six

## - ∞∞ -

On the bow of the command ship stood a man in uniform, grasping the wooden parapet with one hand and holding a small book in the other. He looked about fifty years of age, short but sturdy, his small black eyes alternating between the book and the open horizon in front of him, his lips murmuring almost inaudibly. The sky above him was clear, except for a few scattered white puffs, and the gentle breeze that bellied out the sails carried with it a refreshing spray of seawater.

Every once in a while, he looked over his shoulder to catch a glimpse of the forest of masts that sailed in pursuit, a sight that made his face glow with pride. Contemplating the events of this busy and exhausting, yet glorious chapter of his life, he thought how nine months ago, he had led the same fleet in the opposite direction. In truth, his life story contained numerous chapters, just as successful, but also a few grievous ones. He was by now undeniably the most successful general the empire had seen for a long time. His troops had not suffered a single defeat in years, scoring victory after victory both east and west, on land and sea alike.

There had been one struggle, though, that had brought him an everlasting sorrow: a loss no human sword could arrest, a fate no shield or armor could avert. When the angel of death had knocked on his door a few years earlier, demanding the souls of both his wife and young son, his army of physicians and priests could do nothing to prevent the defeat. Ever since then, he had, in one sense, stopped living. A solemn vow had been made: he would never eat meat or enjoy the pleasures of life from then on. His true desire was to bury himself in some monastery and spend his remaining years preparing his soul for the other world, where he could spend eternity with the only woman he had ever loved, and the only son she had given him.

But desires were one thing, and responsibilities were something altogether different. First, there were a few missions that needed to be accomplished. Crete was liberated, a great success, but his work was far from finished. The Roman armies in the east had been under his leadership for years, but the Cretan campaign required someone no less experienced than himself. Now that the task was accomplished, he couldn't wait to travel east to where more aggressive Arabs were conducting their incursions deep inside Romania without being properly chastised. Though at sea, his mind travelled all the way to the mountains of Anatolia. The vast provinces which during the reigns of Heraclius and Constans had been lost wholesale to the Saracens were being onerously recovered by piecemeal conquest – at least those provinces that were perceived recoverable. Having brought back such an important province into the Roman fold, he had all reasons to be proud. He had directed that lengthy campaign better than anyone else could have, he was certain. Many had failed miserably where he succeeded. There was no arrogance whatsoever in thinking himself indispensable to the empire, only plain truth. Finding an equally skilled commander to replace him was not going to be at all easy.

He had barely closed the book and put it in his pocket when the ship's captain – the droungarios – approached him.

"General Nicephorus!"

"Yes, Nicholas, what is the matter?"

"The prisoner is causing a disturbance on the lower deck. He has refused to eat or drink anything unless he be allowed to pray."

"And have we ever prevented him from performing his accursed rituals?"

"He demands that the shackles be removed from his wrists and ankles so he can kneel and prostrate himself freely."

"This emir, or should I say 'pirate' is going to need all the prayers he can muster before he is paraded in the streets of the capital tomorrow. Release his shackles until he is done with his prayers."

The captain descended to the lower deck, while Nicephorus remained where he was, surveying the blue horizon.

Suddenly, loud shouting and stomping broke out from down below. Amid the confusion, Nicephorus heard one distinct cry, "*Grab him!*" At that same moment, the prisoner scrambled up to the upper deck, running toward the edge of the ship, intending, so it seemed, to throw himself into the sea. By then, one of the general's bodyguards had started toward the prisoner, and, grabbing him at the last moment, prevented the suicidal escape attempt. They wrestled on the ship's deck, until five other guards got hold of the elusive emir and clamped the fetters on him once again.

"You incompetents!" Nicephorus fumed. "You barely remove the

23

shackles and he escapes your clumsy hands? Don't you know that your lives are tied to his? If it hadn't been for John, you would now be swimming in pursuit of this wretch! Send him back below and make sure he remains there until we reach land."

"Yes, sir!" the guards replied, their heads bent in disgrace. They dragged the captive back to his cell while he loudly spewed out curses in his foreign tongue.

Calling upon his clerk, Nicephorus bellowed out, "Deduct two months' wages from each of them!" to which he received another firm, "Yes, Sir!"

He turned to John, who had remained by the ship's parapet, adjusting his clothing after the brief scuffle.

"Can you believe that?! Nice work, John."

"Thank you, Sir. Always at your service," he smiled proudly.

Very often, when Nicephorus would see John, his mind would instantly recall why he had hired the man in the first place. A particular incident at the beginning of the Cretan campaign some months before had convinced him. After the Roman fleet had reached the shores of Crete, the first thing that needed to be done was to quickly go ashore and win the first battle against the Saracens, securing a foothold on the island. The landing was successful, and the first battle won decisively, but after the Saracens fled behind the imposing walls of the city, the Romans proceeded to build their camp outside Chandax. They dug trenches and began a sustained siege both on land and sea.

After a long day of digging trenches around their camp and strengthening their fortifications, the Roman soldiers, all thirty thousand of them, had been eager to get some rest in their tents, arranged in a large square with the general's tent at its center.

In the middle of the night, as silence prevailed, the bodyguards assigned the night shift had also fallen asleep out of exhaustion. Suddenly, they were woken by the sounds of a struggle a few paces away from the domestic's tent. Carrying torches, swords drawn, they went to investigate the matter, and found a most surprising sight: two Muslims, dressed in black from head to toe, lying on the ground with their faces in the mud, subdued by two young Roman soldiers. Each soldier was sitting on the back of his adversary with his sword placed threateningly on his neck. The general, who, as usual, slept very little, appeared a moment later, and, seeing this sight, roared with laughter. The assailants were tied up and interrogated all night. As it transpired from their confessions, the cunning emir had the conviction that the easiest way to escape a possible defeat was to assassinate the domestic.

The next morning, a scaffold was erected in full view of the besieged city and the two assassins were publicly hanged.

Afterwards, the two now-famous Roman soldiers were called to the general's tent. Their names were John Sgouros and Demetrius Syros. They were generously rewarded, and, following a period of special training, were enrolled in the regiment responsible for guarding the Domestic of the Schools on campaign. Being part of that elite group was a source of envy to the others, not only for the prestigious position and proximity to the general, but also for an equally respectable pay increase.

Ever since then, John and Demetrius, who only met during that campaign, became close comrades and served during the following months side by side with distinction and bravery. That night had joined them together on a path far more fascinating than either had ever thought possible.

# Chapter Seven

- 𝔰𝔬𝔠𝔰 -

John rose up from the table quickly. He could only bear to swallow two or three spoonfuls of the stomach-churning fish soup. The lower deck where the men ate their meals was dark and stuffy. The stench of fish and the furious curses of the Saracen emir, refusing to shut up, made it impossible for John to stay another minute. He admitted to himself of being a picky eater but even after his delicate taste had been roughened by months of military life, the meal that day was more than he could handle. He glanced at his comrades, voraciously emptying their wooden bowls and walked towards the cook, Longinus.

He stood behind the two large clay pots. A round-faced, broad-shouldered man with a hearty manner, cooking was definitely not his finest talent. He was generous, though, always filling the boys' bowls to the rim, and always having a reserve of bread and dried fruit.

"Looks like you didn't savor the food today, John." He giggled, knowingly. "It's not like I have the ingredients of the royal kitchen. Besides, your friends seem to be enjoying it just fine."

"Never mind, Longinus. Just hand me some of those raisins you keep."

"That's all? There you go, and half a loaf of bread, too."

Longinus's handful was about twice that of the average person. John took his snack and climbed up to the upper deck. His chest expanded as he took a deep breath of the fresh sea air. The golden hair he had inherited from his mother glistened under the sun, and the color of his eyes, like hers too, matched the deep blue water. The strong jaw and Roman nose gave him a dashing look. His light spirit – possibly the result of being the youngest family member – and amiable character, though far from frivolous, in addition to his good looks, gave him close to magical powers in acquiring friends with little effort. He was quite popular in the army, especially after the famous nocturnal incident. Of course, there were always those who had bitter feelings of envy toward him, but these were in the minority. The other soldiers that knew John had genuine feelings of

26

respect for him.

He threw a few raisins into his mouth to counter the fishy taste then followed them with a bite of the heavy brown bread. He glanced at the bow where the domestic had been standing but the man had gone by then. Time for his midday nap. The swiveling pump used to spew the deadly Greek fire cocktail sat abandoned at the front of the boat waiting for the next sea battle when it would be used to spread devastation among enemy ships.

Leaning on the parapet, he lifted one boot and placed it against the wooden planks. As he threw more plump raisins inside his mouth and chewed slowly, he let his mind wander.

*Back to the city after so many months. I wonder if anything has changed, if everyone is alright. I'm sure they must have written me even though I received nothing. Terrible mail. Anyways, I'll see them now in their flesh and blood. No need for paper and ink to tell me about how they're doing. I wonder how they'll perceive me ...*

He extended his arms in front of him, admiring the favorable changes the past months have left. The daily drills with heavy swords and shields, the marches with backpacks, and the constant exercises had sculpted his body. He never imagined he could gain such outstanding muscular strength that fast. He'd always been a strong lad, even as a child he could run faster than most of his peers, but there was a limit to how far civilian life could build a man's body. The nine months on campaign had made him feel, and look invincible.

The picture of the dromon making its way on the waves, the salty water spray and the sudden squawking of a seagull made his mind shift elsewhere, magically evoking a distant memory.

*Funny how one sound can bring back to life such long buried memories.* On one rare occasion when his father hadn't been too busy at the Palace, he had taken the family on a short boat trip across the Bosphorus. *I must have been about ... eight, Alexander thirteen. Was it my first time at sea? I guess it was. Father bought us candied figs, I would never forget that sweet taste, not in a hundred years. Alexander kept chasing me around the boat until that tough mariner shouted at us to keep calm. And keep calm we did!*

*Father was almost always too busy to take us anywhere, but at least we got to see him every evening before we slept. His little tales before bedtime were really fantastic. And mother ... she always took good care of us. She hardly did anything else besides that ... and praying of course. Now that I think of it, I can't really complain about an unhappy childhood ...*

He put the last bit of bread and the last few raisins in his mouth, brushed his palms together and reached for his belt pouch. His pay and share of the spoils were safely kept elsewhere but in this pouch he kept something else. When the men had stormed the castle of Chandax and laid their hands on its immense treasures, he had picked a beautiful gold necklace from one of the many treasure boxes recovered. Later on, when each of the men showed their comrades what they'd acquired, they all agreed John's necklace had been the most beautiful.

"You have an eye for beauty," some of the men said "You'll sell this for no less than fifty nomismata."

But it wasn't for sale. It was his mother's gift. In fact, at that moment he felt so proud he could offer such a fancy gift to the woman who brought him into this world. He, who only a year before used to gain his weekly allowance from assisting his brother at the fur shop.

*Nine months away and I've gained more than Alexander makes in three years.* It was a fascinating fact. Truth is, money wasn't what enticed him to becoming a soldier in the first place, but that aspect of the military career was certainly welcome. He needed nobody now. He all of a sudden ceased to be the young member of the family who received advice from everyone and depended on everyone. He, like all of his young comrades now could boast his independence in so many ways. For a handsome young man like him, his pockets full of the golden nomismata, Constantinople, with its theaters, taverns and brothels was the place to be. A big smile forged itself on his face.

Demetrius's head appeared from the hatch. "Oh, there you are," he said, climbing the ladder. Demetrius was shorter than John, though by no means a small man. He had a strong body and darker skin more common in the eastern provinces of the empire, and a pair of piercing brown eyes. He took things seriously, sometimes too seriously, as John would often tell him, but after meals his mood usually became merry.

"You look too happy for someone who's had raisins and bread for lunch."

John raised a brow. "I'd rather swim back to Crete than eat that hellish soup. I still can't believe how you swallowed that poisonous liquid!"

"You're just too spoiled, city boy. I even asked Longinus for a refill!"

"Incredible" John shook his head and giggled. "I still think Longinus should be throwing javelins instead of seasoning soup. I told him that last week, he answered he'd rather stand behind clay pots rather than behind ramparts."

Demetrius giggled too, then wiped his mouth with the back of his palm. "Tonight is our last night on the boat."

"Yeah, I heard the droungarious talking to the domestic earlier. One more night at sea and we drop anchor at the capital's harbor."        "I've had enough of waves rolling and rocking us day and night. Can't wait to step on solid ground."

"You will soon, and not just any ground. I can already visualize the celebrations that await us: the chariot races at the hippodrome, the people cheering. I've missed all of that. You'd be surprised to see how greatly the people of Constantinople adore celebrations. You'll see more wine poured, more food - and not like Longinus's food - than you've ever seen in your entire life". A few tough mariners, with arms strengthened by years of rowing, and skin bronzed by the Mediterranean sun hastened to pull the boom of the main sail. The triangular sail turned around the mast and the dromon slightly swerved to the north east.

"We're leaving the Aegean and into the Sea of Marmara." John noticed. Unlike the illiterate majority, of whom Demetrius was one, John's childhood tutor had lectured him on some of Ptolemy's maps from his *Geographia*.

"Let's see what the royal city has in store for us." Demetrius too leaned on the parapet.

The mariners who at other times rowed the dromon's one hundred and eight oars followed the instructions of the droungarious at sea but also fought alongside the soldiers on land.

"Come on, pull some more!" Nicholas shouted from his place at the stern. The favorable wind propelled the ship allowing the rowers some much welcomed rest.

Land could be seen not far on the horizon, and the domestic's dromon, followed by the entire fleet, soon entered the narrow straits of the Hellespont, the natural channel that led from the open Aegean to the closed Sea of Marmara, on whose shores stood the empire's first city.

The fleet sailed with Asia on its right and Europe on its left. Green, densely forested land was a welcome sight to the men who had spent too long at sea.

John knew that their upcoming stay at the capital was going to be a short one. Where they were going to be needed next in that vast empire he didn't know, and really it didn't make a big difference. Whether it was the frigid banks of the Danube, the burning sands of Mesopotamia or the rugged mountains of Anatolia, he would gladly follow his master on the next mission, through the next battle, fighting the next swarm of barbarians as long as he was one of the domestic's bodyguards. His life had turned out to be a truly exciting one, and no one could take that thrill away from him.

# Chapter Eight

- ∞✸ -

Constantinople was within sight of the fleet vanguard, its destination the naval base at *Kontoskalion* Harbor. A crowd began to gather by the seawalls, watching these floating castles glide along the waters of the Sea of Marmara.

Around noon, the first ships dropped anchor at the harbor amid salutes and intense cheers from the assembled multitude.

The emperor and empress were there when the domestic disembarked from the command ship followed by his bodyguard.

"Welcome back, domestic Nicephorus!" the monarch announced, smiling to the man who had just won him a remarkable victory.

Nicephorus carried in his hands a golden tray upon which was placed a large metal key. He offered it to the emperor with a bow.

"This is the key to the city of Chandax, Your Majesty. The island is yours."

"Well done, domestic!" the empress said with a graceful smile, revealing a glimpse of her shiny pearl-white teeth.

Horses were presented to the domestic and his companions and, following the royal carriage, they crossed the short distance to the palace where a formal reception awaited the victors.

At the Chalkis gate, everyone froze with reverence as the young imperial couple disembarked from their carriage and ascended the stairs that led to the palace followed by their guards.

Nicephorus waited before stepping inside, then receiving the signal from the chief of the Varangian guards, he turned around and selected a few men to accompany him; his sub-commanders, the Droungarios Nicholas, and finally, John and Demetrius.

While the other men had visited the place numerous times before, going inside and in the presence of the emperor and empress was almost unthinkable to John and Demetrius. They walked behind Nicephorus on the path lined with guards, believing they were in some kind of a dream. A

30

moment later, they were inside the famous throne room.

The impression such glamour and magnificence left on the young officers, who had just arrived from the tumultuous military surroundings of blood, sweat and steel was unimaginable. By then it was late afternoon and the golden mosaics and palatial chandeliers were gleaming with the rays of the setting sun, flooding through the large windows. The hall was packed with senators, clerics, dignitaries and on the elevated platform sat the two royal figures in their full splendor. It was a scene straight from one of the bedtime stories John's father used to tell him as a child.

After the formal bows and introductions, the young emperor, now seated on his throne addressed his domestic.

"You have been faithful to the duty entrusted to you, Domestic Nicephorus, to the great benefit of our state and the entire Roman commonwealth; succeeding where many before you have failed. For that, you have our gratitude."

Albeit sitting on the throne and adorned in purple and gold, those words sounded out of place coming from a novice, when uttered to the most experienced soldier in the empire, the age of his father.

"I am deeply honored, Your Majesty. I have taken it upon myself to fight the enemies of the empire, both foreign and domestic, and I shall continue this duty with the grace of God until the last day of my life."

"Your father, Domestic Bardas, served my father Constantine, at the head of the army for many years. And now, you continue on this honorable path with yet another victory."

John had heard about Nicephorus's father, a respected old general and his son's predecessor as domestic, but he had never seen him before. Today, the old general was among those present in the hall. While everyone else stood in the presence of the emperor, he alone was allowed to remain seated in respect for his advanced age and long service.

*The domestic looks so much like his father.*

Bardas slowly stood up.

"If Your Majesty would allow me."

"Yes, Bardas." The emperor nodded.

"Thank you, Your Majesty," he said, bowing. "For fifty years, I have served the empire, first as a cataphract, then as a commander, and finally as a domestic under your father, Emperor Constantine Porphyrogenitus, may his memory be eternal. I spent more time on horseback than on solid ground. I do not remember one year passing without having fought a battle or conducted a raid or repulsed an attack. I have lost so much, dear ones, too.

"But now in my old age, as I seek peace in the remaining years of my life, nothing brings me more joy and pride than to see my own son gaining your royal favor and marching under your victorious banner to preserve our homeland and defend the churches of God. May the Lord from the heavens protect Your Majesty and grant you a long and prosperous reign, and our army uninterrupted triumph!"

As Bardas sat down, the emperor moved to deliver an important message:

"There are still numerous battles to be won and swarms of enemies to be conquered. Crete is now pacified and your brother, the general Leo has done a remarkable job defending the eastern front, but now the army should march east and attack the Arabs before they recover from their defeat."

"...Without any delay." The chamberlain suddenly got to his feet, taking up from where the sovereign had stopped.

John was somewhat surprised to see anyone interrupt the emperor's flow of words.

*What does he mean, without any delay? Are we to be sent to the east immediately?*

"Yes, my Lord," said Nicephorus, addressing the emperor. "My men and I shall wait for your orders to march east. Nothing pleases me more than riding against the enemy, but the men do need some rest, with your permission."

"By all means, you may enjoy a period of rest after the long campaign, but this Emir of Aleppo, this 'Sayf' is causing us much trouble and is refusing to relent. You might have to deal with him sooner than you think."

"Certainly, Your Majesty. I promise you that he shall not have a better fate than the pirate of Crete."

"Go now and rest, domestic. Tomorrow we shall meet in the Hippodrome."

The guests bowed in reverence for the emperor and empress, who stepped down from the throne platform and walked solemnly out of the throne room. But just as they were leaving, John's eyes caught a glimpse of Bringas' face. His eyes had been fixed on Nicephorus, who had bowed almost to prostration when the two royal figures passed in front of him. In that split of a second, John could see in the chamberlain's eyes a look so evil it reminded of an iconic depiction of the devil. It was pure hatred, lasting only for an instant, after which his face returned to its normal emotionless state.

# Chapter Nine

- ∞⚮∞ -

While the domestic was being received at the palace, thousands of soldiers were disembarking from their ships and making their way across the city to their camp outside the walls.

John hailed from the capital, and with the domestic's permission, he could stay with his family for a while instead of the camp, taking his comrade Demetrius with him. The next morning, however, they were to take part in the triumphal celebrations at the Hippodrome.

The two men diverged from the line of marching soldiers and headed to John's home. Though the distance was not that far, it was sufficient enough for them to receive praise from the passersby, particularly from young ladies. Indeed, the two comrades were worthy of such admiration; both young and handsome soldiers, their swords by their sides, and their armor gleaming in the ruddy afternoon sun.

John's decision to respond positively to the imperial recruiters who had been calling upon him to join the army precipitated his first experience away from home. After the short training he received in one of the camps just outside the capital's walls, he soon found himself boarding one of the galleys that sailed to Crete. It was a hard decision to make, especially when his family objected to this dangerous choice of career. His father had advised him to work with his brother at the fur shop or start a new business, but to no avail. He was determined to 'save the world' as his brother would sometimes mock him. Quickly, however, the family saw his strong resolution, and the tears his mother shed before his departure turned to prayers for his safe return. But now he was coming back, adorned with glory, and although he did not have the faintest feeling of vanity, he wanted his family to see that he could not have made a better decision about his career and future.

"Is it still a long way to go?" Demetrius asked with some impatience, as they crossed from the busy street into a quieter alley.

"What is it, the armor weighing you down?" his friend replied with a teasing smile "Given how the girls look at you, I'd say it's worth the while! Why, you fought for three long hours wearing it without complaining, and there weren't even any girls there at the battlefield." He chuckled.

"You don't make such jokes to a married man. Besides, most of the shy smiles were coming your direction, not mine," Demetrius said, raising a brow.

"Then it must be your ever-rumbling stomach. I'm very hungry myself. I bet mother has prepared us something delicious."

"Trust me, after nine months of army food, anything homemade would be more than delicious."

"We are almost here. See that house?" John pointed to a neat white house of two stories about fifty paces away.

When John knocked on the door, he could smell his mother's delicious 'keftedes'; the scent carrying him away as if on a magic carpet. Instead of the proud soldier, he was again a ten-year-old boy playing with his friends in the alley in front of the house, the smell from their kitchen drifting through the window and calling him for dinner long before his mother could.

When Anastasia opened the door, her eyes fell upon that same little boy; her little boy who had been out playing war with his friends and was now home for dinner.

***

The reunion was just as John had expected it to be; with the intimate atmosphere, the overwhelming emotions and the sweet coziness of home and family. Yet there was something missing that he could not discern. He felt he had something to do or somewhere else he should be at; but what and where, he didn't know. He had finally arrived home but failed to understand why such feelings of loss and alienation were haunting him during those precious moments with his dear ones. It was as if he were a stranger in his own home.

Regardless, he managed to set those feelings aside for the time being as his brother, having searched for him at the harbor with no success, eventually arrived home and found him there.

With everyone sitting together around the dinner table, the family engaged in a conversation that went most of the time in one direction. John -and to a lesser degree, Demetrius- answered the questions the others were asking in as much detail as he could. They told of the most important and thrilling events that happened to them during the campaign.

Then came the feasting on the various dishes Anastasia and Zoe had prepared (including the famous roasted lamb chops Alexander had predicted), after which they all reclined on more comfortable seats in the living room to have John's favorite dessert.

"Oh, Mother, it's been so very long since I was pampered this much!" said John, dipping his spoon in a nicely decorated china bowl filled with honey, yoghurt and raisins.

"You deserve it, my hero!"

"There is so much to catch up with, John," said Theodore, "but let me first inquire a few things from your good friend here. You come from Anatolia, Demetrius, but where exactly does your family live?"

"Well, sir, I grew up with my family in a village two days' walk from the city of Caesarea in Cappadocia."

"And how did you end up as one of his majesty's soldiers."

Suddenly, a shadow of uneasiness crossed Demetrius's face. He spoke with a heavy heart.

"My father is a farmer. We owned some land and lived off it, fairly well I'd say, until three years ago when famine struck the province. It was a hard winter. Frost remained on the ground for three months."

"I remember that winter," Zoe confirmed. "Even here, it was the coldest winter I ever witnessed."

Demetrius nodded gravely.

"The following summer was cold and rainy, all our crops failed and we struggled to survive. We had no choice but to sell the land to one of the rich local landowners and continue to work it as his tenants."

"That must have been difficult for you," Theodore said, compassionately.

"Not only for us, but for so many of the small land owners like us. The rich magnates roamed the province like vultures seeking a prey. They bought the land at half of its price from the desperate farmers, enlarging their estates considerably.

"As you know, these rich noblemen are every year expected to supply the imperial army with soldiers, fully clothed and armed soldiers in numbers proportional to the size of their estates. And although I had only been married recently, I agreed to be one of the few nominated by our landlord to the military service. It meant a steady salary, and a better life for my family. I thought that, perhaps, with some luck I could someday be able to repurchase our farm."

"You know, laws have been issued by the late emperor giving farmers the right to do just that: repurchase their farms."

Like many other learned men in the capital, Theodore took interest in learning of the new laws that were being issued.

"Demetrius has been hoping to do that with what he gained from Crete," John explained.

"I do hope so," Theodore said. "Has your family always lived around that area? I heard it has fertile soil."

"My ancestors actually came from Syria, hence our family name: Syros," Demetrius replied.

"Interesting," Theodore replied, thoughtfully.

"My father once searched church records and found out that our family had come from Aleppo about a hundred and fifty years ago and settled around Caesarea. Life for our ancestors must have become unbearable under Arab rule, so they chose to abandon their native land and come to resettle in Roman territory."

"This is one reason why I felt the gravity of what we were doing in Crete." John said proudly. "We fought so that people did not have to live under foreign rule in terrible conditions."     "We are fortunate to be living in these times," Theodore said, leaning back in his seat. "Ever since the swarms of Arabs emerged from the desert some three centuries ago, they have been on the offensive. They conquered Syria, Egypt and Africa and besieged this city twice, threatening us with total destruction. Only in these past few years have our armies, with God's grace, been scoring victory after victory, regaining some of the lost cities and freeing their people from the tyranny of these invaders."

"You should see how the locals met us there, 'Brothers!', they would call us," John relayed with much excitement. "To them, we were heroes, angels sent by God to ease their suffering. They would come to our camp after we besieged the Arabs inside Chandax, offering us their food, some to the last loaf of bread in their shabby homes. Their desire for freedom was far greater than that for sustenance. After the liberation, their joy was indescribable."

"To see the cross erected once more above the Cathedral of Chandax was the greatest moment of all," Demetrius added. "Villagers descended from their isolated mountainous refuges where they had lived in an exile of their own making and relished the first moments of freedom after the fall of the city in our hands."

"What amazing things you have witnessed," Zoe said, having listened attentively. "We've had nothing nearly as exciting here in the City. Life's carried on just the same as always."

"While at the harbor looking for you, I saw many soldiers sitting around the docks. Some of them were in so terrible a condition that they could barely walk but had to be carried on litters and in carts," Alexander inquired. "Who are these men?"

"Those poor souls are freed prisoners who had endured months, even years of captivity. You should have seen when we reached the prison and unlocked the cells. The dark dungeons were nothing but tombs encasing those wretched men. Once mighty warriors, they had been reduced to skeletons."

John noticed the sadness his words left on his mother's face. Her father, a cataphract, had been taken captive by the Arabs when she had only been a little girl, never to be seen again. John shifted the conversation to a happier topic.

"I believe it will be crowded at the hippodrome tomorrow."

"That's for sure," Alexander replied.

"Your mother and I will try our luck. Seeing you riding alongside the domestic is something we wouldn't miss for the world."

"You don't have to worry about that, Father," John said, "I'll have my father sit in the front row!"

"You'll have me sit in the front row? I've worked in the palace for thirty years and served three emperors, do you think I will need your connections for front seats?"

"Times change, Father!" he said teasingly. "Your son has become one of the domestic's entourage!"

"Come on, John, enough boasting!" said Anastasia, who valued modesty above all virtues. "You need to rest after this long day. You have another big day tomorrow. Let me show you where you will sleep."

As she stood up, the two men followed her to the inner room.

"Oh, my good old bed!" John sighed, looking around his room. "Didn't know I could miss you that much!"

# Chapter Ten

- ℰℋℭℬ -

Before the city woke up, John and Demetrius headed towards the Golden Gate; the spot from where all Triumph processions entered the city, ending at the hippodrome. They reached their destination, took their positions by the other soldiers and waited for the arrival of the general. For two long hours they stood there and awaited his arrival.

"This is taking longer than I thought," Demetrius complained.

A soldier standing ahead of them with a spear in his hand turned his head and said in a singsong accent that betrayed his Calabrian descent: "He's still at the palace. He'll come once he's done receiving praise and compliments from the emperor and the senators."

"It's worth the wait, trust me," said Andreas, a man of big proportions and one of the domestic's experienced bodyguards. "A Triumph is a once in a lifetime experience. I remember the last great Triumph this city witnessed. When our armies captured Edessa from the Muslims and recovered the holy image of Christ, I was about fifteen years old. It was talk of the people for many years."

"I remember that, too, though I must have been only six or seven," John said. "The festivities and the chariot races were staggering. It was the first time in my life that I saw a giraffe. "

"What is that?" Demetrius asked.

"You don't know what a giraffe is? It's an animal, a huge one, taller than a house of three floors!"

"You can't be serious! Why would they bring such a monster here?" Demetrius's looked bewildered.

"Relax! It's a meek creature! It only eats tree leaves!" John chuckled. "Such wild animals are brought and displayed to entertain the people."

"How would a provincial like me know of your exquisite festivities, you city boys."

Suddenly, there was a commotion at the back of the line.

"Stand straight, here he comes," the Calabrian soldier said

melodically.

Finally, the domestic appeared, accompanied by another group of guards, his face darkened with fury.

*He doesn't look like someone who's just finished being showered with compliments.*

"Is everything alright?" John whispered to one of the guards who had just arrived with Nicephorus.

"There will be no celebrations at the hippodrome. Cancelled!"

"What do you mean, *cancelled?*"

"The emperor ordered that a mere ovation be given to the domestic at the hippodrome but there will be no chariot races, no games or shows, just a parade across the Main Street and a blessing of the patriarch at the hippodrome."

"But why?" John persisted, perplexed.

"That, no one will dare tell you. You will have to figure it out yourself."

There was no time for more questions as the parade began moving. A few hundred selected soldiers, holding their standards, marched in an orderly fashion, each unit headed by its commander. Behind them, on horse-drawn carts, magnificent treasures of gold and silver recovered from the Saracens were displayed to the astonished crowds who were already lining the path on both sides. High-profile prisoners along with their emir were paraded in chains at the end of the procession, provoking curses and laughter from the gloating multitudes.

At the head of this conglomerate parade walked Nicephorus, receiving acclamations from the crowd. John, along with the rest of the general's bodyguards, marched beside him looking with hawkish eyes for any possible threat that might be lurking among the thousands present, his mind busily wondering what might have caused the cancellation of the festivities.

By now, word had spread among the people that the expected triumph had been reduced to an ovation and seeing the domestic walk, instead of ride on horseback, confirmed it, to their great disappointment.

"What else deserves a Triumph if not this?" John heard the murmurs with his own ears. The people had enough insight to speculate as to the reasons behind the cancellation.

"The emperor wants successful but obscure commanders," said an old man at the entrance to the hippodrome.

The procession slowly moved inside the horseshoe-shaped arena, where, in addition to the thousands of spectators, the emperor, empress, the ministers and members of the entourage were present in the lofty royal box. This luxurious balcony, isolated from the surrounding terraces but connected to the palace through a series of corridors and an underground pathway, was where the royal family followed the races and other events that took place here.

The shouts of approbation from the now agitated crowds were quickly overwhelmed with cries of, *Nicephorus Victor!* By itself a pun on the domestic's name which literally meant *Bringer of Victory*. The thousands of people that filled the large open theater unanimously resounded this acclamation with enough zeal and enthusiasm as to convince any spectator it had more to it than mere admiration. A smell of an uprising could be felt in the air, and a wild idea crossed John's mind.

*What if all these volatile crowds, to vindicate their favorite's injured dignity, refused to settle down? There are tens of thousands of angry people here. What if things got out of control? After all, it is not unheard of, nor even uncommon in Constantinople.*

John had more than once witnessed limited riots during chariot races at the hippodrome, but that day seemed to promise more than the customary disturbance. From what his tutor had taught him, the *Nika* riots which erupted four centuries before at the very same place had started in much the same manner. Resentful crowds had gone out of control and although the then emperor – Justinian - had not been toppled, the riots had left dozens of thousands dead and half of Constantinople burnt to the ground.

It was a time of high tension, and those present could feel it. John, who was marching to the right side of the domestic, looked up toward the imperial box, and noticed some confusion there. Members of the Varangian guard had created a human barrier, shielding the emperor from the eyes of the crowd. He immediately recalled a similar tactic he had practiced several times in the army when it was necessary to protect the domestic from enemy projectiles during battle. But what projectiles where these guards attempting to protect the emperor from? Did the emperor really suspect danger?

It looked as if the glorious day could in the blink of an eye turn into a nightmare. The crowds were cheering louder and louder and even the soldiers who marched in the procession began to bang their swords against their shields with a zeal reminiscent of battle times.

Nicephorus, whom thousands of eyes followed to the center of the hippodrome, made a pacifying gesture with his hand. Silence fell over the crowds like a cloak. In a commanding voice, trained by pre-battle speeches and amplified by the excellent acoustics of the hippodrome, he addressed them:

"Roman and Christian men! A dear part of our empire has been liberated from the claws of the pirate infidel. Thousands of Christians have been set free after long years of servitude! We have all been granted this victory from above, all of us! Let us thank the Lord on this day and rejoice, for he has made our enemies a footstool for our feet. God save the Emperor and bless you all!"

The buzz from the crowd began to rise once more as he walked with humility to where the patriarch and some members of the clergy had been standing on a platform at the center of the hippodrome. This time, however, the crowds sounded more curious than angry. Romanus and Theophano, looking from above, watched as Nicephorus prostrated himself before the aged prelate and the latter recited a solemn prayer especially reserved for such events.

Silence fell again once the patriarch began reciting the prayers. The now-peaceful crowd must have realized that they were in front of a man with unique qualities. One who wasn't the kind they'd meet every day, nor was he of the same specimen of men that populated the city's palaces and luxurious villas. He was a man whose humble soul had quickly managed to endear him to their hearts more than any of the city's power-thirsty elite ever could.

"You won't be seeing any giraffes today," John whispered to Demetrius, both standing like living statues.

"I've been concerned more about civil war than about strange animals," he whispered back.

John had been thinking about the same thing. Now he gazed at the mighty commander engrossed in prayer. *He's just as good at preserving peace as he is at waging war.*

4

# Chapter Eleven

- ℰℐℭℬ -

Over the next few weeks, John enjoyed an entertaining stay at the capital, accompanying his master on numerous visits to Constantinople's most revered personages. Almost every day, the domestic would be attending some business at the palace, the senate, or be invited to meetings and banquets at the villas of distinguished men. At most of these events, John would be one of his few companions. Nevertheless, the young soldier would get to visit his family every few days.

The Phocas residence was a beautiful mansion befitting the head of the army, located on one of the city's seven hills, surrounded by a vast well-tended garden and overlooking the sea. The kitchen, guest rooms and the guards' quarters were on the ground floor while the master of the house resided on the upper floor. His aged father, the famous general Bardas Phocas, stayed in a spacious apartment on the same floor. He was by now in his eighties, enjoying a peaceful retirement after a long military life during which he had led the empire's armies on the eastern front for decades in relentless warfare against the Arabs.

The discipline at the camp was somewhat relaxed so that the tired soldiers could get enough rest after long months of campaigning offshore. It was a mild summer in Thrace that year and the soldiers got all the rest they needed, with frequent baths at the close-by seaside and *controlled* visits to nearby Constantinople (where only a limited number of soldiers were allowed to enter the city at any given time). The taverns and brothels of the capital enjoyed a steady stream of thirsty and lustful soldiers flowing through the city gates. Just as there was a time for war, there was also a time for recreation and pleasure.

But as the soldiers were enjoying that period of idleness, John anticipated its conclusion at any time. Everyone talked about how the front in the East had been volatile for the past few years with the Arab Prince Sayf Ad-Dawla escalating his attacks from the capital Aleppo in Syria, on the border cities of Anatolia. He was campaigning deeper and deeper into Roman territory and getting bolder with every victory. There on the front, however, the man in charge of the Roman troops was another distinguished general by the name of Leo, none other than Nicephorus's younger brother. In spite of Sayf's encroachments, things were still under control and the order to leave for the East had not been given yet.

When they had been still in Crete, John and his comrades received news that boosted their morale. Leo had scored a notable victory against Sayf al-Dawla, whose army had advanced deep inside the empire and was retreating after having seized tremendous booty and hundreds of prisoners. At the right moment, Leo ambushed the Arab army from his location in the mountain defiles and achieved another victory that would be long remembered for the Phocas family.

But Sayf wasn't giving up and the absence of the main Roman force, on campaign in Crete, emboldened him to conduct more raids.

***

On a summer's afternoon, John and Demetrius sat on the steps of the porch outside the domestic's mansion as the latter enjoyed his short daily nap upstairs. For a man who spent most of the night in vigil prayer, a midday nap was necessary. Other guards were stationed in various places around the house. It had rained heavily the previous night, quite unusual for that time of year, and the fresh green grass and tree leaves flickered with the gentle afternoon breeze. The two men sat watching the boats traversing the blue waters of the gulf below them, the Golden Horn. Suddenly Demetrius spoke in what seemed like an outburst of long withheld feelings:

"What are we going to do with our lives, John?"

"What do you mean?"

"I mean, while the worst thing that could happen to us is getting maimed or even killed in the next battle, the best thing would be to keep on running with the army east and west, not having any hope of settling down, of having a normal life. Am I right, or not?"

"So, this is what's been troubling you lately, then."

"Come on, John, don't tell me it never crossed your mind."

"I know it's harder for you, being married and all. I don't mean to be cruel, but I thought we all knew that that was how our lives were going to be once we joined the army. Do you remember the first thing they taught us when we were enrolled in the domestic's bodyguard?"

"How could I forget?"

"Before you learn to be ready to kill, you must learn to be ready to die."

There was a moment of silence, as if both were contemplating

43

those words seriously for the first time.

"I had only been married six months when I left," Demetrius said with a dreamy look on his face.

"How could you let go?"

"I didn't have much of a choice. Seeing my father work his own land like a slave, the mere thought that my life and that of my children was going to be forever like that, barely paying our debts to our landlord.

"Besides, even if I had asked to be exempted that year, being my parents' only child, newly married and all, I would have certainly been called the next year."

John nodded.

"I don't think I have ever told you this before," Demetrius said, recollecting what sounded like painful memories. "The day after our landlord sent us word about the recruitment, my wife Eleni came to me and told me she wasn't going to let me go. I remember her coming from the water spring in the early morning after having filled her jar. I was bending down digging the earth around a tree trunk, and when I lifted my eyes, there she was standing in the green field before me, the clay jar on her shoulder, the sun rising behind her and light rays pouring through her long black hair. I can still see her now, standing in front of me, looking so beautiful, but equally downhearted. With tears in her eyes, she said the few words she had wanted to say and left quickly to finish her chores. I remained in the open field, not knowing what to think or feel. But 'a man is not to be affected by such feminine sentimentalities' I foolishly thought. 'A true man ought to be rock solid'. One week later I was marching north with the army, far away from her."

"You did the right thing." John reassured his troubled friend. "You would have just continued to labor in some remote province for bare sustenance, but look where you are now, in the heart of the empire, in the service of the most prominent general, at the beginning of a long path of success. With your pay and your share of the spoils, very soon you could achieve your dream and repurchase your father's farm.

"Once we are sent to the east, you would be close to your home, spending the campaign season on the front and the rest season at your village, with your wife."

"I can't wait for that to happen. I miss her a lot." He sighed. "What about you, John? Have you ever thought when you would get married?"

"Me, married? Ha-ha. I still have a whole world to discover. Besides, there are plenty of pretty girls in the taverns who, with two copper coins, can do the job better than any wife can!"

"Talking of pretty girls ... ha?" said a hoarse voice from behind them with a long deep accompanying laugh. Recognizing the speaker, both men bolted upright and turned around to face him, bowing respectfully.

"Oh, do sit, sit, don't stand for me," Bardas said, waving his hand in the air, then bending down and easing himself into an empty armchair on the porch. "Why did you stop talking, go on!"

"No reason, sir, there is nothing more to say," John replied, still standing.

"Oh, there is always something to say." Bardas looked at them and heaved a sigh. "I was a soldier too, for too long in fact. And both your fears and aspirations I can understand well," said the old man, who appeared to have been around longer than they thought. "It is hard enough for a soldier to stay alive." He pointed to a hideous old injury that mutilated the left side of his face. "Let alone to have a stable life. Between the battles, the camps and the long marches, life is a series of hardships; but trust me, it is a rewarding life. Even if cut short, it would still be worth more than a hundred years of cowardice and obscurity. You only die once, and then in that terrible moment when your spirit prepares to leave its earthly tabernacle, your entire life will flash before your eyes and you will feel pride and satisfaction. I've seen that look in so many eyes in my life. "

"I'm not afraid of death," Demetrius said with youthful pride.

"I can see that. You appear to be more afraid of life than death" the old general replied. "But don't worry, all will come in due time. Once you move with the army to the east, you can rejoin your family and produce children who will then grow up and become soldiers like their father. This is how the world works. My father was a commander before me, and his father before him, and now my two sons are the leaders of the eastern and western armies. You can imagine how proud I am. I see my life as complete. But don't think I didn't pay. I paid dearly."

"But will we continue to fight indefinitely? Will our children and grandchildren be perpetually turned into soldiers? What I mean to say is, where will it end? Is it going to be Baghdad or Damascus ... or even Jerusalem? What do we do after we have conquered the entire world?" asked Demetrius, unreserved in sounding his frustration.

"Listen, my sons. This God-protected city and the empire it rules have never been short of enemies. Persians, Goths, Vandals, Avars, Scythians, Rus and Arabs have all tried, century after century to annihilate us and destroy our kingdom. Some with more success than others.

"As we defeated one enemy, another took its place. In the west, the barbarians flooded the provinces like a deluge that ravaged everything in its path. Some now call themselves Christians and worship the Holy Trinity as we do, others adhere to the Arian heresy, but the empire in the west is no more. There is no western emperor, just chaos, poverty and ignorance. This could have been our fate had this great city not endured.

"In the east, a more formidable and ruthless enemy; the Arabs emerged from their sea of sand, united by their new religion, a vile heresy, and conquered the greater part of our eastern provinces. Syria, Mesopotamia, Palestine, Egypt and Africa have all been lost. But they haven't stopped there. For the past three hundred and fifty years, they have relentlessly tried to subdue us. Had this city not resisted siege after siege with the help of God and the Virgin, our fate would have been far worse than that of Old Rome.

"Were we to blame for this evil? Were we to let them take over our land, destroy our blessed empire and enslave us? We had only one choice: to fight, and fight we did.

"You have to know this. You are still young, but you have to know this very well. We live in a merciless world. If we back off even for one day, the torrent of enemies that surrounds us will devour us like wild beasts. We have to remain vigilant and brave. God will defend us only if we defend ourselves.

"But to answer your question, I'd say the answer is, 'yes'; this will carry on until the end of the world, for this is not the kingdom of heaven that we live in now but the kingdom of men, some of whom are quite evil. Until the Lord returns in glory, we shall have to pray for peace but prepare for war."

The two soldiers nodded in agreement, and Bardas appeared to have finished his sermon at the right moment, as two horsemen, in a rather slow trot, approached the external gate that separated the quiet road from the mansion's front garden. John stood up and walked toward them slowly and cautiously, his hand clenched around his sword's handle, but he soon noticed that they were unarmed.

As he came closer, the visitors saluted him politely and asked, "Is the domestic available?"

"You know I cannot answer that," replied John as two more guards slowly walked toward the gate from their positions in the garden.

One of the two riders, without dismounting, handed John a small square of folded paper wrapped neatly with a golden thread and sealed with a red wax seal.

"Please deliver this to your master."

"And who might I say it is from?" asked John.

"It is from his lordship, Basil Lekapenos," the messenger answered, then, waiting no longer, both men pulled the reins of their horses and slowly trotted away.

John watched them for a moment before turning back with the note in his hand. The domestic was already standing on the porch.

"What is it, John?" he asked.

"They brought you a letter, sir," he said, walking to the porch and handing him the note.

Nicephorus opened the neat wrapping and read its brief contents.

"Tell the men to saddle the horses," he said, looking up. "We have a visit to make."

# Chapter Twelve

- ℰℐℭℬ -

Just before evening faded into dusk, about a dozen men, headed by Nicephorus, made their way across the capital to the palace of Basil Lekapenos. It wasn't the first time that Nicephorus had visited the place, but it was John's. He did not know who this *Lekapenos* was, but the view of his villa gave him the impression that he undoubtedly possessed great wealth and power; wealth for the splendid palace that majestically stood before them, and power for the countless armed guards and retainers that lined both sides of the path, from the remote exterior gate to the very room where Basil was awaiting them. It was obvious that their host commanded his own little army.

Basil Lekapenos was the illegitimate son of a former emperor, but his dynasty was no longer in power. Still, he retained, in addition to a large fortune, a wide network of relations with influential people in the capital, including the emperor himself, whose father he had served as a chamberlain with loyalty and dedication. However, after years of heading the palace officials, and even armies on campaigns, the new young emperor replaced him with Bringas, something which led to a deep animosity between the two eunuchs; each seeking the destruction of the other. The recent resentment between Nicephorus and Bringas was no secret, and only enhanced the old friendship between Nicephorus and Basil.

The host, a rather tall man in his late forties, welcomed Nicephorus to a magnificently decorated reception hall with great hospitality and warmth. In the middle of the hall stood a long table covered with the most tasteful foods, the finest wines and exquisite delicacies. The two men sat at the dinner table while the general's accompaniment was seated in an adjoining room. John stood behind the domestic with his back to the wall, as the former and his host dined and chatted in a friendly atmosphere that on similar occasions lasted for hours.

As always, John overheard most of the conversation, yet he absolutely understood that preserving the secrecy of these private conversations was just as important as preserving his master's own life, especially now, as Nicephorus had become a popular figure and many were eager to find a blemish on his impeccable record.

By the nature of his work, John had learnt a great deal about his master's private life. He saw him wake up every night around midnight and pray at length before the icons in monastic austerity. He knew that the same religious passion drove him to sleep most nights on the cold hard floor instead of his bed. He could tell by the expressions on his master's face what was expected of him. But having all this knowledge stored in his memory was like throwing little rocks into a deep well; once down they would never surface again to satisfy the curiosity of intruders, and that was one of the reasons why the general often confided to him what he had in mind.

"I have been waiting to invite you ever since you returned from Crete, my dear Nicephorus, but I preferred to delay it a while until you have finished your businesses here and there," said Basil in his thin voice.

"A man of great courtesy and intelligence, that's what I've always thought of you, Basil. The timing of your invitation couldn't have been any more convenient."

"So, I assume there are no more dinner invitations coming your way from the senate members."

"Devil take them all!" Nicephorus waved his words away.

"Why the annoyance?"

"These parasites – or most of them, at least - are either busy increasing their huge fortunes, or conspiring against everyone else, including their own colleagues! Accepting their invitations was an evil I could not escape. Imagine this, they all, without exception, found it important to ask me, in some way or another, about my share of the spoils. I became so angry at one point that I even told that greedy Marcianus that whatever my share had been, I had already donated it all to charity. I immediately saw resentment, even disgust, in his cynical eyes, which was more than enough for me!"

"And did you actually do that; donate your entire share?" asked Basil, amazed. He had quite a fondness for wealth.

"Yes, I did, for the establishment of a monastery on Mount Athos."

"That rugged peninsula? A monastery there?"

"But why are you surprised? Do tell me, Basil, what benefit would I receive from amassing treasures? You live here in the capital among the elite, your duties and responsibilities require that you maintain a certain image, to all who know you, but we live in the midst of death. Our lives differ so much from yours. You take pride in these silver plates and forks while we in our bronze shields and iron swords. In this city, everyone is a prince, you all wear your fancy silk clothes, even to the marketplace -as I surprisingly rediscovered the other day- but there we prefer the drape of chain mail. Here wine is poured abundantly, there blood is shed with the same generosity. What benefit would I get from gold and silver? Besides, my estates in the East generate an income that far exceeds my needs."

"Well put, you have all my respect," Basil said, sipping a little wine. "I advise you, though, to make this donation of yours known. So far, every senator, dignitary and official in the city envies you for your share of the spoils, especially Bringas." Basil smirked.

"I couldn't care less about that weasel." said Nicephorus, scowling.

"Honestly, I thought you were on good terms with him, especially when he nominated you to lead the Cretan expedition last year instead of me!"

"Last year was something, and this year is something else, my friend. I've met him a couple of times, official meetings in the presence of the emperor. He seemed to react indifferently about everything I had to say, as if trying to undermine me in the eyes of the emperor. The emperor, on the other hand, would show interest in my suggestions but would never give a final decision. He's clearly depends totally on that creature's advice, which makes me, in fact, pity him. He is undoubtedly at the mercy of his subordinate."

"I agree with you, but the empress on the other hand, despises him and seems to see through his deception. Don't think that because I am not the chamberlain anymore that I don't know what is going on there."

"I'm sure of your superb capabilities, my friend. And yes, she seems to be the one with the royal pedigree not her husband."

Two servants appeared carrying a large oval silver tray with grilled fish and other exquisite seafood and placed in on the table in front of the two men, followed by two others who began to serve them, filling their silver plates with a variety of dishes.

"Do you know what I find surprising?" said Basil as he pierced a piece of crab meat with his fork. "The fact that they haven't sent you away yet. After seeing how the people so warmly welcomed you upon your return, I didn't think you'd stay this long in the capital."

"Do you honestly think I am enjoying my stay in this nest of vipers? I can't wait to get to the front, where at least one gets to confront one's enemies and fight them face to face with dignity and courage. A soldier like me has no pleasure in participating in the political intrigues and sly maneuvers of these corrupt bureaucrats. I have thirty thousand idle soldiers, all getting paid from the treasury and enjoying the best summer of their lives."

"What sort of news are you receiving from the front? Is your brother in control of the situation there? I've heard there were some serious encroachments last summer."

"So far, I've received both good and bad reports from Leo. The Arabs did invade the border provinces and managed to get away with booty and prisoners. But later they were beaten in the mountains. Since then, that accursed Sayf has not been risking raids deep inside our territories but instead has attempted to recapture some forts that guard the mountain passes and did achieve some success. There is news that he is preparing for a major attack. This is why my return to the east with the army could be imminent."

"I understand you totally. Remember that I, too, fought against Sayf along with your nephew John Tzimiskes a few years back and he suffered a bitter defeat at our hands, but it seems he has been emboldened by your absence. "

"It is a tough task to defeat the Arabs. You've been there, and you know. They have an endless supply of men and weapons, but what really makes them a stubborn enemy is their faith. To them, death in battle is nothing to be feared, but rather welcomed as the passage to eternal bliss. They fight to kill or be killed, and rarely flee, even when victory seems impossible. Still, with proper tactics, be sure that even they can be defeated. As they have, indeed, been defeated numerous times before. But the challenge is really about not leaving the young commanders to improvise on their own when facing a sudden Arab invasion."

"And how are you planning to do that?"

"I have undertaken to write down clear instructions in a manual explaining what a commander fighting the Arabs needs to know and do."

"The Arabs among all enemies?"

"They have specific tactics that require a specific manner of defense."

"A marvelous idea. You never cease to surprise me, Nicephorus," said Basil with much interest, "and when will this great work of yours be ready?"

"I have already started the writing, it should be completed before the end of the year. I will have it copied and distributed to the sub-commanders at the front. Everyone is expected to act according to a unified policy, otherwise, chaos will prevail, not to our benefit, of course."

A servant standing beside the table refilled Nicephorus's empty glass. He took a sip of the ruby-red liquor and said, staring at it, "Once I'm there, they will taste my wrath. It will be a new struggle with new rules. My rules!"

# Chapter Thirteen

- ᚛ᚑᚌᚄ -

The chamberlain strode toward the emperor's private apartment with a paper in his hand and a grudge in his heart. His fine cloak rippled behind him in black waves that made the flames from the torches flicker as he passed by.

*Romanus, I have wrapped around my finger like a ring. He thinks he's ruling, the naïve boy.* He smiled to himself. *He can feast and hunt and drink all he wants, I wouldn't want him to change not even one bit! Why, he is the kind of emperor any chamberlain could ask for! As for Nicephorus, he's made of a different material, I won't tolerate his presence here any longer, weaving a web of connections with the city's aristocrats, especially that snake Lekapenos. with thirty thousand soldiers in his pocket ... just too risky. What if he sets his eyes on the throne? Who can stop him then? An emperor like him has no place at his court for a chamberlain like me.*

The mere thought of having to relinquish power made him tremble.

*It is about time that unwashed rustic left the capital for the muddy camps of the East where he belongs. He comes here from the barracks and receives the welcome of a king! I purchased him this glory with my diligence, I and no other put that campaign on its feet and chose him to lead it, and what do I get in return? Nothing. While he gets to be hailed like a conqueror and liberator.*

*But, did he really think I was going to let him have it all? Did he think I was going to let him celebrate his triumph with the ignorant crowds cheering for him endlessly?*

*Does he not know that I am the master of the palace? I suppose he does, but all he can do is run around the city and whine to his sympathizers, but not anymore ... not anymore. His time is over. Very soon he and his filthy soldiers shall be on their way out of here!*

He stood outside the emperor's private apartment, knocked twice and entered. The monarch was sitting in a big armchair wearing his casual clothes and holding a golden goblet in his hand; a familiar sight. On a separate couch sat the empress in a beautiful blue robe. Attended by two young maids, the little boys played on a big round carpet made of tiger's hide.

Theophano looked as if she were about to protest but her husband talked over her:

"What is the matter, Joseph?"

"I apologize to have come at this time, Your Majesty, but I've just received some information about Nicephorus and thought you might want to hear it immediately."

"You thought right, Joseph. What is this paper?"

"It has the names of the people he has been visiting, or *conspiring with*, should I say."

"Hand it to me, let me see."

The emperor opened the note and read out a long list of names, one at a time. After each one, the chamberlain provided incriminating information against that individual.

"Basil Lekapenos ..."

"Rich, powerful and very resentful of the fact that Your Majesty chose me over him as chamberlain. I do not believe he has ever forgotten this insult."

"Constantine Gongyles ..."

"A suspicious man. After your late father, may his soul dwell with the angels, entrusted him with the recapture of Crete, a mission in which he failed miserably deserving a disgraceful release, he has remained embittered."

"Basil Peteinos ..."

"This man is known to have connections with the exiled Stephen Lekapenos, the son of late Emperor Romanus Lekapenos and the half-brother of Basil Lekapenos. His dream of seizing the throne back to the Lekapenos family will only die with his last breath."

The emperor's young face became more serious.

"Is this list accurate, Joseph? Do you really think he is conspiring against me?" He looked genuinely, if only momentarily, concerned. The merry emperor hardly lost sleep over anything.

"I have no doubt about it, Your Majesty. I have tried to warn you of this even before his arrival."

"What then are we to do?"

"With the army at his side, and soaring popularity, it would be too risky to try and confront him, at least not now. I would suggest sending him off to the eastern front as soon as possible."

"And then what?"

"And then we make sure he remains engaged in warfare until we decide our next move. We might even be so fortunate as to have the Arabs turn him into a martyr."

"Fine, I need him and the army to be ready in three days to start moving east to Caesarea," the emperor ordered, then gulped down the last of the wine in his cup.

"If it is your wish, I shall convey these orders to him immediately."

"Fair enough. Send him off. "

It was total victory, until Theophano spoke.

"You cannot believe these 'conspiracy allegations'," she protested.

"I would appreciate it very much, if you left these matters to me, my dear wife," Romanus said with drunken sluggishness. "When you shipped my five sisters off to different monasteries, I did not object to it. You said then that their presence jeopardized my throne; that when married, their husbands would pose a threat. Now, you seem not the least worried when Nicephorus has met with all sorts of suspicious characters."

"Fine, believe what you want! But don't you think it would be inappropriate to send your domestic to the front without seeing to it in person, especially when there is no proof of his misconduct?"

"I will not be here tomorrow to see to him or anyone for that matter," he said as a servant replenished his goblet with the heady concoction.

"Why, where will you be, my dear husband?" she asked, completely disregarding the presence of Bringas.

"Hunting, my dear wife, hunting in Thrace." He looked not toward her, but up at the ceiling.

"I wonder why you need to go that far to kill some innocent animals when we already have quite a few closer by, and more deserving of your arrows."

Bringas knew exactly what she meant.

The gullible, half-intoxicated husband, who probably missed her point, laughed and said, "Is that all, Joseph?"

"Yes, Your Majesty." The Chamberlain bowed and left the room, alarmed at the last words of the empress.

*This innkeeper's daughter is more stubborn than I thought. She is starting to have a say in everything. And Romanus is too soft, he can barely handle her. If I'd let him deal with Nicephorus at his leisure, who knows when he would have ordered him out of here. This list has done the job pretty well. No more worrying about Nicephorus. He can enjoy the company of the Arabs from now on.*

He walked back the same way he had come, without the paper but now with yet another grudge.

# Chapter Fourteen

- ℰℐℭℬ -

The orders to march east were finally announced. John had been at the camp when the news arrived, causing much clamor. The soldiers' pleasant summer had finally come to an end. The tavern owners of Constantinople, the wine sellers, the pimps and prostitutes, however, were just as unhappy about the departure of their spendthrift customers. The men who had come from the remote provinces and impoverished villages throughout the empire had for some time enjoyed all the pleasures money can buy. Now, instead of the capital's entertainments, the hardships of a new campaign stared them in the face.

John asked for permission to go and see his family one last time before their departure. That evening, he went home and dined with them. News of the army's departure had reached home before he did. When he knocked on the door, Anastasia opened with her usual warm motherly smile, but her misty eyes betrayed her true emotions. She led her son inside where the rest of the family anticipated his arrival.

"Nothing lasts forever," Theodore spoke slowly, resonating in his voice decades of parenthood. "From the moment that you returned home, we've had before our eyes your image departing again. That's the life you've chosen. May the Lord of heavens and earth grant you wisdom and discernment and deem us worthy of seeing you again in this life." His parents knew that every time he bid them farewell, it could very well be the last time. It was common knowledge, dreaded and up till then unspoken, one they had by then learnt to live with.

"I won't be long this time, I hope." John answered struggling to keep a smile on his face. "I'll write you more often, I promise.".

If only he had known how long it would pass before he could be able to see them again, he might have stayed a little longer. But he didn't and soon afterwards he was riding back to the camp. There, Nicephorus was planning the march east. He had been expecting this coming march all along, and had made most of the arrangements for departure: the food supplies, the mules and wagons, the shoes and clothing for the soldiers, and a thousand other necessary measures. Now he was finalizing all these matters so that the long journey would be orderly and smooth. In all these matters, John proved himself an indispensable assistant. Nicephorus personally oversaw the packing and loading of supplies and arrangement of the troops. It took three exhausting days.

On the dawn of the fourth day, a seemingly endless column of soldiers, horses and baggage marched through the capital, destined for the harbor where a flotilla of ships was prepared to ferry them across the straits separating Europe from Asia. Dozens of priests stood for hours, sprinkling the soldiers with holy water as they marched past the forum of Constantine and descended upon the harbor like a swarm of locusts. The ships began transporting the army in groups across the few-mile-wide strait from early morning, continuing as the hot August sun soared high in the clear skies. By late afternoon, almost the entire army had moved to the other side of the Bosphorus, to the town of Chalcedon. The last to cross was Nicephorus, accompanied by his elite regiment.

"Careful with the horses!" Demetrius shouted at a mariner who was leading some horses inside a transport. Pointing at a certain brown and white horse, he continued, "This charger is mine, make sure nothing happens to him!"

"For one silver miliaresion, sir, I can guarantee that this fine steed will enjoy the best journey of his life."

"A miliaresion! A bribe, you mean?!"

John, who had been standing next to his friend, grabbed his shoulder firmly.

"Don't be so stern, Demetrius, all the horsemen pay one or two silver coins to these greedy mariners for the safe passage of their animals. You don't want to risk your horse getting injured in these cramped transporters, do you?"

"Here, have these two miliaresions and take care of both our horses!!" John called out, pointing at a shiny black horse, then tossed the two coins in the air, one after the other. The mariner, whose sly smile never left his face, caught the money and saluted the soldiers, then crossed the wooden makeshift bridge into the ship with the animals.

"That cheeky fraudster! I could've broken his teeth!" Demetrius protested, clenching his fist.

"Come on now, let's move. See! The general is through talking to Father Athanasius and is coming to board the boat." John pointed discreetly.

Nicephorus, who stood on the harbor jetty, had just finished talking to his spiritual father, Athanasius, receiving his blessings. The monk, who was only in his early forties but looked much older after years of austere ascetic life, had escorted his spiritual son to the harbor. His long beard and pale face gave him a venerable appearance. The general kissed his right hand then bent his head so that the monk could place a rope necklace round his neck with a small wooden cross dangling from it. Athanasius remained on the jetty next to his helper, a young monk, and watched as Nicephorus and his accompaniment boarded the last boat to cross the strait. The anchors were rolled up and the sails spread wide for the westerly winds, when Athanasius made the sign of the cross in the air and said in a prophetical manner:

"This man is set for the fall and rising again of many."

\*\*\*

John and Demetrius stood on board the boat looking toward the busy city they were leaving behind for the second time in a year.

"I haven't really asked you, Demetrius, what is our march going to be like?" John asked, sinking his teeth into a large juicy peach

"Ah, what can I say? When we last marched from Caesarea, it was about the same time of year. At the beginning, the general made us march from dawn till dusk, only resting at noon to avoid the midday heat. It can be very hot and dry in those regions, you know, and some men couldn't keep up, so the general eventually slowed the pace a little. I remember I couldn't feel my legs at the end of each day. My skin became as black as a moor and my whole body suffered under the weight of the baggage."

"And for how long did you endure that torture?"

"Eight weeks. Eight *long* weeks! But this time, there will be no marching! Riding with the other cataphracts will be a picnic in comparison," he said happily as he, too, munched on a reddish peach. "I'm going to miss these Thracian peaches!"

"I suppose it will be an austere diet these coming eight weeks! Biscuit, biscuit and more biscuit! I'm already dreading that dried bread!" John shook his knapsack.

"We've barely started the journey and you're already complaining about the only food we can carry with us? Listen, if we get lucky, we might be able to do some foraging during our stops. Besides, the landowners whose properties we pass will provide whatever food and drink are available in their stock. Last year, the harvests were abundant and the march through the countryside was not lacking food and drink. But it seems that you got too spoiled this summer with all the banquets you've been attending."

"It's not as if *you* weren't present," John said lightly. "Among all the banquets we attended in the palaces of senators and officers, the food at the palace of Basil Lekapenos was always the best!"

"The man has taste."

"And a lot of money!"

Both of them fell silent for a moment watching the city grow smaller, contemplating the time they had spent there.

Finally, John said, rubbing his palms, "Let's see what awaits us this time. Now it's not just a petty emir and his piratic emirate that we march against. It is the strongest and most cunning leader of the Saracens."

"That 'petty emir' cost us nine hard months of campaign and three battles until he was subdued," he tossed the peach pit into the sea.

"Imagine how things will now be against Sayf."

Their recent victory in Crete and their vast numbers sent the spirits of the soldiers soaring. They were truly a formidable force, led by one of the most brilliant commanders the empire had ever known, and the soldiers who adored him were ready to follow him to the far ends of the earth. In a sense, they were going to the end of the earth, at least to the end of the Roman world and life as they knew it, where a different, hostile and dangerous order had now established itself.

# Chapter Fifteen

- ❧❧ -

For two long months, the massive army slowly marched in a seemingly endless train crossing the hills and snaking up and down the narrow mountain passes. For the first part of the journey, they enjoyed a relatively easy passage through the flat and densely populated Bithynia, where rich landowners provided the army with abundant quantities of food and drink; more out of obligation than generosity, of course. But as their march penetrated deeper to the southeast, the country became less hospitable and more sparsely populated. Gone were the smooth plains and beautiful fruit orchards. The mountains that soon appeared on the horizon promised a much more arduous journey.

As if the rugged terrain and the weight of their baggage weren't enough hardship for the soldiers, several times during their march through Anatolia, dark clouds concealed the midday sun and roaring thunder was followed by torrential rain, pouring down from the sky and turning the dirt roads into quagmires, impassable to humans and animals. Such mountain storms and flash summer floods were common to the area, as the native Demetrius later informed John. There on that rugged plateau, the hot days quickly turned into frigid nights and the flat plains into rocky ridges. However, the beauty of the land's natural flora and landscape was, to say the least, captivating. Had the soldiers not been marching for hours every day, heavily loaded with baggage and armor, they might have been able to pay more attention to the rare charm that God bestowed upon their surroundings. Mountains as high as the clouds stood like mighty warriors crowned in perpetual ice, overlooking the green valleys and the scattered blue lakes in a sublime image. Innumerable streams of crystal-clear waters flowed from the bosom of the earth, bringing life to the trees, birds and to every living creature. Flowers of every color and shape sprouted with dazzling beauty, carrying the signature of a divine florist.

It was thus an unexpectedly less exhausting journey for John and Demetrius. They rode on horseback alongside the general at the head of the column with minimum effort compared to the foot soldiers.

They had set out from Constantinople in early August, and by the end of their march, it was mid-October. Autumn was already upon them. Tall maple and birch trees lined their path as the soldiers ascended the last ridge that separated them from their destination, the city of Caesarea. With each gust of wind, a shower of reddish leaves fell gently upon them and strewed the way with a welcoming carpet of red, orange and yellow. That last ascent was particularly difficult, but finally reaching its top, a vast plain lay beneath them, extending endlessly toward the horizon in a marvelous panorama. In the middle of the plain stood a city with thick walls and high towers, whose might the great distance could not diminish.

"How joyful it is to indulge my eyes with your sight, O beautiful homeland," said the general, looking down toward his birthplace and heaving a deep sigh.

*It looks like a fine place, not too large but strong and secure.* John genuinely admired the walled city from afar, the name of which every little boy knew well. He remembered how, as a child, on the day before Christmas, he would go with his friends, knocking on doors, singing the *'Kalanda'*, the traditional Christmas songs, in return for some sweets, dried fruit or possibly a copper coin. He particularly remembered that stanza that begged their listeners to be generous and take Saint Basil's role as gift bearers:

*The holy Basil's on his way,*
*But he has gifts for none today,*
*He's still far in ancient Caesarea,*
*But you're here, my generous 'Kyria[1]'*

Nicephorus' enthusiastic voice interrupted John's distant memories, "This is the mistress of the plain, the fortress of the brave, and the homeland of saints. This is Caesarea, my loyal men, the capital of Cappadocia that gave us Gregory, Basil, and a myriad of saints and leaders. Now it shall be the base from which you launch yourselves upon the enemy and crush them like a steel rod crushes clay jars!"

*He really did miss home.*

The men began their cautious descent toward the city, following the winding road on the steep mountainside, making the long column fully visible to the city's watchtowers. The chilly autumn wind that occasionally blew reminded them of the harsh season that was soon to prevail on the plateau. When they had crossed about half the distance to the city, a band

---

[1] Kyria: Lady.

61

of horsemen, no more than twenty, appeared to be riding in their direction. As they drew nearer, Nicephorus' face glowed with joy. A horseman who appeared to be at the head of the group hastened to meet Nicephorus, his horse galloping on the dirt road, kicking up a trail of dust. When the two men finally met, they hurriedly dismounted and embraced warmly, slapping each other's back and roaring with laughter.

It took the men only a second to realize that their general was in fact embracing his younger brother, General Leo, who bore a remarkable resemblance to Nicephorus, though taller and better looking.

"It's been more than a year, brother!" said Leo happily.

"Yes, yes, and what a year! A year blessed by God Almighty with victories against the lawless Saracens on all fronts."

"Even after this long march you look as strong and fresh as ever! I have so much to tell you. There are so many things to be discussed."

"We have all winter!" Nicephorus said, patting his brother's shoulder and staring him in the face. "After which we shall take our revenge from Sayf Ad-Dawla."

*Revenge?* John wondered. *What revenge is he talking about? Is it the animosity between two combatants or is there more to it that I don't know?*

Leo nodded grimly, his smile quickly fading at the mention of the Arab emir's name.

"You taught him a good lesson in the defiles and injured his pride, but that hardly pays for the evil deed he has committed. I will not rest until I have wreaked vengeance upon him and his city."

"Yes, looks like we do have all winter indeed. It turns out that the major assault we thought was coming from the south will not come anytime soon. By the time the news of your approach with the army spread in Cappadocia, the Arabs left their outposts and fled south to their border castles. Come now! Let's not stay here too long. It's going to rain," Leo said, looking at the black clouds that were looming from behind the mountains. "We have already prepared the area for your men's camp, right next to that of my army. All they need to do is set up their tents under the city walls."

"Efficient as always," said Nicephorus, who then sent messengers with the news to his sub-commanders marching further behind with the body of the army, that their camp was almost ready. The exhausted men were thrilled by that gesture of hospitality from General Leo. After all, the two armies were now going to be united, and the formidable force that was to emerge was promising a change of fortunes in the ongoing warfare with the Arabs.

"So, you grew up around these regions, hah, so different from where I grew up," John said to his comrade as the entire party advanced at a slow pace to the city through the flat red-soiled plain.

"Well, it wasn't exactly here. My village is about ten miles away, but you're right it's a totally different place than the capital. I remember spending the long summer days outdoors with the other village boys. We played all day long in the fields and the mountains, climbing the high rocks and swimming in the rivers. Some days we even forgot to eat and only felt how terribly hungry we were after we had returned home at dusk," he said dreamily, his mind travelling through time and space. "I remember armies marching south through our village almost every summer, pretty much like us now. The village boys, myself included, would stand by the dirt road and watch with amusement as the thousands of soldiers, horses and carriages passed by our otherwise quiet little village. They looked so brave, so strong, almost like heroes in our eyes. Those summer spectacles were our only reminder that there was actually a world beyond the borders of our village."

Small drops of rain began to fall, just as the city's main gate was being opened wide. The settlement of the army on a flat and elevated area outside the walls was entrusted to the sub-commanders while the two generals and their entourage advanced through the town's main gate to the ancestral home of the Phocas family, situated in the northern part of the town.

The settlement itself appeared to John much like the other towns they had passed through on their journey. Each had a population of a few thousands which could easily fit into one of Constantinople's neighborhoods, and each had high walls that protected the people from the frequent Arab raids. It was understandable that not many people seemed willing to move into the provinces that lay within range of such hostile incursions. Caesarea, being the capital of the Cappadocian province, looked significantly larger and more militarized than any of the other towns. Even before any of Nicephorus's regiments came within its walls, Leo's men had already made the town look like a military base. Soldiers could be seen everywhere. To require such vast troops meant that the targets Nicephorus had set his mind on conquering were extraordinary.

John, riding behind the two generals, could see that they were already engaged in deep discussion. Leo appeared to be briefing Nicephorus about the conditions at the front. He was describing the latest incidents, giving numbers and dates, along with his own assessment of the situation.

Although Leo was the commander of the western armies, and Nicephorus of the eastern, which gave both theoretically equal titles and authority, the latter was nevertheless more senior than his brother, partly due to his distinguished military achievement but mainly because customs granted the commander of the eastern armies the higher position and prestige. Nicephorus had originally occupied the eastern position, prior to the campaign to Crete. Now he was back to assuming full command.

John and Demetrius would be lodged along with the rest of the general's bodyguards in one of the many apartments that were scattered around the Phocas residence, where about two thousand retainers already lived with their offspring, having served the influential family for generations. The house itself was more like a large fortress with high walls and square towers built with huge well-cut stones. It had a deep moat surrounding it, and there were armed men at all times positioned on top of its towers keeping watch of the area. It looked so different than the prestigious 'civilian' residence at the capital. It was a fortified palace befitting its warlike masters in a warlike country, distant from the refinement and civility of Constantinople, both geographically and culturally.

The winter that followed was long and cold, with very little to do apart from frequent scouting campaigns to check on enemy positions. The generals and their sub-commanders spent the entire season planning the massive campaign that would be launched in the spring, aiming to crush the archenemy of the empire, Sayf, once and for all.

# Chapter Sixteen

- ☎☜ -

## Cilicia, Spring 962

"There, behind the wooded hill ... do you see that tower ... the stone tower with the green banner?" Leo said, on horseback with an outstretched sword. A distant stone tower appeared, partially concealed behind the trees, while a green flag with white Arabic inscriptions, waved on the wind.

"Yes, I can see it," Nicephorus replied, he, too, on horseback and in full body armor.

"That is Tarsus's outmost tower. The city castle has been enlarged and fortified during your absence."

"The birthplace of the blessed Paul shall, with God's grace, become Roman again," Nicephorus confirmed passionately, then looked back to the thousands of eyes that were fixed upon him, and with a wave of his sword ordered the army to march forward.

Four months had passed since they had reached Caesarea; their base in Anatolia. But to the soldiers, those winter months were very different from the idle months of the previous summer. Almost every day, Nicephorus personally supervised the drilling of the soldiers, regardless of the cold, mud or snow. It was a long and important period of intense training that preceded the major spring offensive. Now, that March had arrived, and spring had gradually begun to replace winter, the army was again on the march, but where to?

The eyes of Nicephorus had been set upon Sayf's capital, Aleppo; but before seeking that trophy, there was still some work to be done. He had to subdue Sayf's allies and coreligionists who controlled a chain of castles and fortified city-states in Cilicia that would otherwise be at his rear and threaten his advance to his enemy's capital. He therefore set out with his brother from Caesarea at the head of the huge army, aiming to take those cities, one-by-one.

"This is going to be tough!" Demetrius said, the sound of his metal armor and chain mail jangling with every trot of his horse. "Once more, there lies in front of us a walled city that appears impregnable."

"You just said it: it *appears* impregnable," John said, emphasizing every syllable. "No city is really impregnable, except for *the* City[2] of course; never conquered, and never will be. All other cities eventually capitulate. And today, this one will!"

"I'm impressed by your confidence! Is it the smell of the fresh spring air, or the view of the sea that has invigorated your spirits so much?" Demetrius smiled.

"It is the booty, my friend. You among all should know! With every city that we conquer, you get to rebuy one more acre of the farm that once belonged to your father. Besides, it's not as if we're doing this for the first time. We are professional soldiers now. This is just another day at work!"

"Ha-ha. Just another day at work! That's what my father would say in the morning before heading to the fields."

"Of course, dear Demetrius. Most if not all of these soldiers behind you see it that way! And don't tell me they are here just to defend the empire and protect Christendom and all that smart talk. Yes, all of this is really important and honorable, but we are here only because we get well paid, and because we get to lay our hands on a lot of booty. If no gold were involved, you wouldn't see any of these men here."

"That's true, John, we all need money to survive, but you must admit that our job requires courage that few possess and grants great honor that few deserve."

"Smart talk again." John let out a long chuckle, cut short by his friend's exclamation.

"Listen! Can you hear that?"

A bell on top of one of the enemy towers was now ringing loudly and frantically, its sound diminishing through space, yet still audible to the ears of the advancing Romans. The whole army had been marching in the wide plain approaching the city of Tarsus. They were about three miles away from the city walls when the enemy sounded the alarm.

"They've finally seen us," Leo said to his brother.

"It doesn't change a thing," Nicephorus replied confidently, even merrily. "The sea encircles the city from one side and we from the other. They have nowhere to go."

"Then we're heading for a siege."

"My guess is that they will choose to fight us in a pitched battle rather than endure a long blockade. It's still spring and they have consumed their supplies during the winter months. Now, just three

---

[2] The City refers to Constantinople

months before the harvest, they will surely choose battle over famine. Order the men to march in battle formation."

Leo turned and gave the order to the sub-commanders, and the few words he uttered worked like magic. Two men sounded their trumpets in an intermittent call, and immediately the entire host reorganized into a new formation. Instead of the long column, the cataphracts advanced ahead and formed themselves into a wide front of four consecutive lines facing the enemy like a triangle; a spearhead.

Directly behind them rode the domestic and his elite bodyguards, where he could oversee their movements. The foot soldiers with their long pikes formed multiple lines behind the general and on both the cavalry's flanks. Two large wooden towers on wheels were being pulled at the rear by twenty oxen. Several other catapults and battering rams were transported on open wagons. These were the siege engines brought with the army from Caesarea, since the mission involved conquering walled cities and fortresses.

The whole multitude marched toward the city in a concerted movement, the earth rumbling under their feet.

On the other side, more soldiers were seen taking their positions on top of the city walls until there was no space between them. Peasants fled their fields and sought refuge within the safety of the walls, though not all were lucky enough to make it inside before the gates were shut. The less fortunate became stranded outside the walls and were left to meet their horrible fate. The scene of the huge Roman army advancing toward the city and the rumbling sound of forty thousand soldiers stomping the ground brought terror even to the hearts of the bravest of men.

As the army came within one mile of Tarsus, a small gate in the wall opened its shutters, emitting a single rider on a pitch-black Arabian stallion, who galloped toward the Romans. The domestic ordered a halt.

"He must be a messenger," John muttered.

"And he is wearing a white turban, a sign of peace," Nicephorus added to the words of his bodyguard.

"Let's see what he has to offer," Leo said with some optimism, to which Nicephorus replied with apparent disdain, "It is probably a waste of time."

The rider advanced to the front line of cataphracts until he was about fifty paces away. He then dismounted and walked slowly toward them.

"I have come with an offer of peace from my lord, the Emir of Tarsus," he said in perfect Greek, though with a trembling voice.

"Let him pass!" the domestic ordered from behind the lines.

The horsemen moved aside making a gap in their ranks, all the while shooting hostile looks at the messenger, but allowing the unarmed man to proceed on foot to meet the domestic. He approached solemnly and bowed with respect.

"What have you got?" the general inquired.

"I have come with an offer of peace."

"And how is it that you speak our tongue so well? Were you their prisoner, or perhaps a traitor of your people and faith?"

"I am neither this nor that, Your Excellency. My father is an Arab merchant, my mother a Christian slave whom he bought, freed, and married. She taught me her tongue."

"Fair enough. Now what is your lord's offer?"

The messenger took a deep breath, then said what he had to say all at once, in concise mechanical tones, "In return for turning back from our city, the emir promises to break his alliance with Sayf and to relinquish all ties with him. He will ally himself with the Romans, fighting their enemies and befriending their friends. He will add to that a hundred pounds of gold and three hundred pounds of silver. My lord is ready to present these pledges in a written document with his signature."

"Is that all?" Nicephorus sounded unsatisfied, his small eyes getting narrower.

"Yes, Your Excellency. He vows to be your loyal ally if you choose peace, and to show you all the due respect as a guest and a friend, but if it is war what you seek, then you shall only see the blades of our swords."

"Tell your master that I have come here to redeem what is ours and I have no intention of withdrawing before this city is returned to the Roman fold. Now you hear *my* terms. If you agree to surrender unconditionally, you will all be granted a safe exit from the city with all your belongings. If not, then you choose to face our wrath, and neither your arms nor your walls will protect you."

"But, Your Excellency, you are asking for the impossible. If you would only consider the emir's offer, you would find in him a true and faithful ally."

"I'm not looking for allies here. Your master would be wise to accept a surrender and save his people from the bloodshed that will otherwise ensue. The reign of Christ and of Caesar shall be restored in Tarsus."

"It is war then," the messenger concluded grimly, and, bowing again, he walked to his horse, then rode back to the city followed by a trail of dust.

"Hold your positions and prepare for battle!" Nicephorus

thundered.

An hour passed in long anticipation. The cataphracts remained beside their horses, fully clad in iron, and the foot soldiers stood with their long pikes pointing to the sky. There were no sounds to be heard except the chirping of spring birds in the surrounding trees.

"What do you say about assaulting the walls?" asked Leo.

"No … no … not yet." Nicephorus replied. "Let us wait a while. It will not be long before they come out to us."

A few minutes later, his expectations materialized. The three gates facing the Romans were suddenly flung open and a stream of soldiers and horses poured out each amid roaring sounds of trumpets and war cries. It took the smaller Arab force only a few minutes to position itself in the plain between the city walls and the Roman army. Their young Emir Ibn Az-Zayyat was leading his forces, riding an Arabian charger and wearing a black turban. Behind the Arab army stood many drummers, banging the large instruments, hoping to infuse enthusiasm in the hearts of the defenders and fear in the hearts of the attackers. The soldiers on top of the walls also did their share of shouting, adding to the clamor.

Now, realizing that the battle he sought was coming, Nicephorus looked toward his men and said: "Let us pray!" The armed men crossed themselves and bowed their heads as their general began reciting a prayer loudly, articulating each word with reverence and precision.

"Christ our Lord! Look down upon us, your humble servants and save us on this day. Grant us prevalence over our enemies and yours, so that we may praise thee as long as we live, together with your eternal Father and life-giving Spirit, through the intercession of your mother, the holy Theotokos and all the saints. Amen."

A thundering *Amen* resounded from the soldiers who, as if invigorated by a hidden power, looked now more invincible than ever, their eyes glowed with defiance. The domestic raised his head and looked at them, then conveyed his final instructions before the battle:

"Do not advance too close to the walls! Their archers are waiting to hunt you down from above! And do not pursue them when they retreat! Attack them midway to the city! But wait for them to charge first!"

"They are no match for us; they are barely half our number," John whispered with amazement. "Yet they choose to fight. I don't know what to call them, brave or insane."

"Don't expect an easy fight, though. These zealots would rather die than surrender," Demetrius whispered back.

The Roman cataphracts advanced at the order of their general, the foot soldiers in their pursuit slowly maintained their wedge formation until the two armies were separated by no more than five hundred paces. The emir finally bellowed his war cry, "Allahu Akbar!"

Nicephorus in turn gave the order to attack, and the two armies rushed toward a terrifying confrontation. The Arab army, both on horse and on foot, charged with indescribable fury and zeal, their emir boldly leading the front wave of the attack with a drawn crescent-shaped sword held high. But the Romans, whose heavy cavalry charged like a wall of iron, collided with their opponents and crushed them without much difficulty.

Nicephorus, following the cataphracts in their advance, oversaw this as they carved their way through the Arab army, cutting down and trampling them like sickles through wheat at harvest. Shouts of men and clashes of swords drowned out the banging of drums. A cloud of dust stirred by thousands of feet and hooves almost obscured the walls of the city, only a few hundred paces away.

But just when the cataphracts were turning back in order to prepare for the second wave of attack, there emerged from the cloud of dust the fearless emir, surrounded by his elite warriors, about fifty horsemen armed with gleaming swords and heavy maces and who charged straight toward Nicephorus. It would be enough, the emir must have thought, to kill or injure the leader of the Christians for chaos to prevail in their ranks. It was a testing moment for everyone, especially those entrusted with the safekeeping of the domestic.

"Protect the domestic!" John shouted with all his might when he saw the fast approaching force and in vain tried to rally more men to the defense of the supreme commander, but his efforts and cries were lost amid the battle tumult and before a moment passed, intense fighting had broken out between the two sides. The Arabs were desperately throwing themselves upon the general's bodyguard, trying to break the ranks around him. John and Demetrius struggled with the rest of the men trying to fend off the attack. Nicephorus himself displayed outstanding valor as he exchanged blows with the younger emir.

The Arabs must have known that they only had a short time to achieve their goal before the cataphracts returned and the foot soldiers closed in on them from behind. Not before long, both cavalry and infantry were doing just that. Realizing that his chance had gone and seeing the futility of his efforts, the emir broke off the fight and fled with most of his men, sounding the retreat.

"These crazy bastards!" John shouted in indignation, gasping for air.

"I told you!" Demetrius replied, wiping the muddy sweat that had seeped into his eyes.

The remnant of the Arab army was following the emir in a chaotic retreat to the city, the Roman cavalry were assaulting their rear with gruesome results, but nevertheless, still obeying Nicephorus's orders of not coming too close to the city walls for fear of the archers. Suddenly and unexpectedly, Nicephorus reversed his orders "Follow them! Follow them to the gates!" and then looked straight at John whilst delivering a crucial order, "You make sure those gates don't get closed!"

Upon hearing the general's orders, John, Demetrius and a few other men dashed in pursuit of the emir, who was seen retreating to the largest of the three open gates.

Heedless of the arrows that were beginning to rain down upon them, John and the group managed to catch up with the emir as he was about to gain entry into the safety of the walls. There, near the gate, another ferocious fight broke out between the emir and his bodyguard from one side, and John and his group from the other.

"Don't let them get in! Hold on until reinforcements arrive!" John shouted to his comrades, but before he had delivered his orders, an arrow penetrated his horse's neck causing the animal to collapse, and throwing its steel-clad rider to the ground. The impact was so violent that John remained motionless for a moment before he could attempt to stand up again. When finally on his feet, an enemy soldier wielding a bloody sword delivered a blow to his left shoulder. If it hadn't been for the metal armor, his left arm could have easily been severed. Demetrius rushed on horseback to his friend's aid and immediately cut down the assailant. But John was now in a vulnerable position. He had lost his horse, and was weighed down by the heavy armor. He had no choice but to back up against the wall until the rest of the cavalry arrived. Meanwhile, Demetrius had to leave his comrade and strive to fulfill the mission.

With his back to the wall, John saw the catapult officers and archers taking more progressive positions and unleashing their weapons against the enemy soldiers stationed at the walls. This caused the enemy arrows to subside as the shooters were themselves under attack, giving the Romans the opportunity to advance closer to the walls.

Seeing the entire Roman army closing in on them and being unable to shut the gate, convinced some of the defenders to surrender, throwing down their weapons and begging for mercy, while others, including their leader, managed to flee inside the city. Therefore, when John noticed an abandoned horse whose Arab rider had been slain, he seized its reins and mounted it, regaining what no cataphract should lose during battle. A moment later, Nicephorus arrived at the gate with the rest of his bodyguard and more Romans flooded inside the city.

"Good work, men! Good work!!" He saluted those who struggled at the gate and rallied the troops inside the city. "The city is ours! Those who surrender redeem themselves, those who fight, show no mercy!"

By the early afternoon, fighting in the city streets, though slowly subsiding, was not yet over, as some fanatics refused to surrender, receiving courage from the fact that their leader was still fighting. But then, word came that the emir had taken refuge inside the Governor's Palace; a large building in the city's center, with high towers and thick walls.

"Is he still fighting?" Leo, who had arrived from his position in the rear, wondered.

"Not for much longer," Nicephorus replied "Come, John, get the men, hurry up."

They all rode to the Governor's Palace. There they found their own soldiers ramming the gate, violently trying to force entry.

"He has barricaded himself inside with some men," the regiment sub-commander explained.

"What is he thinking? Doesn't he know it's all over? Why doesn't he simply surrender?" John questioned the emir's logic.

"Worthless effort. He will only buy himself another hour or two," replied another soldier.

The ramming of the strong wooden gate continued unabated.

John looked above the gate and saw something that made him gasp. He frantically pointed upward, "Look! Up …!"

When the men lifted their heads, they saw atop of one of the towers, the Emir Ibn Az-Zayyat himself, standing under the green banner. He had taken off his combat attire and armor and was instead wearing a long white robe and a white turban; the traditional Arab costume in the time of peace. The soldiers ramming the gate stopped what they were doing and gazed up with amazement. He stood like a statue, surveying the horizon, his white robe flapping with the wind on top of the lofty tower. Then, in an unexpected move; the young prince stepped over the parapet and, giving the city a final look, dove with arms spread wide open. Everyone heard the gruesome crunching sound of his body colliding with the ground.

"I believe *now*, it's over," John muttered, grimly.

# Chapter Seventeen

- 𝒮𝒞𝒢 -

During the few months that followed, the army continued its conquest of the region, capturing numerous fortresses and walled cities in Cilicia, a prerequisite for the coming invasion of Aleppo. But since Nicephorus preferred a surprise winter attack on Sayf's capital, he returned to Caesarea and dismissed his soldiers for the remainder of the summer, so they could visit home – for most of them had been recruited from Anatolia – returning the next autumn to Caesarea.

Leo, being domestic of the western armies, departed for Constantinople, leaving the bulk of the army under his brother's command.

Demetrius was released to go and spend the hot season with his family in his village outside Caesarea. It was no secret that after almost two years of absence, he was dying to see his wife and parents. He dreamt of the day when he would hug his beautiful spouse again. He had only left her because he wanted a better life for them. He didn't want her to toil endlessly. Now with the money in his possession, he hoped he could make a difference. He hoped he could repurchase the farm with the small fortune in his possession. Perhaps their landlord would be magnanimous enough to agree to sell them back what was theirs only few years ago.

On his way to his village, his anticipation was almost unbearable. He relished the sweet moment of reunion and the happy days he was going to spend there. These rosy visions glimmered before his mind's eye until he arrived at the tiny mountainous village.

Meanwhile, John remained in the service of his master in Caesarea, where he spent his days accompanying him on numerous visits to the notables and landowners in and around Caesarea. Nicephorus, being the military governor of the region, wanted to make sure that the obligations of these magnates to the state were fulfilled, and he made sure of that personally. In proportion to the sizes of their estates, they were obliged to provide the army with a certain number of soldiers, armed and equipped. A portion of their crops was taken as a tax for feeding the vast army encamped nearby and in constant need of sustenance.

It was a new experience for John, traversing that part of the empire in the company of a most prominent figure, learning a few things about the complicated mechanism by which the empire operated and collected its resources. Those tours were enjoyed by the domestic as much as by the young officer, though obviously for different reasons. While Nicephorus, like a lion roaming his natural habitat, took pleasure in enforcing the law on the wealthy and powerful magnates, John, as curious and adventurous as ever, found satisfaction in observing the process that asserted the power and authority of the state he proudly served.

"You shall have to do this on your own one day," Nicephorus would often tell his disciple

***

The date agreed upon for the reunion of the army was one of the year's major milestones, a feast commonly regarded as marking the end of summer. On that day, fires were kindled all night on mountaintops throughout the empire and beyond.[3] Therefore, when some soldiers were ascending the mountains around Caesarea, carrying their burning torches and leading mules laden with firewood, the forefronts of the troops were beginning to arrive at their camp outside the city, announcing the end of their rest period and the resumption of the season of warfare.

On the eve of the holy feast, Nicephorus and Leo attended the vigil inside the Basilica of St. Basil with his usual fervor and diligence, surrounded by a band of his guards, while John stood by the church's entrance, keeping watch.

On the altar was placed a priceless relic; a small piece of wood, the size of a finger, believed to be a part of the cross that once stood on the hill of Golgotha a millennium ago. It was placed in a beautifully ornamented golden box and displayed to the faithful only once a year on that particular day. Hundreds of peasants had been marching to Caesarea from all over the province in order to receive the blessing of the 'life-bearing cross'. Although the basilica was spacious, it did not have the capacity to take in a great number of pilgrims, many of whom stood outside the church in silent prayer while others, mainly women and

---

[3] The Exaltation of the Cross preserved the memory when the empress Helen discovered the true cross hundreds of years before in Jerusalem. To inform her son Constantine, then in Constantinople, a chain of fires on mountain tops was lit extending from Jerusalem to Constantinople. The tradition of lighting fires on mountain tops remained an important part of the traditions surrounding that feast.

children, huddled together and slept on the square's stone-paved floor, resting from their laborious march.

John had been expecting the return of his comrade with the first wave of visitors, as his village was no more than a day's trip from Caesarea. A little before midnight, among the arriving pilgrims, he recognized a figure approaching slowly under the moonlit sky. He looked tired as he dismounted, tethered his horse to a nearby tree, and came to meet his friend.

"You look like you haven't slept for a week!" John said, embracing him.

"It's the road. I had to ride nonstop," Demetrius replied, looking a bit dizzy and exhausted.

"But why hadn't you set out earlier, then?"

"My father. He's very sick. I couldn't leave him like that. "

"Is it serious?"

"Just yesterday, the fever left him, so I set out."

"Go on to your room, go get some sleep," John said in a reassuring voice, patting his friend's shoulder.

"No, I'll not go. I'll just sit here and rest a little."

He walked a few paces, laid down on the floor next to the church wall and, putting his coat under his head, immediately slipped into a deep sleep. The moon was full, and the stars glittered that night. A slight breeze with a bit of chilliness picked up occasionally and rustled the leaves of the large sycamore tree that stood in the middle of the churchyard.

But then came a dream, a deeply strange and unpleasant one. The thoughts that battled inside his brain were manifesting themselves.

Demetrius saw himself riding through a dreary landscape with bare trees and frozen swamps. The sky was overcast, and small snowflakes were whirling through the air. He felt greatly upset, almost suffocating, from the dismal surroundings.

Two other horsemen came out from the woods and joined him, their bodies covered in heavy armor, their heads in metal helmets. They said nothing, their faces concealed behind iron.

As the three men rode silently, these bleak surroundings suddenly changed as they approached a village with attractive white houses, red roofs and colorful flowerbeds. A few children played happily and laughed in the streets. Demetrius felt relief surge in his heart as he passed through that oasis of joy in the midst of the pervading gloom, but, having advanced beyond the village boundaries and back into the grey landscape, he stopped hearing the children's laughter anymore and felt subject to great sadness, something which his silent and anonymous companions did nothing to prevent. He looked over his shoulder and was appalled to see that the village was ruined now, its houses half-burnt, smoke still ascending from their charred walls, and the bodies of the little children scattered around. A terrible sight. He began to cry.

"Who did this? Who did this?" he repeatedly and hysterically questioned the two horsemen but received no answer. Instead, he looked down at his sword and was shocked to see it dripping with blood, his coat and shirt were stained in red, too. The swords of the two other men were also dripping blood. He couldn't believe it. He took off his blood-stained coat and shirt and threw them away along with the sword. Now naked from the waist up, he shivered in the freezing cold and felt immense sadness. He didn't know where he was headed. It didn't seem that his distressing journey was going to end anywhere soon.

"Wake up, Demetrius! Wake up!" He finally felt John's hand shaking him gently.

He awoke drenched in cold sweat and gasping for breath.

"You were shivering, I covered you with my coat, but then you didn't look very well. I think you started hallucinating," John said, kneeling beside him.

"I just had a bad dream," Demetrius explained. "What time is it?"

"It's almost dawn, the service is about to end soon."

"Alright, I'd better get ready then," he said, wiping his face with his hands.

"Go behind the church, there is a little water fountain. Drink some water and wash your face too."

It was still dark, and the huddling families were still fast asleep in the square, but it wasn't long until the first light of dawn emerged, and the church bells began ringing, announcing the end of another long service.

The sleeping ones started to wake up and take their places in the square in preparation for the long-awaited blessing with the holy relic.

Demetrius went to the water fountain, splashed several handfuls of water on his face then straightened up and took a few deep intakes of breath. Upon his return, he found a large crowd already standing in the square, both locals and pilgrims ready to receive the blessing.

*Must be more than ten thousand.*

At the church door stood Nicephorus and the local bishop holding the most holy relic, protected in its golden box. Two steps below them stood John in his military uniform, along with a few other guards forming a semicircle that separated the general and the prelate from the gathered multitude. The climax of the whole feast had come, and the bishop, holding the box which contained the piece of wood with both hands, drew with it the sign of the cross three times in the air over the people who, in turn, responded with a recurrent, "Kyrie Eleison!" They had walked for hours, some even for days, to witness this moment. Many showed their gratitude with tears of joy and repentance.

But the feast also had another aspect, it was the day when the church blessed the produce of the land and thanked God for the harvest of the dwindling summer. And as was customary, there were stacked beside the church hundreds of wooden crates filled with fruit donated by the rich landowners of the province in hopes of a plentiful harvest in the year to come.

A short while after the blessing was given, the multitude began to disperse, each being handed an apple, a pear or a cluster of grapes by the deacons. The locals went to their homes, some of the pilgrims went to the bread shops, and others remained in the square to rest.

Demetrius walked toward Nicephorus, who had come down the few steps after exchanging a few words with the bishop, and was now accompanied by his men, ready to ride home. Being used to austere ascetic discipline, he appeared not the least fatigued by the long sleepless hours of worship.

"Good morning, Master Nicephorus!" He bowed with respect.

"You made it on time, Demetrius, I hope your family is well?"

"Yes, Master." replied Demetrius timidly. "They are doing just fine. Thank you for asking."

"Good, good. Now, come along and get something to eat. You look pale and tired."

Nicephorus had maintained a fatherly relationship with John and Demetrius. He deeply believed they were among his bravest, most honest soldiers, and he also knew very well that even to the toughest of men, a few encouraging and reassuring words meant the world.

Demetrius untied his horse and rode at the rear of the band toward the Phocas residence, but John, who was eager to know what had happened with his friend during his absence, deliberately slowed his horse's pace until he was riding next to him. Demetrius appeared still to be tired, his eyes sleepy and his hair a mess.

"When was the last time you ate anything?" asked John with genuine concern.

"I don't remember. I think it was yesterday noon. Mother had given me some bread and dried fish for the road."

"Here, take this apple." John handed him the golden fruit. "Now tell me about your stay there."

Demetrius stared into space for a moment then heaved a sigh.

"The first day I arrived, I went straight to the field and there I found the three of them, my wife and parents working under the hot sun. They couldn't believe their eyes when they saw me, and the truth is … neither could I. I looked at them and saw what two years of hard labor could do to a person. They looked tired, inside and out, my father's few grey hairs had multiplied. His face looked sickly and weak. Mother looked like she hadn't had a day's rest in months. But what broke my heart was Eleni. I had promised her a good life, one that we could at least spend together. Instead I had left her and gone away. She didn't know if I was even going to come back alive or not.

"My mother later told me that my father had been intermittently sick, spending many days in bed unable to move, and often with fever. With him unable to work most of the time and having to pay the expensive fees to the physicians, they had accumulated a large debt, mostly to the landowner. Most of the money I had with me was spent paying him back. So much for rebuying our farm." He shook his head.

John listened silently.

"Still, we did have a good time together. For me and Eleni, seeing each other again was like heaven. I cannot begin to describe the happiness, the ecstasy we both felt. She begged me not to leave again, but, of course, she knew I had no other choice. Then came the moment of departure. Even in our joyous moments, the thought that we were going to separate again haunted us like a dark ghost. At all times, even in the most pleasant of moments, there was this constant hidden feeling of distress, of guilt, of the temporality of joy and the inevitability of separation. As hard as I tried, I couldn't get that bitterness to disappear."

"Well, now you're here and soon we'll be marching south. If you want to stay alive, all you need to think about is how to fight the next battle."

***

By the second hour of the day, the group reached the Phocas residence. There they found a group of soldiers waiting for them in the courtyard. They'd been sitting on long benches placed under the porticos of the square courtyard. Their horses were being led away by the servants to be fed and watered while they were being served glasses of cold water, reserved for important visitors. A deep cavern close by was filled every year with the winter's snow, compressed and preserved to be mixed with wines and refreshments in summer.

It was obvious that they had just arrived from a faraway place as they hadn't taken off their breast plates. A short, well-built man with reddish blond hair and deep-blue eyes appeared to take precedence among them, although he was no older than thirty-five or thirty-six.

When they saw Nicephorus and his bodyguards arrive, the guests rose to their feet and acknowledged their host with a military salute and a bow.

"Who are these?" Demetrius whispered to his friend.

"I have no idea, but they appear to be the general's acquaintances and he must have been expecting their arrival."

The sturdy blond man approached Nicephorus joyously as the latter dismounted, then embracing him warmly, said:

"So glad to see you again, Uncle!"

# Chapter Eighteen

- 𝔈𝔒𝔒𝔒 -

The newly-arrived John was none other than the famous commander, John Tzimiskes. Nicephorus's nephew was an outstanding soldier and had been given command of one of the empire's most critical border provinces in Anatolia. John noted his excessive self-confidence and high discipline. Now that his maternal uncle and first tutor in military affairs was planning the invasion of the enemy's capital, he called for Tzimiskes to join him on the campaign, along with most of his army. For the last weeks of the summer, Nicephorus kept the army busy with excessive training and daily maneuvers. Then, in October, the time had finally come for the long march south to Aleppo to 'cut the snake's head,' as he put it.

The army marched east for almost two weeks in the muddy countryside of northern Syria, capturing many fortresses and towns along the way and replenishing them with garrisons, thereby securing its return route. In the small town of Doliche, which had been captured that morning, the soldiers were busy setting their tents around its castle after its Arab garrison had simply fled at the sight of the approaching Romans. It was mid-December and winter had returned vigorously that year. Rain was pouring down one evening when Nicephorus and his war council gathered in the fortress' largest hall to discuss their next move. The big room was lit with a few torches installed on the walls. Nicephorus, Tzimiskes, and the sub-commanders were assembled around a heavy wooden table. John stood by the door.

"Men," Nicephorus began, "I have called you to this meeting because it has come to my attention that Sayf has dispatched a large army north to meet us. He is not leading this army, though, and has preferred to stay at home."

"And to where is this army heading?" asked one of the sub-commanders by the name of Romanus Kourkouas, a valiant man in his thirties who had to his credit many successful raids against the Muslim border emirates.

"The scouts who brought us the news reported that it is heading north, more to the northwest, toward Antioch." Nicephorus answered.

"Antioch?!" Kourkouas exclaimed. "But we are going east. If their intention is to intercept us, they ought to be heading northeast instead of northwest. It is either they are acting with superb craftiness or with total ignorance."

"I'd say it's the latter," continued Nicephorus, "their ignorance of our destination, and thus our direction, seems to be complete."

"So far, our advance east cannot be indicative of our true intentions," said Tzimiskes. "In their eyes, we could as well be heading to Germanicia or Hierapolis, or even further east."

"Yes, that is true," said Nicephorus. "So, we should continue heading east, and then make a sudden turn to the south and appear before the walls of Aleppo. Then, I would like very much to see what that arrogant Sayf will do!"

"And the army that he sent for us? What shall we do about it?" Kourkouas asked again.

"Nothing, absolutely nothing!" Nicephorus replied, smiling to his cavalry commander. "We will simply ignore this misinformed and misdirected army of his and head straight toward his capital. I believe the other day I saw you playing chess, Kourkouas, with you, Maleinos, wasn't it?"

The sub-commander Eustathius Maleinos was another member of Nicephorus's war council as well as the governor of Cappadocia. "Yes, General, we sometimes play chess in the evenings. I usually win." He smiled.

"Then you must know quite well that when you surprise your adversary with a checkmate, it doesn't matter how many pawns he still has elsewhere on the board. The dispatched forces can do nothing to save the king. Let our opponent send his armies north and west while we head east and south. In the end, they will be roaming all of northern Syria in search of us while we sack their capital."

"Then, this is your strategy, General?" Tzimiskes asked, seeking confirmation of the attack plan.

"Yes. With the absence of their main army, and by securing our return route, the path is clear for us to strike and destroy Aleppo once and for all. However, you should know that this remains no ordinary campaign. We are seeking to pierce the heart of the dragon and he is going to resist with all the might he can muster. How many men, in your opinion, can be gathered to face us?"

"As opposed to our fifty thousand, I would say no more than ten or fifteen thousand," replied Tzimiskes confidently. "And these troops would have to be gathered from his capital's garrison and its able-bodied men. Taken by surprise, there is little chance he will be able to recruit any more soldiers."

"But then again, let us not forget that we shall be attacking them at home. I would not underestimate the will of fifteen thousand men defending their homes and families," said Kourkouas.

"That might be true, but as the Arab proverb says, 'Numbers defeat courage' let alone that we possess both," Nicephorus answered.

"There is also another thing, commanders," said Tzimiskes, who sat next to Nicephorus facing the other commanders on the other side of the table. "The walls around Aleppo are dilapidated. The scouts we sent earlier this week came back today. They say that the Arabs do not show any intention of repairing them. That, in my opinion, proves beyond doubt that they are totally oblivious to our true destination."

"It could have been the heavy rain that is keeping them from doing the necessary repairs to the walls, for even a slight suspicion must have arisen in their minds that Aleppo could be our target," replied Maleinos

"Oh, but Maleinos, you don't know the man's vanity," said Nicephorus, correcting his sub-commander. "It's arrogance, sheer arrogance. That Arabian prince who rides to war in front of his army, performing acrobatic moves with his spear, throwing it up in the air like a buffoon and catching it in a flourish, playing his lyre as if he were going to a feast, that haughty character cannot bring himself to consider that we might actually attack his capital. He believes that his reputation alone is capable of repulsing us, but this arrogance of his shall soon become something of the past, a distant memory; for by the holy Mother of God, he and his city shall soon be humbled in mud and ashes!"

John looked at the angry domestic and could see that the campaign was as much a war of vengeance as it was one of conquest. Nicephorus clearly had a score to settle with Sayf and he seemed determined to take advantage of the opportunity to its fullest. But why such determination? He had never heard him speak with such deep animosity against any other enemy of the empire, yet more than once, the name of that Arab emir when uttered by Nicephorus had been accompanied by a desire for revenge. Now, John felt almost certain there was something he was missing.

After about an hour of discussion, the war council was dismissed. John left the hall and went outside to the courtyard where he noticed some of his comrades sitting around a small fire, warming themselves and chatting.

"Just the man I was looking for," he said to Andreas, the

bodyguard.

"Me?" the big man answered with an inviting smile. "Come, sit by the fire."

"So, what did they come up with?" asked Demetrius.

"We are marching to Aleppo tomorrow!" replied John to everyone's approbation.

"That big apple is waiting to be picked!" said one of the group to acclamations and cheers from the others. They began to conjure memories from the Cretan campaign, namely the storming of Chandax, where they had conquered an equally large and wealthy city. The talk of gold and women lit up the gathering, wine made it merry and loud.

"What did you want me for?" Andreas turned his head looking curious.

"You have spent more years with the domestic than all of us here. If there is anything to be known about him, you surely know it."

"What information do you require?"

"Do you happen to know why Nicephorus seems to hold such a grudge against this 'Sayf'? I mean, I know he is the Emir of the Saracens, the archenemy of the empire and all that, but inside that hall, I could sense that there was something more, something personal. I've often heard him speak about revenge when he mentions Sayf."

"Do you mean to tell me that you don't know about Constantine, the domestic's brother?"

"He has a brother named Constantine?"

"*Had*," answered Andreas, gravely.

"And what happened to him?"

"How could you not have heard of this before? But then again, it's a forbidden topic. The mere mention of it infuriates the domestic." The buzz of the merry group impeded Andreas's words from travelling further than John's ears.

"Listen, my dear John. Ten years ago, in a winter as harsh as this one, Sayf launched a campaign from Aleppo to the north. He captured many towns and fortresses and was on his way back to Syria, laden with booty, when Constantine Phocas, Nicephorus's youngest brother, blocked his return and inflicted heavy casualties on his army. Faced with an armed barrier, Sayf had to take a long detour back home, then caught up with the Domestic Bardas and his son Constantine near Germanicia. A fierce battle took place, this time Bardas barely escaped with his life, getting that hideous wound to his face for his troubles. Constantine in his turn was captured and carried off to Aleppo."

"They took him prisoner to Aleppo?" asked John, his eyes as wide as saucers.

"Yes, and he languished there for some time until he died in captivity; some say of illness. Others say he was poisoned. Bardas, his grieving father, ordered the execution of many Muslim prisoners, some of whom were relatives of Sayf himself. But alas, what was lost was lost."

"And where was Nicephorus in all of this?" John asked, feeling intrigued.

"He was far away from these border battles. He had been the military governor of Amorion, at the heart of Anatolia. But right after that catastrophe, the emperor relieved Bardas of his duty as domestic and gave the position to Bardas' eldest son, Nicephorus."

"Oh, my God," said John in disbelief.

"Yes, yes, my friend. Now you see why Nicephorus seeks this battle so eagerly."

"This explains much," John nodded.

"He swore to take vengeance for his brother ten years ago. It seems we will see his oath fulfilled very soon," Andreas concluded, throwing a piece of wood onto the fire.

# Chapter Nineteen

## - 𝒮𝒞 -

The next morning brought a halt to the rain, though it remained windy and cold. The roads were terribly muddy and the men put up a tremendous effort pushing the wagons that frequently got stuck in the foothills of the Taurus Mountains. But for the next couple of days as the army pushed south, clearer skies prevailed and the road conditions improved.

The season was a holy one. It was just one week before Christmas, and the devout general had been keeping a strict fast. He often read from his little prayer book as he led his army through the countryside with the deep conviction that he was doing the Lord's work and fulfilling His will. His spiritual father, the elder Athanasius, who was too frail to endure the arduous campaign, had sent in his place his own disciple, a middle-aged priest by the name of Procopius to serve as the general's confessor. Father Procopius soon discovered Nicephorus's huge appetite for theological discussion, as the general would often ask for the priest to ride next to him, thereafter being transported from the physical world to the metaphysical.

As the army happened to pass by the ruins of a once flourishing Roman town, now part of the permanently scorched land that lay between the two belligerent states, Nicephorus asked for the priest to be fetched. Whether seeing its ruins reminded him of the temporality of earthly life, or the fact that there lay a cemetery for the fallen Roman soldiers of previous wars, the general felt an urge to speak to his knowledgeable and faithful cleric. He soon caught up with the general on his donkey.

"Peace be with you!" he began cheerfully

"And with you too, father."

"The weather has improved greatly these past days and the army has been marching at a faster pace." The priest smiled and patted the donkey's back compassionately. "Sometimes, as I am being carried on the back of this meek animal, I get too absorbed in my reading and realize that I'm lagging behind you considerably."

"Well, if you ever change your mind and wish to exchange this donkey for a horse or mule, you only have to mention it to any of the commanders."

"Thank you, General, but I prefer the meekness and obedience of a donkey over the strength and agility of a mule. Besides, a couple of pats on his back are usually enough to make him speed up like a mare!"

"Here we are, father, marching in these parts where no Roman army has set foot in three and a half centuries, since Egypt, Syria and Palestine were lost to the Arabs in the days of Heraclius."

"Your victorious armies have brought the infidel down on their knees in many a place, Nicephorus, and that is because you give God His due reverence and glory. Who knows, it might be in God's predestined future that the emancipation of Jerusalem could come at your hands."

"May God's will be done," said Nicephorus thoughtfully.

"On earth as it is in heaven, but so far, my son, it has been God's will that three of the five Patriarchal seats should continue to languish under the rule of the Ishmaelites: Antioch the city of God, where we were first called Christians, Alexandria, the great city of learning and the birthplace of monasticism, and finally Jerusalem, where our Lord chose to execute the salvation of humanity. Only the New Rome and Old Rome are saved by God's grace from a similar fate."

"Make no mistake, father, old Rome too is under the tyranny of barbaric nations, though they call themselves Christians. They insolently claim the title of Emperor and the bishop of Rome is regrettably complicit in their illegal claims, crowning their petty chieftains as emperors, and forgetting that only in Constantinople is the one and legitimate emperor of the Romans."

"The Latins do have their errors both in the spiritual and the temporal matters as you rightfully mentioned, but out of Christian love, we should pray that they renounce their innovations and adhere fully to the true faith of the one holy and apostolic church. I must say, however, that they do possess a strong and honest faith in God that has not been corrupted by too much philosophy and human learning. We justifiably consider ourselves to be superior to them in matters of philosophy, theology and the rest of the sciences but that can easily lead us to vain pride which is the highway to hell. Let us humble ourselves before God and condemn ourselves first so that we might not be condemned by He who will judge both the living and the dead in His glorious return."

"Do you see these ruins, father?" Nicephorus pointed to the piles of rubble and column stubs that once made up homes and markets. "This is why I called you."

"Here have we no enduring city, but we seek one to come," replied the priest prophetically.

"And I steadfastly hope in the life to come, in the heavenly Jerusalem, but here I am wearing this heavy armor and leading my men to battle, in the stifling heat and in the frigid cold, in sickness and in health, fighting the enemies of God, to kill and be killed, like those soldiers who once fought for the empire, and whose graves you can still see by the side of this road."

The priest inclined his head to the graves which were topped by large piles of stones and blessed them with a sweep of his hand.

"Yet," continued the domestic, "you cannot tell me for sure that if I die today fighting the infidel that my soul will ascend unhindered to the heavenly tabernacles, to be escorted by the angels and guided before the throne of God. And here comes my question to you, father, or rather my protest: why will not the church consider those who give their lives for the safety of their brethren, for the prosperity of the kingdom and the safekeeping of the churches of God, why will the church not consider them martyrs whose sins are absolved and souls are purified? Why will not our spiritual fathers canonize them? Didn't the Lord Himself grant His church the authority to bind and to loose, saying that 'whatsoever ye shall bind on earth shall be bound in heaven: and whatsoever ye shall loose on earth shall be loosed in heaven'? Why will the church not use this divine authority to grant us soldiers a general absolution? Instead, and I beg you father not to regard my words as murmur, instead, we are often refused communion except when on the verge of death! I have yet to taste the holy Eucharist for over three years now, moving from one front to the other and knowing that should my end come unexpectedly, I would depart this life deprived of the holy flesh and blood of Christ which the holy fathers called the medicine of immortality. While at the capital, I asked the Patriarch Polyeuctus to consider this request on behalf of all the soldiers of Christ, and though he did listen to me attentively, he showed an absolute rejection to the idea saying merely that it was against the holy tradition of the church. I obviously have no spiritual authority, and as a faithful Christian, I abide by the decision of his eminence and that of the holy synods. Still, I feel embittered by this rejection which, while risking the earthly life, threatens to deprive us of the heavenly one."

"My son, the church has received from the Lord the commandment not to resist evil with evil, and Christ taught us that if anyone slaps you on the right cheek, turn to them the other, yet on the night when He was betrayed, He asked His disciples to sell their garments and buy a sword. Also when the Lord of all was being tried before the high priest of the Jews, and an evil servant dared slap Him, He replied, saying, 'If I have spoken evil, bear witness of the evil: but if well, why strike me?'. Therefore, never doubt for a moment the righteousness of what you are doing, defending piety, and protecting the weak. And I know for sure that had you for one second doubted the goodness of your deeds as a soldier and commander of his majesty's armies, you would not have achieved such great and distinguished victories."

"Still, our holy fathers, guided by the Holy Spirit, and following the words of the divine Paul have seen it wise that those who kill another human being, created in the image of God, even for the defense of others are not to be allowed communion for their own good, so that eating and drinking the body of the Lord might not turn into a judgment against them. The church, as a caring mother, gives her sons their food in due time and prays for their weaknesses and faults so that united through her, the sinful individuals become holy members in the body of Christ. Therefore, my son, as you march on your perilous campaigns, always be sure that the whole church fervently prays for you and your men incessantly, and her prayers ascend like the fragrance of incense before the throne of God."

"Do you have any idea how many more soldiers would join the army if this decision were taken by the church? Instead of running to monasteries to save their souls, thousands of young men would swell the armies of the east and west and fight the Muslims with the same zeal and impulse with which they fight us. I can already see the results of such a move. Is there any theological argument that you can think of to support this?"

"What am I hearing, dear Nicephorus?" the priest softly reproached his spiritual son. "Are you placing our pure and divine faith on the same level with that of the Mohammedans? Has the lust for victory veiled the message of the Gospel from your eyes? How would we be different than them if we adopted their doctrines? We might as well embrace their religion and then there would be no reason to fight them anymore. We are in a war against them because we differ from them in so many ways, but above all, because the commandments by which we are called to live are spiritual and heavenly whereas theirs are carnal and earthly."

Nicephorus nodded. He had heard enough, at least for the time being. He looked ahead and silently thought of the coming encounter. Battle was the thing he did best and – as weird as that might sound – enjoyed most.

A scouting squad suddenly appeared on a distant hill. They had returned from their assignment, and were soon in the domestic's presence announcing that Aleppo was only a few miles away. Father Procopius, in his usual courtesy, knew when it was time for the spiritual to make way for the earthly, especially on a military campaign. He excused himself and retreated further back along the proceeding column. The commanders were asked to advance and march with the domestic as the encounter with the enemy became imminent.

Soon, Aleppo's protecting walls and towers appeared in the far distance. It was a considerably large city, as Nicephorus and his commanders knew all along, surrounded by high walls and at its center rose a hill with steep slopes. On top of it was situated a strong citadel built by the Arabs.

The short interval of good weather, which coincided with the approach of the Romans, had allowed the population to resume their mercantile and agricultural activities. But the appearance of a massive army before Sayf's capital must have been a total surprise for that Arab metropolis and its famous emir. The farmers who were ploughing and pruning their fruit orchards and sowing cereal fields outside the city, fled in panic to the safety of the walls. Merchants and traders – to whom Aleppo was a major market as well as an important rest and resupply station – were also caught off guard and many abandoned their laden caravans preferring to save their lives.

With more scrutiny, the walls surrounding the city did appear to be as neglected as Tzimiskes had described. Some towers were in such bad condition that they had partially collapsed, with no sign of restoration works being carried out.

*How could Sayf have been sending army after army to raid roman territory, and spending so much wealth and manpower in building fortresses and castles along the borders while leaving his own capital in such a pitiful state of vulnerability and defenselessness,* John couldn't help wondering.

Sayf, in all his acclaimed chivalry, was expected to come out and fight with whatever meager troops he still had instead of cowardly hiding behind his walls. But just as the confident Nicephorus managed to surprise Sayf's capital with his swift and unexpected maneuver, so he too was destined to be surprised. He led his completely oblivious army to what awaited him outside Aleppo.

# Chapter Twenty
- 𝕯𝕺𝕮𝕾 -

The army continued its march through the rolling countryside, as the terrain leading to Aleppo passed through a wide and fertile valley, surrounded on both sides by higher densely wooded hills. The valley widened as they drew nearer to the city, and the hills pushed further away to the north and south, creating a rather broad plain.

Nicephorus, who needed a more unobstructed view of the enemy and the potential battlefield, left Tzimiskes to lead the column and took John and Maleinos the sub-commander. Nudging their horses into a jog, they ascended one of the wooded hills overlooking the city. It took the galloping horses only a short while to carry their riders to the hilltop among the pine and oak trees, but once there, a shocking sight shattered the view. A scene unfolded before their eyes surpassing in horror their worst nightmares. They gazed in disbelief towards the plain beneath them. A multitude of enemy soldiers, far more than the hastily gathered forces Nicephorus and his war council had expected to see, were forging a gallant show, preparing for battle.

With the main Saracen army away from Aleppo, and with the element of surprise on their side, they had raised hopes of capturing the city without much resistance, but what they saw dashed these hopes entirely. Their dreams of a swift operation and an easy conquest quickly vanished upon witnessing the many thousands pouring out from the city gates and assembling themselves in the open field. If they wanted to capture Aleppo, they would have to defeat that mighty army first. Even retreat was not an option anymore.

"There must be over thirty thousand of them down there!" Maleinos cried, clearly taken aback by what he was observing.

"How on earth could they have gathered such an army?" John mouthed, in disbelief.

But Nicephorus continued to survey the horizon silently, lost in his own thoughts.

"Do you see those gleaming shields?" he finally said, pointing at the

90

right flank of the enemy, which from afar looked as if set ablaze by the reflections from thousands of brass shields. "Those are not Arab shields."

"Whose are they, then?" Maleinos asked, confused. In his many years as commander and governor of Cappadocia, he had never seen such armor.

"These are warriors from Khorasan, from Persia. They must have come to the aid of their ally Sayf."

"What are you saying, domestic, is this not the same army sent to intercept us?" John inquired.

"Certainly not. That army must be still searching for us further north. These men have arrived from the east, from far away. I cannot mistake those gleaming shields. Many years ago, while still an officer, I fought against an army of their countrymen. We were defeated that day in one of the bloodiest and most hard-fought battles that I can remember."

"But how on earth did they get here in time? We advanced so quickly, there is no chance they could have known of our approach!" Maleinos wondered indignantly

"My guess is: pure coincidence, a stroke of luck," Nicephorus said with a pensive look. "Aleppo, as you know, is the spearhead of their holy war against us, and it is not uncommon that troops from all over the lands of Islam to assemble here before they attack north. These volunteers have arrived just in time when their ally needed them most."

"Just when everything was heading in the right direction!" John muttered. He had no idea how that mighty army could be defeated. There were thousands and thousands of men down there who had crossed hundreds of miles just to have the honor of killing the idolater Christians, or to gain paradise by dying while trying. They could have remained in their country beyond the Tigris and no Romans would have come near to threatening their land.

The three men descended the hill to rejoin the army.

"What did you see from up there?" asked Demetrius. "From the expression on your face, it doesn't look good. What is it?"

But John had no good news to tell his comrade. He watched his face become clouded with worry as he described to him what he had just seen.

Meanwhile, Nicephorus called upon Tzimiskes and the other commanders. They came on their horses and encircled the domestic.

*He must be explaining the battle plan to them. God knows what plan he has come up with but to defeat that army, it must be a really, really good one.*

The meeting only lasted for a few minutes and Tzimiskes was the first to leave the circle. He rode with a slow trot towards John and

Demetrius, looked them in the eye and said grimly without stopping: "You two take good care of the domestic today."

John followed him with his eyes as he continued to ride towards the cavalry lines. He took about half of the cavalry, close to three thousand riders, and split from the main body of the army retreating in the direction they had approached Aleppo from.

"Where are they going?" wondered John.

"I think I could take a guess," came suddenly from Andreas who was right behind him.

***

The sun had yet to reach overhead, and as the men had only been marching for a couple of hours, Nicephorus deemed them fit to fight that very same day. They only needed a short respite to prepare themselves for battle.

"Brave Christian men!" he thundered. "Soon, your eyes will behold the city of Aleppo, once a Roman and a Christian city, now the capital of the Saracens and the base from which they launch their venomous attacks against your homeland every year. You have come all this distance not merely to win another battle or capture another fort but to eradicate the enemy in its cradle, to uproot him and capture his first city with all its wealth. Another day of battle has arrived! Another time when the enemy tastes the bitterness of your swords. Do not be intimidated by their numbers, for as they say, 'the darkest hour is just before the dawn'! Listen to the instructions of your commanders and follow them meticulously for upon that depends not only your victory but your very lives. They shall now explain to you what you must do to win this battle.

"Today is the harvest and you are the reapers! The denser the crop, the easier the harvest! Put your trust in the true God, the wonder maker, the God of our forefathers and be certain of His divine assistance through the intercession of His most holy mother! Before today's sunset, Aleppo and all its riches shall be yours! Advance!"

The men erupted with enthusiastic shouts and banged their shields with their swords creating a deafening clamor that announced their approach to their still invisible enemy. Nicephorus ordered the men to advance and the whole army proceeded in battle formation. The only things visible to their eyes from the far distance were the city's tower tops and the lofty citadel.

Soon afterwards, the banners of the enemy appeared on the horizon; numerous green standards with Arabic inscriptions, then without much delay the entire Muslim army appeared on the flat plain outside the city, marching to meet them. The thousands of Arab and Persian men marched belligerently and boastfully.

"Is this the hastily gathered army that we were expected to wipe out in an hour?" said Demetrius, speaking for every other soldier who saw the multitudinous enemy approach.

"You handle one man at a time," John replied, looking at the thousands of heads in front of him. "This is where all that discipline we practiced becomes most vital. This is where the endless hours of hard training are expected to pay off. It's going to be a long day."

"A long day is what I pray for now."

The men foresaw a ferocious fight ahead of them. The fire of animosity between the two warring factions was further fueled by the personal grudge between the two commanders. Finally the day had come for their account to be settled.

Less than one mile now separated the two armies. The Arabs had their backs to the city while the Romans faced it and could see the citizens mounting its walls, watching the scene where their fate was soon to be decided. Sayf rode on his white Arabian steed, at the head of an army whose numbers and morale swelled with the timely arrival of the fierce allies. Next to him rode, Ali, who had marched with his men from the faraway lands of the east to join the holy war against the idolaters who worshipped three gods and knelt to graven images.

The soldiers of Ali, distinct by their brass shields and helmets which glittered under the weak December sun, remained as when they were first seen from the hilltop, on the right side of Sayf's army, their concerted movement and costly armor displayed much valiance and strength.

The Roman cataphracts, on the other side, gave off no less an imposing and intimidating aura, providing their enemies beforehand with an alarming idea of what they were about to face. Their posture revealed high discipline and organization, as did their armor and attire. Over mail shirts, they wore long cloaks dyed in their respective unit colors and on their heads, the coned helmets were topped with a tuft of horsehair also dyed in the same color. The superb fighting skills they possessed matched the level of their grandiose uniforms.

Reaching a satisfactory distance, both armies came to a stop and rearranged themselves in their battle formations before the fatal confrontation. Dozens of banners flapped on both sides of the field with the frigid wind that began to blow from the north bringing with it signs of a drastic and imminent change.

The domestic stood on a mound behind the army lines where he had decided to monitor the battle surrounded by his bodyguards. John was in close proximity, his heart beating fast, his senses alert, and his hand clenched on his sword's handle.

*It looks like it's going to be quite a spectacle.*

Nicephorus, without further delay, sounded the famous battle cry *'Deus Nobiscum!'* and the whole army resounded with *'Kyrie Eleison!'*

This cry unleashed the ironclad cataphracts – led by their commander Constantine – on their first wave of attack wielding their swords and maces. Almost simultaneously, Sayf also sounded his *'Allahu Akbar!'* and the thousands of men and horses raced to a violent clash on the plain outside Aleppo.

*They shall see now what we are capable of.*

But instead of a collision he watched as the initial attack turned into a retreat. The typical triangular formation of the Roman cavalry simply crumbled and instead of mowing the enemy down, their first encounter with the Arab heavy cavalry made them turn around and flee. In vain did the commanders call upon them to halt their retreat and face the enemy.

From their elevated position, the domestic's bodyguards watched what looked like the birth of a catastrophe. John glanced at the face of Nicephorus seeking to read any signs but his stern features betrayed little emotion.

He looked back at the battlefield. The cavalry's shameless escape was so chaotic that any attempt of regrouping them into formation appeared impossible to the spectators. This invigorated Sayf's armored horsemen, and the retreating and dispersed Romans, realizing their vulnerability, hastily fled the field to the safety of their impenetrable infantry square, panic stricken.

The Saracens, filled with joy at the scene of the terrified Romans, broke loose from the rigid discipline which they had so far maintained. The Khorasani fighters especially, overtaken by zeal and fanaticism, were the first to break the lines and chase the enemy. Soon, the entire Saracen army was pursuing the Romans to their camp despite their leaders' attempts to stop this reckless charge. After all, it was well known that the Roman baggage train contained great sums of gold and silver reserved for the payments of the soldiers, safely kept at the camp.

Sayf could be seen racing on his Arabian steed, calling upon his soldiers to maintain order, but the desire for loot proved too hard to resist.

John felt his heart sink as he watched the brave men he had fought with side by side in so many battles run like scared children before the enemy. An incoherent deluge of cavalry and infantry raced behind the romans who still had about five hundred yards to cross before they could reach their camp.

But as that was taking place, another plot was unraveling. Suddenly, John felt joy surging up his heart as hundreds of light cavalry, armed with bows and swords, emerged from their hideouts on the surrounding hills and began pouring down to the battlefield with exceptional speed.

*I thought they'd never come!* John took a deep breath, his face glowing.

Tzimiskes and his cavalry descended the hills like angels of death and struck the rear of the disorganized Saracens. The other half of the cavalry who had successfully convinced their enemies of their feigned retreat, suddenly turned around and faced their pursuers, thus completing the encirclement.

"Follow me now!" commanded the domestic. John and his elite regiment plunged straight into heavy combat and quickly found themselves in the middle of the horrific battle where thousands of swords clashed violently, blood splattered, limbs were severed and mighty warriors bellowed with excruciating pain. The Romans were closing in on the Arabs and their allies from front and rear. All that remained was to harvest the fruits of a good plan.

Sayf must have realized that the worst had become inevitable. The battle, Aleppo, along with his reputation were all lost. He had no other choice but to abandon the battlefield which had become a deadly snare, and swiftly flee to the east with a few dozen horsemen.

Some Khorasani and Arab horsemen managed to follow their fugitive emir, but the infantry were not as lucky and were mercilessly massacred, except for those who surrendered, preferring slavery to death.

***

"Kourkouas!" Nicephorus called out to his exhausted sub-commander. "Send your men to secure the prisoners and keep guard while we ride to the city!"

While the capable commander sent his men to tie the prisoners' hands, Nicephorus took one cavalry regiment and rode to the city before the shortest day of the year ended. The scenes John encountered on the road were no less horrifying than on the battlefield itself. The bloodied and mutilated bodies of hundreds of Arab soldiers were strewn everywhere along the road and up to the city walls. There by the gates, dozens appeared to have met a crushing death, trampling upon each other in a desperate attempt to enter the city before the gates were closed.

Upon reaching the city, they found Tzimiskes's soldiers presiding over what looked more like the site of a massacre than that of a battle. Some were sitting near the field of corpses resting their worn out bodies, others fetched water from the nearby river to quench their thirst and wash their wounds.

There, at a safe distance from the city walls, the uncle and nephew met again. Both looked as tired and bloodied as their soldiers. Tzimiskes walked towards his uncle and supreme commander with confident strides. Nicephorus, his face as grave and serious as ever, spoke with noticeable contentment:

"It's over. The coward ran for his life."

"I could see him calling on his men to stop their rash advance. He could sense the coming catastrophe. But as soon as we began our descent, he realized they stood no chance."

"He who fights and runs away may live to fight another day," said Nicephorus. "I want you to take two cavalry regiments and chase after him."

"It will be difficult to catch up with them now," replied Tzimiskes

"I'm aware of that but we shouldn't let him rest. Chase him until the Euphrates if you have to."

"All right. I shall leave immediately, then."

He quickly gathered the troops and set out east after the runaway emir.

John stood there next to the domestic and surveyed the area, amazed by the unbelievable outcome of the battle. There were very few dead Roman soldiers among the thousands of bodies that littered the field.

"John!" suddenly called Nicephorus.

"Yes, domestic."

"Ride to the commander Kourkouas and inform him to bring the prisoners here. I need them to bury the corpses of the dead. The last thing we want now is their stench bringing us disease. They failed to kill us while alive, let them not succeed when dead."

The orders were carried out swiftly and efficiently.

With their backs towards the setting sun, the rest of the army marched from the battlefield headed by the large wooden cross. Dragging alongside them was a long line of prisoners stripped of their weapons and body armor and shrouded instead in misery and shame. They walked in disbelief at the day's outcome. Having had all means of victory, they were now walking weighed by shackles instead of booty. They, who up to that very morning were warriors of the highest esteem, were now subhuman, a mere commodity sold to whoever paid the highest price. Yet, as they dug the shallow graves with their bare hands and buried their dead, at least some of them must have felt fortunate enough to have survived the fate of their comrades. They were still breathing, their eyes could still witness the sun sinking behind the horizon, and that in itself was a great privilege denied to the many thousands who fell in the carnage earlier that day.

The few of them who understood the language of their captors could hear a new expression, a new title which the Roman soldiers bestowed upon their victorious strategos on that fateful afternoon. No one knows who first invented it but by then, it was already reverberating with the news of victory throughout the empire and beyond.

Nicephorus's new dreadful title was: *The Pale Death of the Saracens.*

# Chapter Twenty-One

- *&)C&* -

John was awoken by the bright sunlight reflecting off the tent's canvas wall. He had finally fallen asleep around dawn after hours of tossing and turning in his bed. Demetrius and the other men had already gotten up and left the tent. Rubbing his eyes, he went to one corner and relieved himself in a wooden bucket reserved for that purpose and washed his face from the clean water in another. He then stuck his head outside to remind himself what the place looked like. The city walls with their sealed gates concealed all signs of life within, and the low grey clouds only completed the image of desolation. It was hard for him to believe that there was anyone behind those walls. Turning his eyes to the west, he saw a vast orchard of pistachio trees, Aleppo's renowned product, bare in that season but well pruned, extending in long straight lines that diminished under the heavy fog. From the thousands of tents, many soldiers were already beginning to emerge before the morning trumpets were sounded.

He ducked back inside and sat on his mattress. His thoughts flew all the way to Constantinople.

*Now, father is probably on his way to the palace, mother and Zoe are in church for the morning service, and Alexander is opening the shop doors.*

He unthinkingly compared the stability of their life with the volatile military nature of his. But he didn't mind this life at all. He loved to be exposed to danger. It kept him alive, kept his heart beating. How could he compare the opening of a shop door, and the opening of enemy forts and cities with the empire's triumphant army? He couldn't imagine himself doing anything else nor feeling more content.

The morning trumpets, thrice sounded, abruptly interrupted the flow of his thoughts. He quickly put on his chest plate, picked up his sword and went out. The men were all lined up and ready to take their orders. But instead of the daily action, something of a different nature needed to be done that morning. The Roman soldiers who had fallen in battle the previous day – a small number of about a hundred compared to the few thousand slain enemy soldiers – were carried with dignity and interred in a common grave by the river. There, and under a large oak tree, the priests installed the portable altar, a wooden table, and covered it with its heavily ornamented brocade, then a silver cross and the gospel book were placed on top and in a small drawer underneath, the final component was inserted, without which no services could be performed: holy relics. In this case, they were a few hairs of Saint John Chrysostom; and a finger of the martyr Saint Mamas the Cappadocian. The entire army then joined Nicephorus in the solemn service held in the open air by over twenty priests – who accompanied the army – in their black vestments and long beards. Their faces looked as grim and sullen as the grey skies above them as they prayed for the 'eternal rest of the souls of the departed' and implored 'divine assistance' for the remainder of the campaign. But having offered their comrades their due respect, the eyes of the army quickly shifted to the city which refused to acknowledge her fate and kept her doors shut in a final act of defiance.

After the open-air service, the commanders moved to Nicephorus's tent for a morning meeting in order to decide what to do next. They arrived, rubbing their hands for warmth and gathered around a brazier filled with hot coal.

"The hard part has been accomplished, the easier part is yet to be," began Nicephorus.

"The easier and lucrative one!" added Maleinos. "The soldiers can't wait to lay their hands on the city's riches."

"Let's not get ahead of ourselves," Nicephorus said. "There is still a professional garrison inside the city, a strong citadel, and the numerous inhabitants. Add to that the fact that these walls aren't going to vanish by themselves."

"I sense from your words, General, that you rule out the possibility of the city capitulating to us peacefully," Kourkouas said.

"The reputation that we have gained in Cilicia as merciless conquerors has preceded us. The terrified inhabitants know what awaits them if the gates are opened. They will not hand us the sword with their own hands to slaughter them."

"Then if we must attack, let us do it quickly, General," Maleinos said. "Too much exposure in this harsh season will render the men sick and exhausted, not to mention the prisoners, the majority of whom will most certainly perish before we reach Caesarea if we linger for too long."

"It is still in our capacity to wait at least a few more days before we launch the attack. When the Arabs besieged our capital during the reign of Leo the Isaurian, they stayed encamped outside its walls for two years, sowing and harvesting wheat twice, and enduring three freezing months of snow and ice, and a harsh famine. Did you bring your bag of seeds, commander?" He smiled amiably.

The other men smiled in return and a couple of servants began distributing cups of warm tea to those present. Some food, Lenten food, was also brought inside the relatively spacious tent upon Nicephorus's orders: olives, dried fish, olive oil and freshly baked bread. The men sat on the ground and shared a light meal with their commander, as was their custom.

As they ate and chatted, they received word that a delegation had just arrived from Aleppo seeking to negotiate with the Romans.

"How many are they?" Nicephorus asked, dipping a piece of bread in olive oil.

"Six of them are outside, General," the guard answered. "One quite old, and all wearing big turbans and lavish clothes."

"Fine, let them wait outside till we finish eating."

John had expected the domestic to order the food removed at once and the tent prepared to receive the delegation. He chewed a piece of dried fish and admired the man's way of handling things.

*Keeping the peace delegation waiting in the cold outside for such an insignificant reason as finishing a snack must be his way of indicating how the negotiations are going to be conducted; he is going to talk and they are going to listen.*

A little while later, the food was finally removed and a space cleared for the Arab sheikhs to sit opposite the domestic and his commanders on the ground.

The men looked as dignified and opulent as the guard had described. They were five of the city's dignitaries in addition to their translator; a young man of no more than twenty-five. Nicephorus called for one of his own translators and the talks began.

"Peace be to you, victorious leader," the men said in almost chorus-like unanimity

Nicephorus's face remained grave. He said nothing, but only nodded once.

"I am the grand Sheikh of Aleppo and these men are the heads of the city's four quarters," began the old man who, by way of age and status, appeared to have preeminence over his companions. "Our young translator here, Mansour, is a Christian. We have come to you, Lord Nicephorus, asking that you spare our city the perils of war. You are a man who fears God, so we learnt, and this city has thousands of innocent women and children whom your mercy will not commit to death and destruction. Grant us our city, and we shall forever be indebted to your magnanimity."

Nicephorus, who up till then had listened attentively, now smiled contemptuously.

"So, you, respectable and wise men, have deemed it reasonable and appropriate to come here to my camp thinking that these empty words of yours would make me turn my back and leave? If that is what you were thinking then you are terribly mistaken. The city for which you now seek mercy is the base from which every year your lawless prince waged war against our lands, where women and children were either killed or captured and sold in your markets – for we too have women and children.

"Those who told you I am a God-fearing man perhaps forgot to tell you of what God I fear and worship. The God I fear and worship has sent me here to chastise that arrogant prince of yours."

"And you have, Lord, by Jesus and Mohammed and all the prophets, you have," the old man hurriedly replied. "And with God's will too, there is no doubt about that, for nothing happens against the will of God. You defeated our emir and destroyed his army. You have taken your revenge on him, and that was God's will. For that, your fame as a warrior and conqueror shall reach the far ends of the earth. Let your fame of generosity and magnanimity accompany that of invincibility."

"You are well-spoken, old man, but your words alone will not convince me to turn my back and leave. I did not come all this distance for nothing, and I shall not leave with nothing, either."

"Far be it from us to suggest that you turn away empty-handed! We are happy to redeem every inhabitant of our city with one gold piece; that is fifty thousand gold pieces in total. Would that be satisfactory to you?"

Nicephorus remained silent for a while. He appeared to be truly considering the old man's offer. Those sitting with him studied his face for clues while he passed his hand over his thick beard, his eyes fixed on the ground. Finally, after a few long moments of anticipation, he lifted his head and looked straight at the old man.

"One room of your emir's palace has gold and silver worth twice the fifty thousand gold coins you now insolently offer me. Perhaps you think I am a fool or a beggar, to accept your petty proposal?"

"Lord!" the old man exclaimed. "You most certainly do not expect us to violate the sanctity of our prince's palace and rob him in his absence."

"If it is fear from him that is behind your refusal," said Nicephorus, "then fear from me should overcome it. If you are reasonable enough, that is. If, on the other hand, it is honesty and virtue, then let me tell you that nothing is more virtuous than saving your people's lives."

"Lord, the city is not devoid of soldiers," said the man who sat next to the old Sheikh, and wore a slightly smaller turban. "The city's garrison is still inside and they protect the emir's palace."

"Ah, so now you have soldiers inside," said Nicephorus, having slyly elicited an unguarded revelation. "I thought there were only women and children as your Sheikh wanted me to believe! Now you listen to me," he resumed in a completely different, more threatening tone, "it's time you heard what I am willing to give you. Let it be known that I shall not accept less than the city's handover to me, no later than three days from now. You will be granted a safe passage out with a donkey's, or half a mule's load for every household. Your lives are to be spared but all the gold, silver and precious artifacts shall remain in the city. Now that you have heard my terms, do not waste my time discussing anything less."

Expressions of impotence and helplessness clearly registered on the faces of the Arab envoys.

"But that is impossible! We cannot convince our people of that!" exclaimed a third man, the youngest of the five dignitaries.

"I do not have to remind you, Lord," said the old man with a calm and sober voice, "that inside the city there are more than fifty thousand souls and a strong garrison. Taking the city by force will not be easy."

"We shall see about that, but for now, this conversation is over. You have my terms and there is nothing further to discuss. You have until sunset to send your reply," said Nicephorus with a firm tone and emotionless face

The Arabs got up and were ready to leave the humiliating session, but just before they exited the door, the old sheikh turned back to Nicephorus and threw his last card at him:

"Do not forget, Lord, that over a thousand Christians live in Aleppo. So far, they have not been harmed, but I cannot guarantee their safety should you choose to resume your hostility towards us."

Nicephorus's face suddenly darkened with anger, his features expressed deep fury and resentment at the sheikh's insinuations.

"How dare you threaten me in that pathetic manner? If it wasn't for people saying that Nicephorus killed an old messenger, I would have had your head displayed on a spear! So listen to me carefully: if anything happens to any of the Christians of Aleppo, you will only have yourselves to blame for the ensuing acts of retribution. Now get out of my sight!" He roared while the translator struggled to convert the threatening words into the language of his masters.

The Arabs, realizing the fury they had just provoked, slipped out of the tent, but Nicephorus cried again: "He stays here!" pointing at the translator. The men froze for a moment, then protested, "But he is our translator! This goes against all the ethics of civilized negotiations!"

"I said he stays. Besides, you won't need a translator anymore, we are done talking."

The men were escorted out by a few soldiers, while the petrified translator remained in his place not knowing what to do or say.

Nicephorus, his face still clouded with anger, picked up a waterskin from the table in front of him, took a sip then looked at his commanders.

"Tomorrow morning, we storm the city."

# Chapter Twenty-Two

- ❧❦ -

Aftter the Arab envoys were shown out, or to put it more precisely 'thrown out', the commanders, John and the dumbfounded translator remained inside the tent. Of the four commanders, Tzimiskes was the only one missing as his chase of Sayf penetrated deep into the Syrian Desert.

John felt the few moments that followed to be awkward and protracted but neither he nor anyone else dared interrupt the silence which Nicephorus's appearance imposed. Finally, the domestic himself looked at the young Arab man, and said, "What's your name again?"

"Mansour, Lord. My name is Mansour. It means 'Victor' in the Greek tongue," he replied timidly, his eyes fixed on the ground.

"So, *Man-sour*, did that old Sheikh speak the truth about your religion?"

"Yes, Lord, he did."

"And why did you renounce the heresies of the Mohammedans?"

"I was never a Muslim. I was still a babe in my mother's arms when I received holy baptism. We are Arabs by race, and Christians by faith. My family traces our faith back many generations, long before this country was taken by the Muslims. Three years ago, our bishop nominated me for the priesthood and began teaching me Greek, the language of the Holy Scriptures and the church fathers."

"I see. And have you been ordained yet?"

"No, not yet, Lord. I still have two more years of preparation, at least."

"Do you acknowledge the seven councils?"

"Yes, Lord, I do."

"Then you have no reason to dread our company. Consider us your brothers. Come on, raise your head."

"Thank you, Lord."

"Now, you must be wondering why I kept you from leaving with those whom you had escorted here." He gave the young man a serious look as he spoke, passing his hand over his thick black beard. "They will have one less Christian in their grasp. Besides, I need you to tell me a few things about the city those elusive men would never have confessed."

Mansour pondered this for a moment and the thoughtful timid look all of a sudden disappeared from his face.

He gazed at his examiner, then with some rashness, he said, "Lord, am I given permission to speak freely?"

The audience was somewhat surprised by the man's unexpected surge of courage. His reserved voice and perplexed mind suddenly summoned enough strength to ask the Roman supreme commander for an opportunity of free speech, and Nicephorus, who seemed to admire that, did not hesitate to approve his request.

"Speak your mind," he reassured the young man.

"You, Lord, have come here leading a vast army and are preceded by a legendary reputation. The city and all its inhabitants trembled at your approach, the city where I was born and where I lived my life just as my forefathers before me. Though you and I worship the same God and share the same holy and apostolic faith, I have shared everything else with the inhabitants of that city my entire life. I beg you, Lord, not to ask of me what I cannot give; that is to betray my country, for there is nothing honorable about betrayal."

"Do you consider helping your fellow Christian brothers retake what was once Roman territory and a Christian city betrayal?" asked Nicephorus, displaying considerable restraint.

"It would certainly be seen as betrayal in their eyes. These people have been our neighbors and friends, we have broken bread together and shared the good and the bad times. I cannot collaborate in what will lead to their death and enslavement."

"Would you rather live under the tyranny of Muslims than in the realm of Romania?!"

"Lord, hear my defense, I beg of you. Ever since the imperial authority receded from Syria, we have come to live under the authority of the Muslims. We have had to accept the new way of life – which is not new anymore but is three centuries old by now. Most of us remained faithful to the religion of our forefathers while others preferred the easier path and converted to the religion of the conquerors. There were good times and bad times, good tolerant governors and evil bloodthirsty ones. But we have survived them all and never ceased to call this place home, regardless of who ruled it. You might find this hard to believe, Lord, but the emir Sayf protected us from all aggressions and insults directed towards us by the zealous Muslims, calling us 'People of the Book' in reference to the Holy Scriptures. He treated us fairly as he did with the rest of his subjects. This time of privilege, however, ended yesterday, after God granted you a great victory. Enraged by the crushing defeat, and certain of our helplessness after the flight of our patron, the zealots roamed the city streets claiming that the reason behind the emir's defeat was his leniency towards the 'worshippers of the cross'. Afterwards, an angry mob led by the zealots stormed the Christian quarter, where most of us live, and began attacking its residents. They called us traitors who favored the enemy and sought our extermination so that we might not betray the city as they claimed. Our old and weak bishop being the one who speaks for us, rushed to the site and pleaded with the mob leaders for his flock's safety, risking his own life in the process. He took upon himself to gather all the Christians in the church and to keep them there so that no one would have any reason to suspect them of betraying the city to you. These terms were accepted but not before twenty had been martyred and several homes looted and burnt. We were given one hour to assemble in the church and not leave it until this standoff around the city walls was over. The houses of the Christians are probably being searched as we speak and any Christian found there would probably be killed on the spot."

"And yet, in spite of all these acts of shameless violence, you still want to protect those who murder and enslave your Christian brothers and sisters? If you ask anyone present here, they would tell you that living too long under the tyranny of the infidel has impaired your senses, young man."

"Those who persecute and hate us, Lord, are but a minority, a few hundred deluded fanatics. The vast majority of the city's Muslims have shown us nothing but fairness and good intentions all our lives."

"Why then haven't these good, well-intentioned Muslims stood up to defend you in the face of the more fanatic ones?" Nicephorus questioned the young Arab translator, in an attempt to demolish his argument.

"Some of them did just that, Lord. Some of them risked their own lives to defend us, to hide us in their homes and to protect our property, but the majority, seeing the thousands of Christian soldiers outside of their city walls must have thought that we also deserved our share of the impending destruction that will befall the city by our coreligionists."

"You seem to blame me and my army for this evil committed against you by these fanatics," said Nicephorus, still displaying remarkable tolerance and patience    "I certainly do not blame you, Lord, nor do I justify what they are doing to us, but I do understand why they are doing it. They feel they are threatened by a vast and powerful enemy, they look around and see our small Christian community, the only thing  which they may direct their anger and frustration.

"From the one side, we rejoice at the approach of a victorious Christian army, but from the other, we fear the destruction of our home city. By our fellow Arab kinsmen, we are treated as Romans, and by the Romans as Arabs. If your army, or I should say *when* your army, conquers Aleppo, it will mean a double calamity for my people whose persecution has already begun. The thousand souls crammed inside the church are vulnerable to any attack. They cannot leave the church on pain of death, and yet one torch could easily turn them all into ashes ..." he finished his last words with difficulty.

"So, the Christians of Aleppo are now gathered in the church?" repeated Nicephorus, having listened attentively.

"Yes, Lord, all of them, my family too, my parents and siblings, my wife and little daughter!"

"That cunning old man mentioned nothing of this when he came seeking peace and mercy." Nicephorus showed signs that he was beginning to lose his temper.

"Listen here, young man." He pondered for a moment. "Most, if not all of the men present here already, consider your attitude foolish at best and treasonous at worst. But I, from my side, admire your deep sense of integrity and frankness. No wonder your bishop nominated you for holy orders. I shall not ask you for any information; not the number of soldiers nor the strength of the gates and walls. I realize how, in your heart, you consider this as treason. In any case, we shall conquer the city with or without anything that you might tell us. But above all, I shall do everything I can to ensure that our Christian brothers and sisters inside the city survive unharmed."

"May God bless your soul, Lord. I knew I could talk freely in your court. Only a man of your qualities can understand the complex situation in which we find ourselves," he said passionately, leaving a deep impression on those present. For he had successfully advocated the cause of his people.

It was already noon and the general dismissed his guests. John was the last to leave the general's tent, but he had barely stepped outside when he heard his name called by Nicephorus.

"Yes, General," he replied with his usual readiness, though his heavy eyes and pale face betrayed great exhaustion.

The general's tent was modest. It had a sleeping mattress laid in one corner, two or three sheepskin rugs, a wooden table with two chairs, and an icon stand. An oil lamp burnt in the opposite corner, flickering every time the wind blew from outside, and a round iron container filled with hot coal which gave more a sensation of heat than actual warmth.

Nicephorus, sitting on one of the two chairs, thought silently for a moment, then looked at John. "Are we going to save those people or not, John?"

"You mean the Christians trapped inside the church? We can certainly try, Sir."

"What do you suggest?" asked the wise general who nevertheless valued the judgment of his young disciple.

"We could negotiate their release in exchange for an equal number of prisoners. We have over ten thousand prisoners tied up out there."

"I don't think that's a good idea. Once they realize how much we value them, they would hold on to them more dearly, they would use them to bargain with us. I very much doubt we could secure their release through negotiations."

"Well, if that's the case, there is only one way left; sending a few men inside the city before the start of the general assault to secure the church and those inside it."

"Precisely my thoughts. But how do you think this can be done?"

"There is always a way, no matter how impossible it appears, Lord."

"I'm glad you think so because I will not find a better man than you to lead this mission, John."

"At your orders, Sir."

"You pick the men you want, and take that translator with you, let him be your guide, he seems like an honest lad."

John nodded twice. He was finally dismissed, but not without a new mission which he had no clear idea how to carry out. He walked sluggishly towards his tent, hoping to get some much-needed rest when he came across Mansour in conversation with some of John's comrades. It looked like a lively discussion, of which the young Arab himself was most prominent.

"… but how can you live among these filthy pagans?" John heard Demetrius ask Mansour

"You might be surprised, my friends, but they are not filthy nor are they pagans."

"What are you saying?" Andreas interrupted, clearly not liking what he was hearing.

"They wash five times a day before prayer and they worship one God, the creator of heaven and earth," Mansour explained. "But that their faith is corrupt, is true. They do not acknowledge our Lord and Savior Jesus Christ as God incarnate or Son of God, but they highly honor him and his holy mother as the holiest people who ever walked this earth."

"Still, they are pagans, heretics at best," complained another soldier who sat mending his leather boots, unconvinced by Mansour's arguments.

"But you didn't tell us how you manage to live amongst them?" Demetrius persisted.

"Well, my brothers, it is simpler than you think. There are laws that govern us and others that govern them."

"What laws?"

"First we pay the tax imposed on all Christians. That's the most important thing to them. Pay your religious tax or face death or expulsion. Then, we should never carry weapons nor keep them at our homes, preach or display symbols of Christianity in public like crosses, or ring the bells of churches under pain of death. We can only bury our dead during the night and must never sell wine or pork to Muslims. If we keep to these laws and a few other similar ones, then we are free to practice our faith and live freely within the boundaries of our homes and sanctuaries. On the other hand, they are not allowed to harm us or take our property without a reason. They cannot force us to convert to their religion as long as we pay our taxes, though I must say these laws are not always respected. There are always some zealots who detest us and seek to harm us one way or another, no matter how obedient and peaceful we are."

"Then who protects your small society from these zealots?" asked another man. "You yourself said you are no more than a thousand in a city of more than fifty thousand."

"Indeed our numbers have been gradually decreasing, for many prefer to live under the rule of a Christian king, thus travelling to the north and settling in Roman lands. But in spite of our small numbers we remain an industrious and energetic community. Many Christians are wealthy merchants and famous scholars whose expertise and knowledge is sought by the Saracen princes. Many goldsmiths in Aleppo, for example, are Christians, and these pay great sums to the emir as taxes on their prosperous businesses. It is thus in the emir's interest to preserve and defend this industrious community, granting him a steady flow of taxes."

"In other words, you purchase your lives with your hard work," concluded Andreas, crossing his arms and staring at Mansour.

"Quite so. I must say, though, that it is not an easy thing to live like a stranger in your own country, to be frequently looked down upon by men inferior in learning and wealth. But most of us have decided to stay in the land of our ancestors and endure these hardships as a cross which our Lord, in his great wisdom, has given us to carry."

"When we conquer the city," said one man resolutely, "these

bastards will pay."

John finally had to step in and interrupt the conversation. He needed to know who was willing to join him on his upcoming mission. The truth is, once he mentioned it, and though lacking all details, it wasn't difficult at all to recruit the few men necessary as almost all present expressed their eagerness to take part.

"We will need you to come with us tonight, Mansour," said John.

"I will not remain here while you risk your lives to save my family."

"You will not have to fight. I only want you to guide us through the city."

"It's too painful to explain what I felt seeing my wife and daughter being taken with the others to what could ultimately be their grave. To tell me to go back by their side, even if it meant facing death with them, comforts my soul. When do we leave?"

"Before dawn. Be ready."

# Chapter Twenty-Three

## - ℰℴℭℬ -

In the final hour of the night, the small team embarked on their mission, crossing the distance to the walls with quick steps and diligent senses. Not too many guards appeared to be keeping watch as only a few flickering torches were visible along the city's circuit walls. Mansour led the men to the section in the wall that surrounded the Christian quarter. Looking up, he could see a small window, wide enough to fit one man at a time and located about twenty or twenty-five feet above ground. With a grabbling hook, Andreas, showcasing unique dexterity, managed to lodge the hook itself between the large masonry blocks. John caught the rope with both hands and began to pull himself up while supporting his feet on the stone protrusions. After a laborious ascent, he finally grabbed the window sill and pulled himself inside the dark vault, the house of an acquaintance of Mansour's. The owners were being held in the church with the rest of the Christian population of the city but the men feared that some looters might have already occupied the place. Because of the complete darkness, John had to depend on his other senses. He kept quiet for a moment. A strong smell of wine filled the house, but the complete hush reassured him that it was indeed empty. One by one the men climbed up the rope then sat in the pitch-dark room awaiting the arrival of daylight.

When the first light rays appeared less than an hour later, the men explored their surroundings. The house they were in was made up of no more than two rooms. It was clear that someone had ransacked the place in search of valuables. Some clothes were scattered across the floor, trails of olive oil and flour extended from one corner of the house to the outside door, indicating that the food storage had also been looted. A stone-carved urn placed in one corner had been shattered; the wine contained therein spilling everywhere, which explained the striking odor.

John went to the door, opened it a crack and peeked outside. The view reminded him of his own neighborhood in Constantinople with its closely built houses of two or three storeys and narrow roads. But what was different in Aleppo, he noticed, was that so many houses were adjacent to the walls, their flat roofs reaching just under the wall parapet and serving as platforms which the city defenders could mount to repel invaders. Indeed, the roof of the house they were in served such a purpose. He closed the door again and went to the window where his other comrades were observing the Roman preparations to assault the city.

As they waited silently, they could see both the defenders and the attackers assembling for the coming confrontation. Gradually, more men began to appear on the walls but only a few looked like real soldiers, the rest were ordinary men with no armor or proper weaponry. The professional soldiers carried long bows which they put into use as soon as the Romans began to draw nearer to the walls. The others threw javelins and rocks on the increasing number of assailants. The attempt to take the city had already begun.

After exchanging missiles, the heavy siege towers came crawling closer to the walls under an incessant shower of arrows. Inside them stood dozens of soldiers, protected, and ready to jump and occupy sections of the walls once they had gotten close enough. They had done the same thing numerous times during their conquests in Crete and Cilicia under the victorious banner of Nicephorus.

Meanwhile, numerous ladders were thrown against the walls for the boldest of soldiers to begin the perilous ascent. The Roman archers were then dispatched to more advanced outposts and ordered to shower the defenders with a cloud of sharp missiles, giving the ladder climbers a better chance to succeed. One of the ladders extended right beside where John and his band were situated. Soon they heard the hurried footsteps of the Arabs on the roof above them and their confused cries, rushing to repel those who had successfully reached the top. The men inside the little house could hear the tramping of fighting feet above their heads.

As amateur as the defenders were, they did manage – with guidance from the few professional soldiers – to topple some of the ladders along with the men scaling them. Soon afterwards, balls, the size of watermelons, which appeared to have been made from a mixture of hay and tar, were ignited and hurled towards one of the siege towers causing its dry wood to catch fire instantly and forcing its occupants to a hasty evacuation before it turned into a fiery grave. It took the blazing tower a little while before it plummeted to the ground in a wave of burnt debris.

But those obstructions were insufficient to stop the waves of soldiers who encircled the city and scaled its walls with remarkable courage.

Until then, the defenders held their positions, repelling the early attempts of the Romans, but John realized the impending change and turned to his comrades.

"The Arabs will not be able to hold out for long. We should leave now." Then, directing his words to Mansour, he asked, "How far is the church from here?"

"Not far, I'd say three or four hundred paces."

"Come on then, we can't linger anymore."

They carried their weapons and headed to the door, but the quiet streets that John had seen earlier that morning were now in turmoil. A deluge of people flooded the narrow streets with great agitation.

"Mansour! You lead the way!" John ordered as the group descended the long and narrow stairway that lead to the busy street below.

Running downstairs, Demetrius looked over his shoulder to the roof of the house they had just left and could see a heated struggle between the Roman and Arab soldiers contesting each other's control over that stretch of the wall. More Roman soldiers were streaming in between the wall merlons until the defenders were finally overwhelmed. The city was falling. There was no doubt about it.

***

Outside the walls, Nicephorus watched from his commanding position as the banners with the double-headed eagle flew over one tower after another and the Arab defenses quickly fell into disarray. Within a short period of time, all resistance seemed to have collapsed and now he waited for the moment when the gates were going to be opened from the inside for the final takeover of the city. Before the inevitable happened, he felt it important to give them one final warning.

"Hear me!" he roared to the thousands of soldiers gathered. "As soon as the gates are opened, the city and all its riches are yours. The gold and silver of its palaces shall be equally distributed among you! One thing you must know, though! Refrain from shedding innocent blood! Spare the women and children. Obey my words and live or you shall find me as good a judge and executioner as I am a commander!"

"He doesn't want to see another carnage like the one in Tarsus last year." Kourkouas leant closer to Maleinos. "You must remember how disgusted we all felt walking through the streets of the captured city among the bloodstained bodies of women and children."

"It was a horrible scene, even to a fierce man like him, but who can control thousands of frenzied soldiers? Not even the mighty Nicephorus can."

All of a sudden, one of the gates was finally flung open, and the men rushed towards it with drawn swords and releasing dreadful cries. To them, it was the climax of the campaign when the fruits of their hard work would be finally reaped. The other gates were soon opened one after the other and the pursuit of the remaining armed defenders continued up to the citadel; the city's central fort.

***

Meanwhile, John and his squad had made it to the city's main square. Amid the great chaos, they hardly cared about concealing their identity for the greatly frightened and mostly unarmed population were only concerned about finding a safe place to hide, if such a place did exist. They arrived just as news of the city's fall was beginning to reverberate. There at the main square, the great mosque stood with its pointed domes and tall white marble columns, many people flocking inside it believing it would offer them a better refuge than their own homes. Across the square, they noticed a more familiar form of architecture, though of smaller proportions. It looked exactly like a basilica except that no cross topped its roof, and no bells could be seen in the adjacent tower.

"There is the church!" Mansour pointed, his face pale and barely able to utter the words as his eyes fell on the place where his entire family languished.

John noticed a few men by the building whose attitude differed from the rest of the confused and disoriented population. He estimated their number as about ten or twelve, and they all were armed. The squad concealed themselves behind the large, rounded water fountain, in the center of the square.

"They are twice our number!" John observed.

"These zealots are not as brave as you think!" Mansour said, his face expressing great resentment. "They only display their cruelty on the unarmed. They would never stand a chance in an equal fight."

As they looked from behind the fountain and waited for the right moment to attack, a tall bearded man came running towards the church with a torch in his hand, shouting in Arabic what Mansour immediately translated to the rest of the group, trembling as he uttered the terrifying words:

"The city is falling! Kill the infidel! Burn the traitors!"

His companions stood petrified by the news of the impending catastrophe, but quickly regained composure and proceeded to fulfill their vow without too much hesitation. Each of them grabbed an unlit torch from a stack near the church wall and proceeded to ignite it. But at that moment, John and his squad made their move. To act a second later would have been fatal for those held captive inside the building. The zealots were taken by surprise, not the least expecting the ambush. They were quickly cut down by John and his brave companions, but one of them managed to throw his burning torch on top of the church's wooden roof before Demetrius's sword pierced his heart. The roof slowly began to catch fire and that prompted John to complete the mission quickly and evacuate the church.

The men removed the large crossbar that kept the gate closed from the outside and opened the two large shutters. Light flooded in through the open door revealing a fully packed building. The faces of the men and women inside appeared to reflect the grave, even gloomy, expressions of the saints' images which covered the dark walls up to the domed ceiling. It appeared that those inside where in the middle of deep prayer, totally disconnected from the clamor and fighting that was taking place outside. The right side of the church was reserved for men, and the left for women, who upon seeing the group of armed men at the entrance, instinctively held their children closer to them and began to sob loudly.

An old priest with a thin face, long white beard, and wearing episcopal vestments and carrying a crosier stood at the end of the aisle facing the newcomers, not sure whether to salute them or to implore their mercy. But at that moment a woman in the crowd cried out: "Mansour! It's Mansour!"

Recognizing the voice of his wife, Mansour dropped the sword he was carrying and rushed to embrace her and his little daughter. The frightened faces quickly showed signs of relief. They had just realized that their coreligionists had indeed conquered the city and that these men had come to their rescue.

John strode purposefully along the aisle, the eyes of the people following his every step until he reached the altar where the old bishop stood. He knelt before him receiving his blessing.

"Who are you, my son?" asked the bishop, making the sign of the cross in the air over the bent head of the warrior.

"My name is John. I am one of general Nicephorus's men. He sent us to your rescue and now you must all leave before fire devours the place."

He stood next to the bishop and addressed the people:

"We have been sent to rescue you," he began, the bishop repeating after him in Arabic.

"Follow my comrades outside and assemble in the square. Do not leave the square or you will be in grave danger." The smell of smoke was beginning to fill the air as the fire on the church roof spread further and became visible to the crowd below. They rushed to leave through the only open exit and gradually gathered in the square outside as they had been instructed.

The saintly prelate, instead of following his flock to safety, hastened inside the sanctuary.

"Where are you going, Father?" asked John.

"Come here and help me!"

He walked to the small cabinet where the holy Eucharist was kept, opened its small door and took out a beautiful golden chalice. He quickly consumed all of its contents and then thoroughly cleaned the inside of it with a white piece of cloth, placing it on the altar.

John stood impatiently by the bishop watching the spread of the fire. A burning plank suddenly fell from the roof to the marble floor below.    Unfazed, the bishop then went to the easternmost part of the apse and with his frail hands attempted to remove a large icon in a heavy wooden frame hanging from the wall.  John saw what the old man was trying to do and hurried to assist him, though he couldn't help but think: *the entire church is in flames and this silly old fool is worried about one icon.* But once the big painting of Christ was removed, it revealed a vault in the wall, inside of which a wooden box had been carefully concealed. The bishop took the box out and put it under his left arm, then grabbed the chalice from above the altar and handed it to John.

"Bring that with you!" he said, pointing to a hefty book with a richly ornamented gold and silver cover

"Shall I help you carry this wooden box, Father?" John asked with concern

"No! This box remains with me!" he replied sharply, like a child refusing to share a toy. He then bowed one last time before the altar he had served for many years and with John's help made his way through the burning debris to where the rest of his congregation anxiously awaited his exodus. When he came out, John saw Demetrius and the others trying to control the crowd, making sure that none of the people left the building. Many of the now rescued Christians demanded to go back to check on their homes and belongings but they were informed that there was nothing to be found, that all their possessions had already been looted or lost to fire.

"Come here, my son," the bishop called on Mansour who stood a few yards away holding his one-year-old daughter and watching the blaze.

"Yes, Father." He approached

The old prelate put his hand on Mansour's head, blessing him and his child and whispering words of gratitude.

"I did nothing, Father, it was these brave men who risked their lives to save us."

"God bless them and their commander, the God-fearing

116

Nicephorus."

The crowd stood in the square and watched their church turn into smoldering ashes. Dozens of smoke columns could be seen rising to the sky from different parts of the city. It was as if they had taken refuge on an island surrounded by raging seas. As long as they remained there, they were safe, and nothing else mattered, not houses, nor belongings.

John, who stood with Demetrius near the bishop, couldn't help but notice how the frail old presbyter held on dearly to the small wooden box. He presumed it contained the church money, but had there been metal coins in that box, it would have been much too heavy for him to carry, he thought. He came closer, with the intention of satisfying his curiosity as to the box's contents, but just as he was about to express his thoughts, a cavalry regiment entered the square headed by Nicephorus himself.

The general paid his respects to the prelate and his scared congregation, promising them safe passage out of the city. Without much hesitation, they walked out of the square through the main street in a long column escorted by the armed horsemen. Yet the screams and sickening smell of burning human flesh had a demoralizing effect on the spirits on these new refugees. Their faces expressed deep sorrow and their mouths remained silent the entire distance.

The truth was that all around the city, there prevailed chaos, bloodshed and looting. The professional soldiers of the now fugitive Sayf shut themselves up in the fort and swore to fiercely resist the Romans. But the Romans couldn't care less about the fort nor its helpless and surrounded occupants. Their attention had been directed all along towards another building: Sayf's own palace.

The magnificently built and decorated structure had been the apple of the emir's eye, as it contained treasures of gold and silver and exquisite artifacts of unmatched beauty. After stripping the palace of its riches like a swarm of locusts strips a tree of its vegetation, the soldiers directed their spree of plunder towards the city's other houses and palaces. They gathered themselves into groups of ten or twenty and broke into the houses whose appearance betrayed signs of opulence, emerging laden with loot.

The wretched citizens had nowhere to run to. Whether by death threats, the torching of homes or the rape of virgins, the rabid soldiers used every imaginable way to extort the riches out of the Arab inhabitants without heed to human or divine restrictions. It was their right, they fully believed, to punish the city that had fought them for so long. In a few hours, Aleppo had turned into a place of horror.

# Chapter Twenty-Four

- 𝕰𝕺𝕮𝕽 -

As the day grew darker, the procession exited the city walls and made its way to the camp where food and shelter awaited the Christian refugees, and fetters the Muslims. The Roman soldiers retired from the looting with the approach of night and made their way outside laden with booty and dragging thousands of new captives of both sexes and all ages.

As the prisoners and refugees marched, they often looked back to catch a final glimpse of their hometown. The numerous fires that raged in the city assured them that even if returning were possible, it had become meaningless. The cold and agile westerly wind which carried the smell of burning matter, now brought with it fine snowflakes descending from the thick dark clouds that lashed their tired faces.

John and Demetrius lagged behind their general at the head of the long column. The Roman soldiers mounted the old and sick Christians on mules and in wagons that were recently requisitioned and the whole train proceeded towards the camp.

"I had the same dream once again last night," Demetrius suddenly said.

"What dream?" the exhausted John asked.

"It's the third or fourth time that I've had it, and every time it is the same. Only the faces of the children change, there are new children every time, and every time their faces turn lifeless."

"What's the matter with you?"

Demetrius kept going on as if talking to himself.

"The smell of smoke coming out of the charred houses feels just as real as what we're breathing right now."

John outvoiced his comrade. "We have just defeated our most stubborn enemy, conquered Aleppo, and all you can talk about is some dream!"

"I didn't mean to make you angry. After all, it's just a dream as you said."

"Soon enough, we will be out of this desperate place and back to Caesarea laden with booty. You'll hug your wife. You might even get to buy back your family's farm. Now these are things to dream about. For now, I think I'll go around to the rear for a little while."

John abruptly turned the reins of his horse and retreated towards the back of the column. He was simply too tired to talk, let alone play the role of a consoler.

Riding against the current of desperate human beings, he began to see clearly the amount of pain and suffering on the faces of the men and women as he passed them one by one, family after family. They were marching to the unknown. Mothers carried their babies in their arms, toddlers and young children clung in fear to their parents' clothes as everyone trudged along in the cold.

He passed by a group who sang as they walked. There was a rare warmth in their voices that battled the frigid winds. Though the language was incomprehensible, the melody was somewhat familiar to John.

*Isn't this the Christmas troparion?* He was almost certain.

It was Christmas Eve and the hymn sounded like an Arabic translation of the Greek original that John knew by heart.

*So much for 'peace on earth'.*

John's eyes continued to survey that trail of sorrow when suddenly he caught sight of one young woman helping a man to walk. The man appeared more sick than old, struggling to keep up with the others. The fading daylight was just enough to reveal how exceptionally beautiful the girl was. John pulled up, mesmerized.

A set of almond-shaped eyes, the color of emerald, shimmered under curled, velvety eyelashes. Her elegant nose and bow-shaped rosy lips looked like the work of an artist. A black glossy mane escaped her hastily wrapped head scarf and dangled to one side of her fair face. Her loose robes tied around her tiny waist did well to display her attractive figure.

He felt a certain sweetness just by looking at her. As exhausted as he was and, in a time and place greatly inappropriate for such sentiments, a hidden force that he could not resist was pulling him, captivating him.

The girl raised her head from the path to see him staring at her.

John quickly looked away.

"Come here and give me a hand!" he cried to one of the soldiers who was walking by, admiring the gold coins he had just acquired. The man quickly put the gold coins back into his pouch and ran to John's assistance.

"We need to put this sick man on one of the mules. Go fetch one." The soldier disappeared for a moment then returned pulling a strong animal after him.

"Allow us to help you," John said to the sick man who stopped walking and allowed himself to be carried and placed on the back of the mule.

"It is you who helped us today at the church, wasn't it?" the man said in broken Greek.

"Yes, I was there with the other men."

"May God reward you for your bravery," he said in a weak voice. "Ever since I fell ill, my daughter has been looking after me. She's an angel. Then came the war and so many hardships, so much loss ..." Tears rolled down his face.

"Don't exhaust yourself, Father," the young girl said, all the time avoiding looking in John's direction.

*Even her voice is heavenly.*

He rode beside the old man while his daughter held the reins of the mule that carried him.

"Don't worry," John assured. "We shall shortly arrive at the camp and there you will be given food and shelter."

"Do you think we would have needed your food or your tents had you not invaded our country and robbed us of everything?" The girl directed all her pent-up anger and resentment on John. "We lived just fine before you showed up!"

"Mariam! Don't be rude to this good man!" cried the father, his weak voice struggling to express his annoyance.

John was somewhat taken aback. Someone so pretty was only expected to converse gently, he had mistakenly thought.

"We have come all this way, a Christian army, to save you from the tyranny of the Muslims."

"Pillage and plunder, that's what you came for!" She shot him a hostile look.

"That's enough!" The father's irate expression conveyed deep disapproval.

She snorted like a wild mare.

"Please, son, do pardon her volatile temper. She has just lost not one but two dear ones. You have done more than enough to help us, I beg you to let us continue our way alone."

"I have no intention of disturbing you any further."

He left them and proceeded to his former position at the head of the column, not knowing what had hit him. The girl's image had already embedded itself deep in his infatuated mind. Her strong character and wild temper somehow made her irresistibly attractive in the young man's eyes.

She was as unique and unattainable as a wild thorny flower blooming on the top of a high cliff.

By the time he reached Demetrius, the party had almost arrived at the camp and a thin layer of snow was beginning to cover everything around them.

"Oh, here you are again. Well, your round didn't take too long," Demetrius said with a little sarcasm. Ignoring him, John watched the flickering lights of the camp they were approaching.

"What's happened to you?" Demetrius continued. "You look like you've seen a ghost!"

"More an angel," his friend replied with a pensive look on his face

"An angel?! Now that is something I didn't expect to hear! You only left for a moment and managed to get yourself charmed."

"It's your turn to mock me, but that's alright, you can say all you want. Bring it on."

"Not at all. I'm just curious to know what happened."

"Not now. We've just got here."

The general entered the large tent followed by his guards. After them, the bishop of Aleppo, Agapius, with a few selected men from his congregation. It was a gathering called by Nicephorus himself. The warmth inside the tent was a deep contrast to the freezing weather conditions.

As the notable guests were seated and given something warm to drink, the bishop still clinging to his small wooden box, Nicephorus began to talk:

"I admit, brothers, that I would have rather met you under different circumstances where you did not have to mourn your dead and lament the loss of your homes and livelihoods. As great as our God-granted victory is against the deniers of Christ, I know that it brought inevitable and undesirable results on you and your families. I have no power to resurrect the dead, only God can do that as he will resurrect us all on the final day. Your beloved ones who suffered death at the hands of the infidel shall then shine like the stars in the sky and be dignified with the crowns that only the holy martyrs enjoy. As for your earthly belongings, it is something that can be compensated. You shall be taken to a new land, a Christian land and there, you will be given new homes and new farms. When we leave this place in a few days from now, you shall accompany our army to Caesarea and spend the winter there until the season is more favorable for your relocation."

The men listened to the words that drew the shape of their future and only looked at each other every once in a while to gauge their comrades' reaction.

"Where will this new home of ours be, Lord?" asked the old bishop with a trembling voice

"Anatolia," replied Nicephorus

"We shall be moved to Anatolia? But we are craftsmen and traders. Most of us are not farmers, or shepherds."

"Anatolia has flourishing cities and a bustling trade. I advise you not to worry now about what will come in the future but instead to rest in your allocated tents and to tend to your families' needs. In Caesarea, the head of every household shall receive twenty golden pieces."

Although almost every family's losses had been much more than twenty nomismata, the men sitting opposite to Nicephorus said nothing. It was not the time to complain but to be thankful for their safe exodus from the ruined city; a time to remain by each other's side. After all, their new lord was the God-fearing Nicephorus and the Roman emperor which gave them some sense of security. Their whole life had just been transformed. They no longer were compelled to abide by foreign laws or pay taxes so as to maintain their inherited faith. They were now Roman citizens under the rule of a Christian emperor, and the consequence of that, although not fully comprehensible to them, was more than money.

Had it been their choice to make, they would never have left their city nor relinquished their churches and homes in a time of peace, but war liberated them from the burden of free will. They had so far considered it their mission to remain in the land of their forefathers, to keep the body of Christ present in that part of the world where the disciples were first called Christians, but now it wasn't their choice to make. It was an act of God that wiped out the entire city and made them the luckier group of refugees where instead of death and slavery, they faced a brighter fate and shared the victory of the conquerors.

The bishop stood up, though old and weak, with a body accustomed to standing throughout the long hours of services. In a language borrowed from old books rather than the streets, he said:

"We are confident of your generosity, Lord, and we have no doubt that we will be shown brotherly hospitality as is evident from this first day. We can only be grateful for God the Almighty who has sent us a pious and wise ruler. As you have now mentioned, many of us are bitterly mourning our beloved ones who were martyred just yesterday, all of us lament the loss of our homes and belongings, but we are men of faith and we know that we have no enduring city here but are looking for the city that is to come. We know that in this life we shall see hardships and sorrows as our Lord promised us. Of earthly belongings we are completely devoid. Other than the clothes that cover our bodies, we own nothing. One thing, however, which we consider more precious than our own children, a thing both earthly and divine we do possess; a treasure we have been found worthy by God to preserve throughout the ages. This spiritual jewel, we offer you willingly, knowing that you will cherish and protect it until it is taken to its new home in the Queen of Cities, the Second Rome to bless the faithful there."

He handed the wooden box to Nicephorus. The general received it with reverence, but like the rest of the Romans present, he was still ignorant as to what its contents might be. Some thought it might be a relic of a local saint but they never expected something of such significance. Nicephorus opened the box revealing a yellowish weathered piece of clothing which he took in his hands and displayed in front of everyone. It was a tattered old tunic made of camel hair.

"Lord," said the bishop, humbled by the presence of the holy object. "You are holding in your hands the tunic of John the Baptist, the greatest prophet born of women, the forerunner and baptizer of our Lord Jesus Christ."

Sounds of amazement and surprise broke out along with many *Kyrie Eleison* and *Hosanna*, and the men moved closer to get a better view of the one-thousand-year-old piece of clothing. The domestic, holding the relic with the care a mother would hold her own newborn, printed a kiss of adoration onto the rough fabric then returned it to its box and closed it again.

"You have presented me with something money cannot buy. His majesty and all of Constantinople shall forever be grateful for your pious generosity."

Prayers of thanksgiving were to be incorporated in the next day's Christmas liturgy as ordered by the general in honor of the newly recovered relic. The general's guests were excused and John left the tent with Demetrius. It had stopped snowing and the thin layer of white on the ground had become frozen under the now cloudless and frigid skies. The prisoners captured both at the seizing of the city, and at the battle with Sayf the day before, were in the thousands. They lay tied with ropes, gathered like sheep inside a pen at one side of the camp, guarded by strong army regiments with nothing to protect them from the bitter cold but a few open fires which they desperately huddled around.

"The fires are still raging," said John, pointing towards the city.

"The soldiers have retired for the night, though. Tomorrow is another round of pillage."

Demetrius gave his friend an inquisitive look.

"Now will you not tell me about the *angel* you saw earlier? Is she an Arab captive, young and curvy? It's not one of Christmas's angels, that's for sure!"

"I'll tell you that later, meanwhile, do say a little prayer for me."

"You want me to say a prayer for you? First you see angels and now you want my prayers? This is clearly a Christmas miracle!"

# Chapter Twenty-Five

- ∞∞ -

John left Demetrius standing by the general's tent and walked in the torch-lit pathways of the camp towards a section where the new Christian refugees were lodged. If he could be lucky enough, he might find out the girl's name, he thought. He almost slipped twice on the frozen mud but eventually made it to the far end of the camp where they were settled. By that late hour, there was no sound of crying children or of sobbing women, barely any sound of human activity. But as he drew nearer, he saw a group of men, some young, others older, all standing around an open fire, in the bitter cold, murmuring in their foreign tongue what sounded like anything but cheerful chat. When he heard the language of the Saracens being spoken in the camp of the Romans, something inside him spontaneously felt revolt, unable to accept that the speakers were friends and brothers. To him, the years of strife with the Arabs had embedded in his mind a subconscious link between those sounds and the enemy.

Though the men talked to each other, their eyes were fixed on the city. They watched the numerous fires and must have been trying to guess their exact locations and the destructive effects they were having. Among those bearded frowny faces, John noticed a familiar one.

"John!" cried Mansour with genuine surprise. He had not expected a visit like this at such an hour.

The men all stopped talking and gazed at the newcomer.

"It's John, Nicephorus's own bodyguard." It didn't take them long to remember the man who had rescued them just a few hours earlier, and the praising comments showered upon him by a thankful gathering were translated by Mansour. Though John had gotten used to such plaudits, he nevertheless blushed every time. His fair skin always betrayed his embarrassment or agitation, but the dim light of the torches came to his rescue.

Just as Mansour had been questioned before by the curious Roman soldiers, John now found himself in a similar situation. The men, especially the younger ones, bombarded him with questions about the life of a Roman soldier – as under Islamic rule, they were never allowed to bear arms or join the army – about Constantinople, its streets and palaces, its pleasures and delights, about jobs in the great metropolis and so many other things which John struggled to answer. It seemed like those men, unable to get any sleep and watching the city burn, found John to be the perfect person to help satisfy the curiosity and concerns they were having about the life that awaited them.

Eventually, a little boy of about eight came running out from between the tents with a message to deliver. "Uncle Mansour, they want you to help put grandpa in bed."

"Come on, John, give me a hand with my sick uncle, will you?" It was a timely rescue from the ongoing inquisition. John left the men as he had found them, gazing towards the city, and followed after Mansour.

"The boy's father was my cousin, so the boy calls me uncle. He is showing remarkable resilience following his father's death. I think he still doesn't fully comprehend it."

"His father died?"

"Yes, he was one of those murdered yesterday by the angry mob in the Christian quarter. He left behind this adorable young boy and a grieving widow, not to mention a sick father and an unmarried sister. Quite a burden for the old man, especially now that we had to leave our homes and possessions. This is by far the worst ordeal we have ever been through."

John, who had wanted to inquire from Mansour about the girl he had seen earlier that day, thought the time was inappropriate, not with all the misery Mansour had just described.

With the boy running ahead of them, they got to the tent which stood only a few dozen paces away. From outside, a lamp indicated that the people inside were still awake, unlike the other tents whose residents either slept or simply possessed no means of producing light.

The boy slipped inside the tent and ran to his aunt who was sitting on the ground next to the sick man with her head in her hands. "I got uncle Mansour and another man, a soldier!" he spoke with excitement. "Don't speak so loudly," she reproached him. "Your grandfather is sick, and your mother isn't feeling too well either."

John, who entered the tent behind Mansour, was taken by surprise; a surprise only matched by that of the young woman who had just finished speaking to her little nephew.

"What is *he* doing here?" She shot to her feet.

"This good man came to give us a hand," Mansour said calmly, unable to understand the reason behind his cousin's sudden irritation.

"Did you have to bring a Roman soldier to help us? Look in the direction of the city and see the amount of help they've provided already!" The outspoken young woman continued in the manner John had witnessed a few hours earlier.

"You don't see *me* looting and burning, do you?"

"Mariam, when will you learn to be respectful?" the old man, who lay in one corner, said suddenly. "Twice this man has come to our help and twice you have insulted him!" he went on in withering tones, his condition appearing to have worsened with the hardships of the travel and the cold.

"Twice?" muttered Mansour, struggling to understand what was going on. "Ah, I see now, so it was you who gave a helping hand on the way here! They said a soldier had assisted them but not that it was you!"

"If they hadn't come here, Saliba and Gergis would still be alive today! What about you, Salma, say something! It was your husband who was killed!" She was beside herself with rage, hugging the terrified little boy. The sick man's face became overwhelmed with sorrow and tears. The boy's mother looked like she hadn't yet recovered from the shock of her husband's loss.

"Let's get this thing over with so I can leave you in peace," John said, trying to suppress his own sorrow and disappointment. They lifted the sick man, and placed him on a makeshift bed on the other side of the tent.

Mariam didn't say any more, probably after seeing how her angry words had upset her father. Instead, she tended to him after his relocation, covering him with an old blanket and sitting by his side.

Before he left, John reached for his pouch, extracted three golden coins and offered them to the father. "Here is a little sum to manage your needs. I know you have a heavy burden and a lot of sorrow in your heart. I hope this will at least help in some way."

"I, to receive charity?! Never did I think things could get this bad! Everybody knew me in Aleppo, they'd tell one another 'go to Jabra's shop if you want the finest jewelry'. I made the golden bracelets and necklaces that Sayf's wives wore."

"Don't trouble yourself with such thoughts," Mansour said softly, "just rest and recover so that you might regain your strength in time for the march to Caesarea."

John left the grieving family, made his way out of the tent, and walked back to his part of the camp, all the while cursing himself for ever thinking that anything good could have come from seeing that resentful girl again. He had barely gone past the next tent when Mansour came running after him.

"Hold on!" he said, grabbing his shoulder "I'm sorry I brought you to that place. I had absolutely no idea of your previous encounter."

"Don't be sorry, my friend, you actually brought me to the one place I had been seeking. You see, I met your cousin on our way out of the city and, to be honest, I liked her a lot, but now I know better than to harbor any hopes or dreams about her. She is in perpetual sorrow and anger, and I don't blame her. The two people she mentioned before must have been dear to her, one I suppose was her brother?"

"Yes, and the second her fiancé, both killed in yesterday's riots by the Muslim fanatics."

"That's terrible."

"If you had only known her before these calamities befell us. She was the flower of the family, always cheerful, always kind and considerate. Having to deal with the murder of her brother, the loss of her home and the turning upside down of her entire life is too much to handle. The people here have had their lives shattered."

"I don't blame her, really I don't. She found someone to direct all her anger at, and that person was me. I don't take it personally."

"Thank you, John. You are a real gentleman. Good night now."

They parted. Mansour walked back to his uncle's tent where his presence was greatly needed.

Demetrius was still standing in his place, outside the general's tent. In an instant, he sensed his friend's agitation. It made him refrain from making any smart comments or even asking any questions. One sentence, though, escaped his tight sealed lips:

"This anger of yours might prove useful in tomorrow's assault."

"What anger? Who said I was angry? And what assault are you talking about?"

"The citadel. The general wants it captured."

"I thought we weren't going to do that."

""We most certainly are. What's more: You're leading the attack."."

128

# Chapter Twenty-Six

## - ∞∞ -

At dawn, a regiment of five hundred men made its way towards the city, headed by John, who only hours earlier had been elevated to the position of *Kentarchos*; a division commander by the grateful domestic. Most of the fires had died out during the night, in part due to the falling of a little more snow, but the smell of burning matter still filled the air. In contrast to the day before, the sky cleared up that morning and the Roman soldiers were already resuming their activities of ransack and pillage from where they had stopped the day before.

The citadel, situated high on the snow-covered hill, glittered under the morning sun and looked as invincible as ever. Nicephorus must have known that the prospects of its capture were quite modest, but the men riding behind John had a different opinion, sounding their war cries and advancing with unique exhilaration and unmatched confidence. A rumor had spread amongst the soldiers that Sayf had hidden his finest treasures within the safe confines of the citadel. Needless to say, the effect on the men was intoxicating. They hurried behind their leader on his first official mission through the deserted streets.

Their horses penetrated a once bustling market, now a dreadful place where the bodies of men, women and children lay motionless and half-frozen.

John was given instructions on how to conduct the attack: the main force would assault the front of the castle and keep the defenders preoccupied while a smaller force ascended the hill and scaled the walls. Soon enough, the archers were assembled and their deadly projectiles began raining down on the defenders. Some scenes from the previous day repeated themselves. The combatants took turns in shooting their projectiles in the direction of the other party, although the steepness of the hill made it particularly difficult for the arrows to have the desired effect. A few hours passed. By which time the second part of the plan was implemented. John gave the signal to the nominated soldiers, wishing them success in scaling the walls of a less turbulent, less protected section.

Naturally, the attack that morning on the citadel drove John's thoughts away from the incidents of the previous evening as he focused all his thoughts and energy on accomplishing the mission. Mariam was a bittersweet figure. He did his best and almost succeeded in shutting her image out of his mind and instead continued to do what he did best: warfare. He could not afford to squander his attention while on his first mission, a mission that looked in no way a picnic. He was resolved to securing the capitulation of the last Arab stronghold in the city.

The Arab soldiers showed no signs of retreat or surrender. They continued to hurl their projectiles, preventing the Romans from coming closer to the walls or even attempting to ram the gates, and by noon the squad that had set out to scale the walls returned empty-handed. They had been rebuffed after suffering serious casualties. But to John, who was eager to succeed on his first mission, that stalemate was unacceptable. He called on the soldiers to bring the battering ram, and filled with rage, ordered them to direct the device to the main gate of the citadel.

"But we are completely exposed!" protested one soldier.

"Are you defying your superior's orders? Follow me and don't be a coward!"

Ten men in mail coats and metal helmets, with John rallying them on, pushed the heavy wheeled device, and under a shower of arrows the large gate shook with the first blow. The second blow followed quickly and proved that the gate was not as sturdy as had first been thought. But then a rock hurled from above smashed one soldier's helmet and his skull beneath it. He collapsed motionless, drenched in his own blood. Another soldier quickly replaced him, pushing the ram for the third hit, but from a small hatch above the gate, liquid fire came pouring down on the Romans. The two foremost soldiers were immediately engulfed in flames and flailed around desperately in a dreadful scene like men possessed. No matter what their comrades did, the fire proved unquenchable and the two wretched men succumbed to a painful death. The ramming device itself, being little more than a tree trunk on wheels, also caught fire. John, who burnt with a different fire, was forced to sound a temporary retreat and backed away from the gate.

The citadel wasn't going to capitulate easily, and the attack turned into a disaster after the attackers' preparations clearly fell short of the strong fortifications. Was failure going to be the fate of the new *Kentarchos* on his first mission? John surely wasn't going to let that happen. He looked up at the citadel's high walls and could see the swarthy faces of the defenders, partially showing from behind the merlons and metal helmets. If the rumor had indeed been truthful then Sayf's choice to place his finest treasures at the citadel could not have been more appropriate.

After a score of failed attempts, John's men appeared to have lost heart. Witnessing two of their comrades burn to death, the nauseating smell of their burnt flesh filling their nostrils, had deprived them of the will to go on. But before he could think of a way to overturn their fortunes, a sudden and violent strike from behind threw him face down on the slushy mud. It was as if a thunderbolt had pierced him, leaving him completely helpless, as if suddenly all his strength had been drained from him. He didn't know what had struck him but amid the confusion, some nearby soldiers cried out his name along with the word 'arrow'.

The men, who realized all efforts to conquer the citadel were, to say the least, delayed, carried their commander and placed him in an open cart, on his right side. They knew better than to try and remove the arrow themselves. Instead, the long shaft which had penetrated his mail coat and continued through his left shoulder was still protruding from his back. No time was wasted and the cart soon made its way down the steep hill accompanied by a few horsemen, to the military hospital inside the camp where the injured soldiers were treated. John knew where they were taking him. It was nothing like the hospitals of Constantinople with their spacious wards, comfortable beds and talented physicians but merely a large tent, overcrowded with groaning soldiers, and a few overworked physicians.

As they descended the hill, the pain became more excruciating, until John felt he could not bear it anymore. His whole body shuddered and his sweating face reflected the deep anguish he was experiencing. But the worst pain he felt by far was that of defeat. He had failed on his first mission as a division commander, and to someone like John, that was unforgivable.

With every jolt the cart made on the bumpy road, he felt as if a chisel hammered at his back.

"Hold on, it's only a few minutes until the healer sees you," said one man riding with him in the cart, confident that Nicephorus's favorite would get the best treatment available as soon as they reached their destination.

But those few minutes proved to be too long for John to endure. The blood flowing from his deep wound seeped down his back and through the cart's wooden planks, leaving a dotted red trail on the dirty snow. His senses began to wane and his mind stagger. Then, though it was still midday, he felt a gradual eclipse taking over his mind until complete darkness, complete silence prevailed.

# Chapter Twenty-Seven

- ဆဝငဆ -

John recalled slipping in and out of consciousness. He couldn't remember much of what had happened very clearly, only flashes of faces crowding around him, the strong smell of vinegar and the clanging sounds of metal remained imprinted in his memory.

John's eyelids trembled slightly then exposed his eyes to the dim light coming from a few lanterns hung from the ceiling. He realized he was still lying on his right side, his knees bent towards his stomach. However, the change of scenery and the soft material beneath him soon made it clear that he wasn't lying in the wooden cart anymore. He had no clothes on from the waist up, but a wide linen bandage was wrapped around his back and chest, and he was covered with his own blanket brought from his tent. The first thing he saw was another person sleeping on a mattress opposite with a blood-stained bandage wrapped around his head. He tried to roll onto his back but the feeling of a dagger piercing through his shoulder-blades quickly convinced him otherwise. Upon his attempt to move, a few familiar faces appeared in front of him.

"The one time you go into battle alone and this is what you come back like?" Demetrius smiled, holding in his hands a long shaft with a sharp metal head.

"Looks like my new title is nothing but bad luck!" John forced out a smile of his own.

Demetrius, Mansour and Andreas had waited by his side, hoping he would wake up.

"The general passed by an hour ago to check on you but you were still asleep. He asked to be informed once you had regained consciousness."

"Was the citadel taken?" John asked with genuine concern, though with a weak voice.

"Forget the citadel for now," Demetrius replied, waving his words away.

"I'm thirsty."

"Of course you are, you bled like a slaughtered bull. Wait a little, I'll get you something to drink, and then I'll inform the general."

One of the men poured some water from a clay jug into a tin cup, but as Demetrius held his friend's bare arm trying to help him sit up, he was struck by the amount of heat his body emitted.

"You are burning with fever! I better call the physician." He quickly went to search for the man amongst the many patients and visitors that filled the place, returning with him a few minutes later. But by then, someone had already informed the general, and soon enough there he was to check on the soldier who had once saved his life, magically turning the clamor inside the large tent hospital into reverent silence.

"I'm glad to see you awake, John," he said in a fatherly voice and patted his shoulder only to recognize what Demetrius had discovered a moment before.

"Fever," he observed. "Did anyone call Cosmas?"

"Yes, Sir, Demetrius is fetching him now."

When a soldier suffered a bad injury, fever could only have dire ramifications. Most died not instantly on the battlefield but from fever and sickness a few days later. John knew that.

Cosmas arrived promptly. Small in stature, he wasn't too old to accompany a military campaign,    and had the necessary experience of a healer. His reddish hair and long beard made him look slightly comical. He wore a long black robe  under a thick woolen grey vest. His demeanor was typical of a learned, well-paid employee of the government; that is confident, haughty, and acting as if he were only second to the emperor.

"How are you feeling, lad?" He felt his forehead with the back of his palm

"I'm fine, I just feel a little dizzy."

"He is with high fever just as I expected," Cosmas said gravely to the domestic. "I will try to break it, but he will need to have constant care and diligent supervision, which my overworked staff might not be able to provide. Moreover, there is always the possibility that things might get worse."

"How do you mean?" asked Demetrius.

The doctor glanced at him, curious to know who it was that dared interrupt his prognosis. He answered bluntly, even a little cruelly, "A lot worse. He might not live out another two or three days."

This time Demetrius did not answer but he had quickly established a solid hatred for the man.

*What an arrogant bastard.*

Dismayed by the answer, Nicephorus asked:

"Other than the towels of water and vinegar that your assistants apply to the bodies of the soldiers, is there anything else you can give him? A medicine perhaps?"

"After we have removed the arrow head from his flesh, there is nothing much we can do, General. He is a strong young man and should be able to overcome the fever ... hopefully," he said, twisting his lower lip.

John noticed that Mansour had been trying to say something all along, and now he seemed unable to stop himself anymore. He mustered his courage and looking directly towards Nicephorus implored:

"Sir, I know someone who can surely make him well."

In genuine amazement, the general stared at Mansour. "You know someone who can make fever disappear? And who might that be?"

"He's a physician, a great one, up till yesterday we were neighbors."

"An Arab?" Cosmas protested with apparent disdain.

There was a meek look on Mansour's face. John could see Demetrius who stood next to Mansour squeezing his hand without anyone noticing.

"And what more can an Arab physician do?" inquired the general.

"He was renowned in all of Aleppo for his skill and expertise, and with the medicines he prepared, he did heal a great number of people who would have otherwise succumbed to fever. Not that John actually needs such imminent help." He turned his head towards John who all the while listened to the discussion about his condition without uttering a word. It was an opportunity to hear the truth without pretense or consolation.

"Interesting. Where is this man now?" demanded the general.

"Well, this might be a bit of a problem, Sir. I did happen to see him in the midst of yesterday's chaos. I recognized him immediately in spite of the miserable condition he was in. He and his family were being led by the soldiers, their hands tied. I believe he could be outside with the thousands of other Muslim prisoners."

"If I may say something, General," interrupted Cosmas. "This is all nonsense. You certainly will not allow a barbarian magus, an infidel to practice his obscene magic in our midst!"

"Enough already," Nicephorus said decisively, looking towards John and rubbing his beard. "I'm sure you will be just fine by tomorrow. Cosmas will see to it. A special service will be held tonight for the recovery of all the injured. Now we shall leave you to get some rest. You, Demetrius, can stay here if you wish." He turned and left, the others following him, except for Demetrius and Mansour.

"You two can leave as well. I'll be alright." John looked at his friends.

134

"And do what? There isn't much to be done around here now. Besides, you heard what the domestic just said."

"This damned fever is making me shiver. Can you throw another blanket on me?" He suddenly started shaking like an autumn leaf.

Mansour said nothing but his anxiety was apparent even to John.

*If only the general would allow that physician to come. He could work wonders.*

A moment later, Cosmas reappeared with a young assistant of his carrying a bucket of strong smelling vinegar. He then dipped some towels inside, squeezed them and placed them on John's forehead, wrists and ankles.

"These need to be wetted all the time. Do you think you can do that?" the doctor asked facetiously.

"Sure, I'll stay here beside him," Demetrius answered.

"Well, tomorrow morning, we will know if he will ..."

A furious look from Demetrius made the callous physician leave without uttering another word, but John didn't have to hear it to know that his time on earth could very much be running out fast.

# Chapter Twenty-Eight

- 𝑒𝒿𝒞𝑔 -

The next morning, just before the wake-up trumpet was sounded, the Roman camp witnessed an unusual buzz at such an early hour. Hundreds of cavalry were admitted inside the fortified perimeter, to be welcomed with enthusiastic cheers by the awakening soldiers.

Tzimiskes was finally back after three days of chasing Sayf deep into the Syrian Desert. The Emir had managed to cross the Euphrates with a handful of men who had escaped the onslaught outside of Aleppo. The once fearsome leader had been reduced to a fugitive. Tzimiskes saw his mission through as best as he could and now his travel-worn men raced back, certain of the fall of Aleppo, and eager to lay their hands on their share of the loot.

"Don't worry!" Nicephorus assured his nephew, pointing to a heap of treasures and artifacts inside an enclosure, guarded by a few soldiers. "All the spoils shall be evenly distributed amongst all."

The uncle and nephew briefed each other on the busy events of the previous three nights. Tzimiskes explained how the chase had to be conducted carefully, especially when the cunning Sayf chose to escape through rugged gorges and narrow passes, perfect for ambushes. Finally, by the time the terrain opened, they realized that Sayf had been in full flight, and had successfully crossed the great river to be sheltered by his ally bedouin tribes. Nicephorus, in turn, described how the city had been besieged, stormed and swiftly taken after negotiations with the Arabs had failed. He showed his nephew the holy prize they received from the city's Arab Christians which Tzimiskes admired greatly and adored with excessive reverence. He did not forget to mention John's infiltration inside the city prior to its fall and his role in saving the holy relic and the small Christian community. When Tzimiskes asked about John's whereabouts, his uncle informed him of his condition.

"He is lying in the field hospital, burning with fever. We thought he'd get better, but he has only gotten worse."

John had always reminded Tzimiskes of himself back when he was still a young officer, before he rose to prominence. Apart from the name, there was much in common between them, and he genuinely liked the brave soldier.

"What did that little doctor say, what's his name ...? Will he survive?"

"Cosmas? Well, he doesn't seem very optimistic."

Tzimiskes shook his head with disappointment.

"I'd like to see him before it's too late."

"Then let us go now."

Both commanders walked to the field hospital, a couple of hundred paces away. It was a brilliant morning, the sun was shining brightly and quickly melted whatever snow had remained on the ground.

Tzimiskes looked towards Aleppo and saw the citadel still flying its green banners, unsubdued after the failed attempt the day before. The rampage and looting continued unabated. The once opulent city was being quickly and completely stripped of everything of worth by the relentless conquerors.

\*\*\*

On the other side of the camp, meagre food rations were being distributed to the prisoners. The men were ordered to stand in long lines and receive their families' morning meal whereas the women and children sat in small circles on the ground and eagerly awaited the arrival of what most of them would not have even considered tasting just a few days previous.

One family, a father, mother, and three children, sat quietly eating their impoverished meal inside the large pen, when they were interrupted by a squad of Roman soldiers, who grabbed the head of the family roughly and made him stand up. The middle-aged man with an exhausted face, a thin beard and wind-mussed hair took a look at the aggressors and quite unexpectedly recognized one of them. "Traitor," he said in Arabic, almost inaudibly and spat on the ground.

The guards, who appeared relieved to have found the man after an apparently long search, escorted him out of the enclosure through the long rows of tents and towards the field hospital while his wife and children shouted and cried out desperately.

"I haven't done anything to deserve what you just called me," Mansour said to him in Arabic.

"And what do you call dealing with them and serving them, those who burnt your city? But you Christians, you have no loyalty but to one another!"

"The city is captured and we had nothing to do with it. We suffered just as much as you did, in fact we were so close to being annihilated. But now let's put these events behind us. What's done is done. You, dear neighbor, have a real chance of reversing your fate. Just look towards the future, not the past."

The uncomprehending Roman soldiers ran out of patience hearing that 'revolting' language. After making their sentiments clear with an angry look, they ended the heated debate there and then.

A moment later, they were outside the hospital where they saw Nicephorus and Tzimiskes walking alongside a few of their guards.

"Listen to me, Jafar, I want what is good for you," Mansour whispered into the man's ear. "This is the domestic. Behave well and you shall be rewarded! Fail to do so and you will not live long enough to digest that meal you just swallowed."

He received a look of contempt from his captured neighbor.

Inside the tent, John lay on his bed almost unconscious, surrounded by his comrades. The usual silence that always followed the entrance of the domestic soon prevailed, and from in between the many patients and visitors rushed Cosmas.

Not wet towels, nor rubbing him with vinegar had been able to break the fever that battered John's injured body since the previous evening. Tzimiskes saw his condition, and sadly remarked to his uncle:

"Perhaps it's time to summon a priest to administer the last rites while the poor fellow can still swallow."

At that moment, the band of soldiers made their entry, proud to have succeeded in finding the wanted man. All bowed before the general except for the captive Arab who stood upright, earning himself a punch in the stomach from one of the soldiers that forced him down to his knees.

"Who is this?" Tzimiskes asked.

"If I am right, this must be the Arab physician we were advised to employ," Nicephorus replied.

"For a physician, you are ill mannered!" Tzimiskes said, with Mansour delivering a prompt translation.

"I only bow to God!" he said, struggling with pain, yet not the least losing his fierce look.

"Well, that's honorable, but sadly you are not in a position to impose your beliefs," Nicephorus replied. "In any case, we didn't bring you here to humiliate you. On the contrary, we were told that you have talents useful to us. If that turns out to be true then you will see that we can be just as useful to you."

"What do you want from me?"

"You see this man, can your medicine make him better?"

The Arab looked at John, lying with his eyes closed, taking rapid, shallow breaths. He pondered for a moment.

"I can try, but what do I get in return?"

"You get nothing for trying, only for succeeding: you and your family's emancipation and twelve golden nomismata."

"How generous! First you rob us of our freedom and belongings, then in return for achieving what your helpless doctors failed to achieve, you bestow upon us a fraction of what is ours," he said in a calm voice, his eyes fixed on the ground.

"He says, you are very generous, Sir," was the only thing Mansour translated.

Nicephorus nodded.

"Let me first examine him and then I can then tell you if he will live or die."

With a signal from the domestic, the soldiers released the physician and he began to examine the patient in a way never seen by those standing. He first checked his wound thoroughly, then moved on to check every orifice in his head. Afterwards, he put his ear on the man's chest and listened at length to his heartbeat, appearing to be doing some sort of calculations as he did so. Finally, he stood up and faced the group of men who all the while had watched him with much curiosity.

"He will live, but only if a certain treatment is administered to him. You must bring me all the components I need to prepare the suitable medicine ... oh, and one more thing: make them thirty gold pieces."

"Let's see if your talent matches your greed. Get him what he wants," the domestic ordered

"You will not be disappointed."

The commanders left giving Cosmas the chance to swallow his pride and order his helpers to fetch the Saracen physician the ingredients he asked for, which they did quickly, albeit deeming the use of some of them for the healing of humans as quite unusual. Certain herbs, citrus leaves, olive oil, starch, honey, ivy berries and a few other strange ingredients were brought to him, and he began mixing and grinding them with a pestle, with the eyes of everyone fixed upon him. In a short while, the medicine was ready.

With an attitude not lacking assurance or command, he lectured the attendants: "A measure is to be applied to the wound and another to be swallowed twice a day. Do that, and his life will be saved. Now, since I will not leave my family alone out in the cold, already a victim of fear and agony, who of you will be performing this treatment?"

"I will," answered a determined feminine voice that no one had heard before. The few men that surrounded John's bed turned and looked in bewilderment at the beautiful young speaker standing by the entrance.

"Well, then, watch how it needs to be done," the doctor addressed her, not the least concerned about the fact that the she was a woman. He must have thought that she was a relative of the patient's, perhaps his wife. It wasn't uncommon for high-ranking soldiers to bring their wives to the front with them. But Mansour looked at his cousin, not quite believing his eyes. "You, of all people?" he whispered to her, but she just glanced at him; her expression revealing nothing.

"A Saracen makes the medicine, and a woman administers it. The obscenity of this whole affair is now complete. Let it be known to all that from now on, the health of this young man is not my responsibility," Cosmas declared, storming off in a fit of rage.

Jafar, the Arab physician, not understanding what had just happened, gestured for Mariam to come closer and watch.

"You can speak to her in Arabic, she is my cousin," Mansour said to Jafar.

Jafar glanced at Mariam and nodded twice, his face grim.

He removed the bandage and painted the wound with the greyish ointment he had prepared, then opened John's mouth and successfully made him swallow a spoonful of it. "This is what you will do this evening, and tomorrow morning. Continue until the fever goes away." And looking at Mansour, he said, "Now take me back to my family, and when he gets better, remember that my part of the deal is done."

The soldiers escorted him out, leaving Demetrius and Mansour equally confused. The former wondered who that woman might be, while the latter could not understand the sudden change of heart that drove his cousin to nurse a person she openly despised.

But the most astonished of all was John, who although in delirium, and barely able to speak, could see that Mariam's presence next to him was a reality. He didn't know what to make of it, neither did his health give him the capacity to think straight. One thing he was sure of, though, that at that dire time of his life, her presence beside him was more than welcome.

# *Chapter Twenty-Nine*

- 𝒮𝒪𝒞𝒮 -

Cosmas's striking rage convinced everyone that the proud physician was not going to take part in John's therapy anymore, and the young patient was moved to his own tent, with Nicephorus's approval. The domestic also received word that one Christian Arab girl was staying by John's side, taking care of him. Upon inquiring, he was informed that John had helped the girl and her sick father the previous day and that out of gratitude, she was now repaying him. In Nicephorus's devout mind, it was perfectly conceivable that a good deed received the deserved reward. He could relate to that from his own life. God was quick to punish him for his sins, but even quicker to reward him for acts of faith and mercy.

For two days and nights, Mariam sat by John's side placing cold wet towels on his forehead only to remove them a while later, scalding to the touch, as if they had been inside an oven. She watched his delirious body shudder under the crushing weight of fever. She administered the medicine the Saracen healer had prepared, exactly as she had been taught. Demetrius and Mansour were obliged to leave, the former to attend to his night guarding shift, the latter to his family at their new temporary home. Moreover, neither of them had had any sleep the night before and both were exhausted. But they left knowing that their friend was being well taken care of.

Just before dawn, after four days of fever, John finally opened his eyes. It didn't take him long to realize he was in his own tent, lit by a lonely oil lamp. His eyeballs didn't feel like they were going to explode anymore nor was there that shattering headache. His wound wasn't throbbing painfully with every heartbeat either. He could finally see clearly. His body had been freed from the thrall of fever and delirium.

At first, he thought rainwater had wetted his bed but he quickly realized it had been his own sweat that was soaking him and the mattress. With fever breaking, he had shed tremendous amounts of water to the degree that his throat felt as dry as an old piece of wood.

Lying on his side, with his face toward the tent's canvas, he tried to lift himself and find something to drink. Meanwhile, his mind slowly began to recall incidents from the last time he had been conscious. His surprise was immense when he turned and saw Mariam sitting next to him. She had fallen asleep herself after a long and grueling night.

He looked at her tenderly. It brought him much pleasure to watch the sleeping beauty in his tent. The woman who had captured his heart, had been without doubt his nursemaid. The reason that drove her to his service was a mystery to him. He cautiously tried to reach for the water jar without waking her up but the light sleeper suddenly opened her eyes, startled like a wild gazelle when it sees a hunter, accidentally knocking the jar out of John's hand, sending it shattering to the ground.

"I'm sorry if I scared you," he apologized.

She was surprised to see him sit up in bed and speak. After four days of staggering between life and death, it was certainly an astonishing development.

"I'll fetch some more water." She brushed his tender words aside, then wrapped herself with a woolen shawl and went out for a moment, soon returning with another clay jar.

"There you go, drink!" She extended a hand towards him, avoiding eye contact.

"Thank you," he replied, staring right at her and taking the jar from her hand.

"Listen," she said, folding her arms across her chest. "Just so that you do not misinterpret the motives behind my presence here, you must know that not for a moment have I stopped feeling hatred and anger towards your people, and probably never will."

"What are you doing here, taking care of me, then?"

The girl heaved a deep sigh then looked at John with a sad face.

"It was my father's wish that I come here and look after you. His health has improved, and on hearing what had happened to you from Mansour, he made me come and look after you until you got better. I would not say no to my father even if it meant my death. He is the last person I have in this world. So don't you ever think that I did this of my own will."

"I'm glad you listened to him." A faint smile pulled at his lips.

"Now that you know, I hope this will be the end of our conversations. At any rate, you have made a fast recovery already. Soon, you won't be needing me, or anyone else for that matter."

He admired her angry, but charming features and appealing curves. "Your obedience to your father is truly admirable, but I still think that your rebellious soul would not have condoned this ... subjugation, unless part of you believed what you did here was the right thing."

"It doesn't look like your appetite for quarrel has been affected at all. I don't think you need my help anymore, now that you are able to spare so much energy for argument."

"Why do you avoid the truth? You are only here because deep inside your heart, you know you are repaying my kindness." He quickly realized that wasn't the best thing to have said.

"Your arrogance knows no bounds!" She raised her voice "You and your friends have caused us all this misery and all you can do is boast about your kindness?! My brother, and the man I was supposed to marry were murdered."

She suddenly choked on her words.

"Why do you blame *me* for that? I risked my life to save your people. Weren't you too among those in the church?"

"If you hadn't come to our country, none of this would have happened!"

"But we did come, and did not intend to cause you or your family any pain. We came to defend the empire and ..."

"And plunder, and rape and murder."

"You're just trying to convince yourself of our evil intentions, but truly, were we supposed to be defeated so that you might be satisfied? We could have either emerged victorious, or be ruined by this war. God saw us deserving of victory."

"What do you know about God!" she protested angrily, her big eyes getting even bigger.

"I do not claim vast knowledge but I do know a few things."

"Things like, love, peace and mercy? I think not!"

"I know that he commanded us to love and forgive our enemies, our personal enemies. As to the enemies of the motherland, the enemies of Christ and emperor, these shall be shown no mercy."

"Big words from someone who a few hours ago was closer to death than life."

"Thanks to God, and to you, here I am now closer to life than ever, not that death scares me, but ..."

"But what? Before I go, I must remind you to honor your part of the deal with that Arab physician who saved your life."

"Wait a second, what happened to him? I do remember him preparing the medicine with his pestle."

"Well, good thing that you did."

He looked at her and saw beyond her anger.

"Mariam," he spoke gently. "I could never do anything to harm you. If you would only get to know me better."

Having survived that heavy illness, John was determined not to keep his feelings for himself any longer. The eighteen-year-old beauty looked at him, a strange look appeared on her face.

"Perhaps in another world, in another time that might be possible."

She turned around and left.

The walls of resentment that she surrounded herself with were hard to climb, her stubborn defenses were truly invincible.

*A different time, a different world,* he contemplated, staring at the yellow flame that danced in the oil lamp next to him

His thoughts were eventually disturbed by Demetrius, barging his way into the tent, his face glowing with joy. He must have heard the quarrel and come to see if everything was all right.

"You didn't think you were going to get rid of me that easily, did you?!" John smiled to his jubilant friend.

Fate had provided the medicine of an enemy doctor, the dedicated care of a resentful girl, and granted John a new life.

# Chapter Thirty

- ဆင်္ကြ -

Mariam stormed out of John's tent taking quick strides back towards that of her family's. She had succeeded in maintaining a tenacious façade. No Roman soldier should ever see her cry. But the moment she was safely far away, she quickly buried her face in her hands and burst into tears. If she hadn't done so, she felt she could have exploded the next second. She didn't want her family to see her like that either and so she stood for a while all alone, among the lines of tents that extended into the quiet darkness. She wept silently while the pitch-black night made way for the first sunrays, slowly coming from behind her ruined home city. The chirping of birds ended the silence around her.

*Another day begins, another day of suffering. How could this have happened? How could fate have turned against us so cruelly?* She gazed in disbelief at the place where she had been born and raised.

Memories of the sweet life in Aleppo came floating back. The feeling of safety within the walls of a warm home, the moments shared with loved ones, the frequent visits to the covered souk with friends, the afternoon walks beside the Belus river. Then sprang images of food, the delicious tastes her city was famed for, and her stomach started growling. She hadn't had anything to eat since the previous day. She wasn't used to this kind of harsh life, being deprived of all things beautiful, of all means of comfort. She had grown up a pampered child. Her father had done all he could to compensate her for the loss of her mother, and while he often overdid it, the crafty little girl understood this and took advantage of his kindness.

*What's the use of having these thoughts now ... That life is never coming back again. Who knows what fate has more in store for us ...*

She had left her sister-in-law, Salma, to take care of her recuperating father and obeyed the latter's will to go and tend to John. Now she was going back to where her family stayed. A lot of work awaited her, she was sure.

*I'll take George and we'll go gather some fire wood. Then we'll go fetch some water from the river.* These were chores she wasn't used to doing but now, everyone had to do their share to survive, even her little nephew.

A cold breeze gave her a shiver. She wrapped the shawl more tightly around her shoulders and hugged herself. *I'd better get going.* She hastened towards the tent, wiped her eyes clean of tears, removed the tent flap and went inside. Everyone was still sleeping. Her father's breathing didn't sound as heavy as it had been a couple of days before. *A good thing.* Little George slept peacefully in his mother's embrace.

Mariam sat in her corner, removed the pin that held her hair in place and shook it out. The long, silky hair fell down freely on her shoulders, relaxing her tension a bit. She quietly began to peel off the half-dry mud from the hem of her dress. When they had been forced to take refuge inside the church then leave Aleppo, she had left home with only her clothes on. She had been wearing her favorite – once beautiful – dress her late fiancé Gergis had given her as a present the day he had come to ask for her hand in marriage. She felt the soft fabric between her fingers and sighed. *He brought me something every time he came to see me, expensive things too. He spared no money.*

The first time she had seen Gergis was when he had come with his father and uncle and asked for her hand from her father. She had never remembered seeing him before in town. Well, at least she had never noticed him before, but he definitely had noticed *her.*

*I must have looked really beautiful when he saw me on that Palms' Sunday, standing in the churchyard with my girlfriends, waving our olive branches.*

A couple of days later, Gergis visited them at home and proposed. She said yes. He hadn't been exceptionally handsome but had come from a rich and respectable family. Any Christian father in Aleppo would have only been too happy to marry his daughter off into a rich merchant family like Gergis's. Besides, the majority of her friends had already gotten engaged by then, mostly to men they had never talked to before.

Her brother, though, had advised her not to rush into anything. *How many times did he tell me to think things through carefully. You're still young, he would say, don't get married just yet. Wait another year. Listen to your heart. Could he have realized that I wasn't head over heels in love with Gergis? Perhaps he could. Perhaps they all could. Why then would Salma tell me that love often comes after marriage?* She sniffed. *Perhaps love does come after marriage, who am I to judge? What do I know?*

All she knew about love, she had learnt from the, secret conversations she and her girlfriends whispered to each other in their bedrooms, amid suppressed, shy giggles. She had heard a few things from poems too. One poet, famous in all Arab lands lived in her city. Aleppo's streets reverberated with his poems She had memorized a couple of stanzas from one of his love poems.

*The fire of love is about to burn my ribs and above,*
*Sparkling by emotion, unquenchable by any potion.*

When she had compared those words to her feelings towards Gergis, there had been hardly any resemblance, but then again, one mustn't believe every poet's fantasy and exaggeration, she had thought.

She took a deep breath, slowly letting it out.

From the other side of her thoughts came John's image before her mind's eyes. *He wants me to get to know him better? Is that why he's been acting so kindly to us, giving father money and all, trying to gain my favor? I could tell he's attracted to me from the look in his eyes. Well, he and the other soldier friends of his did save our lives at the church and that was even before he'd seen me. They rescued us from a fiery death. He must be really distinguished, the chief commander of the Romans was coming in person and asking about his condition. And brave too, having led the assault on the citadel, receiving that injury which nearly cost him his life.* She pondered for a moment.

*And he's really handsome too.* A dreamy look appeared on her face.

The two previous nights, she'd taken care of the young soldier who lay mostly unconscious, bare from the waist up; a blanket covering his chiseled back and strong arms. He had the body of a true warrior, the face of a Greek God. It had been the first time Mariam had been alone with a strange man, albeit in delirium. She remembered removing the bandage off his shoulder to apply the ointment. Touching his warm, smooth skin had sent a chill down her spine, and now she felt the same chill again just by thinking about it. A short while ago, he sat in bed talking to her, replying gently to her angry protests. His deep-blue eyes surveyed her, she could see that. She noticed his lustful, captivating looks .

She shook her head in panic. *What am I thinking! I should get ahold of myself.* Then crossed herself with her muddy fingers to expel the wanton image. *How could I let myself drift like that. These feelings are to be resisted, to be buried here and now! Gergis's body is still warm and I'm having day dreams of the vilest sort.* She abhorred herself.

She promised never to let that image of John captivate her senses again but little did she know that it would be harder thought of than done.

Salma made an incomprehensible sound. Mariam looked at her and saw that she was still sleeping. Everyone was still sleeping.

*Let them rest a little more. They need all the strength they can get. Soon we will begin the march for the land of our conquerors. Soon we will behold Aleppo no more.*

# Chapter Thirty-One

### - 𝒮𝒪𝒞𝒮 -

On the first of January, the grand army began its journey back north leaving behind a devastated city and a ravaged countryside. It was a clear message to the Arabs that the Romans were now unstoppable, that nothing could prevent them from returning and inflicting as much devastation as they pleased, whenever they pleased. All the other cities saw the fate of Aleppo and shuddered.

The march north went at a leisurely pace as countless wagons filled with loot and thousands of prisoners traipsed behind their Roman captors. After passing the narrow gorges of the Taurus Mountains – the natural border between the two realms – the long column proceeded along the Taurus River. The fact that their march took place in the middle of winter meant that there were days when heavy rain or high winds caused delays, which was inevitable for the weaker members of the party. The sick, injured and the prisoners, among which were large numbers of women and children, couldn't keep up with the agile march of a veteran army and had to make frequent stops.

The campaign against the Arabs had ended in such a remarkable victory as only few had predicted, and the army deserved a period of rest. To soldiers whose villages lay on the road to Caesarea, it was the end of the journey, and Demetrius was one of these. He had been eagerly awaiting the day when he could settle the issue of the farm. But this time, he wasn't going alone. John was going to accompany him.

John had spoken of going back to Constantinople. Demetrius had sworn to accompany him as the loyal friend he was, should he decide to do so. It'd been a year and a half since John last returned home, which was only natural for a soldier on campaign, but now, since the war was over, and he was in no position to take part in drills, at least for the time being, the most suitable course of action was to go home and recuperate. The only thing that made him reluctant about leaving was Mariam. He still harbored some faint hope that she might return his feelings of affection.

By the time they left Aleppo – or what was left of it – John's health had notably improved. Though feeble in comparison to his previous self, his wound was slowly healing and the fever that had come close to ending his life was completely defeated. He could once again mount his horse. The recovery was so astonishing that Nicephorus emancipated the Arab physician and his family, as the deal had been, and made him join the medical team that accompanied the army, earning in addition to the thirty golden pieces he had demanded and deserved, a salary of twenty pieces a month. Of course, Cosmas hated the fact that he now had a rival for a colleague, and indeed an infidel rival who had proven to be superior in knowledge. But Nicephorus couldn't care less about what Cosmas felt as long as the lives of his soldiers were being saved and their health better maintained.

Jafar, the physician, was encouraged upon his emancipation to embrace the faith of the Romans, his new masters, something which would have brought him countless advantages. He, however, preferred to continue following the religion of his forefathers, relying on the pragmatic tolerance of his patron, the supreme commander.

The first thing John did after his recovery was to seek his benefactor, Mariam's father. He searched the marching Christian refugees for the one family he knew well, but to find them among the thousands of soldiers, prisoners and refugees was no easy job. He rode up and down the line, trying to locate them.

Eventually, he spotted them: Mansour carrying his little daughter, his wife beside him. Behind them traipsed Salma holding her son's hand tightly. And finally, a few paces behind, came Jabra and his daughter who held the reins of a mule that carried their few belongings.

John dismounted, grabbed the reins of his horse and approached them. Mansour appeared glad to see him.

"You look fine today, John. What brings you to this part of the line?"

"I haven't had the chance to thank Jabra and Mariam for looking after me."

Jabra, who looked like his health had improved significantly, held John in high esteem. The man who had recently lost his son, and the man his daughter had been promised to, found consolation in John's visit.

"I did nothing worth your praise," he said, modestly.

John looked at Mariam, and could see that she felt uneasy about his presence.

"Father, I'm going to catch up with Salma now." She said, then glanced brusquely at John. Her flashing eyes were like a blade that cut through him.

"Go with God."

She left them and advanced a few steps ahead.

"I know you like Mariam. I've noticed the way you look at her," Jabra said in all honesty.

"I can't say I don't," John replied with the same frankness. "But since you've mentioned it, I must assure you of the pureness of my intentions."

"I never had any doubts about that. You certainly are an honorable man, John. But Mariam has been through so much," Jabra confided. "Slowly I can see her returning to her kind and loving self. I remember when she lost her mother. She was only seven years old. Her sadness and anger were immeasurable, and lasted for a long time, but when the wound in her soul finally healed, she was once more the joy of the house."

John pondered on that for a moment then said: "What do you think I should do? You certainly know her better than anyone else."

"I would be happy to see my daughter married to someone as kind and generous as you, but right now, I think the best thing would be to take a step back, perhaps even to go away for a few weeks. Allow her to overcome her grief on her own, to check her heart."

"Actually, I've been thinking about returning to Constantinople for a couple of months, to see my family," he said reluctantly.

"Are you in good shape to travel that far? Constantinople is not a bowshot away!"

"I feel just fine. Besides, I might stay with a friend of mine for a few days at his nearby village before I set out for home. I'll see you back in Caesarea in springtime … I hope by then …"

"Sounds like a good idea to me. In your absence, she will be more capable of assessing her feelings alone, as she is used to. Go home and see your parents, but don't be long. We will miss you around here."

"Thank you, Jabra." His departure for home had now gained more reason.

"This war has brought so much destruction, you must understand, John, not only to cities and buildings, but to our very souls. We are all shattered from inside. We need time to heal, some more than others."

John looked at the man and couldn't help but think:

*He must be about the age of my father, yet their lives couldn't be more different. One lives in peace and dignity, the other deprived of both.*

"We've left behind the homes we built, the trees we planted, the familiar neighborhoods of our childhood, even the bones of our ancestors. Part of our hearts will forever remain there."

"In Caesarea, a new life awaits you, a new hope."

He dearly wished that his words would come true. After all, would these Arabs really  assimilate with their new surroundings? Would they forget their old home? How fast will they stop being Arabs and start being Romans? But above all, will the new home soften Mariam's heart? He had absolutely no idea, only hope. A new beginning might prove better than one expected.

# Chapter Thirty-Two

- 𝒮𝒪𝒞𝒮 -

Two young women sat in the sun chatting and watching a group of children play catch. The rare warmth of that winter's day was more than welcome.

"I can't believe how, after such a long and exhausting march, they can still run and skip like they had been sleeping all along," said the younger of the two.

"They've had an hour's rest. It's more than enough for children their age to replenish their vigorous little bodies. But you'll experience that firsthand once you've had children of your own, my dear Mariam."

"Oh, Salma, please." She heaved a sigh. "After what happened to us, I don't know if I can think about those things ever again."

"*Because* of what's happened, you should consider these *things* more than ever. Your father will not be around forever, you know."

"Salma, I beg you, don't start now." Her voice was already beginning to quaver.

"Start what? You know I want what's best for you. You keep on pushing that young soldier away, though I don't really know why. What is it that you hate about him? He is not to blame for this war. In fact, he might very well turn out to be the only good thing to happen to you as a result of it."

"Listen, Salma. It's not that I don't find him attractive or kind, but he's one of *them*." She simply couldn't let go of the fact that John was part of an invading army.

"This is nonsense, Mariam. Soon *we* will become Romans like them. Why do you think they are resettling us in Caesarea? We are Christians, most of us speak Greek, and they need the likes of us to populate their borderland. In fact, whether we like it or not, we are already Romans in their eyes!"

"And what happened to us this winter? Shall we just forget about it, like nothing happened, like we never had a life before we set out on this miserable march north?"

152

"Who said we should forget? But for the sake of these children, we must learn to live the new life we have been given."

"Salma, I'm still there in the middle of the fighting, I can still hear the shrieks of the children and smell the burnt flesh. Every morning I recall the moment when we saw the Romans surround our city. Every day, just before evening fades into dusk I remember that afternoon when the angry mob of fanatics snatched Saliba and Gergis and ..." she trailed off into silence.

A boy kicked the cloth ball the group had been chasing after towards the two women. Salma grabbed it with both hands and tossed it back to them.

"You think I don't know?" Her eyes were quickly filling with tears. "Saliba was your only brother, but don't forget he was my husband, the only man I ever loved and the father of my son. Just a month ago, he was with us, taking care of us. Just a month ago I thought I was the happiest woman in all of Aleppo. He used to talk a lot about your coming wedding. He couldn't believe his baby sister was getting married. Therefore, I tell you Mariam: don't take life for granted. A time spent in love is much better than that spent in hatred. Give this man a chance to prove he is as sincere and well-intentioned as he claims to be, then you can judge."

"Not now, I can't. Not like this"

"As you wish, Mariam, it's your life, but I'm not sure how long he will keep on trying"

"Well, speak of the devil," Mariam said, glancing at her sister-in-law who quickly wiped her eyes.

The man they were talking about was walking straight towards them.

"Good afternoon, ladies," said a revitalized John, wearing his military uniform and his breastplate for the first time since his injury.

"I saw you sitting in the sun and thought I might come and say goodbye."

"Why, where are you going?" Salma asked, shading her face with her hand.

"Demetrius's village is right behind that mountain, a few hours' ride. You know Demetrius, don't you? "

"Yes, Mariam told me he was your closest comrade. "

Mariam shot Salma an angry look.

*She's been telling her things about me.*

"I will spend a few days at his village, then from there head to Constantinople."

"Constantinople?! That's so far away. To me, it is more like a fantasy than a real place," Salma said with amazement, trying to compensate for Mariam's silence.

"Well, in many ways, it is a different world indeed, so different from anywhere else. It's a beautiful city, with so much to offer, though it can sometimes be a cruel place, for with beauty often comes cruelty." He glanced at Mariam.

"Is your commander sending you there?"

"Not really. I'm just visiting my family for a while. I was born and raised in the *City*. As for you, have no worries, the general Nicephorus will make sure you are properly housed and provided for upon your arrival to Caesarea."

"John! We need to get there before dark," came a voice from under a nearby sycamore tree. It was Demetrius, on horseback, holding the reigns of his and another horse. Both mounts were loaded and ready for the journey.

"I must get going. Please give my regards to Jabra." He gave Mariam a final look and began to walk away, but in a sudden change of heart, he turned back to face the two women again.

"I will be back to Caesarea in the spring. Will I ever see you again, Mariam?"

"Who knows, you might," she finally said something, but avoided looking him in the eyes.

"Do you want to see me again?"

"I'm not sure." She sounded like a confused little girl now.

"You're not sure?" he repeated with an inquisitive smile on his face. He could feel there was more in her heart than her lips expressed.

"John!" shouted the impatient Demetrius, but John acted as if he hadn't heard a thing.

"I will be away for about two months before my return to Caesarea to rejoin the domestic Nicephorus. It will not be hard for me to find out where you have been settled. Until then, peace be with you. Look after yourself."

"You too," Mariam said unexpectedly, looking down at the rocky soil under her feet. John looked at her trying in vain to see behind her words. Her eyes were like two green forests that refused to reveal their mysteries.

He bowed then turned around and walked away.

"May the holy Virgin protect you wherever you go!" Salma said loud enough for him to hear.

He waved a hand, striding then mounting his horse.

"What was that all about?" Demetrius asked, having watched from a distance what looked like an argument.

"I wish I knew. Perhaps time does heal wounds, after all."

They set out on a narrow rocky path that led them uphill, away from the encamped soldiers below. Both had returned alive from that tough winter campaign, hardened by battle, enriched with spoils, yet both had so much on their minds.

*Is it a wise decision to leave for home now? Perhaps if I stayed, I might be able to draw Mariam closer to me? She does seem to have softened up a little. But her father said it's better to go away for a while, and he certainly knows her far better than I.*

*These few months will give her time to think, time to heal. She will have experienced her new life in a Roman city. She will see other Romans, normal people, simple people not just war-waging soldiers. Perhaps by then, she will not be so withdrawn. Perhaps by then, she will see me for who I really am.*

While both silently rode towards the setting sun, myriad thoughts crowded his mind. He knew there was no point in letting them out, that it was better for them to remain unspoken, at least for a while.

As the sun was about to slip behind the snowy mountain tops, the small village of Nazianzus appeared in the not so distant foothills.

# Chapter Thirty-Three

- ℰℭ -

Demetrius hadn't seen his family since the end of the previous summer, almost six months before. Back then, they had been laboring in his absence trying to make ends meet. His wife, whom he had left shortly following their marriage, had been without him for two years, a long time for a new couple. *How many two years are there in a person's life?* he wondered bitterly. He had hoped to buy back the farm his family once owned, but the money he had gained was not enough, and most of it was spent on paying the family's debts to their landlord.

Yet, at least he had left them better off than before. With the remaining money, he had hired help, making sure his sick father didn't have to work so hard, and now with his pay, and his handsome share of the spoils from the latest conquest, there was no doubt in his mind that he could finally achieve his goal. The long hard days he had spent fighting in distant lands were finally going to pay off. Every drop of sweat and blood he had shed was worth the sacrifice. His family was going to become the masters of their own destinies. There would be no one getting on their backs anymore, no landlords, no despots.

He was proud that at such an early age, he had become his family's hope, their true savior. At least, that could justify to his Eleni the long lonely nights spent apart.

He had left them with the approach of autumn's chilly gusts and gloomy skies. Now, and after the greater part of winter had passed, he was on his way home, to that same place where everyone and everything he loved existed. The cold and rugged terrain of Cappadocia in mid-February proved not to be an initiator of the rosiest thoughts, but in the middle of those colorless and dismal surroundings, a few clusters of purple cyclamens appeared beautifully between the rocky outcrops, reminding him that spring was just around the corner. Perhaps, he thought, just like the approach of the previous autumn had brought separation and disappointment, the approach of spring might bring a rebirth of happiness.

That was one cheerful thought he clung to until he arrived home.

***

When the two riders reached Demetrius's house, it was almost dark. The house John saw before him was no more than a medium-sized wooden cottage with a pitched roof covered with flat clay bricks. A chimney billowed with a continuous stream of grey smoke.

They dismounted, led their horses inside the low wooden fence that surrounded the cottage and tethered them to a big tree. The faint lights coming from the house's windows illuminated their steps.

John followed his friend to the front door, a strong wooden door that allowed only the passage of one person at a time. He knocked twice.

The door opened and an older version of Demetrius appeared. Eutychus looked like he had seen more hard times than good ones in his life of about sixty years. Demetrius embraced his father warmly then walked inside with John behind him greeting his hosts respectfully.

Inside sat the two women. His mother, Isidora, had a big wooden bowl in her lap filled with spinach leaves. Next to her sat Eleni, knitting. She looked just as Demetrius had described her to John; a beautiful fair face with a pair of wide dark eyes, a small round mouth, and hair as black as night.

She rose up quickly and wrapped her arms around her husband. John noticed her slightly rounded belly.

*She's pregnant!*

Demetrius kneeled in front of his wife, held her belly between his hands and planted a kiss on it.

"What month?" he asked her, looking up, his eyes shining with joy.

"Fifth," she answered with a shy smile.

John could sense the bond between the two of them. For a couple that had spent more time away than together, they seemed truly *one body* as the epistle read during the wedding service says. He had heard that segment of the New Testament dozens of times during his life as it was read at every wedding but could only name a few couples who seemed to possess that sublime union. His parents were one example. Demetrius and Eleni seemed like another rare case. He hoped he could one day have that kind of union with a special person. The image of Mariam floated before him.

He watched how happily his comrade's loved ones quenched their yearning for him with warm embraces and kisses that flowed directly from their hearts. There were tears of joy in the eyes of all four of them, their faces glowed like meadows freshened by a drizzle.

He himself was welcomed by the old couple with no less hospitality

157

than that given to their only son. They had heard a lot about John, and wished to repay him for hosting their son at his home in Constantinople the year before, let alone for protecting him in battle.

The five of them enjoyed the simple meal that followed: spinach stew, olives and black bread. Demetrius's mother kept on lamenting the fact that her son and his precious guest had to eat that for a welcoming meal.

"Food is the last thing I care about right now," he said to her with filial affection, sitting next to his wife and clasping her hand in his "All I care about is to see you all well."

"Tomorrow, I'm going to go and see that haughty Mardarius. He is going to sell us back our farm."

"That cruel man hasn't once looked kindly upon us, not even when your father was sick. May the Lord repay him for his wickedness on the day of judgment!" Isidora said, looking up, her hands extending to the sky imploring divine justice. She was clearly embittered.

"Have you earned enough money? He wanted two hundred nomismata last time," his father asked, full of hope.

Demetrius produced a hefty bag, placed it in the middle of the table and opened it to everyone's amazement.

"There are more than four hundred nomismata here." The golden coins glimmered brightly.

"You can buy the neighbors' farms too!" John chuckled.

"That is the greatest amount of money I have ever seen in my life!" Eutychus said humbly and jubilantly.

"John has an equal amount in his bag. In this house there is more gold than all of the village's houses combined!"

"Believe me, we deserved every one of those coins," John said.

"But what if he refuses to sell?" Eleni asked, concerned.

"The law is on our side, my love. He is obliged to sell us should we offer a reasonable price."

Suddenly John glanced at Demetrius's father. He had been staring at his son with great pride and satisfaction. He felt really happy for the old man.

As John had expected, his friend and his wife retired early to the privacy of their room. The old couple went to bed as well in the cottage's second bedroom but not before Isidora, Demetrius's mother, had laid a mattress of soft sheep wool beside the fireplace for John. He blew out the single oil lamp and quickly fell into a deep sleep.

# Chapter Thirty-Four

- ಬಂಡ -

Rich old Mardarius lived in the next town and Demetrius wasted no time riding there with his father and John the very next morning.

He owned a big country house which bustled with his offspring. With eight sons and dozens of grandchildren, the prolific patriarch had established an entire colony of his own. Yet, in spite of the abundance of helping hands, there he was doing the work of a gardener, pruning the vines that climbed on a long pergola.

When they reached the open outer gate, he stopped what he had been doing and waddled towards them under the colonnade.

"He hasn't changed one bit in the last five years," Demetrius whispered before he dismounted.

"If it isn't Eutychus and his soldier son!" he said, standing by the gate. "And who is this handsome young man?"

John looked at him carefully. His drooping lower lip and saggy eyes gave him a revolting appearance. For some particular reason, John thought he had seen that face before.

"This is John, my comrade and best friend," Demetrius replied coldly.

"And what has brought you and your best friend here on this day? I have a feeling you didn't just come to check on your old landlord, did you?" He looked anything but thrilled to see them.

"We have come to buy our farm back."

"The soldier has brought back some money, eh? And quite quickly too. How long has it been, two, three years? Had I known you were that skillful in warfare, I wouldn't have nominated you for soldiery. I should have sent that clumsy son of Michalis instead of you. He would not have returned in a decade, not alive at least. The governor demands me to provide him with two men annually. He never stresses that they be skillful."

"We have brought your money in full. Now please give us the deed," Eutychus said to his landlord.

"And what makes you think you have the exact amount?" The old man raised a brow, adding more wrinkles to his weather-beaten forehead.

"Two hundred nomismata. Isn't that what you asked for the last time?"

"Oh, but that was last time. With our army scoring one victory after another – of which you must know all too well – pushing the borders of our blessed empire further from here, more families have begun flocking to our province. Arab raids have become something of the past thanks to you and your comrades!" He sounded cynical. "The price of land has doubled! I will not accept less than four hundred nomismata."

John looked at the man with unbridled fury.

*What a greedy old villain!*

"We sold you the farm for a mere one hundred nomismata. Now we offer you two hundred, much more than its actual value and you demand four hundred?" Demetrius protested furiously.

"Well, this is my price!" he said with an evil smile.

"Listen, old man," Demetrius began threateningly, but John suddenly raised a hand, silencing his friend. A certain memory had flashed through his mind.

"I've seen you before," he addressed the landowner.

Scowling, Mardarius turned his head towards John.

"I wouldn't find that strange. I'm famous around here, I own more land than any other man in Cappadocia."

"And that is why last summer, you were among the group of landowners who had been summoned to the domestic's house in Caesarea to answer for some serious tax evasions. I stood next to the domestic and listened to him while he chastised every one of you.

"You, in particular, had reported three thousand bushels of wheat when your land had produced over five thousand bushels."

"Who did you say he was?" The old man looked at John with narrowed eyes. John had an idea.

*Time to mix reality with some imagination.*

"I'm the domestic's logothete and assistant. You know how his Excellency is fond of enforcing the law, especially on magnets like you who often *forget* to report their true earnings. One word from me to the domestic and you will have a hundred inspectors here by the next harvest, staying in your house, at your expense, scouring your fields and recording the true quantities that you produce. I advise you to set your greed aside for today and accept the offer these good men have made you."

The landowner was clearly burning with rage. He shook his head in dismay and said:

"Wait here!"

Then waddled away under the long colonnade and into the big house.

"How did that happen?" Demetrius asked, amazed.

"I think we were lucky today!" John smiled heartily.

The man soon returned with a yellowish paper in his hand. It was the deed to the farm and on it was written the name of Eutychus Syros.

"Let me see your money," he demanded and when the pouch was extended to him he jerked it violently and began counting the coins.

"... One-hundred-ninety-eight, one-hundred-ninety-nine, two-hundred nomismata. Fair enough. You have received what you came for. Now don't let me see your faces around here again. Get back to your village before you get buried in the blizzard."

*What blizzard? There's hardly a cloud in the sky. The old man must be hallucinating.*

Demetrius proudly gave the deed to his father. Tears sprang to Eutychus's eyes as he read his name on the piece of paper. He then put it in the inner pocket of his coat and the three of them rode back to the village.

By the time they arrived, the sky had turned grey and strong gusts threatened to throw them off their feet. What had begun like a sunny day ended up with a cold winter storm.

*That avaricious old man sure has an eye for the weather.*

\*\*\*

Inside the cottage it was warm and cozy. A pot of chicken soup had been simmering on the stove and was ready to be served when the three men entered in triumph.

"We have the deed!" Demetrius shouted with glee. "Show it to them, Father!"

Eutychus took the deed out and displayed it to the two women who let out a series of joyous shrieks.

"Thank God for his great mercy!" Isidora cried and embraced her son in tears.

Eleni, who waited for her turn to embrace the family's hero, said to him, looking into his eyes, her arms wrapped around him:

"First you show up yesterday unannounced and now this! Such pleasant surprises!"

"Hear one more surprise," Demetrius said as serious as could be. The change in tone made everyone look at him with real anticipation.

"I'm not going back to the army. I've decided to stay home and work the land, our land." His eyes glowed with joy, looking at his wife who stood petrified.

*Quitting the army? Is he out of his mind?*

John couldn't believe what he was hearing. He certainly hadn't foreseen this.

*It must be the intoxicating effect of retrieving the farm. He will soon return to his senses. Who quits a post like that to work the fields?*

But Demetrius continued.

"I shall ask to be released from the military and come back to settle home. I've always wanted that. There is no reason now for me to be away. My only desire is to be here with all of you."

John shot an inquisitive look at Demetrius. *What are you talking about?* But Demetrius wasn't going to discuss it with John, not then, not in front of his wife and parents.

Dinner was served, and the delicious meal was enjoyed by the happy family. It was the first meal they had had in over five years as free landowners instead of tenants bound to the service of a landlord. John could see the great happiness that shone from their eyes. For the first time in a long time they felt really free, safe, and secure. They had recovered not only their land but their full dignity.

It was unusual for the family of farmers to stay up late. There was always a lot of work to be done at sunrise, and getting a good night's sleep was the only means by which they could endure the hard labor of the following day. But that night, they were too excited to go to sleep. They stayed up late talking, confessing old dreams they thought would never materialize. A regained property, a reunited family, prospects of progress and improvement with the small fortune Demetrius had brought with him, and plans of building a separate house for the young couple were just some of the things they discussed.

Close to midnight, the older couple finally retired to their room and were soon followed by the pregnant young wife of Demetrius.

"I need to have a word with John," her husband told her lovingly. "You go ahead and rest. I will follow you shortly."

She planted a kiss on his cheek and left for the couple's room, her long shadow diminishing in the darkness of the bedroom.

Demetrius didn't have to guess what John was going to talk to him about. They sat opposite each other, not far from the waning flames of the fireplace.

"First of all, congratulations once more on today's achievement," John began in a low voice, close to a whisper, sounding very sincere. "Ever since I knew you, this has been your dream, but what's this talk about coming home for good? You have caused quite a stir in the family and raised them all up to the sky."

"You are the best friend I've ever had, John. I'm sorry I haven't said anything about this before but it only really sprang to my mind today after we had left Mardarius and headed for home. I'm tired, John. Eleni and I are going to have a baby in a few months. I want to be here and watch my child grow. I've had enough of battles, not knowing whether I would see Eleni again or die alone in a foreign land."

"You are destined for bigger things, Demetrius, can't you see that? Don't quit now."

"I don't want bigger things." He shook his head. "I will settle for this, the simple pleasures of life are just fine for me."

In John's eyes, Demetrius was doing no less than throwing his life away, resigning from a glorious military post to the obscurity of a tiny village in the middle of nowhere.

"Do you think the domestic will let you go that easily? You are one of his best bodyguards. You can't just walk away!" He now tried using a different tactic.

"I'll ask him. He will not refuse my request. I'm sure of that. He will not keep me against my will, not to mention the fact that I am the only means of support for my wife and the only son of my ageing parents."

John stared at his friend's face and saw true determination. He saw a man who knew what he wanted.

*It's not like he hasn't tried the other life. He has been there and seen it all, both its hardships and pleasures.*

"I love her, John. I need her as much as she needs me," Demetrius said earnestly. He stood up, walked past his friend towards the bedroom, patting his shoulder on his way.

"Goodnight."

John could clearly see what was happening. Demetrius had won the most difficult battle in his life and now he was determined to fight no more.

***

That evening, after Demetrius followed his wife to bed, John stood by the window watching the snow fall heavily. The wood logs in the fireplace, thick and large earlier in the evening, had been reduced to a heap of red, glimmering ashes that provided the room's only source of light. In the dead of night, thoughts came rushing to John's mind.

*I've never seen Demetrius more resolute about anything than returning to civilian life. His parents must be thrilled by the idea that their only son is going to escape the perils of war and come to live among them again. I could see their glee. As to Eleni, her heart is clearly dancing with joy. I can't even begin to imagine the depth of her happiness. Everyone except me seems to be more than fine with Demetrius's decision.*

*Am I thinking about what is best for him or best me? Perhaps he has finally found what he has been looking for, a stable life close to the ones he loves, in the land where he grew up and where he knows every rock, stream and tree.*

He was still not fully convinced of his friend's move but he definitely was going to support him, if that truly was what he wanted. Finally, the inseparable friends were going their separate ways.

***

It must have snowed all night!" Demetrius said, looking out of the main door, pulling on his heavy leather coat.

"I watched from the window until long after midnight," John confirmed, standing right behind him. "Never have I seen such big snowflakes."

"You stayed up that late, ha?" Demetrius shot John a probing glance, one that told his friend he could read his mind. "Come now, let's not keep the door open for long."

The snowfall had stopped but not before a fluffy white covering, a foot thick, had fallen from the sky. Under the grey clouds, they walked to the other side of the garden to a small storage cabin in order to fetch wood for the stove. Two blackbirds jumped nimbly on the overburdened branches in search of buried treasures.

"I built this storage cabin with my father back when I was twelve. I can remember every step of the construction like I'd done it yesterday."

"Fine workmanship," John said, admiring the small structure.

"And those two cypress trees, I planted them after my grandfather had died." The two slender trees stood like two brides dressed in white.

"You love this place, don't you?" John asked, certain of the answer.

Demetrius ducked down and passed through the low door of the storage cabin. He picked up two logs and handed them to John.

"There's no place like home. Trust me, it's the truth."

To John, home was fine, family was important, but unless he explored the world, his life wasn't worth living.

"It is farewell, then?"

"Not so fast." Demetrius smiled "I'll still come with you to Constantinople."

John waved his words away.

"I'm perfectly capable of travelling alone. Two weeks on the military road and I'll be in the city. There's no need for you to come all the way."

"I will hear none of it." Looking serious, he dropped the logs in the snow. "I promised I'd come with you. Did you forget that you carry your share of the spoils? Only a crazy man would travel alone with that sum of money."

"And how will you get back? Have you thought about that?"

"There are regiments leaving from the capital to the front all the time. I will leave with one of them."

"You seem to have thought this through."

"You haven't fully recovered. How could I let you go alone?"

"Alright, alright." John conceded to the chivalrous stubbornness of his friend.

"You're a true friend, Demetrius."

"I know you'd do the same for me."

John nodded.

"And after my return here, I will head to Caesarea and ask the domestic to release me from duty."

There was no changing his mind. He was fixated with that one idea, linking its realization to his happiness.

# Chapter Thirty-Five
- 🙢🙠 -

The week they spent in the village passed quickly for both men. Demetrius and Eleni made sure to savor every moment together. The young soldier who usually left the common tent in the morning before anyone else did, now would not emerge from the conjugal room until the third or fourth hour of the day, with a big accompanying smile on his face.

John, on the other hand, enjoyed a solitude he had been deprived of for the past few months.

The slow and peaceful rhythm of life in the countryside was a sharp contrast to the violent and exhausting front, something which had a calming effect on the healing soldier, both in body and spirit.

He would wake up every morning and go for long walks around the small village. His favorite destination, however, was the top of a hill overlooking the area where a small chapel crowned the summit. From that spot, one's sight could travel unhindered for many miles in all directions, past hills and valleys of forests, farms and tiny villages, all covered in a thick white blanket of snow.

Peace of mind had been something John enjoyed up to recently. He could remember himself overcoming every difficulty, facing hardships with a smile and with the rare confidence that relief was just around the corner. He went to battles and looked death in the face with a light heart. But now things seemed to have changed for him. The woman he adored was out of his reach, like a castle that refused to surrender, like a closed paradise that had no door. Never before in his life had he imagined that he would feel that helpless before a woman. To compound his frustration, his best friend had decided to take a different path in life.

The fearsome warrior who nevertheless had the spirit of a child suddenly matured, seeing life in its true colors. It looked like he had no more lucky strikes, no more happy endings to wild adventures.

But that week on the snowy mountain gave John all the time he needed to accept this new reality. Alone, he settled the disputes of his soul so that by the day of his departure, when he came down from his idyllic hilltop for the last time, he had come to terms with things. If Mariam was truly going to loath him for all eternity, then there was really no point in pursuing a mirage. But if for a second he felt he would ever have a chance to win her heart, then he wasn't going to miss that opportunity. In either case, he wasn't going to see his beautiful tormentor any time soon. A couple of months in Constantinople with all what the big city has to offer was exactly what he needed.

***

By the time the two companions left Nazianzus for Constantinople, the weather had improved considerably. A couple of sunny days caused streams of melted snow to trickle down the mountain slopes, feeding the rivers that raged in the valleys.

After nearly a year and a half away from home, John was on his way back. He begged his friend a final time to let him travel alone, but Demetrius showed no signs of relenting. Two years of close comradeship made it unthinkable for him not to escort his recovering friend on the long journey home.

They followed the military road, riding during the day and resting at night in one of the many inns and monasteries along the way. Being members of the domestic's bodyguard, they had obtained prior to their departure special documents allowing them to travel freely throughout the empire without any hindrance.

For two weeks, their journey took them across the greater part of the Anatolian peninsula until finally, the deep blue waters of the Sea of Marmara appeared on the horizon. Only a few miles of water now separated them from the imperial city.

They advanced to the port of Chalcedon, intending to take a boat to cross the Bosphorus. The town was beautifully situated by the sea in the midst of lush green pine forests. Its proximity to the capital made it a favorite refuge for the city's elite who built on its shores numerous luxurious palaces and donated great sums to establish and adorn magnificent temples. Five centuries before, the fourth general synod of the Church had been held in that sea town, and ever since then, the town's name had become linked with confessing two natures in Christ; human and divine.

The town was also a natural route for travelers and merchants coming from the east and wishing to be transported with their merchandise to the ever-hungry markets of Constantinople.

When the two soldiers arrived at the harbor, there was a bit of a clamor, a small crowd had gathered by the waterfront.

"Pardon me, but what's the matter, why the stir?" John asked a tall, well-dressed merchant, one of the many assembled.

The man turned his head and flashed a resentful look. "You seem to have just arrived, as to us, we've been stranded here for a week. One whole week with no ships crossing the straits. High winds, too dangerous for sailing. Just this morning, it finally calmed down a little – thank Christ! – one brave captain finally decided to set sail and as you can see, everyone is attempting to secure a place on his boat."

"What's the hurry? It's not like your spices are going to go bad or anything," came unexpectedly from behind them. They turned to see a plump, middle-aged man with a fleshy nose and two beady eyes buried in his chubby face.

"I'm in no mood to endure more of your repulsive comments, Callinicus!" the tall man said with indignation

"My comments?! You should have heard yourself this past week, fuming and cursing day and night!"

"Just get out of my sight!"

"I'm afraid that won't be possible! We will still share the same boat!" The fat man chuckled so hard his belly bounced. It looked like he enjoyed teasing the short-tempered merchant who could take no more and moved away, fuming.

The mariners finally extended the gangway and the passengers pressed on and shoved to go first. The two strong soldiers pushed their way forward and made it on board without much difficulty. Two copper pieces was the fare on each head.

Up on the deck, the two comrades sat on a bench, resting their legs and enjoying the sun. The imposing walls of Constantinople appeared on the horizon, the dome of Hagia Sophia rose above everything else.

Out of nowhere came the same fat merchant waddling towards them and then sitting next to Demetrius.

"A fine day today, isn't it, boys?"

"Not too bad," Demetrius answered dryly.

"If I'm not mistaken, you two are soldiers, right?"

"Yes," he answered with the same indifference, looking towards the sea instead of his interlocutor. But the merchant either failed to take the hint or was simply going to talk anyways. He leaned his head closer to Demetrius's ear and whispered something to which the latter erupted in fury.

"Why would you think that you foolish old man?"

"What did he say to you?" John asked, alerted.

"He thinks we're deserters!" the infuriated Demetrius replied, talking through gritted teeth.

John drew his sword and stood in front of the man who by then had realized his blunder and cowered fearfully. "If you mention that word again, you silly old fool, you will feel this sword cutting through that fat belly of yours. Do you understand?"

"I do, I do! Forgive me, I was just trying to be humorous!" he begged, blood draining from his face, turning it as yellow as a lemon.

"Is that so? Well, you should work on improving your humor before it gets you killed one day," John said, returning his sword to its scabbard, to the relief of the other passengers who thought they were witnessing the last moments of the merchant's life.

"My wife, dear Katerina says the same thing all the time!"

"Perhaps you should listen more to your wife, then!" John concluded, unable to resist cracking a smile at the sight of the terrified man.

The two soldiers soon realized that they had nearly caused the frivolous man's heart to stop from fear. A second look at his trembling limbs convinced them he was completely harmless, and with their feelings turning from anger to sympathy, they now tried to calm him down.

"My name is Demetrius and this is John. We have fought under the command of the Domestic Nicephorus. Just watch your tongue, and you'll have no reason to fear us." He patted his shoulder.

The man gulped and said reluctantly, "I'm Callinicus, a merchant from Nicomedia."

Quite amazingly, as if nothing untoward had happened, Callinicus was magically back to his talkative self. He began to relay to them his journey back from Armenia where his mules carried a considerable amount of tanned leathers and textiles. And when John mentioned their last campaign and how they had been with the army that defeated Sayf, the other became exceedingly excited and began to describe an incident that happened to him a couple of weeks before.

"Returning from Armenia," he began, "my caravan stopped to resupply with food and water at a Muslim city. There, in the city's market, a cortege of some distinguished person passed in front of us with much clamor. We watched the large number of servants penetrate the busy market, carrying their master on a litter. He looked sickly and very weak but behind his pathetic face, one could see a noble origin. When I inquired from a bystander in Arabic – which I speak fluently, by the way – about the man's identity, I received an answer with much censure: 'Who doesn't know the Emir Sayf?' the man standing next to me said, not quite believing how anyone could fail to recognize the distinguished prince. Seeing my ignorance, he volunteered to add that 'after his defeat in Aleppo, he has been reduced to a mere shadow of his glorious past' and that 'his body was collapsing under the blows of sickness and remorse'."

"What city did you say that was in?"

"Martyropolis, the Arabs call it Mayyafaraqin. It is the last city you encounter in Anatolia, right by the frontiers of Armenia."

"The vanquished Emir fled that far, to the edges of Armenia!" John laughed. "No wonder Tzimiskes could not catch up with him!"

Delighted with the information they had just stumbled upon, the two were in a jubilant mood when the boat finally made it to the other bank of the straits. To their, and everyone's surprise, the harbor of Constantinople was desolate. Apart from a few guards, there were no ships spreading their sails, no fishermen steering their fish-laden boats, or fixing their nets.

*On the first day of good weather following a week of high winds, one would expect a buzz in the harbor,* John thought, looking out from the parapet

John and Demetrius were among the first to disembark, looking around them in wonderment. They headed towards the gate in the sea walls where a few guards stood with their hands on their weapons, displaying the silence and inanimate qualities of the many statues that adorned the city squares. A peek towards the usually busy street behind the walls, now completely desolate, was enough to convince them that something was amiss. But what might that be? During his entire life, never did John see his birthplace so empty and deserted. It looked as if some power had robbed the largest city in the world of its citizens and left it lifeless.

"What's the matter? What's happened?" John directed his question to the guards, one of whom, tall and frowny, looked at him and uttered coldly the few words that left everyone in shock:

"The emperor has died."

# Chapter Thirty-Six

## - ೲೞ -

No one could have imagined that they would hear those words, not for a few decades at least. The healthy twenty-four-year-old had inherited his father's role as sole emperor of the Romans barely four years before. His beautiful wife had already produced him two male heirs, and with all the great victories his armies were achieving both in the east and west, the future seemed to promise him and the empire a long and prosperous reign. His untimely death now cast thick and morbid shadows over the imperial city.

The two comrades quickly made it to John's house through the empty streets of the capital. There was much eeriness in seeing the bustle of the city turn into a silence more befitting a graveyard.

"He's not much older than we are," John said to his friend. "Never thought one had more chances of dying in the palace than on the frontline."

"Everyone knew he was a merry man, liked his wine a lot. Perhaps he overdid it?" Demetrius speculated.

"Let's see what the people have to say about this."

To his family, the series of unexpected events which had begun with the death of the emperor the week before, and continued with the surprise arrival of their son, did not stop there.

"What happened? How did the emperor die?" was the first thing John said to his father after a warm embrace.

"No one knows, son. One night we heard he was very sick, the next morning all the church bells began ringing in slow monotonous mourning,"

"Some people say it was divine judgment for hunting and feasting during Lent," Anastasia said from inside the kitchen, hastily preparing a meal for the two unexpected guests. "May God forgive his sins."

"Others say he was poisoned, like his father before him." Alexander raised a brow.

"Why is it that when an emperor dies, the first thing that pops into people's minds is poison?" Zoe wondered.

"Who would want to poison him?" John thought his father might have an idea, having spent the greater part of his life in the palace.

"There are those who say it was the empress," Theodore replied. "But in my opinion, this is nonsense. What would she benefit from killing her young husband, the man who made her empress and the source of her authority and power? Besides, just two days before Romanus's death, she had been in labor, giving birth to a baby girl. What woman in that condition would be capable of doing what these crazy people suggest?

"Then there are those who insinuate that it was the chamberlain Joseph Bringas."

"But he can never be emperor. He's a eunuch." Alexander said, folding his arms across his chest.

"Well, being head of the Regency Council, he shall be the real ruler of the empire until the two little caesars become old enough to govern; that gives him at least ten or twelve more years of undisputed power."

"What Regency Council?" Demetrius asked. Theodore began to explain. His words came out slow and bitter.

"The late Romanus had left in his will the names of those he wished to take over the rule of the empire: Joseph Bringas, the empress Theophano, and the patriarch Polyeuctus. These three shall govern the empire until the Caesar Basil comes of age. However, he gave precedence to the chamberlain. He was to be the first among the three."

"Couldn't he have just died of natural causes? People who look young and healthy die too," Zoe said.

"I would like to believe that." Theodore sighed

***

Demetrius had thought to stay a week or so before he returned back home. Until then, he went about the city with John and watched it slowly recover. Day by day, the streets regained more of their buzz, and the shops opened their doors hoping everything would eventually return to normal.

Almost ten days after the emperor's death, there were no looming signs of riots or looting. The regency council seemed to be doing a good job in maintaining stability and providing the daily needs of the people. But when things looked to have taken a turn for the better in Constantinople, it suddenly became clear that the city's sense of security had been false, that there was fire under the ashes.

It so happened that John and his friend were spending the morning down by the harbor. It was a beautiful sunny day, and watching the boats from the top of the sea walls was something the young officer had always enjoyed ever since he was a little boy.

"This death of the emperor, I cannot comprehend. What, he just fell sick one day and died the next?" Demetrius said with some uneasiness, leaning on the thick brick wall.

"I'd advise you not to rack your brains trying to find the answer. Looks like no one will ever know what really happened, after all," John said, surveying the horizon from between two merlons. "The emperor died, but the empire lives. Look at these massive walls we are standing on. Do you know which emperor built them?"

"No, who was it?" Demetrius wasn't a person who knew a lot about the past.

"Theodosius, more than six hundred years ago. He is long gone now but his work has since kept this city safe."

"I wonder what the Arabs will do once they know of the emperor's death. Do you think they will attack?" Demetrius said, shifting his weight from leg to the other.

"After the lesson we taught them at Aleppo, I doubt it," John replied. Enjoying the view from above.

"I doubt it as well. If they have any strength left, they might as well use it to rebuild their devastated city."

Among the many boats on the Bosphorus that day, one stood out.

"Look at that dromon, Demetrius." John pointed at a large military ship that was sailing fast from the Asiatic shore. Demetrius tuned around and looked to where John pointed.

The large vessel advanced with the power of a hundred rowers. In a very short time, it had crossed the Bosphorus and was dropping anchor at the Kontoskalion harbor, right under the walls where the two of them stood. On its deck, they could clearly identify, though not without great surprise, a man they would not have missed even among a thousand others.

Nicephorus in full armor, surrounded by his guards, had arrived in the capital.

"The domestic!" Demetrius shouted in disbelief then both ran down the steps and headed straight towards the gate, almost colliding with two soldiers who were ascending the same flight of steps to begin their watch.

The domestic and his men disembarked from the vessel and went through the open gate in the sea walls. There, no sooner had the identity of the guest become known, than cheering and welcoming sounds filled the harbor. The people of the capital could not have wished for a better visitor.

The darting eyes of Nicephorus did not fail to see the two

comrades among the dozens of people who flocked at the gate. The loyal soldiers approached their commander and welcomed him with a military salute, but Nicephorus, who treated them as the sons he never had, embraced them warmly, and they immediately followed their commander as if they had not left his side at all.

"What on earth brought you all here?" John asked Andreas whose head rose above all others.

"The empress sent for the domestic. She said that even though the city is grieving over the loss of the emperor, the domestic's conquest of Aleppo deserves a Triumph."

"A Triumph? The last one that was supposed to take place was cancelled," John said, and raised a brow.

"This one will not. This one will be a real Triumph." Andreas sounded confident.

"Where are we going now?" Demetrius asked.

"The general has vowed to visit the grave of the emperor before he does anything else."

The domestic with an entourage of about twenty men rode up the Mese Street. As word of his return spread like wildfire in the capital, hundreds of people followed the beloved commander until the procession reached the church of the Holy Apostles.

The temple had been the final resting place of some of Christ's apostles – hence its name – as well as most of the emperors including the late Romanus. Though smaller than Hagia Sophia, the still large church had the footprint of a cruciform topped with five beautiful domes, and was by no means inferior to the Great Church with regards to the beauty of architecture or the lavishness of ornaments, and certainly not in the degree of sanctity.

When the party entered, it was around midday, and the faithful were gathering for the prayers of the sixth hour. Inside the church, lining the walls could be seen mausoleums of the departed emperors covered in brilliant slabs of marble and decorated with reliefs of biblical scenes, personal achievements and conquests. One particular tomb appeared to have been freshly constructed; the marble shone in full luster and the gypsum plaster that filled the joints didn't lose its whiteness to the fumes constantly ascending from a thousand oil lamps and candles. It didn't take them long to realize it was the tomb of young Romanus, whose body had been interred there only recently. Beside it stood two black-clad monks reciting psalms; something which was to be carried out incessantly over the dead monarch's body for forty days after his demise. At the entrance, the general stood for a moment and marveled at the place where the successive rulers of the world, beginning with the Great Constantine, were laid to rest. With people continuing to flock in and filling the vast space under the five domes, he advanced to the mausoleum and began a silent prayer. The bells of the sixth hour soon began to ring and the bishop who had to start the service on time, regardless of the celebrated visitor, initiated it with the well-known exclamation:

"Blessed is the Kingdom of the Father and of the Son and of the Holy Spirit, now and ever and unto ages of ages."

No sooner had the people responded with the usual *'Amen',* than a detachment of armed soldiers flung open the gates, and though fully armed, did not hesitate to advance inside the cathedral. The worshippers stood astonished by the abrupt and crude trespass of the holy place.

"Nicephorus Phocas!" their leader declared, interrupting the service. "By orders of the governing Regency Council, you are to leave the sanctuary and accompany us at once!"

But Nicephorus didn't abandon his devotional silence, neither raising his head nor even turning to face the armed aggressor. The eyes of the people were all directed towards him and the few men who surrounded their master appeared ready to defend him with their lives should it become necessary. Apart from the frequent shouts of infants, cutting through the silence and echoing under the domes, everyone held their tongues, waiting to see whether the domestic would allow himself to be arrested or not. Finally, he concluded his prayers.

"What do you want?" he asked in a calm voice, turning to face the soldiers.

The detachment commander repeated the previous words: "By orders of the Regency Council …"

"You mean by orders of the eunuch Bringas, don't you? You go back and tell that fox that I'm going nowhere, that I have come with an invitation from her majesty. As to you, it's wiser that you take your men and leave this holy place or you will not live long enough to regret it."

But the commander paid no heed to his words and the tension only escalated as men on both sides showed more belligerence and stood their ground.

John drew his sword like the rest of the general's bodyguard and stood ready for what looked like an inevitable and bloody confrontation.

*Has the empress invited the general here so she can have him arrested? Why would she do that? Could she have become worried that he might lead a usurpation? Unless it is as the general just said, that Bringas is the one behind this. But can Bringas act without the approval of the empress? If he's the one to send these soldiers, then it must be with her consent. And what about the patriarch Polyeuctus, the third member of the Regency Council? Would he have allowed the soldiers to invade the church like this? What on earth is happening!*

Nicephorus stood surrounded by his men while the soldiers remained close to the entrance, having surrounded the building.

The bishop and his clergy now reacted; they came from the altar and approached the soldiers demanding that they leave the sanctuary and settle their disputes elsewhere: "This is a house of prayer, a house of God." He directed his reproach to the military. "You have already disrupted our prayers and violated the sanctity of the place! Aren't you ashamed of yourselves? Is this becoming of Christian soldiers? Leave or you will soon find yourselves excommunicated by the patriarch!" But the commander simply declared that he had orders and that they needed to be implemented.

"What do we do, General?" Andreas asked.

"Nothing. Just stand your ground," Nicephorus answered firmly.

The two monks beside the tomb continued to mumble psalms beside the emperor's tomb, unaffected by what went around them. An hour later, the stalemate had not changed.

"I've never fought inside a church before!" John whispered to Demetrius.

"I hope we won't have to, but if we do then it will be just like any other place ... perhaps I'll cross myself before I start cutting those lawless soldiers to pieces." He looked furious.

Finally, in the middle of the tense silence came the sounds of hooves trotting on the stone pavements outside the church. Two messengers, clearly unarmed, dismounted and ascended the few steps that elevated the church's entrance above the adjacent street. One of them handed a paper to the commander at the door and the other made his way inside the church and delivered his letter to Nicephorus. "Her majesty the empress invites you to the palace under her protection, in full immunity. You are her majesty's guest."

"If so, then take this letter and give it to the bishop. Let him place it on the altar for all the people to witness," Nicephorus replied.

The bishop took the letter and saw the empress's seal. He raised it so all the people could see the royal signature and seal of their empress. The detachment commander, looking rather relieved, ordered a retreat, quietly rounding up his men and leaving by the way they had entered.

"Now, I'll come with you," Nicephorus told the messenger. then made his way out of the building, heading to the palace where a warmer welcome was expected.

# Chapter Thirty-Seven

- ∞∞ -

Earlier on the same day, the residents of the palace had felt an unusual stir. Messengers were rushing with important letters to deliver, summons were being sent to important members of the senate and clergy and indeed many special guests did arrive and were shown in to one of the palace's great halls where the small devious schemer, who had been orchestrating these steps with his usual efficiency, dictated more letters to his small army of clerks. Around noon, his sole guest was the patriarch Polyeuctus, an old venerable prelate, only second in honor to the Pope of Rome though by no means less powerful or influential in his own jurisdiction which extended from the borders of Armenia in the east, to Calabria and Sicily in the west.

"You see, your eminence, for these reasons, this man needs to be stopped. At this precarious time, his presence in the capital is a danger to us all, a danger to the safety of the royal infants and the continuity of the Macedonian dynasty. Under the guise of devotion and piety, he has left the frontier and come here, but why, and for what reason, to honor the dead, to visit the emperor's grave? A mere show. Should the army follow him here, which it most probably is doing right now, then only God knows what evils will befall us."

The old patriarch was known to be very pious and austere, to the point that many of his opponents called him, without much injustice, narrow minded and dictatorial. He cleared his throat after he had heard the chamberlain's sermon, looked him in the eyes and said with the same fluid voice that echoed with hymns every day in the Hagia Sophia:

"My son, your concerns are logical and legitimate, army commanders don't usually come to the capital and leave empty handed. History tells us that many men in Nicephorus's position have seized the throne with the power of arms. "

"And don't forget, Your Grace, that his brother Leo is Domestic of the West, which makes two brothers in control of the empire's armies. This is too dangerous to ignore. "

"But!" the patriarch interrupted. "Those were men whose thirst for power blinded their conscience. Nicephorus is no such person. He has confided to me on more than one occasion that his only wish is to retire in the monastery now being built on Mount Athos with his own generous donations. I doubt that he has any interest in seizing power for himself."

"Your grace, did you really believe that? I admit that he's very clever and very convincing but a man of your wisdom shouldn't be deceived by this show of his."

"What makes you think it's a show? Do not judge or you too will be judged, says the Lord."

"The Lord also commanded us to be as wise as serpents," the Chamberlain replied, clearly running out of patience. "At any case, your eminence, I have invited you here to inform you of what I'm intending to do, all for the safety of the kingdom and the two little caesars, so that you might know firsthand, and not through a third party."

"And what might that be, exactly?" The patriarch's weary eyes narrowed.

"I have already ordered his capture, upon which he shall be stripped of his title and expelled from the city. "

"You have gone way too far, Joseph!" The old prelate raised both hands up in protest. "You will never get my approval for this, nor that of the empress who invited him in the first place!"

Bringas, remaining clam, though talking in a louder tone now, said defiantly:

"I mean no disrespect, but I don't require your approval."

The patriarch's face flushed.

"Don't think that because you are head of the Regency Council you can decide on your own! You need the approval of the rest of the members, not to mention the members of the senate. "

"Which I'm in the process of obtaining. Besides, if you would take a second look, you would surely see that the interests of the Church are better served with the steps I'm taking."

"How so?" demanded the patriarch furiously.

"If, God forbid, this man becomes emperor, he will not content himself with governing the state but will surely start meddling in ecclesiastical affairs. The first thing he will do is enforce an old wish of his on the church; to consider all fallen soldiers in battle as martyrs. You will soon find yourself, Your Eminence, forced to ask for the intercession of a myriad of new saints whose sanctity is solely derived from their shedding of other men's blood. Their pugnacious icons will adorn the church walls and the iconostases. Then he will turn to church property, most of which he will undoubtedly transfer to the benefit of the army he so much adores. I've been doing you a great service, making sure that a person with such extreme and corrupt views doesn't come near the imperial throne."

"You let me worry about matters of the Church!"

"And you me about the matters of the State."

It was at that moment of high tension that the door was opened by the guards and the empress Theophano appeared in all her finery. Though she was dressed in her mourning clothes, and her face looked tired, her beauty couldn't be easily suppressed.

"Why hasn't anyone informed me that his eminence is here? I surely would have liked to receive his blessings."

"May the Lord be with you, my daughter," the Patriarch blessed the empress who walked towards him gracefully.

"And with you too, Father. It appears that ever since the departure of my husband, I've been missing a lot of what has been going on around here." She gave the chamberlain a fiery look. "How dare you offend me and send troops to arrest my guest?"

"I have meant no offense, but your highness should've known better than to invite a power-thirsty figure such as Nicephorus to the capital. It's like entrusting a flock of sheep to a wolf!"

"Watch your tongue, Bringas. Nicephorus only came here because I invited him. Otherwise, he would have remained on the frontiers defending the empire as he has his entire life. What is irresponsible is your order to arrest him which brought the city to the brink of an uprising. I had to annul your order and arrange for him to be escorted to the palace in full dignity. How do you think the people view the performance of the regency council? Full of divisions and discord is the only way they see us now."

"You invited him here to the palace?" asked Bringas.

"Yes, I did. The man deserves a Triumph."

"Has he complained to you? Has he asked you to call him here and honor him with a triumphal entrance?"

"Try to oppose the people of the city if you can. Try to convince them that the commander who conquered Aleppo and whom the whole empire rightfully calls 'The Pale Death of the Saracens' should be denied a Triumph."

"I will do no such thing, not now that he's already here. I shall allow the triumphal celebrations although I can hardly think of any decent reason behind your invitation. It's, to say the least, scandalous. But let it be known to you that this is the last time I will allow anything like this to happen behind my back, you have my word on that."

"Are you threatening me, and in front of his eminence?" She was furious.

"Your Highness. I have been trying to convince the chamberlain that his idea about Nicephorus is flawed." The patriarch explained his position.

"It seems I need to remind both of you once more that *I* have the final say on matters of government. It was the will of the emperor that I should hold this position and I will religiously observe it."

"You poisoned the mind of my late husband against Nicephorus. God knows what else you poisoned, " she all but shouted.

Bringas's eyes narrowed with anger. "I reject and abhor what you are insinuating. We all know his majesty died of natural causes, unless you have information in your possession to the contrary!"

"What is natural about the death of a healthy twenty-four-year-old? Tell me, chamberlain, or should I say Head of the Regency Council! You seem to be the only one who has benefited from the death of your sovereign!"

"I shall not stand here and listen to these despicable allegations!"

"Then leave!"

"You are mistaken, Your Majesty. It is you who shall have to leave if you continue to spew these poisonous claims against me."

"What do you mean by that?" She shot him another fiery look, albeit, not without genuine concern.

"I mean that the fate of your sisters-in-law hangs in the balance should you cross the line once more."

The mere thought that she could be shipped to a convent like her husband's sisters terrified Theophano.

"Did you hear that?" she cried to the patriarch who remained in his place, speechless.

"This is your final warning!"

The furious Bringas turned and left the hall, but as he walked angrily towards the door, the guards announced the arrival of Nicephorus. It was one of those fateful moments which seem frozen in time.

Both men passed by each other, the one leaving, and the other entering. There was no exchange of pleasantries but the looks on their faces betrayed what a thousand words could never have expressed.

# Chapter Thirty-Eight

- ℰ✺ℂℬ -

The Triumph celebrated a few days later was of the like the capital had never seen before. Unlike the constrained ovation a couple of years previous which was more of an insult than a reward, this Triumph was as magnificent and lavish as the victory it recognized was stunning. Nicephorus brought out all the treasures his army had won in the last campaign and paraded them in the streets of the capital, while he, in the absence of an emperor, enjoyed the dignity and attention usually bestowed upon the monarch and his family on such occasions. It was the first time the people saw a General of the Army take precedence in a Triumph, earning the deserved honor instead of an often idle emperor. The thousands of people who lined the streets chanted 'Victor' as he passed by them. They knew very well that it was Nicephorus and none other who had crushed the empire's arch-enemies in the south. Still, Nicephorus's piety wouldn't allow him to assume the ultimate place of honor. He firmly believed that the first place belonged to providence, the dispenser of victory, and so, in front of the domestic, and on a beautiful carriage pulled by two white horses was placed the precious relic of John the Baptist for all the people to see and adore. A torrent of religious emotions swept over the people as their eyes met the tattered piece of clothing which once covered the holy body of the forerunner of Christ. Tears of joy and piety washed the faces of men and women alike as the relic passed before them on the crowded triumphal route. Sick children, hopelessly weak men, and barren women presented themselves before the relic and poured their souls out in prayer asking for miracles, which on that day God seemed to grant abundantly.

In the days that followed, the general visited his old friends: the patriarch Polyeuctus, Basil Lekapenos, and top members of the senate, not to mention his spiritual father Athanasius, who happened to be in the city at the time seeking to purchase construction materials for his monastery. But the one person whom Nicephorus remained almost in daily contact with was the empress Theophano. Even to his personal escorts such as

John, very little was known of what went on in those meetings conducted behind closed doors. But the results soon created an atmosphere of confidence and mutual understanding when Nicephorus was reaffirmed in his position as domestic by the Regency Council after having signed a document in front of the patriarch and the senate promising to protect the lives and rights of the two orphaned caesars and their mother.

Bringas, though the head of the council, could not oppose the wave of cheering and celebration which overwhelmed the populace, the Church and the Palace. He was almost alone in his objection, and couldn't face the popular domestic, not there and then. But the crafty chamberlain had in no way given up. In fact, seeing Nicephorus's influence and popularity soar, he couldn't be content with merely standing in a corner and gnashing his teeth. He successfully concealed his deep animosity under a pretense of neutrality.

Easter arrived once again to the imperial city and the domestic remained there for the religious ceremonies and celebrations then made plans to return quickly to Caesarea where his army was enjoying a period of rest before the next autumn campaign.

While John was eagerly waiting for the journey back to Caesarea, where he would no doubt see Mariam again, Demetrius hoped the journey for the borderland would be his last one as a member of the military.

A few days after Easter, he approached the domestic while returning from the Palace on horseback, mustered his courage, and said:

"General, if you don't mind, I want to go home."

"Once we're back in Cappadocia, you can spend the summer at your village like last year."

"I mean, I wish to go home for good."

Nicephorus looked at him in confusion. "Why do you wish to leave us so fast, Demetrius? Are you bored of our company?"

"On the contrary, Sir. I just wish to settle down with my family. My wife is giving birth soon and my parents need my support."

The domestic nodded and said:

"Fine, I shall appoint you closer to your home. I reckon you will make a fine 'Komes' in the Cappadocian theme."

"I have no desire to remain in the military, Sir."

"I see. And how will you make a living?"

"I intend to cultivate my father's farm and live off the land. We own enough fertile land to grant us a decent livelihood."

Nicephorus valued the service of his brave soldier yet he wasn't going to keep him against his will.

"If this is what you want, then I grant you the release once we get to Caesarea, but only on one condition." He suddenly looked serious.

"What is that, General?"

"You must promise to bring a lot of children into the world who will grow up to defend the empire as bravely as their father did."

Demetrius smiled. Nicephorus sounded like a father who wished for grandchildren.

"You must know, though, that your place with us is reserved should you ever change your mind."

Demetrius nodded with appreciation. Finally, he could dream freely of the life that awaited him back home with his beloved wife.

But the plans of departure with the domestic back east never materialized. Two days before he left the capital, and as he and John kept guard around the domestic's mansion, they were summoned to the reception hall where their master had been sitting with his father Bardas and confessor Athanasius.

"Come in, come in," he said, welcoming the two soldiers. They entered, and bowed down with respect in front of the three distinguished men.

"As both of you know, father Athanasius has been building a monastery on the chersonese called Athos."

"With your generous donations and pious support," interrupted the monk.

"He has been in the capital procuring building materials for the past month which will then be shipped to the construction site. The last time he made such a trip, a pirate ship chased them but thankfully, they made a narrow escape. Now, this time, the ship will be carrying rare and expensive materials; finely carved wood for the iconostasis, brass chandeliers, lead for the roofs, and paint for the icons; a full ship's load. I, therefore, wish that you two travel to Athos with this holy man when he leaves next week and be as obedient to him as you are to me. You shall have twenty men under your command in case the pirates attack.

"After the ship has unloaded, you shall return with it to Constantinople then make your way back to Caesarea.

"This will be your last mission, Demetrius. As to you, John, you look like you have regained your strength. You know that I admire the bravery and intelligence the two of you possess. You make a great team. That's why I want you and none other to carry this mission out for me. Do you have any questions?"

Surprised as they were by this sudden commission, John was quick to respond with a cordial appreciation of the general's trust.

"I told you to stay in your village! You didn't listen to me. Now instead of Cappadocia, you shall be travelling to Athos!" John whispered to Demetrius as they walked out of the hall.

"I've waited two years to return home and never leave again. I can wait another month."

The short meeting was over but from then on, the two men became fully involved with this new mission of which they had no previous experience. For four days, they remained at the harbor making sure the goods were being properly loaded and stacked for the journey.

Two days after the Domestic had left the capital shrouded in glory, they set sail with the loaded ship and headed to the west to the place which took its name from a mythical giant that the ancient Greeks believed had been buried there.

The ship made its way through the closed Sea of Marmara then out to the open Aegean Sea by way of the Hellespont straits. Since the liberation of Crete, the attacks of the Saracen pirates had almost vanished, but there were still few times when they would come from the shores of Syria and Egypt and attack the Roman ships.

The passengers, who in addition to the ship's crew and the soldiers, included a couple of younger monks with their Abbot, prepared themselves for a week at sea. During that period, John and Demetrius came to realize why their general highly esteemed the monk Athanasius. They experienced firsthand what a meek and peaceful person he was, one whose appearance displayed a touch of divine grace. They learnt from one of the two younger monks, about the same age as them, that Athanasius had been a teacher of literature at the capital, famous and renowned for his eloquence and great wisdom, even at an early age. Nicephorus and his brother Leo had gotten to know him during their regular confession visits to their uncle; a famous and pious monk himself. They soon became good friends, after Athanasius had forsaken the world and embraced the ascetic life. The two brothers made him their spiritual father, with Nicephorus expressing his wish to spend the rest of his life in the monastery he encouraged and helped Athanasius to build.

Nicephorus had always been seen as a truly pious man, but his soldiers had never heard before of his intention to become a monk. It was quite surprising to them, to say the least. Why would a man at the summit of his success want to leave the world behind and retire to an isolated monastery far away from all civilization? And when was the great leader intending to fulfil this wish? For the past month, he had appeared fully focused on the situation in the capital, deeply involved in its politics and power struggles, which did not quite fit the submissiveness and selflessness of a monk. But who knows? They had heard about important men, powerful men, even emperors who abandoned the glamorous and deceitful world seeking a life of truth and serenity.

After a week at sea, with no sign of pirates, the steep and lush slopes of the chersonese began to appear. It looked like a giant pier of land protruding far into the sea. Their destination was close to its southernmost tip, where a small port had been constructed a couple of years before on the rugged shore to allow the transportation of people and goods to the desolate peninsula.

The ship anchored at the port and a number of men, both monks and paid laborers, came running down the narrow path from the hill above where the incomplete walls of the monastery were beginning to rise. They all bowed before their abbot and received his blessing with much reverence.

Then the unloading of the ship began and continued for a couple of days. The monks, looking thin and sickly, were by no means feeble. Even the older monks whose laymen peers enjoyed a tranquil retirement in the capital showed an extraordinary strength, carrying the heavy goods and plodding uphill with no murmur or complaint.

John ascended the hill himself and saw the great undertaking which Nicephorus had been funding. The external walls whose circuit covered the area of a small village were still under construction along with numerous protection towers, but in the middle, the small church was already complete along with some temporary huts for the accommodation of the workers.

*This is really impressive. I wonder how it will look like when it's complete.*

A little before sunset, when everyone finally retired after a long day of labor, there were no more sounds of stone breaking or wood hammering. The place was exceptionally serene and beautiful.

*No wonder Father Athanasius chose this place for his new monastery,* John thought, sitting on a rock overseeing the ocean. It was simply ideal for a life of solitude and devotion. Even a vibrant soldier like him felt a hidden attraction to the place, and for the first time he could understand the beauty of the ascetic life behind the coarse rags and the austere asceticism.

A few days later, they were on their way back to Constantinople. They had completed their mission and receiving the blessings of the holy abbot, they set sail for home. By the time their destination appeared, they had only been away for a little less than a month, but they never imagined what dramatic changes could have taken place during so short a period. While the city appeared to them from afar unchanged, they were soon to learn of a force which threatened to turn everything upside down.

185

# Chapter Thirty-Nine

## - &)C3 -

"I think it's about time I made my way east. God knows how much I miss Eleni," Demetrius said, surveying the city from on top of the roof where John liked to sit.

"We have barely returned from a week at sea and here you are talking about leaving again. I'm as eager as you to set out, but I say we rest a couple more days."

"We've had three days of rest. Besides, I don't want to delay my return too long. Eleni must be worried sick already. I told her I'd be away for a month and it's been two months now since we left Nazianzus. Actually, I'm thinking of leaving tomorrow. Besides, don't you want to see that wild girl of yours again?"

That wasn't far from the truth. John thought constantly of Mariam. The Christian refugees had already been resettled in Caesarea, so Andreas told him. Was the period that he had spent away enough for her to have gathered the shattered pieces of her soul? Had enough time passed for her to be able to look at him as someone who loves her and might be worthy of her love?

"Yes, I'd like that. I think it's about time I figured out where I'm heading."

\*\*\*

In the other side of the city, Theodore was already on his way home from the palace. Unlike his placid demeanor, he walked rather hurriedly, looking behind him every once in a while as if he had committed a crime. He passed by his friend's shop without making his usual afternoon stop and seemed oblivious to the existence of Cyril who called out to him twice in vain, leaving him confounded by the side of the road.

He reached home, entered quickly and made sure to fasten the door behind him, then went upstairs to where Anastasia was preparing dinner. When she saw his face, she knew something terrible had happened; it was beyond any doubt.

"John! Come down and see your father."

The truth is, the royal tailor had been witnessing troubling things which portended no good, and he had been confiding what he saw only to his wife. On the outside, everything appeared to be fine: the Regency Council was again running the empire with efficiency and in complete harmony, but as an insider, Theodore had been aware of the abnormal conditions imposed in the palace after Nicephorus's departure.

Recognizing discomfort in his mother's voice, John climbed down the wooden stairs where he found both his parents looking awfully distressed. Theodore gave his son a sympathetic look, his face conveying terrible sadness. John knew his father was a worrier. Any deviation from his daily schedule was a cause of anxiety to this habitually ordered person, but the look on his face was something John had never seen before.

"What's the matter, Father?"

"Come, come to the back room, I have something important to tell you, and you too, Demetrius, you too come along."

The two puzzled men followed Theodore to the somber room to find out what he was so anxious about. In a voice not far from a whisper, Theodore began describing what had happened to him that morning at the palace.

"As usual, I went to work this morning, and nothing untoward happened until I was summoned to meet the empress. Normally, I would receive summons once or twice a month to present her highness with my work, but lately, after the emperor's death, she has rarely called for me. Although I did meet her briefly yesterday for the first time since the demise of the emperor. I, of course, conveyed my family's condolences and she received them with her usual kindness. Somehow, your name was brought up during the conversation and I mentioned that you had just returned from Athos. At the time, it didn't seem to have much of an effect on the empress.

"But once more, I was summoned today, and just like the day before, I walked guided by two guards to the private imperial apartment in the Boukoleon palace." He paused for a moment. "I should probably first tell you about the new arrangements at the palace before I continue with my story." He took a deep breath and then went on. "After the Domestic's departure, and upon the chamberlain's orders, the palace has been turned into a sort of a castle: Varangians are deployed everywhere closing the palace doors in the face of all visitors and confining the royal family to one section of the palace. 'For their own safety,' as he said. The empress together with her children have not been seen in public ever since, and only a few people have been allowed to visit them, myself included."

"Are you serious? When did this happen?" asked John.

"A week after Nicephorus had left."

"And why haven't you said anything, Father?"

"It's not my job to go around spreading news of the Palace. How do you think I've managed to stay there thirty years? It's because I've kept my mouth shut. Now let me tell you what happened. When I was led to the empress's chamber, I found her sitting by a window overlooking the sea. She stood up and, although acting normally, I could see that she was exhausted. The guards followed me inside and stood by the door watching every move and listening to every word. The empress talked about ordinary things, she asked me about the black mourning robes my artisans had been busy making for her and her maids. Many things we said were a repetition of yesterday's session. She seemed to want to prolong the conversation on purpose, asking me all sorts of unnecessary details, which must've sounded all too important to the ignorant guards. I picked up on her intention and went along with her in extending the duration of our talk. After almost an hour of discussing fabrics and patterns, I noticed that the guards were beginning to lose interest. Their eyes were growing less and less diligent and they appeared to have become tired of the seemingly endless, incomprehensible talk. At one point, as the empress was checking the black silk robe I had brought with me, she produced an envelope from her left sleeve."

Theodore took out a small envelope sealed with the empress's royal seal.

"And as quick as a bird, she inserted it in the robe's pocket and whispered, 'Let your son take this to Nicephorus as soon as possible'. I was momentarily stunned, my senses paralyzed, but somehow I managed to muster my strength without the guards noticing anything unusual and the conversation resumed for a short while afterwards until the empress dismissed me as she usually does. The guards escorted me outside and closed the door behind me. I could hear the sounds of heavy bolts securing the door as I made my way with the two guards to the workshop, my heart pounding so hard I thought they could hear it."

John, amazed, took the letter from his father's hands. The paper was of excellent quality, neatly folded, and the red seal was intact.

"She wants me to take this letter to the domestic?" he asked with great astonishment

"That's exactly what she said. She is virtually a prisoner in that palace; there is no doubt about it anymore. Bringas has tightened his grip around her, around all of us."

"Then there is no time for us to waste." John had a determined look on his face as he turned to Demetrius. "Looks like we'll be leaving tomorrow, after all."

# Chapter Forty

- ಏಂ೧ಙ -

Two horsemen faced the rising sun as they raced across the plains of Bithynia, on a path that was becoming all the more familiar. The Domestic needed to know more than the vague, insubstantial reports that he regularly received from the capital. He needed to hear the appeal of the captive empress. His being the empire's savior was nothing new, but that was now truer than ever with one difference only: that the empire's enemies whom he had fought so far were external, whereas this time they were domestic. His only way of knowing the true events that were taking place in the palace of Constantinople lay in the hands of those two men, who tried, before it was too late, to fulfill the mission entrusted to them. True, it was John whom Theophano named to convey the secret message, but by now, even when the two friends determined to go their separate ways, fate had intervened.

They had crossed the straits before the break of dawn and began the long journey to the south-east. While it took them two weeks to get from Caesarea to Constantinople, they strived to make the return journey in only half that time. It was the beginning of summer and the longer days and warmer weather were in their favor. But after three days of steady progress, crossing almost half the distance, they and their horses were in desperate need of a break. It was time they found themselves a place to rest, and possibly have a few hours of uninterrupted sleep.

By the side of the military road, on the outskirts of Ancyra stood a small inn, whose owners the soldiers had gotten to know when travelling in the opposite direction a few weeks previous. The middle-aged and childless couple lived in an apartment on the ground floor and let the remaining rooms of the two-story building to frequent passing travelers. When John and Demetrius reached the inn, it was well after sunset. The owners happily informed them of the availability of a room. They sat in the kitchen downstairs at a big table beside the stove where some stew was cooking slowly. Apart from a place to sleep, their energies were replenished with a fine home cooked meal of lamb stew, brown bread and some local red wine, their horses were watered and fed and all that for eight copper pieces. The precious letter had all the while been kept close to John's body. His mother had sewn it inside a small cloth sack, more like an amulet, which he wore around his neck under his clothes. When they eventually went to get some rest, the hardness of the mattresses did little to prevent them from falling into a deep sleep the moment they threw their exhausted bodies down, and the much-needed slumber lasted till after sunrise.

John was the first to wake up and realized they had had more rest than they could really afford. They hurriedly put their shoes on, and were about to set out again on the remainder of their journey when Demetrius discovered his saddle had been badly damaged. After three long days of riding, the girth was so worn out it was on the verge of tearing.

"If this gets torn with you on it," John said, "you're doomed. It must be fixed before we continue."

"I don't know why these things happen only when one is in such a hurry." Demetrius sounded frustrated. "Why don't you go and buy us some food while I fix the bloody saddle?"

Indeed, they were in need of supplies for the remainder of the journey.

Demetrius asked the innkeeper's wife for a sewing needle and a strong thread and sat down fixing his saddle.

"I won't be long." John headed down the road to the village.

The tiny outpost was close by and from its only bakery he bought a four-day hoard of heavy black bread before making his way back. True to his word, he returned in less than an hour, anxious to resume the journey to Caesarea as fast as possible.

The lonely inn stood on the side of the road, one could see it from afar as the only man-made feature in that part of the hilly and wooded landscape. When he got close enough, he could see Demetrius standing up next to his saddled horse, talking to a group of travelers who must've just arrived at the inn. They looked like they were asking him for directions but when he got closer, it was evident there was little friendliness about Demetrius's new companions.

*What in God's name are these Varangians doing here?* He wondered, but before he could figure out what was going on, he heard Demetrius yell at him frenziedly: "Run! Go! Don't stop!" At which point, two of the men attacked him while the other three jumped on their horses and went after John.

John's first impulse was to draw his sword and charge, something he would've done had this situation occurred a couple of years before, even when he had had no idea how to wield a sword, but time in the army had taught him how futile that would've been even for a distinguished soldier like himself. It was impossible to defeat three Varangians by himself. Instead, he listened to the logic in his friend's call and fled, carrying the precious letter with him.

"I will come back for you!" He sent out a final cry before turning his horse in the other direction.

They galloped along the road that went uphill towards the town of Ancyra. It was impossible for John to take a different escape route as the three horsemen would eventually catch up with him. Instead he chose to flee towards the town in hope of eluding his pursuers.

The medium-sized town was located on top of a hill surrounded by imposing mountains and verdant forests. The high wall encircling it gave it the appearance of a fortress. Anyone standing on its western wall would have noticed John's brown horse speeding up the rocky hill and kicking a trail of dust as three huge Norsemen with gleaming axes were on his tail.

John followed the road to the nearest gate, but once inside, it wasn't only the smooth cobblestone-lined roads which forced him to slow down. Swarms of people filling the street made a speedy flight impossible.

*Where did all these people come from?*

He found himself entering the town's busiest market. Stalls of vegetables and fruit, grains and oil, clothes and tools lined both sides of the street and hundreds of shoppers roamed the place with their children and livestock. He had no choice but to draw his sword, wield it in the air and ferociously threaten: "Move aside!". But even that had little effect. Abandoning his horse and disappearing in the midst of the crowd seemed like a good idea at first, but without his horse, there was no way he could get to Caesarea.

His pursuers were less wary of the safety of the inhabitants. Several people were trampled ruthlessly under horses' hooves as the riders attempted to seize John. The townspeople watched the chase proceed through the dense market with great astonishment and horror.

As the distance between the hunters and the prey shrank, it appeared as though it was only a matter of time until the ferocious Varangians got hold of the elusive soldier.

The small town with its beautiful stone houses, numerous water springs, and fresh mountainous air was a place to John's taste. Under different circumstances, he would've enjoyed wandering about its markets and taverns, but now he was beginning to see that it might be the place where his life, or at best his freedom, would come to end. He struggled to carve out an escape route. But just when all hope of survival seemed lost, when he began to foresee his doomed fate, an idea flashed through his mind. He reached for the pouch tied around his waist, extracted a handful of golden coins and flung them over his shoulder, then did the same a second and a third time. The effect was immediate, almost incredible. The luster of the golden coins had a magical power, the sweet dinging sound on the cobblestones overshadowed the fearsome noise of the Varangians' horses. In but a moment, dozens of peasants flocked between John and his pursuers like a human barricade, each determined to gather as much as possible of the incidental treasure. There was no way the Varangians could penetrate that human dam. Not their incomprehensible bellows nor gleaming axes could break the ranks of a greedy crowd. The chaos that ensued was all that John needed.

Looking over his shoulder, he saw the barrier he had created. He rode across the town and speedily exited the city from the eastern gate, thanking God a thousand times for the miraculous escape. He was prudent enough, though, not to continue his journey on the military road but instead to seek Caesarea through mountainous paths and shadowy forests away from the eyes of stalkers and pursuers.

After the initial shock had subsided, and in its place came feelings of safety offered by the forest's seclusion, John's mind began to consider the series of events. He couldn't figure out how their secret had been betrayed.

*How did Bringas know of the empress's letter? Who tipped him off?*

It was impossible for anyone else to have known of their mission. As far as he knew, only the empress, and his parents knew of the letter. Did something change at the palace causing their secret to be revealed? Is it already too late for the empress? And what about his parents? Are they safe? He almost lost his mind juggling all these terrible thoughts.

But the image that persisted was of Demetrius being thrown on the ground by the two Varangians. The look on his face still showed defiance and determination. But for how long will he endure the beatings and torture that were surely to come? What if, instead of running away, he had fought against the attackers? Would he have had the chance to save his friend? There was only one answer to the question and he knew it very well. Still, his mind was tormented by these thoughts, by his ignorance of his friend's fate, of the fact that he had abandoned him. What was he going to tell Eleni? The poor woman finally had hope of a peaceful life after years of hardship and pain, and now he was going to announce to her the capture of her husband. How did they get entangled in this struggle for power? If only he could stop those tormenting thoughts. But it proved impossible.

He was sure of one thing, however, that his friend's only chance of survival lay in the hands of Nicephorus, and that gave him further motive to advance across the uninhabited mountains and swamps to where the domestic resided. It was a longer, but a safer road, and though the nights on the plateau were frigid, he dared not light a fire. He squeezed the last drops of energy he possessed both in body and mind so as to reach his destination before it might be too late.

Finally, on the morning of the seventh day of that arduous journey, the walls of Caesarea appeared before his eyes.

# Chapter Forty-One

## - 𝕏𝕆ℂ𝕊 -

John stood before the gate of the Phocas residence in the heart of the city. Anyone else would not have even dreamt of securing an immediate meeting with the domestic, but the guards on the gate recognized their comrade and seeing the miserable shape he was in, they sent word for Nicephorus who let him in immediately.

Once in the presence of Nicephorus, he wasted no time relaying what had happened to him and Demetrius ever since he was entrusted with the letter and until his arrival at Caesarea. Up until then, the general held the unopened letter in his hand and listened carefully to all that the exhausted Kentarchos had to say. After John had finished his narration of the events, he stood and watched as Nicephorus unsealed and read the letter.

"I should never have left Constantinople in the hands of that wicked man!" the domestic growled. "It was my mistake that I did not rip his throat out a long time ago!"

He looked furious, pacing the room like a caged lion.

"As for Demetrius." He stopped and looked resolute. "Have no doubt, I'm as eager to save his life as you are if not more. Both of you are like sons to me. I will not let him be another sacrifice on Bringas's altar of greed."

"I'm sure of that, Sir. But I can't help but wonder who betrayed us. I don't know what will happen to my family." He shook his head in despair

"Go now and get some rest. I want you to resume your duties with your comrades as soon as possible." Then turning his head to one of the servants he ordered: "Take care of his needs."

"I wanted to ask you for something else before I left, General."

"Speak up."

"I wish to travel to Demetrius's village and inform his wife and parents of what has happened. They are expecting his return any day."

"Right, right, I will send them a messenger."

"I would rather inform them myself, if you don't mind, Sir."

"Fine, you go ahead, but don't flog yourself. This is not your fault, John."

John was dismissed. As he walked down the hallway with a couple of other soldiers, the figure of Tzimiskes appeared. Sweaty and dusty, he looked like he had been leading the soldiers' drills.

"Is that you, John? I thought you were in Constantinople. What are you doing here?"

"I wish I knew, Sir."

Tzimiskes, who was responding to the general's summons had no time to stop and chat, but John's answer left a bewildered look upon his face.

***

"Have you called for me?" the commander asked his uncle as he entered the spacious and airy room.

"Yes, we seem to have some kind of situation. I've just received an urgent appeal from the empress Theophano."

"Delivered by John Sgouros, I suppose?" Tzimiskes quickly made the connection.

"The man almost lost his life bringing it here and his companion was captured by Bringas's agents."

"What is it?"

"It's serious. Bringas has locked her up in the palace and is denying her any contact with the outside world. Even this paper, she had to smuggle out."

"Has that monster gone out of his mind?"

"On the contrary, he seems to know exactly what he's doing. The empress suspects he's preparing to ship her to some remote monastery and take full custody over the minor caesars. This is why she has offered me her hand in marriage."

"She has offered you her hand in marriage?! Splendid!"     "Not so fast! I'm not going to rush into this."

"What are you going to do about it, then?" Tzimiskes's initial excitement was beginning to fade in the face of his uncle's reluctance.

"I have no choice but to march on the capital."

"As emperor?"

"Certainly not. I will not be another usurper."

"But she has offered you her hand! Finally, the empire shall have the capable emperor it deserves. You mustn't deprive us of this!"

"Not so fast, John. You have known me all your life. My desire of a monastic end to my days still stands. I will not trade the heavenly kingdom to win an earthly one."

"The lives of so many are on the line, the safety of the empire you have spent your entire life defending is in the balance. You cannot back down now and hand everything to a eunuch. The empire needs you now more than ever!"

"I must think things over. I've never hesitated in waging war, but civil war is the last thing I want to do."

"With all due respect, general, I think you're making a big mistake. The wide path to the throne is paved before you. "

"You know I've always preferred the narrow path and still do. But I promise you I will seriously consider it and pray that the Lord might guide me to what is best for all. Pray for me."

"I will." Tzimiskes gave his uncle a pensive look. "You just mentioned that John was almost captured trying to deliver the letter. Do you have any idea who might have informed on him?"

"John and his father risked their lives trying to bring the empress's appeal to me."

"What if it was the empress herself?"

"The empress? Why would she do such a thing?"

"Imagine the empress being threatened with exile, Bringas's men coming to snatch her away. What would be the first thing that she would do?"

"She would use the last weapon in her possession. I suppose she would let Bringas know that she contacted me and that help was on the way."

Tzimiskes saw his uncle arrive at the same conclusion as him.

"This is precisely what I believe happened. I think she had no other choice but to threaten Bringas with you. He, however, sent his men in pursuit of the letter and came close to intercepting it."

Nicephorus pondered on that idea.

"I don't think we have much time, Domestic. Whatever your decision is, it has to come fast."

Tzimiskes uttered those last words and then headed back to the barracks. Contrary to what his uncle might have thought, he believed these latest events could be manipulated to serve the interests of the family. He needed to try and convince him to seize this unique opportunity but he also knew his uncle's stubbornness, consulting everyone and in the end doing as he wished.

Two days later, a private messenger came seeking Tzimiskes. He arrived from the capital, and strangely, had ample knowledge as to the whereabouts of Tzimiskes's residence, heading straight there. Under the cover of darkness and in extreme discretion, he delivered his message and left.

As great as Tzimiskes's surprise was to learn the identity of the sender, it was nothing compared to learning what the letter actually said.

# Chapter Forty-Two

- 𝒮𝒰𝒞𝒮 -

John had to carry out the loathsome task of bringing to Eleni the news of Demetrius's capture. With the first light, he rode to Nazianzus with a heavy heart.

He thought how Demetrius had only left on that journey for the sake of his safety, and here he was now, going to tell his loved ones that he didn't even know where their son and husband was.

He wasn't good at delivering bad news. What would he say to an old couple and a pregnant woman desperately awaiting the return of their hero?

He didn't know where to start, but in the end, his small and anxious audience heard the truth. He spelt out the few bitter words, and saw the devastating effect they had.

"Demetrius was captured."

There were a lot of questions of why, where and when, and he couldn't answer them all. He did his best, though, to pacify their anxious hearts and didn't leave until they had a beacon of hope.

"The domestic assures you that he will spare no effort to save him and set him free," was the last thing he said before he bade them goodbye.

"Where are you going? It is late now. Come and spend the night here at least," the father called out to his son's comrade in vain. Even in the darkest of times, a villager's hospitality could not be compromised.

He waved a thanking hand and left.

Wandering aimlessly, he found himself on the road ascending to the top of the hill where the little chapel guarded the horizon. It was a different scene than the last time he had been there. He tethered his horse by a tree and laid down to get some rest on the fresh grass.

Under the shadows of the little chapel, he spent the night and glancing at the metal cross topping the pitched roof, he swore by all that is holy to save Demetrius or die trying.

The next morning he was again on horseback riding to Caesarea.

\*\*\*

Back in the city, the nearest tavern attracted him like a moth is attracted to light. He needed to drown those terrible thoughts which pounded his head mercilessly, and what would do the job better than a few glasses of cheap wine? Quickly intoxicated, he fell into a deep sleep on the wooden table.

Sometime later he felt a hand shaking him vigorously from his slumber. It took him longer than normal to identify the person who stood above him. With drowsy eyes and fuzzy hair, he sluggishly said, "Mansour?!"

"Stand up, John." Mansour helped him up and out of the place.

They walked a few paces and sat down on a stone ledge in one of the narrow streets outside. The sunlight and fresh air began to have a positive effect. There was a lot of catching up to be done. Mansour informed John that he had been appointed translator for the imperial army and lived close by with his wife and daughter.

"What an unfortunate thing to happen to Demetrius," he said after he had heard the full story. "And now what? What will happen with the empress and the caesars?"

"I don't know but I suspect that it will not be long before Nicephorus does something to oppose that wicked Bringas. He needs to be stopped before anything bad happens."

"Absolutely."

He rubbed his face with both hands then heaved a sigh. "Tell me about yourself, have you settled in?"

"Not only I but all the Christian refugees are getting adjusted to their new home. Come on, let's walk, it will do you good to sober up. I have something to show you."

The two continued to chat as they walked down the narrow streets of Caesarea.

"What about your plans for the priesthood?" John remembered.

"I have put these off for the time being. There seems to be more need for translators than priests in Caesarea!"

"I'm glad to hear you are doing well, Mansour, but I'm afraid darker times are in store for us. Civil war is the worst that can happen to a country."

A few minutes later, they reached their destination; a small shop on a quiet street. Inside, John easily recognized the shop owner's face; it was Jabra, perfectly healthy and resuming his work as a goldsmith.

"How great to see you again, dear John!" His face shone with joy as he embraced him.

"Likewise, Jabra. I see that you have gone back to your old

profession."

"And the locals are stunned by his great skill and fine taste," Mansour said proudly. "They had not seen such beautiful work before. I bet he will soon become the most prominent goldsmith in all of Caesarea."

"I'm so happy to see you have recovered both your health and your life, Jabra."

"You once were a great consolation to us after we had lost almost everything. For that I will always be indebted to you." His eyes brimmed with tears

"I knew he wanted to see you, that's why I brought you here."

"You did well, Mansour. It is so wonderful to see you again, Jabra. Give my regards to Salma and her little champion, and also ... to Mariam."

"Why don't you come and join us for dinner tonight? I will be closing soon."

"Well, that's kind of you, but I don't want to intrude. Besides, I'm in no mood for gatherings."

"But I insist! It is just a humble meal. I'll depend on you, Mansour, to bring him with you."

"Alright, uncle. We will not take more of your time, see you in a while then!"

The two of them left the shop and walked aimlessly around town.

"I've been meaning to ask you about Mariam, how is she?"

"And I've been waiting for you to ask. You shall see tonight for yourself. She has become more of the person she used to be in the past, before the destruction of Aleppo."

"I haven't seen that Mariam yet."

\*\*\*

When the shop owners began closing their doors for the day, both John and Mansour headed to a small house near the goldsmith's shop. And while he couldn't wait to see Mariam again, John's concern over the fate of his family and best comrade was getting the better of him.

Inside the humble abode, the whole family were gathered. There were Mansour's wife and daughter, Salma and her son who had grown considerably taller in only a few months, and of course the host Jabra and his daughter Mariam. Their life as a family seemed to have regained some form of normality after all the hardships of the previous winter. They all seemed happy to see the soldier again.

Though he was mostly absent-minded, he still noticed some change in Mariam's attitude towards him; a kind word, a friendly gesture, things he had never seen before. And when after dinner John and Mansour went up on the flat roof terrace to have a breath of fresh air, they were soon followed by gentle footsteps. Mansour excused himself and went back downstairs, leaving the couple to settle their account alone.

She took small steps towards him, her feet guided by the silver rays descending from a giant moon. Only the faint buzzing sounds of crickets cut through the silence on that summer evening. He looked at her as she came closer to him and could see that her approach was not merely physical. He felt she was coming closer in more than one way.

"You barely escaped with your life trying to get here, so Mansour tells me," she spoke in a voice close to a whisper, staring at the moon in front of her, "chased trying to deliver some important letter to the general, your friend being not as lucky."

"Is that what he said to you in Arabic back at the table?

"Yes, but he didn't tell me all that had happened."

As unexpected as her concern sounded, John duly answered. "There is trouble at the capital, the emperor has died."

"Yes, I've heard of that."

"The widowed empress, as if the loss of her husband hasn't been enough a tragedy, is confined to the palace, imprisoned by the chamberlain."

"Why?" she asked, facing him.

"Greed, lust for power." He himself was wrestling with the reasons why. "The letter I carried was a cry for help."

"And she has chosen you and none other to deliver that dire message?"

"Huh! Sounds like a privilege, doesn't it?"

She shrugged. "And your friend? What will befall him?"

He knew that question was coming. He looked away to mask his anger. "He's in their hands now, but not for long, I hope. I promised I'd go back for him." His jaw clenched and released.

"How ironic! You two have risked your lives east and west fighting the enemies of the empire, only to be pursued, hunted down by your kinsmen."

"Ironic indeed. Not all Romans are of one heart and one mind, though. The quest for power often takes men down an evil path, and while they struggle to win influence and glory, they end up losing a lot more, most of the times, everything."

"I wonder what it is that's worth pursuing." She mumbled to herself. But John was quick to pick up the uncertainty in her voice.. He answered like someone who had given the matter much thinking. "Happiness, adventure, thrill, but above all love, true love, a love beside which all other things look trivial, meaningless, useless." He couldn't have sounded more genuine. "And these words come from someone who had thought such love never existed until he saw your face."

He fixed his captivating blue gaze upon her. From the look on her face, he sensed an urge to step closer to him that didn't materialize, as if part of her wanted to succumb to his charm but another resisted. The latter won, at least for the moment. She merely heaved a deep sigh.

"It was around this time of the evening that I first saw you," he said, looking into the big green eyes of the nineteen-year-old beauty.

"And what did you see?" She sounded like she genuinely wanted to hear the answer.

"I saw the most beautiful girl I had ever seen. I saw a person that captivated my senses and left me intoxicated ever since. This is what I saw, Mariam. Ever since that moment, your face has accompanied me even in the darkest of moments." She stared at him, looking resolute.

"Do you want to know what I saw back then?" she replied. "I have already told you what I perceived in you: a lustful, bloodthirsty invader, a ruthless enemy who deprived me of my dear ones and wrecked my entire world. Even with all the kindness you showed me and my family, in my eyes you remained one of those evil men who turned our lives upside down. Because of you I lost everything. There was no other way I could see you, and don't be deceived, I still believe that the motives that brought you to Syria were not all that chivalrous. I know why empires go to war, but the difference now is that I simply do not take it personally anymore. It's the only way I can forgive and move on with my life. I'm sure you didn't have my family or my home in mind when you besieged Aleppo, and so you didn't really deserve all that hatred and resentment from my side. I admit, that my vision was blurred with all the sorrow and pain that engulfed me, but looking back at those few terrible weeks during our exodus from Aleppo, I can now see things more clearly."

"Your words sound like a dream to my ears."

"Isn't life just one long dream? I often wake up at night and wonder where I am. I imagine I would open the window and see our old neighborhood in Aleppo, and hear my brother singing in the garden like he used to. If they hadn't killed Gergis, I would have been married to him by now."

"Did you love him?" he suddenly asked.

There was a strained, uncertain look on her face.

"I must have," she muttered. Gergis had been her first experience, the first man with whom she had any kind of relationship in her conservative society. Now he had become a martyr, a saint, at least to her and her community, just like her brother and the other men who lost their lives at the hands of the fanatical Muslims. For that reason, she adored his memory, more like a worshipper adores a saint than a girl her lover. Had he remained alive, she couldn't tell how their relationship might have developed.

"And loving me, is it something you could ever bring yourself to do?" He held her hands in his. "Ever since our paths crossed, I've had no desire for anyone or anything but you."

She gently pulled her hands away and dipped her chin.

"I feel hollow inside, as if in the place of my heart there is … nothing. I don't think I'm capable of love anymore, not you, nor anyone else."

She glanced at the sky then back at him. "When you laid there battered with fever, looking so vulnerable, flitting between life and death, I felt a little sorry for you. I was surprised at myself. And then when you left before our arrival to Caesarea, I felt a new sadness creeping into my heart. I didn't want to admit it but somehow, it felt safer with you around."

"Do you feel safe now?" he asked her, his words gentle and reassuring.

"I do," she answered reluctantly.

"Then your heart is not lost forever, Mariam. It is there somewhere. If you allow me, I will help you find it. We will find it together, you and I."

She looked away, on the verge of tears.

"I know my actions will mean much more to you than these simple words. I promise you I'll stand beside you, to love and cherish you until you have regained that smile which everyone who knows you tells me can melt rock."

"You've never seen me smile, ha?" Tears sprang to her eyes.

"No, I haven't, not a real hearty smile."

"I don't remember the last time I smiled."

*She's been through a lot. What if I put my arm around her? Will she push me away?*

He mustered his courage and wrapped his arm around her shoulder. To his surprise, she let her head rest on his chest and wept silently. The young woman who had resembled an angry lioness was in fact just a little girl, a tired little girl in desperate need of rest. Finally, John wasn't the enemy anymore. She could finally see his true self. Under the starry sky, John might as well have been the happiest man on earth if only there weren't another thousand things that he had to worry about.

The only girl he had ever loved and whose rejection had caused him so much pain was now in his arms. True, she probably wasn't head over heels in love with him, not yet, but at least the abyss of her hatred had been bridged. All he needed was more time in Caesarea with her, a few more visits to sooth her soul and touch her heart. Little did he know that his stay in Caesarea was going to be a lot shorter than he had imagined.

# Chapter Forty-Three

## - ℰↃℭℬ -

Feeling exuberant, though not without a twinge of bitterness, John returned to the Phocas residence through the narrow streets of Caesarea. He had just spent the most wonderful evening of his life on that little terrace with Mariam, quite unexpectedly. Her image didn't leave his imagination with her eyes, clearer than cove water, her lips, more luscious that a pomegranate's flower, yet with sadness matching her beauty. The war had spared her body but her soul had been deeply scarred. If he wanted to gain her heart, he was going to have to walk with her down the long path of healing where there were no guarantees of a full recovery.

On the other hand, his sense of responsibility towards his captive comrade would not leave him in peace. It kept on pounding his conscience like an invisible hammer. He had never felt this confused before.

Exhaustion eventually overcame excitement and anxiety, allowing him a few hours of sleep. The next morning, he was back on duty.

"Why, if it isn't John!" Andreas, who had been keeping guard in the hallway outside the domestic's room – his head nearly touching the ceiling – welcomed his comrade cheerfully. "Everyone's been talking about your journey back from Constantinople, with Bringas's men in hot pursuit, about Demetrius being captured and all, but no one has managed to get hold of you!"

"I had to go and tell Demetrius's family of what has happened."

Andreas's face darkened. "That eunuch in the palace needs more than his balls cut off!" Even without being so exasperated, Andreas's figure alone inspired fear.

"It all depends on what the general will decide to do. He must do something, and fast."

Andreas looked right and left making sure no one listened then said low: "I've heard Tzimiskes try and convince him to declare himself emperor, to seize the throne, but he strongly refused. I heard their conversation with my own ears last night."

"Ah! But the general has already pledged to protect the thrones of the two young caesars in front of the senate and the patriarch Polyeuctus. It is not easy for a man of his piety and honesty to break such solemn oaths and promises by declaring himself emperor," John replied, whispering.

"I don't see how else he can protect the two caesars and their mother. They are Bringas's prisoners, for God's sake!"

"Let's wait and see. I have a feeling the general's decision will not take much longer."

"I sure hope so. I'm going to go now and get some rest." He yawned, his chest expanding like a ship's sail. "Been here since midnight. The domestic is inside the room. Let me know if you hear anything."

John nodded. He watched Andreas walk away, the sound of his footsteps fading in the distance. As he stood in the hallway outside the domestic's bedroom, keeping the guard, he could hear Nicephorus pace the room. A little later, a chance to speak to the man finally presented itself and he knocked on the door.

"Yes. What is it?"

"I'm sorry to have interrupted you, Sir, but they have brought the ink and paper you asked for."

Nicephorus seemed glad to see John's face through the crack in the door, standing next to a servant carrying an inkwell and some new papers.

"Bring it in," he ordered.

John took the writing things form the servant and placed them on a small table in one corner of the room. His face revealed deep anxiety which Nicephorus was quick to notice.

"What do you think we should do, John?"     "Why, march on the capital, rescue the empress and remove that tyrant."

"You believe then that the solution would be to conquer our own capital, perhaps even besiege it first and subject it to the shells of catapults?" His cynicism was too obvious to miss.

"The city and its inhabitants are the hostages of that wicked man. How else can we free them?" John defended his position.

"This is what I have been studying, John. There is more than one way to solve this. I just need to know which is better: force or diplomacy."

"What do your advisors think, Sir?"

"My commanders think like you. They believe, especially Kourkouas, that I should march straight to the capital and free the empress before it's too late. Truth is, I'm inclined to do exactly that but not before I have studied all other options."

"Options like what?"

"Bringas might not be a saint but he is no fool either. I will try to reason with him, convince him, or threaten him. The last remedy of all is war."

Suddenly, the door flew open and Tzimiskes stormed into the domestic's apartment like a winter's torrent. It was the first time John had seen anyone act like that in his presence. He grabbed his sword's handle, just in case.

"What's the matter?" Nicephorus asked, alarmed at the sight of his nephew.

"I believe this will change your mind, uncle." He held in his right hand what looked like an opened letter, fury had turned his fair face red.

"And what is this?"

"It's a proposal, a preposterous proposal. Here, read for yourself. All I need to do is betray my uncle, says the letter, and the path to fame and glory would be paved before me. Not only would I be appointed domestic, but even the throne of the empire would, with some patience, eventually become mine."

Nicephorus looked with amazement at his nephew's hand which carried the piece of paper. He raised a brow and asked:

"And who might be this patron who favors you so much as to make such a grandiose offer?"

"It's not the will to elevate me which has prompted him, as much as the will to destroy you."

"Bringas?"

"Who else!"

He handed him the letter which contained a clear promise for Tzimiskes of his uncle's position and beyond if he would turn against him and successfully send him in shackles to Constantinople.

John listened as the letter was read out by Nicephorus. He could hardly believe what he was hearing.

*Has that despicable person now resorted to such methods? Is he that desperate to get rid of Nicephorus? Had Tzimiskes agreed to this unholy alliance, God knows what might have happened. Perhaps, I might have had to actually use this sword instead of just grabbing its handle.* He imagined a group of soldiers headed by Tzimiskes barging into the domestic's room, seizing him at best, or ending his life at worst, had Tzimiskes succumbed to the seductive luster of power.

"This time he tried to lure me, your nephew and loyal commander. A terrible mistake on his behalf. The next, he will approach some other general whose loyalty might buckle under the weight of golden promises. The next conspiracy might bear fruit. You must act fast, Domestic. You cannot allow him to continue weaving conspiracies around you with full impunity."

But the domestic seemed to be deep in thought. John had never seen him so reluctant. When it came to defending the empire, he acted with outstanding boldness and resolution. Now, when he himself was the target, he was less than decisive. *What is he afraid of?*

"Do I have your approval for what I am about to do?" Tzimiskes looked at the domestic with fiery eyes, determined to get an answer.

Finally, the answer he sought came firm and clear.

"Go ahead. I shall chase that weasel out of his burrow." It seemed like those words were all Tzimiskes needed to hear. Looking more than satisfied, he exited the room with long strides. John too turned to leave but before he left the supreme commander to his solitude, he saw him walk towards the icon stand in the corner and kneel before the shrine.

*Seeking divine guidance ...*

Both men went out into the hallway. The door was shut.

"Brace yourself." Tzimiskes looked all too serious. "Today, we shall have a new emperor, the emperor our great empire deserves."

There was no need to explain any further.

Tzimiskes departed, but about an hour later the two commanders Maleinos and Kourkouas arrived in haste, behind them a great number of officers, and the entire guard of the domestic, John's comrades. Nicephorus came out wearing his best uniform and breastplate then the whole party marched to the camp. They arrived to the sounds of trumpets calling on all soldiers to present themselves.

Regiment after regiment, the whole army began to assemble outside the walls of Caesarea. Tzimiskes stood inside a large pavilion orchestrating the whole operation.

When 'The Pale Death of the Saracens' appeared to the assembled troops, the plain shook with the shouts of forty thousand men acclaiming him emperor. Their concerted, unanimous cries could not have been coincidental. To John, they acted like they had clear instructions which they were more than happy to implement.

Amid the deafening clamor, the domestic was raised by his closest men on a large shield. It was the first time John had participated in anything like this, which he later learnt had been an ancient roman custom resurrected on that day after centuries of oblivion.

John found himself lifting the large shield with a dozen other bodyguards while the soldiers shouted *Nicephorus Basileus!* The feeling was, to say the least, thrilling. The bravest, most valiant person he had ever known, a man who acted like a second father to him had finally agreed to lead the empire.

After the deafening cries subsided, the soldiers looked at their supreme commander, now their sovereign too, and listened to what he had to say. Nicephorus, girt with a sword and supporting himself with a spear, took his stand under the open sky on a conspicuous and lofty height and spoke:

"My fellow soldiers, the fact that I didn't assume this imperial regalia through any desire for rebellion against the state, but was driven to it by compulsion of you, the army, you yourselves bear witness who forced me to accept such a responsibility for the empire. I call as my witness Providence, which guides everything, that I'm ready to lay down my very life for your sakes. You, who could not bear that the madness of the eunuch and his rabid insolence should govern our empire and control the fate of the royal family, but have chosen me instead as your ruler. Thus I will show you clearly that I knew how to be ruled and now know how to rule securely with the help of God!

"Your struggle is not against Arabs or Scythians or any barbarian people but against the God-protected capital of the Romans. Yet, in this struggle I am convinced that you will have as your helper the Almighty and His saints for it is not we who have broken the agreements and oaths but the deceit of Joseph who has sought my destruction even though I never wronged him.

"You, faithful men, have followed me from victory to victory, now follow me without hesitation wherever God may lead us!"

The troops again erupted in enthusiastic cheers. They were a formidable force that was headed not towards enemy territory but towards their own capital, the heart of their kingdom.

The first decrees of the new emperor were issued right there and then. In front of the vast army, he appointed Tzimiskes Domestic of the East, entrusted him with the safety of the empire's eastern frontier then ordered an immediate march on the capital.

Now things were beyond the point of return. Soon, under the walls of Constantinople, everyone's fate was going to be decided.

Any hopes John had fostered of coming closer to Mariam quickly evaporated. There was another, more pressing, issue that needed to be settled first. The matters of the heart would have to wait.

# Chapter Forty-Four

- 𝒮𝒰𝒞𝒮 -

By Cyril's shop door, the two old friends sat on low wooden stools watching people go by on Constantinople's busiest street. It was already high summer and the afternoon breeze that blew from the sea infused the air with a much desired coolness. Theodore saw Cyril as his best friend and confidant. After years of close friendship, Cyril had gotten used to Theodore's worrisome nature. The two of them always had something to talk about, thoughts and doubts to confess, and events to discuss in the ever-busy capital.

In truth, Theodore hadn't had a moment of peace since his son left with that secret letter a month before. His days were desolate, his nights sleepless. It was in the company of his old friend that he managed to rid himself of some of that burden and not carry it all home to his equally worried wife.

Last week, there had been this deep yet obscure feeling around the city that things weren't right. Strange rumors were beginning to circulate that the grief-stricken empress had been thinking of abandoning the world and retiring to some remote monastery. Other more plausible rumors conveyed a different story claiming that she had in fact been a captive in her own palace. The object of the rumors never came out to confirm or dismiss them, something which made gossip spread like wildfire. The populace wasn't sure what to believe. All they knew was that more soldiers stationed in around the city wasn't a good sign. An atmosphere of uncertainty and suspense enveloped the capital of the Romans, which in some weird way thrived on rumors and found in them an exciting source of entertainment.

Of course, when such rumors were already being spread, Theodore became justifiably more worried. After all, the people who were allowed in the palace those days were limited, himself included. He, therefore, requested some time off from work thinking it would do him good to stay away from the palace for a while until things settled down.

Finally, the day before, the fateful news arrived at the capital that

Nicephorus had been proclaimed emperor by the army and that he had already set out from Caesarea. This confirmed that John had successfully delivered the empress's message, and that he, himself was safe. It was a huge relief.

The news sent shock waves throughout the city, raising the level of excitement, anticipation and anxiety to new heights. The people welcomed the news that finally the most capable and popular commander was going to lead not only the army but the whole empire in a triumphal procession. But the people also expected that a great deal of evil was bound to occur. Bringas wasn't going to step down without a fight, and a fight meant death and ruin, the extent of which no one could predict. Everyone held their breath and prayed for the quick dispersion of the black clouds that were beginning to accumulate in the skies over Constantinople.

In front of the two friends suddenly appeared a vanguard of soldiers that penetrated the Mese Street. Hundreds of cavalry and infantry led by their distinguished commander Marianos marched through the capital to the great amazement of the people. True, they were used to seeing troops pass through their city on their way to the eastern frontier, but this time it was different. These were Macedonian troops, stationed in the European provinces of the empire and had no business whatsoever at the capital, nor were they going anywhere. Constantinople was their final destination.

"He's done it! He's called in troops from the western provinces!" Cyril said, full of astonishment

"I told you Bringas wasn't going to give up easily," Theodore said in a low voice. "Now all the forces of the empire are converging here, pointing their swords towards each other while our borders are left for the barbarians to ravage. What a disgrace!"

"War is imminent, and where? Here in our midst! I knew it was only a matter of time until the whole situation erupted. This power-thirsty Bringas would do anything to obtain full authority. And who will stand in his way? The empress? She is no more than a prisoner now. Polyeuctus? That old monk is barely capable of managing his own realm, let alone standing in the way of a tyrant. If that monster manages to seize the scepter, may God have mercy upon us."

"He still has to overcome Nicephorus and his army first." Theodore reminded his friend.

"That castrated fox will not depend solely on the troops at his disposal. He will resort to all means possible to achieve his goal, and by that I mean conspiracy, bribe, assassination. Anything and everything!" Cyril, like the majority of Constantinopolitans, wasn't especially fond of

Bringas. "Some customers confirmed to me that Leo Phocas, Nicephorus's brother has been placed under house arrest. Imagine, the strategos Leo, who has won so many great battles against the Saracens, being treated like a prisoner! This makes me more convinced that a confrontation is imminent."

"I must get going now," Theodore said, with a concerned look on his face. ".If I stay any longer, Anastasia will begin to worry."

"Alright, you take care, I'll probably close early today, the soldiers have left no room for shoppers."

Indeed, the marching troops removed any hope the people had had of a peaceful resolution to the power struggle. They knew their city was being turned into a fortress so it could repel an army whose triumphs it had celebrated so enthusiastically. Now, the target of the mighty Nicephorus was none other than Constantinople.

Theodore had barely stood up before a group of Varangians arrived at the shop led by Paul, Theodore's assistant.

"Which one is he?" growled one Norseman with a heavy accent.

"That one." Terrified, Paul pointed towards his master with a trembling finger.

Theodore looked like he had been anticipating this all along and was the least surprised of all. His eyes met Paul's for a second, and with a nod of his head expressed his conviction that coerced collaboration was what guided the informant's steps.

He was then quickly seized, his hands tied behind his back without any respect for age or status. Cyril didn't speak a word. He knew better than to oppose or protest the actions of those ruthless barbarian mercenaries. Instead, he remained rooted to the spot and watched as his friend of thirty years was dragged away.

Paul was set free from the tight grip of the guards, but was still subject to the crushing weight of remorse at what he had just done.

When Theodore and his captors vanished in the crowds, he looked at Cyril and said, his voice quavering with grief:

"They threatened my two-year old son! They said they would enjoy watching him fall down the sea walls! I had no choice"

\*\*\*

Theodore had no doubt as to where he was being taken. A few minutes later, his captors dragged him through the Chalkis gate, with hands bound like a criminal. He couldn't help but notice the great number of soldiers and guards stationed at the entrances, on top of the walls and in every corner of the palace. It looked as if there was an undeclared war going on.

They finally arrived at the Boukoleon palace, to a medium-sized, windowless room containing nothing but a desk and a couple of chairs. Lots of papers were strewn on the desk next to an inkwell and what appeared to be an unfinished letter. All but one of guards left and closed the door behind them, more than enough to restrain the aged prisoner should he attempt to resist. A moment later, the door opened once again and the infamous Bringas entered, a sly smile on his face.

"How are you, tailor?"

"I'm fine, Your Grace," replied the resentful Theodore, still maintaining the courtesy he had acquired through years of court life.

"You see, Theodore, I have always thought of you as an honest, hardworking person but never as particularly intelligent. Lately, I learnt that even the aspect of honesty has been corrupted. The problem is that when the head of a household commits a crime, all his family ends up suffering one way or another. When, for example, he bets on the losing horse, he sometimes has more than his money to lose; he might end up losing his life."

"I don't understand, Your Grace."

"But of course you do, even the slowest of criminals would immediately remember their mischief once apprehended by the authorities."

"I never knew it was a crime to be loyal to the royal family, to the empress and mother of our caesars."

"You see how you once again prove to be naïve, you trust the wrong people and your foolish son has taken after you. That same woman, for whose sake you risked your life and that of your son, was quick to betray you. How do you think I knew of the letter? Oh, look at yourself! I mention the letter, and you shudder!" He clicked his tongue. "She thought they had run far enough then boasted that she had sent word to Nicephorus, but what she didn't know was that no one can beat the speed of the royal mail."

"Why are you telling me this?"

"Oh, I haven't told you much yet. Do you know what happened to your son's co-conspirator? Only a harsh beating was enough to make him confess every detail. It turns out he's not as tough as you thought he is."

"I can hardly believe a word of what you say, Your Excellency."

"Believe whatever you want to, but there is still a chance for you to save your neck. Tell us what we need to know and you will be pardoned by reasons of old age … and ignorance."

"I have nothing to tell you."

"Don't play games with me, tailor. You may be talented with

fabrics, but you have no ability in concealing the secrets of the soul. I can read you like an open book, so talk and don't force me to resort to more … convincing methods."

"What do you want to know?"

"I want to know where your son is."

"I have no knowledge of that whatsoever."

Bringas nodded his head twice, strolled around the room then turned to Theodore and said: "When my men searched your house, your terrified wife said the same thing, but for some reason I don't believe her either."

"What do you want from us, leave my wife alone!"

"Nothing for now, but since we might need you later on, you shall remain our guest. Who knows, you might receive a revelation and remember something." He looked at the guard and said with a cunning smile:

"Throw him in a cell and administer what might refresh his memory."

# Chapter Forty-Five

- ℰℑℂℬ -

## Chalcedon, August 963

The numerous soldiers who manned the sea walls of Constantinople could clearly see the host of flickering lights that shone from across the Bosphorus. Nicephorus and his army had finally arrived at the Asiatic shores after a long march and now it was only a matter of hours until they moved into action. The plan that Nicephorus had put forward was to besiege the city and force Bringas to capitulate. Taking the city by force wasn't Nicephorus's goal. It was too dear, too sacred to be attacked by its own children, and too strong. It had never been conquered before in spite of the seven times it had been put under siege by godless invaders. But Nicephorus was no infidel. He was the city's loyal son, an emperor proclaimed by the army, and adored by the people. He and his forty thousand men knew that by the time they stood outside the gates, Bringas's iron grip would begin to shatter of its own accord. But what they didn't know was that Bringas wasn't going to allow them to display that show of power in the first place.

A few hours earlier, after the army had crossed the last few miles on land, the newly proclaimed emperor took his commanders and guard and advanced to the port of Chrysopolis to inspect the vessels that were to carry him and his army to the other shore the following day. The numerous boats and dromons between the two shores could be relied upon to ferry the soldiers to their final destination.

Yet to his and his companions' great surprise the harbor looked as desolate as the beach of some remote island. Only the sounds of waves and seagulls could be heard. There was nothing else, not a single boat and not a single mariner.

"What is this? Where are the vessels?" Maleinos was the first to voice his concern.

The seriousness of the obstacle that lay ahead of them displayed itself fully and clearly. Without ships to cross, Nicephorus's campaign could advance only so far.

"This is no coincidence. All the ships have been driven to the other side," Nicephorus said. "That sly fox is one step ahead of us!"

John shot a bewildered look at the empty harbor.

*We are stranded, then.*

"Does he really think he can keep us here forever? What is his plan?" Kourkouas wondered angrily.

"He knows he can't face us in the field so he intends to keep us here and buy more time until he has brought in troops from the west, or until he has exiled the empress or forced her into some monastery. God only knows what's going on inside that devil's mind."

Nicephorus held his nerve. "Hear me, men, we have only arrived. Let the army rest for a while until we discuss our options. Come on, let's get back now."

By the time they returned to the camp, it was dark already. News of the situation spread quickly among the soldiers who had prepared themselves for an imminent confrontation, but now had to settle for a period of anticipation. John, who all the way from Caesarea had been weighed down with anxiety over the fate of his loved ones, now left the camp and went for a walk under the starry sky to clear his head. Between the twinkling of lights on both shores there extended the pitch-black sea, only visually passable. The city he grew up in and loved so much had become a prison to its inhabitants, the royal widow and orphans were under the mercy of a ruthless and cunning warden, while the empire's greatest army headed by the acclaimed emperor stood only a few miles away, watching helplessly.

It had been a long, hot day and the sound of recurrent waves dying on the sandy shore was too tempting to resist. He took off his clothes and plunged into the refreshing waters. It had been quite a while since he had bathed in the sea, or anywhere for that matter. The six weeks of forced march from Cappadocia to Constantinople were exceptionally hard on everyone.

He lay there floating in the water, allowing himself to drift and be rocked by the gentle waves and gazing up at the firmament, so brilliantly dotted with a thousand tiny lanterns. It reminded him of a black velvet cloak richly embroidered with the many white pearls he as a child once saw his father work with. His thoughts floated further to the remote Anatolia where Mariam was now. She had been so close yet so unattainable, like Constantinople had become. He hadn't had the chance to say goodbye to her. That same day when Nicephorus was declared emperor, he rode beside his monarch on the journey back to Constantinople. There was so much business that needed to be settled, and no time to waste lingering in Caesarea.

An hour must have passed as he soaked in the water when all of a sudden, a faint ghostly light approaching on the surface pierced the darkness. As he mustered his senses, he heard two oars splashing through the water with energetic rhythm.

*Perhaps it's time I got out.*

He swam to the shore, dressed hastily, and grabbed his sword just as what appeared to be a little rowing boat finally reached the shore. In the dim light he could see two figures.

"Who's there?" His threatening demand was met with the sound of swords being drawn.

With his natural fearlessness, he walked barefoot on the sand towards the two men. "Unless you identify yourselves, then you'd better say your final prayers."

A familiar voice replied unexpectedly, "Aren't you supposed to be guarding the new emperor, John?"

The speaker raised the lamp closer to his chin as he spoke, illuminating a well-known, yet exhausted face.

"Your Excellency!" John stumbled for words.

"Take us to the emperor."

With the torch as the only source of light, John led the way to the camp. The emperor and his generals were in session when the guest entered unannounced.

"Good evening, gentlemen."

"Good Lord!" Nicephorus cried out, then hurried to embrace his brother Leo while everyone else stared at them speechlessly. "I've been worried sick about you!"

Leo appeared tired, his face pale.

"God is merciful, my dear brother."

"How did you get here?"

Leo sucked in a couple of deep breaths, he closed his eyes for a moment.

"I managed to sneak out under the cover of darkness, crossed the sea in a small boat, but father wasn't as lucky."

"What do you mean?! Did anything happen to him?"

"I was cautious enough to not be at home when Bringas's men came for me last night, so they took him away instead. He is being held in the palace. If that coward dares to harm him in anyway ..." he said through gritted teeth.

"He's doing all he can to harm you and convince you to retreat. He has arrested so many people for the mere suspicion of sympathizing with our cause. The city is under the grip of the Macedonian troops and their commander Marianos whom he has brought over from Thrace."

"What about the empress and the caesars?"

"Hardly anyone knows anything about them."

Even to John, who knew little about the politics of the palace, it appeared clearly a game of power. Whichever party could withstand more pressure was going to emerge victorious, and it seemed that Bringas had all the right cards in his hands. He had the empress and her children in his grasp, he had completely cut off Nicephorus's army on the other shore, had his aged father locked up in a cell and was controlling the city with dissident troops.

Leo continued to describe the dire situation in the capital, frequently interrupting the coherent narrative with bursts of anger. By then it was no secret: to many it seemed like Nicephorus's bid to the throne was going to be written down in history as another failed usurpation.

John could have sworn then that even Nicephorus himself must've started having doubts about whether he was going to sit on the golden throne after all.

# Chapter Forty-Six

## - ರಿಲ -

For the past three years, John had witnessed firsthand the methods to which the domestic owed his victories. By virtue of his swiftness and agility, he had attacked his enemies before they had time to catch their breath. Now, as an uncrowned emperor, he didn't seem intent on changing his methods. He guessed that Bringas was experiencing a premature euphoria of triumphalism, believing that he had successfully blocked all paths in the face of his adversary. His guess was right. For the next morning a messenger crossed the straits in a small boat carrying a message from the chamberlain. It was short and clear: in return for his safety and that of his family, Nicephorus was to send the army back east and come alone to the city. There in the Great Church of the Holy Wisdom and in front of all, continued the letter, he was to renounce all claims to the throne, acknowledge his error and accept the holy orders, thereby residing permanently in the Athonite monastery he had founded.

Nicephorus scribbled a reply on the back of the letter. *First release my father and then we might talk*, he wrote to the de-facto ruler of the empire, and didn't forget to remind him how base and degenerate he was, "exacting vengeance upon an old man".

The messenger left carrying Nicephorus's letter to Bringas signed: 'Nicephorus, Emperor of the Romans'.

Meanwhile, he called John and few of his colleagues to his tent by the beach where he entrusted them with a task of huge importance.

"You must carry out this mission with the utmost care," he exhorted the young guards after he had told what he wanted them to do. The words of the mighty Nicephorus instilled ineffable ardor into their souls. "Upon your success lies not only the salvation of one man, but that of all of us. Your success will deprive our enemy of his most significant bargaining tool. You have John as your leader. He is not the eldest among you but he has proven himself time and again as a capable and intelligent soldier. Follow his directions and you shall do well."

"We shall do all we can to justify your confidence, emperor." John talked on behalf of himself and his comrades.

"Go with God!" He sent them off on their mission.

*\*\*\**

That evening, a warm August evening, a small boat, provided by a local fisherman, set sail under the cover of darkness carrying four men towards the city. It avoided the sea walls and rowed far to the west where the massive land walls protected the peninsula's only land front, not far from the Golden Gate. There the nocturnal travelers abandoned the boat and spent the remainder of the night in the nearby woods waiting for the approach of daylight when the gates would be opened.

"I never thought I'd have to enter Constantinople this way," Said Procopius, one of the four and a fine soldier who knew well how to wield a sword.

"That is if we manage to get inside in the first place. How are four young, able-bodied men entering the city supposed to avoid the hawkish eyes of the guards?" Andrew, possessed of exceptional height and bulk, justifiably wondered.

"We *will* get in. We'll just have to be clever enough and wait for the right moment," John replied, trying to reassure the small group they weren't committing suicide.

The right moment didn't take long to arrive. An hour later, the approach of some Thracian farmers transporting their famous peaches to be sold in the capital's markets presented the infiltrators with the opportunity they wanted. Two wagons piled with fruit and a dozen peasants passed through the Golden Gate arousing no suspicions whatsoever. A hundred paces past the gate, four of those who had been pushing the loaded carts quit their laborious task and vanished in one of the narrow streets after handing a few gold coins to their temporary colleagues.

"That wasn't difficult, was it?" John said with a smile.

"Which part, fooling the guards or bribing the peasants?" Andreas replied, all the while trying to avoid running into people in the narrow alleyway.

"With three golden coins, my friend, you can convince a peasant to dance on his head."

"I hope your plan to enter the palace works, or else, we'll be flayed alive." Procopius said with a shudder.

"But even if we succeeded in getting inside the Great Palace, how on earth are we supposed to find Bardas in that huge complex, and how will we get him out of there unnoticed?" Andreas continued picking holes in the scheme.

"Just quit grumbling you two. Nicephorus is a public hero. I'm sure we'll find people who want to be remembered for having assisted the emperor when he needed their help," John replied, inspiring confidence in his comrades. Still, there was a lot in their plan that had been left to chance, and he knew it.

The men continued to walk through the city. Squads of the Macedonian soldiers could be seen everywhere; in the markets, in the plazas, outside the churches and up on the walls. That, however didn't seem to bother the citizens who appeared to go about their business as usual. John walked the streets of the city he loved, yet for the first time as a fugitive.

Walking by the Forum of Constantine, they passed through the quarter of the Artopoleia, where the city's bakeries worked day and night to provide bread for its half a million inhabitants, then headed north. John glanced to his right where the hideous Noumera, the city's prison stood. A strong contingent kept guard around the building. *Demetrius must be locked up inside there … that's if he's still alive.* That morbid thought brought him much distress and he shook it off quickly. *If only I could do something before it's too late. You'll have to wait, my friend, just a little while longer.* Finally, the small group made it to their destination in the northern part of the city where many luxurious villas were scattered close to the Golden Horn. In time, they reached a beautiful mansion surrounded by a high marble wall. John had been here more than once before and although it had been only two years since the last visit, it felt like an awful long time ago.

"Is this the place?" Andreas asked, marveling at the view before him.

"Yes," John answered. "Here we can be sure of receiving the help we seek. The enemy of our enemy is our friend."

John handed a guard standing by the main gate the letter he had been carrying to be delivered to the master of the house..

Their wait for a response didn't last long, for a moment later they were called inside.

"His grace, the lord Basil Lekapenos, will meet you now," an elderly servant announced and led the four men into the same hall they had dined in two years before.

The former chamberlain entered the hall holding between his long fingers the opened letter. He looked exactly the same. The passing of time had not affected him in the least.     "I'm sure you haven't had the time to eat," he said graciously and clapped twice. "Bring the men food and wine." A couple of servants rushed to carry out their master's orders.

"Please sit down. How may I help you, officers?"

The men bowed before him.

"Your Excellency, as you know, our great Domestic, Nicephorus, has been acclaimed emperor by the army," John began. "He is now emperor of the Romans. Yet, Joseph Bringas has responded insolently by denying his sovereign access to the city. Moreover, he has taken the emperor's father captive, displaying actions befitting of criminals and robbers."

"I'm aware of all of that you have mentioned, Nicephorus has asked me in this letter of his to give you all possible help, which I am more than happy to give to his loyal men, but you haven't yet told me how I can be of assistance to you."

"Actually, we were hoping you could facilitate our entrance to the palace," John replied.

"If your plan is to assassinate Bringas, forget about it. His bedroom is virtually a fortress. My friends at the palace tell me there are more than fifty guards that never leave him day or night."

"That's not our desire, Your Excellency. We know better than to aim that high, though we're sure he will meet the fate he deserves some day. Our mission is only to liberate the emperor's father."

"I see." He passed his hand over his beardless cheeks. "And when are you intending to make your move?"

"The sooner the better. Who knows what might happen to the old general if we wait any longer?"

"You act fast like your commander. I like that. I can arrange your entry and exit this very night. With some cosmetic modifications to your appearance, of course."

"We are deeply grateful. The emperor will be deeply grateful as well."

"And what are you intending to do afterwards? What will you do with the most dignified old man in Constantinople, whose face every senator, merchant and guard recognizes?"

"The emperor ordered us not to leave the city without his father, and we are intending to do just that."

# Chapter Forty-Seven

- ࿐ -

That afternoon, the four soldiers who had entered Basil Lekapenos's palace never came out. In their place emerged four monks in shabby black cloaks of coarse linen, with wooden crosses hanging from their chests. It wasn't unusual at all to come across monks, young monks too, visiting the Roman capital with its magnificent shrines, numerous monasteries and unmatched collection of holy relics.

Instead of heading to a church or monastery, the great palace was their destination. When they finally arrived in front of one of the smaller, rather concealed gates, there was someone waiting for them there, but not just anyone. It was the Papias himself, the palace official responsible for the opening and closing of the palace gates, an old friend of Basil's, and to whom he owed his ludicrous yet prestigious job.

Although he had a numerous staff of ushers and workers under him, the high official came himself to welcome the monks into the palace and lead them to the royal chapel.

"Come in, come in, holy brothers." He ushered them inside the premises. "By sunset, all the gates will be sealed till dawn, no one will be able to enter or exit. The new instructions of the chamberlain."

*His Excellency, the chamberlain, seems to be looking over his shoulder.*

"We wish to spend the night in adoration and worship beside the holy relics," the *monk* John told him.

The Papias nodded.

"You don't have to tell me the details of your visit, holy brothers. His Excellency, Lord Lekapenos already informed me of your noble purpose."

They walked through the garden led by the high official whose presence gave them a sense of security in a place crawling with guards.

"I learnt that you are also interested in knowing the whereabouts of a certain living relic," the papias whispered after they had entered the quiet chapel, a sly smile on his face.

"Quite so," John answered, displaying a serious look.

"You remain in here and try to act like real monks," he whispered. "Just before dawn, I will send someone to take you to his room."

"What about the guards outside his door?" John knew that any confrontation with a guard would be guaranteed to attract a hundred others.

"The guards outside his door are already enjoying a gift of the fine aged wine they adore. They could only dream of such a liquor back in their frigid countries. Now, they can't go without it." The papias smiled knowingly. "Just don't make a lot of noise and all will be good."

"What about the other guards? Is there any way we can avoid them?" John asked the man who knew the palace better than anyone else.

"Don't be too worried. You'll not see too many of them at night when the palace gates are closed." The smile suddenly vanished from the papias's face. "I've waged everything on your success. If Basil hadn't assured me of your ability to pull this off, I wouldn't have risked everything: my position, my fortune, even my neck." His hand encircled his thin neck. "When everything is over and you're out of here, don't forget to mention me to the emperor."

"You sound pretty confident of the outcome," John said to him.

"I've always trusted Basil. He has a good eye for things. Years of his friendship have only brought me favorable results. Now you make sure this business of yours follows that pattern. I'll wait for you by the same gate. Don't be too late." He turned and left, making sure to close the door behind him.

*Let's see.*

"To prayer, men." John signaled, and the four men knelt on the marble floor before the richly ornamented chest of relics and put up a convincing image of piety should any prying eyes observe them. The princely shrine wasn't especially large but every golden mosaic and every marble column was a manifestation of royalty.

Some court officials, and later a couple of talkative court ladies, visited the chapel, paying little attention to the four prostrated monks in the corner. As the long summer day finally came to an end, the visits ceased.

"Now we wait," John whispered.

The chapel was dark but for a few oil lamps that burnt constantly before the icons of Christ and the saints. The four men stood in the shadows and waited. Hour after hour passed, the men occasionally hearing the heavy footsteps of the guards traversing the hallway outside their door. After midnight, those footsteps became less frequent until silence finally prevailed.

John, stood in the darkness, too anxious to be fully aware of the passage of time. He marveled at the icon of Christ the Pandokrator – the Ruler of All, with the diadem on his head and the scepter in his right hand, looming through a veil of incense. It had been so splendidly painted he had never seen a more majestic yet sublime depiction of the Heavenly King. The glamour of the portrait moved him from fake to real, sincere prayer. With his drowsy comrades alternately slipping in and out of sleep, he alone stood in the corner and muttered.

*I know I haven't been your most faith follower, especially lately, being busy with never-ending missions and ever-growing troubles ... I feel embarrassed that I should seek your help now when I haven't bothered to talk to you for a long time. But then again I haven't really bothered you with any supplications either. Now, however, it seems like we will need a miracle to pull this off ... and that's when we'll need you more than ever to look down from the sky and help us. You've silenced the storm, healed the sick and raised the dead. I'm not asking for that big a miracle, though. A deep sleep for the guards, the kind you caused to fall on Adam when you created Eve will do just fine ...*

A soft knock on the door disturbed John's thoughts. He was a little startled but quickly pulled himself together. An usher carrying a lantern silently beckoned to them through the door. "Come on, men, let's go!" John said to his comrades.

They all bolted upright and followed after the young man as quiet as a pack of panthers. Silence was absolute in the minutes preceding the break of dawn. A corridor, then a flight of stairs, a turn right then another left, and out into a courtyard. No sign of the guards so far. *The imperial quarters where the empress and her children reside are on the other side of the palace.* John remembered from his few visits to the palace with Nicephorus. *That's where the horde of guards is probably amassed.*

The usher's steps froze at the beginning of a long arcade that formed one of four sides of a rectangular courtyard. The arches, supported by round columns made up the courtyard's perimeter. The usher, without uttering a word, pointed to where two still shadows could be faintly seen at either side of a door. He then produced a key that could fit into a man's palm, gave it to John, turned around and disappeared.

*Here we go.*

The men wasted no time and proceeded to where they had been shown. Underneath their ascetic clothing, each of them had their concealed hands wrapped around a dagger, in preparation for the worst. As they drew nearer, they began to better discern the nature of the two shadows they were approaching. Piled on the floor lay two massive but unconscious Varangians. A couple of empty wine jars revealed just how merry the previous night must have been for them.

John put the key in the door. "Easy now!" Procopius whispered as he and the others stood ready to slay the guards should they show any signs of rousing themselves. The key smoothly turned inside the lock. It felt like the it had only recently been oiled. He pushed the door and entered the spacious, albeit poorly furnished room. With the light of the room's lonely candle, he tip-toed with his monk's sandals across the marble floor to where a man appeared to be sleeping deeply on a bed. *I hope the guards weren't generous enough as to share their wine with him.*

"Don't make a sound!" he whispered to the old man after covering his mouth with his hand. Bardas opened his eyes in terror to see a monk towering over him. "We've been sent by your son, the Emperor Nicephorus, to get you out of here," he said slowly and clearly. In the dark, and dressed as he was, Bardas didn't seem to recognize the face of his son's faithful bodyguard, but at hearing his words, the terror in his eyes quickly disappeared. He nodded twice. John slowly removed his hand from the man's mouth and then helped him out of bed. "Come on, General, we must get going fast.". From a cloth sack he had been carrying, John produced another monastic habit. "Here, let me help you put this on." Bardas, with his long face and white beard could easily be taken for a real man of the cloth. John looked at Andreas through the open door, standing readily above the guards. He signaled to him. All was clear.

A moment later there appeared four young monks and their abbot walking hastily across the courtyard. So far they had been lucky enough as to encounter no guards, save those two who slept like hibernating bears in a Nordic winter. Two more, sober, they managed to avoid as they exited the last door that led to the gardens. As they reached the small gate, John felt his heart nearly leap out of his chest when seeing the papias anxiously awaiting them. His bulgy eyes had now turned red, apparently from lack of sleep. It was still dark, but he nevertheless turned the key inside the lock and allowed the five men to slip out into the street.

"See? I told you you'd make it! Go now, go! But don't forget to mention me to the emperor."

"We most certainly will not," John affirmed.

The group was already out of the palace with their big prize safe and sound.

"We made it!" Procopius said, wiping cold sweat from his forehead.

John looked up towards the sky that had begun to brighten with the first rays of dawn. *Thank you.* He breathed out.

"I can't believe my son has resorted to monks to do this!" the old man said in wonderment.

"General, It's me, John, the emperor's bodyguard!"

Bardas gazed at him then suddenly realized who he'd been talking to all along. "Why, of course it's you! Nice trick you pulled off there, incredibly brave too!"

"Where to now?" Procopius asked, still anxious. They had already walked a bowshot from the palace's fence and were about to step into the Mese Street but they were still far from being safe. Suddenly, a commotion broke out from behind them. John looked and saw a group of frenzied Varangians rushing out of the palace gates. They looked like ferocious beasts, ready to tear down to pieces whoever fell into their hands.

*Time to run!*

"They must must've found out what happened. We need to hide, fast!" John said, alarmed, as they quickly sheltered behind a corner.

"We can't get far, not with them looking for us." Andreas warned the rest as they stood behind the stone wall. "In a few minutes, the entire Macedonian contingent as well as the Varangians will be hunting us down. Forget about trying to reach the harbor or leave the city."

"Then where are we supposed to go? Someone answer me!" Procopius asked, looking right and left.

"There is only one place right now," Bardas said, confidently. "And it's right in front of you!" He pointed a bony finger towards the largest and holiest building in all of Constantinople.

# Chapter Forty-Eight

- 𝓔𝓞𝓒𝓑 -

The bells of the adjacent Hagia Sophia were starting to ring on that Sunday morning, and the great edifice acted like a human magnet, attracting people from all directions. News quickly spread – as they usually do in Constantinople – that General Bardas had been kept inside the palace against his will but had managed to escape seeking refuge at the Great Church. The worshippers entering the cathedral could clearly see him sitting on a chair inside the sanctuary, right beside the stone altar. There, he was untouchable. According to ancient tradition, he was under the direct protection of the Church and the people. Even usurpers and traitors could take refuge at the holy site in order to escape the wrath of emperors, and in many instances, they did receive a fair chance, after the initial fury of the monarch had subsided.

But in this case, Bardas hadn't done anything deserving of punishment except being the father of Bringas's arch-enemy. He stayed in his place during the entire service, and the worshippers, packed inside the spacious cathedral, kept their eyes on the father of their acclaimed emperor who had spent his entire life fighting the Saracens in the east, but was now forced, at such an advanced age to run for his life.

John and his comrades stood inside the safe haven and watched. *Let's see what Bringas is going to do now. We've taken Bardas from right under his nose! Now all his fury and all his soldiers can do nothing for him. Perhaps we haven't succeeded in getting Bardas out of the city, at least not yet, but this is the second best thing. If only Nicephorus could be informed somehow …*

When the liturgy was but a few minutes short of ending, with long lines of worshippers waiting to receive the holy communion, the sound of stomping feet echoed under the great dome, overshadowing those of the psalters. John turned to see what up  until a few minutes he had thought impossible.

*What is going on here? This can't be happening.*

The four monks stood beside one of the giant columns and watched the unprecedented scene unfold.

228

The service was rudely interrupted by a detachment of fully armed Macedonian soldiers headed by their leader Marianos. Unlike the last time when Bringas attempted to arrest Nicephorus in the church of the Holy Apostles, the soldiers didn't merely content themselves with threatening from a distance. Before anyone realized what was going on, they headed straight to the sanctuary, pushed the clergy aside, snatched Bardas from his seat and dragged him off towards the exit. In vain did the patriarch and clergy protest to this crude and unjustified behavior.

"Let him go!" Polyeuctus cried at the soldiers with apostolic zeal. "You will suffer God's wrath for this!" The men looked to their commander for guidance. The patriarch's words had made their hands falter for a moment, but Marianos's stare threatened a more imminent wrath should they hesitate to carry out their orders.

"We don't take our orders from you, Your Grace." Marianos answered scornfully. "We are taking this man back to the Palace where Lord Bringas wants him to be. Carry on what you're doing men!"

"Let go of me!" the old man protested. "You have no right, you cheap mercenaries!" The stunned worshippers froze and looked on like a flock of sheep as one of their own was being devoured by wolves.

But before the soldiers could exit the building, another voice interceded.

"They can't just come and carry him away from the sanctuary! He has the right of protection!" John shouted to the petrified crowd. He was beside himself. *They can't do this!*

"Will you allow these insolent mercenaries to abduct an old man before your very eyes, a man whose entire life has been spent fighting the infidel for your sake?" The crowd looked and saw the young monk crying at the top of his lungs.

"What Romans are you if you allow the father of your emperor to be humiliated before your eyes? What Christians are you if you allow injustice to prevail amongst you? Rise up, faithful men and rescue an honorable man who has taken refuge in the house of God!"

"He's right, the monk is right!" shouted one man. "This is scandalous!" protested another.

The monk's angry incitement finally had an impact on the people. What started with a murmur, and escalated into a clamor, quickly ended up becoming a full scale attack, halting the soldiers before they could depart with their prisoner.

Although unarmed, the people had the advantage of numerical superiority, and the hundred soldiers couldn't resist such an angry human deluge. Bardas was rescued from their hands and the perpetrators and their commander were ejected outside the cathedral without much difficulty.

It happened very quickly. The four sturdy monks took hold of Bardas amid the great chaos that ensued and rushed him back inside the sanctuary.

It looked like total victory.

The old man had been more resilient than anyone could have imagined. There was a gloating look on his face as he was being carried back to his refuge by the altar.

Inside the sanctuary, the Patriarch Polyeuctus and his clergy watched the return of Bardas to safety with a look of indignation. He, being the empire's most senior prelate, must have been burning with rage that the words of a novice could achieve more than his own, regardless of the fact that the outcome had been agreeable to him

"What monastery are you from, who is your abbot? Identify yourselves at once!" he demanded of the four men in black robes who bowed with respect.

"We are not monks, Your Grace. We are men of his majesty, Emperor Nicephorus," John answered, taking off the monastic habit.

"I see." The Ecumenical Patriarch's head went up and down. "So Nicephorus sent four men, dressed as monks, believing they could stand in the face of an army. Is he that desperate? There must be hundreds of soldiers now surrounding the church. Where do you think you can run to? You won this round, that's fine, but I know the chamberlain, and he will not give up that easily."

"We only need one thing from you, Your Grace, to keep this honorable man here inside the sanctuary, and the faithful people of this city will do the rest."

"I will not allow this holy place to become the battlefield for the struggle over temporal power," he fumed. "But I will respect the ancient right of refuge. That is all I can grant you. At least, this is what I will try to grant you. I have no army of my own. May God have mercy upon us, all of us!"

The patriarch glanced at Bardas then at John, and then left the church with most of his clergy heading to the nearby house of the patriarchate, leaving behind him a full building.

"He fears the retribution of Bringas if he sides with us wholeheartedly," Andreas said, watching the group of black-clad clergy walk away. "One way or another, he will have him removed, if not from this world, at least from the patriarchal throne."

The people, nevertheless, seemed unwilling to leave the father of Nicephorus to his fate. Instead, as he stayed inside the sanctuary, they remained in the church to guarantee his safety.

"And now what?" Andreas asked.

The sun soared in the middle of the sky, the people who had been fasting from the previous day in order to receive the Holy Communion, were beginning to wane.

"Nothing, we wait here with the people." John was trying to think of a way out of this stalemate.

"Until what? He will send more soldiers the next time and…"

"… and turn the church into a bloodbath? I don't think so." John sounded confident.

As it transpired, they didn't have to wait much longer to find out. A clamor soon arose from the other end of the vast building. The tall western door was pushed open and to everyone's surprise the well-known figure of Bringas appeared. He penetrated the crowds like a hot knife cuts through butter, his mere presence causing them to clear a path before him.

"He is here!" John warned his comrades.

The infamous chamberlain advanced with a hellish look on his face. Instead of the sanctuary, he walked straight to the ambo then and ascended the platform where the priests read verses of the holy scriptures during liturgy. But in place of sacred, consoling words, Bringas had prepared a speech far from comforting. The eyes of thousands were focused on him when he opened his mouth and began spewing invective at them.

*The devil is going to preach now? Boy, did we make him angry! He simply can't tolerate losing his best bargaining tool and has now arrived to put the fear of God into those who dared interfere with his plans.*

"What do I see here?" he said as he surveyed the crowd. "I see a rabble, thousands of worthless troublemakers who think they know better than their masters and lawful governors! What interest have you in supporting the usurper and his father? Do you think I'm unable to drag that conspirator out of here by force of arms? I certainly am capable of more than that but have only refrained in doing so out of piety and respect for this holy place of God! I warn you, though! Don't try my patience! If Bardas the fugitive is not handed over peacefully, then you shall see the full extent of my fury.

"You insolent multitude! I shall discipline you like a horde of stray dogs! From now on, there will be no food for a disobedient and rebellious people. The bread shops in the capital shall be closed as of today by my order! Repent or else!"

He stepped down fuming with anger and walked arrogantly out of the church amid the murmuring crowd.

"Look at that!" Andreas said indignantly "Does he really think he can threaten the entire city with starvation? Who does he think he is?"

"It doesn't look like he's joking," Bardas said from behind them.

John had a concerned look on his face. *I hope the people will not bow to his threats. We need them here. They're our only support.*

"Don't let him scare you!" John shouted to the people who by then knew his true identity. "If he could do more than spew empty threats he wouldn't have hesitated for a second, but this is the furthest he can reach."

An old woman responded with a husky but resolute voice: "Man shall not live by bread alone! Even if he withheld the bread, God will provide." Her words brought much approbation from a people who now openly loathed the chamberlain. They had made their decision, and were going to defend the cause of their new emperor till the end.

Hours later, when Bringas's threats failed to produce the desired effect, the crowd witnessed firsthand to what great lengths the resourceful chamberlain would go to get what he wanted.

# Chapter Forty-Nine

- ℰℑℭℬ -

The standoff continued for the rest of the day and the following evening. With the soldiers surrounding the edifice, John and his small band spent the night inside the sanctuary by the side of Bardas while a few thousand people slept on the hard marble floor.

It seemed to John like the least worried of all was Bardas himself. He even looked like he enjoyed the fact that he was the most contested person in the empire. He slept well, snoring loudly all night, had a big breakfast in the morning sent by the patriarch and even asked for his favorite wine.

"The emperor is cut off on the Asiatic shore, while we're surrounded here. This doesn't look like it is going to end well." Andreas expressed what everyone else thought in secret.

Words failed John who, like his comrade, realized the gravity of the situation they found themselves in.

"Never leave room for pessimism! If you believe in victory, then victory will knock on your door when you least expect it," came from Bardas, who by then was enjoying his third glass of wine. He leaned forward in in his chair, the brass cup in his hand, and sounded like he were still the powerful strategos lecturing an obedient army. "I was once surrounded in a fort in Armenia with no more than a handful of soldiers for about two weeks by an army of three thousand Saracens. Yes. Three thousand! We were this close to capitulating. We almost ran out of food and water but fate smiled on us when the besiegers were caught up in a rainstorm. They began to suffer while we enjoyed the safety and warmth of our castle. The downpours continued for seven days and seven nights, nonstop until the Saracens finally left of their own accord preferring to lose the day than their lives. We have to be patient. Besides, think of the rewards my son will bestow upon you if you pull through." The old man was clearly becoming boastful of his son's ascension to the imperial throne. The fact that Bringas, the walls of Constantinople and the Bosphorus stood between his son and the throne didn't seem to bother him at all.

But while the besieged practiced patience, someone else wasn't endowed with that virtue. There were still people lying on the floor when soldiers burst into the church for a second time.. But they hadn't come in to fight. Indeed, no emperor or governor had ever dared risk having his name written down in history as the desecrator of the Great Church. It was an unthinkable infamy, especially for someone who had his eyes on ruling the empire. The soldiers who rushed inside remained by the gate while the people gazed at the astonishing view that unfolded.

Bringas had returned. This time, however, he wasn't alone; he held the hands of two children. Ordinary children they were not; but rather the little caesars Basil and Constantine. It was the first time in weeks anyone had seen the princes and now it was an immense shock to see them brought in the midst of such turmoil.

Bringas and the princes, whose faces shone with child-like innocence, walked to the sanctuary where Bardas and his makeshift entourage of four stood waiting for them.

"How dare you involve them in this?" Bardas shouted in the face of his enemy. But Bringas remained unmoved.

"Remove these men out of the sanctuary at once so we might talk," Bringas demanded.

"We're not going anywhere!" John responded defiantly, his eyes burning with fury.

"I see that you're back, John. Is your master so afraid to come himself that he is sending us his minions?"

"Watch your tongue, eunuch, my master is your master too, and master of the whole ecumene, the emperor Nicephorus."

Bringas maintained his calm and said low to John's ears:

"I advise you, in particular, tailor's son, to leave me and General Bardas to settle our issues alone, that is if you wish to see your father again." He flashed a malicious smile. "Not to mention that comrade of yours whom you left and fled in cowardice."

John looked as though he was about to jump on the little man and tear him to pieces. His jaw clenched and released several times, but Bardas looked him in square the eyes, signaling his desire to be left alone with the chamberlain.

The four men moved a few steps aside leaving Bardas, Bringas and the two little princes inside the sanctuary.

"What does that bastard want now bringing the two boys into this? What cunning words is he telling the old general?" Andreas whispered with frustration.

"There's no doubt about it." John replied. "By this holy place, he must be blackmailing Bardas into submission. He's threatening him with the lives of the two boys. Why else would he bring them here?"

Only low murmurs could be heard, nothing discerned.

"The patriarch has failed us! How could he! So much for the right of refuge. He has to take responsibility for this!" Andreas once more protested

"Bardas will not fall for this. He would never give up that easily," John said, but it was only wishful thinking rather than the reality of the situation, for he had barely finished his sentence when the small group gathered inside the sanctuary appeared from a side door through the iconostasis. With Bardas leading the way, Bringas followed, still holding the hands of the two princes, a faint smile upon his face. It was nothing John and his comrades had expected, let alone those gathered in the church.

"Where are you going, General?" John shouted, agitated.

Bardas glanced towards him, but said nothing as he continued to walk towards the exit. Bringas, however, looked at John and said with a sly smile: "I'll give your father your best wishes when I see him!"

After the initial shock had subsided, the clamor of the people gathered inside the church began to rise. They were resentful and frustrated at having been deceived so easily. They knew they had to do something but didn't know what or how to go about it. John, encouraged by his own indignation, seized the golden opportunity. He ascended the ambo.

"Hear me, faithful men and women!" he cried to the assembled multitude. "Polyeuctus has failed us. He has failed to protect an honorable man who spent his life fighting for God and country." The whole church shook with shouts of disapproval once the name of the patriarch was mentioned. "But we shall deal with that later. Now, we have a more urgent matter at hand. We mustn't let that fox snatch our victory so cunningly!" If the name of Polyeuctus made the crowds agitated, the mention of Bringas sent them into a violent frenzy. "Stand behind your rightful emperor and great leader Nicephorus! March to the Palace and fear no man for God and his saints are on our side! March to the Palace and cleanse it of the traitors!"

Those few words were enough to turn a crowd of peaceful worshippers into an army of fierce fighters. It was clear by now that John was the leader they desperately needed. Perhaps it was his sincerity, his passion, or youthful daring looks. There was just something about him that gave magical authority to his words.

An angry crowd had gathered in the square outside the great church and their new chief was ready to lead them to the nearby palace to intimidate Bringas and his men into releasing not only Bardas but all the other prisoners, perhaps even the empress. It wasn't going to be easy, though. A crowd of noncombatants armed with sticks and stones were marching to meet the empire's elite soldiers. There was surely going to be a lot of spilt blood and everybody knew it. They also knew that if the spontaneous insurrection of theirs failed then all of them would be destined to a dark fate. Yet, the people's sense of justice, their faith and love for Nicephorus overcame their fears.

When the bells of the sixth hour began to ring, the crowd headed by John and his comrades moved against the heavily guarded palace. Several hundred Varangians and Macedonians guarded the gates motivated by loyalty and discipline, no less than by hefty pay.

The two sides stood belligerently, preparing for battle. The Varangians, headed by their giant-like chief, took their positions by the Palace walls and waited for the attackers to approach in order to unleash their fury. Everyone was charged up, anticipating the throwing of the first stone or the shooting of the first arrow. Suddenly, a familiar voice cut through the tension.

"Stop! For Christ's sake stop!"

The figure of patriarch Polyeuctus emerged from behind the soldiers guarding the Chalkis gate. He wasn't alone, beside him stood Bardas.

John looked on in amazement. *Not bad at all! Polyeuctus must have heard that we were going to come for him afterwards. The crack of a whip will make the lazy mule spring!*

The Varangians quietly made way for the supreme religious leader and his companion. The crowds raised their primitive weapons in the air and let out triumphant shouts. It was something no one had expected from the old and timid bishop, who must have estimated the grave repercussions of having the aged general denied the right of sanctuary.

"Take him home!" John ordered his newly acquired army. About a hundred men volunteered to rush the old general to the Phocas residence and keep guard around him there.

*Bardas is now secure. The first knock on Bringas's head. Now, time to go for the big prize.*

He cried passionately to his crowd. "We still don't know where our empress and caesars are!. We, the people of Constantinople, demand to be assured of their safety, don't we?"

"We do!" the crowds roared.

"So many of our brothers are locked in dungeons only a bowshot away from here for no reason other than their love and support for our brave emperor. They need to be set free, don't they?"

"They do!" the crowd roared once again.

"This is your day today! No army can stand in the face of your rightful and holy anger! Bringas's mercenaries and their leaders are trembling at the sound of your shouts. They run before you like mice! Cleanse the city of their treason and prepare it as a bride for your rightful emperor!"

*I didn't know he had such oratory skills,* Andreas thought to himself with much wonder, noticing the way everyone's eyes were fixed upon the young rebel leader.

The human deluge, swelled by more newcomers, advanced. They seemed confident of their strength, and the justness of their cause. A few yards away at the gate, the Varangians stood there waiting for them, determined to prevent anyone from taking one further step closer.

John gave his signal to the people behind him to stop and then approached the Varangian chief.

"What do you want, troublemaker?" the giant Norseman began in broken Greek

"We demand to see the empress and the royal infants. We want her to come out and show herself to us."

"Is that all? I can assure you that the royal family is perfectly safe."

"I'm going to need more than your word, barbarian. If you don't want your men to be trampled under the feet of an angry crowd, you'd better produce the empress and the caesars right now!"

The Varangian chief looked at John then at the thousands of angry men assembled behind him, thought for a moment and then said: "Wait here".

He walked back inside the Palace, and the great Chalkis gate was shut behind him. As minutes passed, the crowd grew ever more restless and some men attempted to climb the high iron fence that surrounded the Palace, only to be shot down with arrows by the guards. The whole situation teetered on the brink of explosion.

Without further delay, the empress appeared with her three children, surrounded by her maids at the Chalkis gate. The appearance of the royal family after a long period of absence thrilled the crowd. Theophano waved to her subjects with a gesture of appreciation and received from them shouts of love and support. Her eyes, sad and wet, were quick to catch sight of John at the head of the crowd. She signaled to him. He came walking towards the gate with long strides then bowed before her.

He looked at her tearful eyes and suddenly realized she was about the same age as him.

"I'm sorry I caused you all this trouble, John," she said softly.

"I'm glad I was able to help, Your Majesty."

"Nicephorus and the army are still unable to cross the straits, aren't they?"

"Yes, Your Majesty. Marianos and his troops are occupying the harbor and preventing any ships from sailing in or out."

"Then you must head to the harbor at once."

"Agreed. But I need to gather more professional troops to defeat Marianos's soldiers who surely must have fortified their positions there."

"Listen, John. This must be done quickly for something dangerous is about to happen." She sounded more serious than ever and continued in a voice close to whisper. "Bringas has seized the royal treasury and is on his way out of the city."

"Are you sure, Your Majesty?" he said, hugely disturbed.

"From my window, I saw his men carry wooden carts full of gold, more than three hundred, and stack them into carriages before they set off. If he sails to Syria or Egypt and defects to the Arabs with all this gold, may God have mercy upon us. With such riches, our enemies could buy the service of innumerable barbarian tribes, while we wouldn't be able to pay our own soldiers. No one can ever know to what ends this man's hatred could lead him, and us with him. Don't worry about me. I'm perfectly safe here. You mustn't let him leave the city, John."

She turned around and walked back inside the palace with her children, leaving John at a loss.

*An impoverished empire, enriched enemies.*

It was a dreadful idea.

# Chapter Fifty

## - 𝄃𝄃 -

Three days had passed since the four men left their leader in Chalcedon and sailed to Constantinople on their onerous mission. Ever since then, the city had been in turmoil. The man who for ten years was the mightiest in the whole empire and whose ascent up the ladder of glory had been so far unhindered, now stood helpless for the first time in his life in the face of a mortal enemy. He gazed anxiously with his commanders towards the reigning city which, though but a few miles away, looked so far out of reach.

On the morning of the fifteenth of August, the great feast of the Mother of God, the liturgy was coming to an end and Nicephorus exited the cathedral of Chalcedon and headed to the seashore where he had been spending most of his time during the past few days. His commanders awaited him inside the tent for the daily morning meeting.

Everyone stood up and bowed as he entered under the rippling roof of the open-sided pavilion.

"Any news?" he asked.

"Nothing," Maleinos answered grimly. "Only that insane letter of yesterday."

He nodded twice and said, "Let me look at it again."

It had arrived the morning before with Bringas's messenger, and read:

*To the usurper Nicephorus,*

*You have once more shown a severe, improper assessment of circumstances which only confirms what I have always believed; that your late military conquests were not the result of your intelligence and valor as much as the ignorance and cowardice of your enemies.*

*I have ordered you to send the army back east where it belongs and to come to the city and beg the forgiveness of God, of the people, and of the Regency Council which is*

239

*the only legitimate power in the land of the Romans. Instead, you have defied us and sent a pathetic band of mercenaries believing in your feeble mind that they could alter the course of events. Those whom you sent have met the painful death they deserve, their fate should teach you not to commit more gullible men to the same miserable end.*

*Your father is still my guest, though given the present deterioration of his health, it does not look like he will stay with us for much longer. I would hate that he ends his life in this manner because of your stubbornness.*

*This is my final warning to you. Heed to logic or meet my wrath.*

*With the Grace of God, Head of the Regency Council*

*Joseph Bringas*

He tossed the paper onto the table in front of him and sat down on a chair facing the sea. Constantinople's walls appeared far in the horizon.

It occurred to him that Bringas could've been bluffing but he couldn't be sure of anything. The news that John and his group had been killed brought sorrow to his heart but it also meant that his scheme to smuggle his father out of the city had failed miserably.

"Perhaps we should feign a retreat and send the army a few miles back?" Kourkouas suggested. He had followed that tactic many times in his raids against the Arabs.

"I will not submit to the wishes of that eunuch, not even in pretense!" He slammed his fist against the table.

"This is a mad man, the empress, the caesars, the General Bardas and the entire city are at his mercy," persisted the commander.

"Listen to me!" Nicephorus began, controlling his temper. "Bringas is only in such a powerful position because he's head of the Regency Council. As you all know, he can never become emperor himself, no eunuch can. If anything happens to the caesars or the empress, he will bring doom upon himself. He can't risk harming them."

"Still, he can maneuver," replied Maleinos. "He can force the empress into a monastery and become the sole guardian of the caesars, ruling in their name, can he not? Isn't this what the empress expressly dreaded in her letter? Didn't the late emperor Romanos force his five sisters into convents to secure his throne?"

"And what will he do with us, what will he do with forty thousand soldiers encamped under his sight?" Nicephorus said. "He knows there is no escape from negotiating with me."

"Yes, Your Majesty, but he also knows that we cannot stay here with forty thousand men indefinitely. Our supplies are already running out."

The new emperor nodded, his face grim, conceding that they weren't in the best situation.

"Let us wait until tomorrow and see. Perhaps you could approach the admiral of the fleet and try to convince him to join us, instead of standing here idly. Find a way to reach him! Find a way to get us and the army to the other side!" he bellowed impatiently.

The commanders looked at each other helplessly. There was nothing anyone could do and they all knew it. Nothing was on their side, least of all time.

***

The meeting was concluded around noon. Nicephorus sat alone in the shade watching the waves die on the sandy shore and ruminating on what could be taking place in the city, the ignorance of which tormented him.

Having spent the previous night in a sleepless vigil, his eyes slowly closed out of exhaustion and he dozed off in his chair.

Almost immediately, he was visited by two luminous figures. He looked to his right and saw both of them in white; a woman and a toddler holding hands and walking towards him by the shore with the shallow waves washing their bare feet. The brilliant vision brought a surge of joy to his heart. When they drew nearer to him he began to discern their faces.

"Stephano! Is that you?"

She continued to walk closer, a halo of light surrounding her as she came to stand in front of him, her fair face and black hair a contrasting image of day and night.

"I know you have missed us so we came to pay you a visit," she said in a sweet voice.

He embraced them warmly. The little boy angel smiled to his father then sat by the water and began to play on the sand. It had been so long, many years since Nicephorus's eyes beheld those two dear figures. They had appeared to him in dreams before but never looking so real, so close, so vivid.

"So much has been going on with you since we left," she said, caressing his face.

"Life's been cruel without you."

"Do you remember when we were just a young couple living together in happy obscurity?"

Her words took him back to the hills of Cappadocia where once he had a wife he loved, a son to carry his name and a humble home to shelter them.

"How could I forget those days? You still look as young. Only I grew older in your absence."

"I was never absent. I accompanied your fearless soul in traversing the empire's breadth. In Crete, in Tarsus, in Aleppo. Everywhere you went, I was there, little Bardas too." The infant, hearing his name, looked up and giggled merrily. His face was his mother's small replica.

"I wish you had stayed here, or I had come with you."

"You still have a lot to do, many big tasks to accomplish, more enemies to conquer."

"How can that be, with us stranded here, with evil men now in positions of power?" He sighed heavily.

"The things which are impossible with men are possible with God," she answered confidently.

He wrapped his arms around her, and whispered in her ear: "I've missed you so much, Stephano."

"I've missed you too, darling." She whispered back. "We shall meet again but not just yet. For now, I must free you from your oath. You have kept to your celibacy scrupulously for so many years already."

He pulled himself back, held her two shoulders firmly and looked into her eyes. "Is this what you came to tell me, that I can marry again?"

"Yes. In all these years, I've felt your love. It reached me in my resting place. But you're not a ghost. Your spirit still inhabits a bodily tabernacle. When the time comes and everything hangs in the balance, don't let my memory prevent you from doing what's right, what's honorable, what's sacred in God's eyes."

"But I will always love you."

"I know you will." She smiled softly. "We must get back now." She kissed him on the cheek then carried her son in her arms and walked back along the shore. The little boy looked from over his mother's shoulder and waved his tiny hand in farewell.

Nicephorus stood there and watched them disappear, a second time.

# Chapter Fifty-One

## - ಬಂಡಿ -

In spite of the astonishing success that Nicephorus's supporters had achieved so far, the situation was still precarious. Bringas was still active, he had the imperial treasury at his disposal as well as hundreds of fierce soldiers who would do anything for gold. His forces were in control of the harbor forbidding any vessel to sail to the stranded emperor on the other shore of the Bosphorus.

There were not enough professional men under John's command that could carry out that mission. Time was passing quickly and he couldn't make up his mind on the next step they should take. That's when an important guest paid him a visit.

At the forum of Constantine where John led the crowds, an unexpected visitor, a man all too famous, showed up with a few hundred armed men. His arrival stirred up a clamor among the militia. Nicephorus's old friend Basil Lekapenos had finally decided to intervene. He rode surrounded by his bodyguards towards the center of the large circular forum.

*Finally, he's showed up. Better late than never. Something tells me he must have realized where the winning horse is. And, it's about time he settled that old account with Bringas. What better opportunity will ever present itself for him to exterminate his enemies and earn the patronage of the new emperor at the same time?*

He reached the center of the forum, people making way for his entourage.

"The last time I saw you, you came to me asking for assistance and left my house disguised as a monk. Two days later, and here you are making the entire city dance to your tune." Basil addressed the young leader with a faint smile on his face.

"Life is anything but predictable, Your Excellency."

"Well, Nicephorus couldn't have made a better choice for an assistant, but now you must finish what you have started."

"That's what I'm trying to do. Bringas is attempting to escape with the treasury."

"I have learnt that and it is the reason why I have come here. An emperor with an empty treasury can be sure to alienate the army and the citizens against him in no time."

John nodded.

"Not to mention the horrendous thought of him defecting to the enemy with all that gold, but I don't have enough men to storm the harbor. I've received news that it has been well fortified."

"With our combined forces, that shouldn't be a problem. Take your men and move to the harbor from the eastern side. I will bring mine and come from the west and meet you there. We shall close in on Marianos and his employer."

"Alright, let's not waste any more time then."

"Here we go again," Andreas mumbled before they left the forum, confident that a bloody battle lay ahead of them.

John took the men and rushed to the harbor of Kontoskalion, making a detour to the east which passed through his own neighborhood. What's more, he was destined to pass through the very same road where his home stood. He had been trying to reach home ever since he set foot in the city three days before but there was no way he could do it.

The little army he commanded advanced through the streets of the city, racing against time. Passing by that little two-story white house made John's heart beat fast. He looked at the windows trying to see if anyone was inside but the stone walls were high and the wooden shutters closed.

He had almost reached the end of the long, narrow road. Not much separated them from the harbor. It turned out, however, that crossing those remaining few hundred yards was going to be more difficult than they had ever imagined. Out of nowhere, a detachment of Macedonian soldiers suddenly appeared, blocking their path.

"Oh Lord, not now!" John cried, eager to intercept Bringas.

The soldiers looked prepared for a fight and were aware of the advantage of their position.

*They didn't wait for us to come to them. They came to us. They want to finish us off here, or at least keep us busy until Bringas escapes.*

John knew that in such a confined space numerical superiority played little role in deciding the outcome of a fight. The soldiers with their large shields and long spears formed an impassible barrier.

"We have to retreat if we want to get to the harbor in time!" he shouted to his comrades.

But that too quickly proved impossible as another detachment of soldiers blocked their way back. John and his few hundred men realized they were trapped in the alley.

"To hell with these bastard mercenaries!" Andreas bellowed in anger.

The soldiers attacked from both ends of the road. As best they could, the rebels fought back, but with Marianos orchestrating his soldiers' maneuvers, the prospects of victory appeared slim.

Many of John's men fell helplessly under the professional strikes of the Macedonian soldiers but they were not defeated yet. Assistance came from the inhabitants of the surrounding houses who began to shower the supporters of Bringas with whatever objects they could lay their hands on.

John's men put up a brave fight and with the assistance from above, they even came close to breaking the ranks of the Macedonian soldiers.

But the Strategos Marianos couldn't stand and watch his men suffer a defeat. To tip the balance, he rushed towards John. The man who had been hardened by a hundred battles seemed determined to crush the head of the rebellion with his own hands.

In the blink of an eye, John found himself repelling violent, successive blows. The younger man tried to hold out against the older, more experienced strategos and both fought ferociously amidst the chaos that surrounded them. John was taller and his blows stronger. Killing Marianos meant his force would flee and the day would be won but should the opposite happen, then the flame of rebellion would be extinguished.

Well into his forties, Marianos showed greater endurance than John had expected. He fought with great talent and dexterity as he had done for years against the barbarians and the Bulgars on the northern frontiers of the empire, and in the end that experience paid off. A hard blow from Marianos's sword sent that of John's flying from his hand, then followed by another from his shield, leaving the leader of the insurrection lying on the ground at the feet of his adversary.

It was so furiously ironic that he who had been to the far ends of the empire and fought so many battles against foreign troops would meet his end in the same alley where he grew up, by the door of his own home, and at the hands of a roman strategos. It was as if destiny mocked him, saving him from so many deaths only to make him perish in the same spot where he had once taken his first steps. His short life looked like a complete circle, beginning and ending at the same place.

While his men strived to save their own lives, he lay on the ground helpless and watched the long blade rise up before it would settle inside his chest. He tried to say a final prayer but the incoherent images of his childhood, of Mariam, of his parents, and of bitter, bloody battles passed before his eyes in a torrent of emotions that enfolded his entire being during those last seconds of his life. He thought of the sheer darkness that would follow the descent of the blade in contrast to the glaring sun that almost blinded him. There was nothing he could do other than resign himself to his fate.

Marianos raised his sword above his head and said with overflowing contempt:

"In your juvenile mind, did you really think you could pull this off? Pay now the price of rebellion."

But before the cold blade could pierce John's helpless body, a flying object descended upon the executioner, smashing his head. He collapsed immediately to the ground and a fountain of blood came surging from a crack in his skull. In a moment, the roles were reversed.

Amid the violent chaos, with the sun in his eyes, John couldn't see where the object had come from but he looked down and saw what had hit his adversary's head sitting right next to his motionless body. It was a heavy metal platter, but not just any platter. He recognized that very same utensil as one he had eaten from countless times at home. When his mother's voice cried his name passionately from above, he saw her crying face in the window, and knew the identity of his guardian angel. He looked at her speechlessly. She had been the most peaceful person he had ever known in his life, yet there she stood like a lioness ready to devour anyone who threatened her own.

John finally recovered from the shock, jumped to his feet and picked up Marianos's sword which lay in a pool of his own blood. It only took a moment for the Macedonian soldiers to realize what had befallen their commander and abandon the fight. Some were captured and others were the object of retaliation by the gloating rebels who themselves had lost many of their comrades.

The fighting subsided but not before the narrow road had become covered with the bodies of countless combatants from both sides.

The leader of Bringas's loyal troops lay dead and the men who didn't surrender were being hunted down throughout the city.

The victorious men covered in their own blood and that of their victims stood among the piles of lifeless bodies, raised their weapons in the air and let out a series of vigorous shouts, recalling times in the distant past and displaying a crude humanity unchanged by centuries of civilization.

\*\*\*

Anastasia opened the front door and ran towards her son, behind her followed her daughter-in-law. She embraced him and wept.

"Thank you, Mother," was all his trembling lips could utter.

"They've taken Alexander too, they came last night and took him away," Zoe cried helplessly.

He took a deep breath. *I hope we're not too late.* "I must go now. We must get to the harbor and stop Bringas. After that, if we're successful, we'll head to the prison and free our men. Do say a prayer for us."

"May Christ and all his saints be with you, my son!"

John left the two women by the door and rallied his men, those who had remained alive and were able to fight, to resume their advance towards the harbor.

News suddenly arrived on the way. A few men came rushing from the harbor. Bringas's escape attempt had been thwarted by Lekapenos who had recovered the treasury. Bringas himself had taken refuge inside the sanctuary of Hagia Sophia.

The men raised their weapons in the air once more and rejoiced.

"Let that snake creep and hide behind the altar!" Andreas shouted with pleasure.

"We must change course, there's no business for us at the harbor anymore."

"Where to?"

"To the Noumera! All march!" John commanded the men.

John speculated that the Noumera, the city's main prison, had been the place where Bringas had kept his prisoners. The infamous building was adjoining the hippodrome and had always been guarded by a strong infantry contingent, but by the time they arrived, the guards had abandoned it leaving the rebels the easy task of unlocking the doors.

Dozens of prisoners were set free, soldiers, senators and even priests. Many of them appeared in terrible shape; some had bruises on their faces, some limped and others had to be carried away. The gathered crowd welcomed them as heroes who had endured a short but ruthless reign of terror. John stood by the outer gate and watched the men leave one after the other in agony until the familiar faces he had been eager to see finally emerged.

Demetrius came out supported from either side by Theodore and Alexander. Whilst the other two looked fairly well, Demetrius himself was in a miserable condition. He limped and his face was swollen almost beyond recognition. Seeing John in command of the field, he forced out a smile.

"Not bad!" Demetrius struggled to utter the few words as he gazed at the militias his friend commanded.

John did his best to conceal his shock.

*He's alive, and so is father and Alexander. This is all that matters. Everything else can be fixed, every loss can be compensated.*

He embraced his comrade and whispered to his ear.

"I told you I'd come back, didn't I?"

# Chapter Fifty-Two

- 𝒮𝒰𝒞𝒮 -

When Nicephorus woke up, it was early afternoon. Stephano had been long gone. He was alone with the sea and the sand. The guards had left him undisturbed for the most part but their faint whispers finally made his eyelids flicker. He looked at their faces and could easily discern that something out of the ordinary had happened.

"What is it? Speak up?"

"Look, Your Majesty." One of them pointed towards the sea.

For the first time since their arrival at the Asiatic shore of the Bosphorus, the men saw a vessel sailing towards them from the European side, the side where the capital stood.

Nicephorus's sight followed the lone dromon as favorable winds pushed it gently and speedily until it docked in the empty harbor.

"Go and find out what this is about," Nicephorus ordered two of his men. They ran to the nearby harbor and came back with a scroll of papyrus.

*Another letter from Bringas!*

Nicephorus couldn't take any more of this condescending correspondence. His face became clouded with anger. His eyes were as red as flames, his nostrils flared as he untied the thread to release the scroll. But when his sight fell upon the handwriting, his face suddenly softened. A smile slowly forged itself on his stern features.

*Theophano and the caesars are secure at the palace ... Bringas is seeking refuge at the sanctuary of Hagia Sophia ... Marianos is dead, his Macedonian soldiers surrendered ... father is now safe at home ... this is incredible ... they did manage to smuggle him from the palace after all!*

"Fetch me Leo!" He shouted at the guards. "Go on, run!" His eyes greedily scanned line after line of the long letter.

*Basil Lekapenos took part in this, I wouldn't have expected any less from him, his men forced Bringas to abandon the treasury and seek refuge ...Demetrius is alive ... the fleet will be dispatched tomorrow to ferry the army ...*

Nicephorus finished reading John's letter with great satisfaction, then began reading it all over again. Soon enough, Leo arrived, looking exceedingly anxious.

"Is it bad news?"

"No, dear brother," Nicephorus replied with a smile. "On the contrary." He handed him John's letter.

"Read this and rejoice!"

He waited a moment then gave orders to his brother.

"I want you to return with the ship to the capital and prepare for my arrival. I will spend one more night here."

"You'll make a great emperor, brother." Leo embraced him. "The city is eager to welcome you, as emperor this time. The son of the tailor has done a great job. He's been worthy of your confidence."

Nicephorus nodded, satisfied. "Go with God now!"

Without much delay, Leo boarded the ship and sailed back to the city.

***

Nicephorus spent the last night at Chalcedon before he received the regalia and ruled all the lands stretching from Calabria to Armenia.

After dark, he sat in the pavilion by the sea watching the flickering lights of the city and pondering on what lay ahead.

He dreaded the idea that being adorned with the most magnificent earthly crown could draw him one step further from the heavenly crown, the only crown he really desired. His life and his destiny were not going to be his own anymore. He couldn't just walk away now and retire to his monastery, spending the remainder of his life in devotional serenity. There was a whole empire awaiting him to administer. There were millions of people whose survival and wellbeing depended on him, millions of souls which he held in the hollow of his hand. The endless shores, the vast provinces and the long borders were his responsibility to keep and maintain. And above all, he had become the one man appointed by God as a ruler of humanity and steward of the Church.

But then again, when had he ever been the master of his own destiny? Had he ever been free to do what he really wanted? The necessities of war imposed themselves year after year. The administration of the empire's striking arm had been his responsibility for some time now. Was anything really going to change? Besides, monastic life was all about surrendering one's will, for the good of others, and was, therefore, also expected of the emperor. Could he be a vigorous emperor and a humble monk at the same time? Could he practice his supreme will over others yet submit his own personal will to God? So far, he had managed to be a most successful army commander, while living the austere life of an Egyptian hermit. But now, even that wasn't going to be enough anymore.

The visit of Stephano came glimmering before his eyes. It felt so real, so true. Why would his departed wife want him to marry Theophano? Did she come to confront him with his true desires which he dared not admit? Theophano was surely one of the most beautiful women he had ever seen in his life, if not the most beautiful. Would his attraction to her prove stronger than his loyalty to his wife? How could he abandon his vows of celibacy, he who has remained faithful for decades and feared the judgment of the living God?

But the vision couldn't be lightly esteemed. His wife had left her divine dwelling place and come to absolve him of his vow. God must've sent her, for she couldn't have come against His will. God Himself must be absolving him of his oath for the salvation of his soul and the safety of the empire. There could be no other explanation.

His legitimacy as emperor couldn't be validated unless he married into the royal family, he knew that very well. Certainly, no one would blame him if he did. After all, matrimony was a holy sacrament. Perhaps the monastic life should wait. Perhaps it was time he for once, pleased God, and himself.

***

With the sun shining high in the first light of morning, Constantinople, the star among cities, sent her ships to bring home her hero. Nicephorus and his commanders lined the shore and gazed in amazement at the flotilla of ships that was heading towards them.

The conglomeration of vessels was something no one had seen the like of before; dromons, merchant ships, fishing boats, horse transporters all sailed in one vast parade. Ahead of them, the royal galley could be distinguished. It was the emperor's own prestigious vessel reserved solely for the transportation of the monarch and his family. Now crossing the Bosphorus, it only meant one thing.

Quickly, the entire army flocked to the beach. It had only been a few weeks since they had clothed their idol with purple and now all that remained was to see him installed on the throne in the reigning city.

It didn't take long for the boats to reach the nearby Chalcedon, but as numerous as they were, many had to throw anchor far away from the now crowded harbor. The sailors roared with cheers and acclamations that were echoed by the army on land.

The royal galley, however, was allowed its due precedence and docked at the harbor where Nicephorus and his commanders stood. Apart from the mariners, aboard it were only a handful of men. Nicephorus could discern the faces of John, of his father Bardas, of Basil Lekapenos and a few other old friends of his aboard the ship. Once the vessel had come to a complete stop, the walkway was extended and John was the first to descend and present himself to the new emperor.

"I send you off in a rowing boat and you return with the royal galley," Nicephorus said, embracing him warmly.

"I did nothing unusual, Lord. God's help and your good name did all the work."

Conquering the capital and defeating Bringas's troops had been a major accomplishment that John's humility couldn't downplay, Nicephorus knew.

"How is Demetrius?" Nicephorus asked, looking genuinely concerned.

"His face is badly bruised, a deep cut to his leg, Emperor. But Her Majesty sent him her physicians. A few days' rest is all he needs, so they said. He'll be alright."

He nodded. "And what about your father? Is he in good health?"

"He is, thank you for asking."

Nicephorus leaned forward, his eyes fixed on John's face, leaving no doubt about the sincerity of his words. "I'll make Bringas pay for all that he has done."

Basil Lekapenos and a few other dignitaries followed suit down the walkway looking in high spirits. Acknowledging the vital assistance Basil had provided, John said:

"Your loyal friends, Your Majesty – now your loyal subjects – have proved worthy of your confidence. Without Lord Basil's help we couldn't have done much."

Basil, disciplined for decades in palace etiquette, bowed with respect before the sovereign he had helped to the throne and declared:

"The city needs its new emperor, Your Majesty!"

"And the palace its new chamberlain," was Nicephorus's grateful reply. Basil's role had been vital in the transfer of power, Nicephorus had been informed, and the most appropriate reward was to give the eunuch his old job back as chamberlain. It was hard to think of anyone more knowledgeable or more loyal for the position.

Nicephorus then ascended to the ship amid the cheering of the soldiers and mariners where his father was seated comfortably. The old man saw his son arrive with John walking behind him and opened his arms widely.

"You have safely found your way to the palace!" Bardas said proudly.

"As you have safely found yours out of it!" his son answered, embracing him and roaring with laughter. Bardas brought his mouth closer to his ear and whispered: "Without that brave bodyguard of yours, it would've been much too difficult for me to get out and for you to come in. I suppose you know that already." Nicephorus nodded expressing full agreement. "Make sure he's properly rewarded!"

Nicephorus smiled and asked. "How's Leo doing?"

"Oh, he's quite busy preparing for your victorious entry, reestablishing peace in the city and enjoying every bit of it. The best part for him, I daresay, must've been that moment when Bringas passed before us in shackles. I know it was the part *I* enjoyed most!"

"That vile creature has gotten what he deserved!"

"*Tu vincas* Nicephorus!" Bardas roared gleefully. Thousands of men responded in sea and on land alike "*Tu vincas*, Nicephorus!". More acclamations rose so loud that it wouldn't have been surprising had they been heard across the Bosphorus.

"Let's not linger here for long," said his father. "The whole city is waiting for your arrival."

With the emperor's orders, the captain of the ship began to shout his orders for departure. Nicholas, Nicephorus's faithful droungarious with whom he had sailed to and back from Crete assumed the ship's command. "Cast off the lines!" he shouted. The large white sails bellied and the hundred or so oars below provided more thrust. Little by little, the ship moved away from the quay toward the capital carrying its new master. A vast armada moved in accord with the empire's victorious army on board. To most of the soldiers, so far it had been an unforgettable summer. Its climax was yet to come with the crowning of Nicephorus in the reigning city.

For many years, the army had not had an emperor lead them into battle. Only the older commanders remembered a time when an emperor led them in person into the fray. Now the younger generation too would experience fighting under the command of one man who controlled all of the empire's resources, a man who valued them above all others. They knew their future with him was going to be full of glorious days. That particular day, however, was the inauguration of that happy era. The men, thus sailed with their emperor to his capital intending to make his day as glorious as could be.

# Chapter Fifty-Three

## - ನಿಲ್ಲ -

At the house of Theodore Sgouros, the family gathered in the middle room for their morning meal. Around the table sat Theodore after an absence of many days. Next to him was Anastasia, unusually somber and silent. Alexander was across the table, next to his wife Zoe who rested her palms on her curved belly.

Along with them sat someone considered no less than family. Demetrius's right leg was bandaged, there were brown, yellowish bruises all over his body. The suffering he had endured in those few weeks of detention in the dungeons of Bringas was all too clear, yet his face showed relief, the relief of someone who had just awakened from a nightmare realizing it was over.

"Who could have imagined one week ago that the mighty Bringas would be seeking sanctuary?" Alexander said, spreading some butter over a piece of bread.

"But sanctuary was denied him like he denied it to Bardas. Now he can have a taste of his own medicine," Theodore continued. "With what measure you measure, it shall be measured to you."

"I wasn't surprised at all when I heard he occupies one of the cells we stayed in," Demetrius said, laughing.

"Now it's up to the emperor to deal with him. What do you think will happen?" Zoe asked.

"Mark my words, Nicephorus will not execute him," Demetrius said. "I'm almost sure he will banish him to some remote monastery or island but he will not shed his blood."

"We cannot forget Bringas's role in the conquest of Crete. After all, it was he who arranged the campaign and even nominated Nicephorus to lead it." Theodore tried to be just. When everyone else spoke ill of something or someone, he usually reminded them of the overlooked good qualities. He felt bad if he didn't do that, although he knew it would cause a few eyes to roll.

"But then he got overtaken by greed and thirst for power. He was ready to fight everyone to maintain his authority, and look where it got him." Alexander took a bite of the buttered bread.

"Who knows, perhaps he had something to do with the death of the emperor. I can't bring myself to believe that his death was merely divine punishment for hunting during lent. It is just ridiculous," Demetrius said aloud what most of the city had been discussing behind closed doors.

Theodore glanced at his wife who hadn't uttered a word. He put his hand on her shoulder and caressed her gently.

"Is this how a woman who has saved her son's life and the empire is supposed to be feeling?" She gazed into space, her palms clasped around a warm cup of herbal tea. Two tears came trickling down her cheeks.

"I don't know how I got the courage to do what I did. I just saw him down there about to be murdered and ..." she finally said with trembling words.

"Any mother would've done the same, my dear. You have put an end to that carnage and saved the lives of many. Look at us now. John has gained great fame and success, Zoe is with child, I am back home and even Demetrius whose body has been trampled like an old rug in those dark dungeons looks jolly now!"

She looked at the young soldier, her son's comrade, his smile was contagious indeed.

"Not all mothers are as brave as you, trust me," he said to her kindly. "When I was nine, I fell off a tree in our garden, blood gushed from my forehead like a fountain. My mother saw me fall but instead of rushing to my help, I saw her gather her dress and run in the other direction! She couldn't bring herself to witness the bloody scene. She ran to my father who had been in the back cutting firewood. He carried me to the village healer while she stood and looked from afar, sobbing and terrorized. I'm glad you were at the window and did what you did!"

There was a knock on the door. Alexander went to open it. A few soldiers appeared on horseback.

"We have an order from his majesty the emperor to fetch Demetrius Syros," one of them said.

"The man can barely stand up, take a look at him." Theodore, who followed his son, protested in vain.

"I'll be fine, don't worry!" Demetrius settled the debate fast. It was futile to try and oppose an emperor's order.

The soldiers carried the bruised man, placed him on a horse, and left.

"The emperor's coronation is due in a short while. I wonder what he wants with Demetrius at such a time," Alexander wondered.

"Come on, let's hurry or else we will miss the Triumph." Theodore rallied the family.

***

The nearby Mese Street was overflowing with the thousands of citizens who had gathered on either side to witness the great entry of their new emperor to his capital. Banners and flags hanged along the famous avenue, drums and trumpets played non-stop and the loyal soldiers who had witnessed so many bloody days by their leader's side preceded him to the city and stood with shining armor to welcome his entrance.

"Let's stand here, Alexander. I love this spot," Zoe said to her husband, her eyes glowing with joy and her hands feeling her slightly curved belly. Alexander knew her thoughts and smiled. He remembered how four months before, she had stood in that very same spot when the relic of John the Baptist was being paraded throughout the city and begged God to grant her what she had been praying for ever since she had been united with him in holy matrimony. She later confessed how the moment her eyes met the holy relic she felt a flame burning inside her.

"If it's a boy," she said with a smile, "we shall call him John."

Her husband smiled back at her and both then looked at the jubilant parade that was taking place before them. Thousands of armed soldiers were wending their way to the sounds of drums and the cheering of the citizens. Right before noon, the city's idol finally appeared through the golden gate, the city's famous triumphal entrance in a scene that had become all too familiar by now. He wore a golden breastplate that glittered under the August sun and rode on a white steed accompanied by his loyal men. Three Triumphs had been celebrated in two years, each one surpassing its predecessor in splendor.

John who, on board the royal galley, had been appointed 'Komes' by the emperor now rode behind his master while numerous other bodyguards kept back the people who crowded close from the path of the procession. He could see many familiar faces and even heard his name being cheered amid the torrent of 'Nicephorus Emperor!'

"You have built yourself quite a reputation in the city, John!" Nicephorus said, turning his head towards him with a smile.

Next to him rode Demetrius as well, looking terribly bruised but smiling nevertheless. The emperor had ordered that he take part in the Triumph in spite of his injuries.

The people's excitement was sent soaring as Nicephorus's henchmen flung gold nomismata to them. The gold coins that rained down on the crowd still bore the image of the deceased Romanus but the people seemed to care a lot less about images than about the shiny metal.

Sack after sack were emptied in the people of Constantinople, that wa festivities. The usual scuffles soon brok nothing was serious enough as to cause t There was enough for everyone.

The procession continued until the Grea elite had assembled. Men and women of the highes filled Christendom's greatest cathedral to bursting p dismounted outside in the square, crossed himself at th Sophia and proceeded to enter with magnificence befitting th world.

From inside the edifice came the scent of rare frankincense a singing of a hundred chorists barely overshadowing the buzz of the my assembled.

By the altar stood the dignified Polyeuctus with his long white beard, dressed in his pontifical vestments and holding the golden crown in his hands. Had he not intervened in favor of Nicephorus and his father during the turbulence of the past few days, some other bishop would have been holding that crown.

At his right stood Theophano and her two little sons, gazing at the man with the golden armor walking proudly towards them. There by the altar, and before the crown was placed on his head, the eyes of the most valiant of men in Constantinople met with those of the most beautiful of women. The patriarch, innocent as a dove but prudent as a serpent, could well discern the kind of look he saw. A month later, he would join the two in holy matrimony.

The crown was placed and the edifice shook with shouts of jubilation and thanksgiving. The crowning of the devout and strong emperor in the minds of so many was no less than a foreshadowing to the millennial reign of Christ. Everyone could have sworn that many years of prosperity were ahead of them, that peace had permanently resided in their midst, but as the history of mankind has proven time and again; nothing lasts forever, neither curse nor bliss.

hat fashion over the thrilled crowds. To
s their favorite part of the coronation
out in struggle for the coins but
e intervention of the soldiers.

Church where the city's
r ranks of society had
oint. Nicephorus
e gate of Hagia
e ruler of the
d the
ad

ohn glanced at the river
hed. An imposing stone
e waterway.

well, it's — have been a dry one. But what do I know? I spent most of it in an underground dungeon deprived of sun and air," Demetrius recalled, somewhat sarcastically.

John rolled his eyes.

"Here we go again. Is this — what? — the fifth time you bring up your incarceration today?"

Demetrius let out a roaring laugh.

"This is going to be a long trip to Caesarea!" John shook his head in frustration.

"You should see your face when I mention it. It carries more guilt than that of St. Peter after he denied Christ!"

"I'm glad I can somehow bring joy to the heart of a badly bruised man."

"Alright, alright! I quit. I promise." He chuckled. "At any rate, a few more days and you'll get rid of me permanently." Demetrius's chin dipped; his smile suddenly left his face. Now, their comradeship was only days short of ending. There would be no more surprises, no more diversions from the plan, no more obstacles preventing his return to his village, his parents, wife and newborn child.

The slow trot of their mounts sounded different when their hooves began to clop on the bridge's cobblestones. Keeping some distance behind them was a regiment of a hundred cataphracts. Their commander, the 'Komes' John, was leading them back from Constantinople to Caesarea in adherence to direct imperial orders. The grateful emperor was quick to reward his most loyal bodyguard with a prestigious position and an appropriate salary to go with it.

The two dismounted at the center of the bridge. John beckoned and two men rushed over. They led the two horses of the komes and his companion down to the river to be watered where a hundred others already lined the bank, their necks bent down, quenching their thirst.

The sudden appearance of so many men and animals didn't seem to startle the tall pink birds with their arched necks and large beaks. They merely moved a little upstream or flew to the other bank and quickly resumed their diligent scouring of the shallow waters for food.

The two men leaned on the bridge's stone parapet and gazed down at the water passing underneath them.

"You thought you'd be home in time for your child's birth." John glanced at his friend whose face still bore marks of the beating he had endured.

"True, but then again I'm lucky to have come back at all." He sounded serious. Though he often heard him joke about it, John sensed firsthand how that ordeal and the cruel torture had impacted upon his friend.

"At least you'll be home for the vine harvest."

"Right, but with this bandaged leg, at least a month will have to pass before I can be of any use at the farm."

"Don't tell me you're going to earn your bread with the sweat of your brow." John's eyes narrowed. "Why, you're a wealthy landowner now. You've got enough gold to hire all the working hands you need. You'll just sit like a lord and boss them around."

"Do you honestly think that'll make me happy? Granted, I'll have to hire enough men to work the big farm. My beautiful Eleni will not have to lift a finger anymore. But nothing gives *me* more pleasure than to dig the rich brown earth with my own hands, to trim the branches of my trees, then to sit under the shades of one after hours of hard work." His expression was that of a man talking not about his trees but about his children.

John looked at him, a faint smile on his face.

"I've never seen you as a farmer. I try to imagine you digging the earth or pruning a tree but all I can visualize is you wielding a sword and dashing through enemy lines."

Demetrius smiled. He pondered for a moment.

"Do you see those big pinkish birds, the phoinikopteres?" His eyes glinted.

"I've never understood why they stand on one leg," John wondered.

"Do you know their color is white when they hatch?"

"Seriously?" It was hard to imagine that those flame-colored feathers could at any point be white.

"Absolutely. They turn reddish because of what they eat and where they live. Once, our parish priest found an injured bird in the church yard. It had blood-red feathers. I must've been nine or ten back then. The pacifist priest felt sorry for the poor creature, put it in a big empty cage which once hosted turkeys, and gave it the same food to eat. A month later, the bird had turned as white as snow. We children could not believe it."

John raised a brow. "A white-born farmer turned into a red soldier," he muttered.

"The blood of the battles turned me red. The earth will turn me white again." He sounded so confident, so full of hope.

"I will probably stay red all my life." John smiled. He had already discovered his passion. Being a soldier was the only thing he ever wanted to do, and right then he felt the joy of being able to live it to the full.

"You were born red. You just didn't know it," came from the person who had shared with him his entire military career so far.

John marveled at the beautiful birds which he rarely saw beyond their home-river, then looked down at his reflection in the water. His hair had grown longer, his blond beard had become thick. Gone was that boyish look which he had possessed when he first joined the military. He was by now a 'Komes', a regiment commander, and he looked like one. He had been given the command of a hundred cavalry and entrusted with guarding the borders south of Caesarea from any future Arab raids, a challenging post, one to his liking.

Mayhem had ceased in Constantinople with the accession of the new powerful emperor. The hostilities had ended with the downfall of Bringas and his henchmen. Life was back to normal in the capital of the Romans, and John's head turned east and west for the next adventure. His heart, however, had been fixed to the east. He picked the new post there favoring it over another in the capital without hesitation.

In his saddlebag, he had a copy of Nicephorus's book *On Skirmishes*. He could very possibly have been the first officer who carried with him that treatise to the front. With its beautiful leather cover, neat letters and colorful illustrations – the work of the Studite monks of Constantinople – it contained the military experience of the Phocads: Nicephorus, Leo and their father Bardas. Decades of warfare tactics against the empire's southern enemies had been put on paper for the army's benefit. Nicephorus had summoned John to the throne room and given him the book personally before dispatching him east.

Leaving the emperor behind him, he knew it wasn't going to be long until Nicephorus followed him. True, the domestic had inherited the palace and married the gorgeous Theophano, but his passions could hardly be satisfied at the capital, of that John was almost certain. To him the saddle was a thousand times more comfortable than the throne. Sooner or later, the warrior emperor would find his way to the front. Not only he but the entire army awaited the time when Nicephorus would lead them into enemy territory, as emperor, from now on.

"It's not only you who's going back home." John all of a sudden swung his gaze towards Demetrius. "Our friend Bringas is on his way home as well." He smirked.

" Huh! Being locked up in a fort inside the jungles of Paphlagonia isn't exactly my idea of home."

"He was born and raised in those parts, wasn't he?"

"As if that means anything." Demetrius exclaimed. "When he was put on that ship that took him to his exile, I was told he had the empty stare of a man who'd been sentenced to death. Not that I feel sorry for the monster."

"After being the most powerful man in the Palace, being humbled like that must be causing haughty Joseph excruciating pain indeed." John said.

"This is probably why Nicephorus spared his life. This way, he makes sure his enemy suffers more alive than dead."

"And the merciful emperor doesn't get to dirty his hands with his blood. Quite clever of him."

"It must be a living hell, even for a heartless beast like him, for what is hell other than being deprived of the only thing one desires?" John's words came slow, uttered almost absentmindedly, as if talking to himself and gazing at the snaking river and the green hills that encompassed it. A fresh afternoon breeze made the tree leaves rustle, and he took a deep breath.

Guarding a segment of the borders from the Arabs wasn't the only mission he had on his mind. There was a far more serious mission that occupied his thinking and required his full dedication, one whose successful accomplishment meant the world to him.

Ever since he set out for Caesarea, it had been almost impossible not to think about Mariam every hour of the day. Everything he saw around him reminded him of her; the pure whiteness of a fluffy cloud, the sweet scent of a flower, the laughter of a child, but now, the Halys reminded him of her the most of all. Just a few months earlier, it flowed vigorously, its waves crashing against the banks, swelled by spring downpours and molten snow rushing in through a hundred tributaries. Now flowing peacefully, its waters conjured up the silent tears she generously shed that evening on his chest. If people could be rivers, Mariam certainly was the Halys.

He would often remember that evening and sweetness would surge in his heart, but he wasn't going to fool himself. He would immediately stop himself from prematurely rushing into an imaginary blissful world. He thought of the thorny path that led to Mariam's heart, a path that could very much turn out to be a maze of uncertainty and peril. But that wasn't going to deter him from trying.

When in ancient times King Croesus crossed that very same river John was crossing, it meant war with the Persians, a war that eventually cost him his reign and later on his life. John, who had heard that story among many others from his childhood tutor, must have felt not much different than the bold king when he had crossed into Cappadocia fifteen centuries before. A strange mixture of glee, pride, determination and uncertainty filled him as he drew nearer to the place where he had experienced all those feelings as he had never before.

He was leading his force to Caesarea of Cappadocia, to a borderland province where the mountains of Anatolia met the plains of Syria, where one empire touched another, where war looked peace in the eye. All what Caesarea represented to the empire, it represented for him too on a personal level. He was heading there, mustering his personal strength to overcome the challenge. He was placing himself on the borders of love and hatred, of happiness and sorrow, of peace and war. Yet, he wasn't going to stand by and watch. He was going to throw himself right in the middle of the fight. He had learnt firsthand from years at the front that to make peace, you sometimes have to make war first.

John made his way once more to the borderland. He who had been found worthy to survive the fiercest of battles was determined to fight this one till the end.

# Chapter Fifty-Five

- ℬↃↅↈ -

Mariam came down the narrow flight of stairs that led to the street below. A jasmine shrub planted in an adjacent pot filled the air with a captivating scent. She gave a surveying look to her new neighborhood, the clusters of stone houses, two or three stories at most, tightly packed together and penetrated by a mosaic of narrow twisting cobblestone roads. Few plants of vivid colors in earthenware pots scattered on the windows and stair tops stood in beautiful contrast against the white stony background.

Ever since she and her family settled in Caesarea, her new life had, to some degree, taken her away from the calamities of the previous winter. Their new neighbors were extremely kind. The ladies of the neighborhood often visited them to see how they were doing, offering advice about everyday needs, good shops with reasonable prices and more. Which also helped improve Mariam's Greek considerably.

Yet, behind the comely appearance of neighborliness, some of these women had an ulterior motive, as people often do. Few of them had young unmarried sons who had their eyes set on the beautiful newcomer. One after another, the mothers expressed their wish to have Mariam for a daughter-in-law and one after another, their proposals were turned down by her.

"Do you want to become a spinster?" Salma would reproach her, concerned as ever, to no avail.

No one could understand her rejection of each and every suiter, not even she herself. And when a young Arab fellow proposed to her, one whom she'd known since their days in Aleppo, and she turned him down, that's when she had no more justifications to give, no pretext to explain her refusal.

"I'm not ready to get married, not yet," was her only answer, something which troubled her father. He began to think that his daughter might have been damaged irreversibly by the horrendous incidents of war.

But Salma had other thoughts, thoughts that only an experienced woman's mind could generate. "You're waiting for John, you just don't want to admit it," she had once whispered to her as the two sat kneading dough. But Mariam dismissed the thought as nonsense and then her fists punched through the dough with remarkable vigor. When she glanced at her sister-in-law, she saw her biting her lower lip to prevent herself from smiling. The puzzle had been solved.

But how could Salma's allegation be anything but nonsense, she thought. Having been confronted with that idea by someone else other than her own self made her consider them more seriously, though. Salma's words sank deeper and deeper inside her with every day that passed.

Lately, she had started thinking a lot about John, not that she had stopped thinking about him ever since the time she had been his nursemaid. But his memory had recently become more persistent, more pleasing too, and she was becoming less reserved about it. They had had the chance to meet only once the previous summer, but it was a meeting that changed everything.

She had first met the handsome Roman soldier when her world lay in ruins. He and his comrades had been responsible for all that misery, she believed. But was he really? And even if he was, was it unforgivable? She had felt a compelling attraction to John, ever since the touch of him in that tent outside Aleppo made her shiver. But she fought her feelings and even refused to acknowledge them, until she saw him again after her life had settled a little in Caesarea.

What was it exactly that she felt that evening on the terrace under the starry sky? The memory of John wrapping her in his protection, the side of her face pressed against his warm chest felt sweet. She could remember her heart beat fast, a flash of heat taking over her entire body.

She'd never felt that way before, not even with the man she'd been supposed to marry, had their world not been torn apart.

Her late fiancé, Gergis, was a good man, and from a wealthy family too. But never once, in all the times they'd been together had she felt the same way as she did that evening when John touched her. However, back then, there was still too much hatred in her heart, too much resentment. That wall of hostility which had secluded her heart had been slowly crumbling during the past months. She was finally coming to accept her new life, her new home. And as her despair melted away, her desire to see John again grew more and more. Perhaps Salma had been right after all, she began to think.

John had told her he would come back in the spring, and he did. But by then, the emperor had died and everything had turned upside down, especially for John who found himself in the eye of the storm. Later on, the news of what happened far away in Constantinople was spreading throughout the empire, albeit with different versions. What all the stories conceded to, however, was that a bodyguard of Nicephorus, a young officer by the name of John had led the population of the capital in a successful rebellion against the chamberlain while the acclaimed emperor and his army watched as victory was being made from the other side of the Bosphorus. She had been quite sure as to the identity of that "John", but she did have doubts about him returning to Caesarea, having risen to prominence in the capital so astonishingly. After all, what officer would want to serve in a remote province when he could wallow in the luxuries of the Palace? Perhaps she would never see him again.

She walked down the narrow, almost empty road that led to her father's shop, surrounded on both sides by an unbroken line of the white stone houses. Between her hands, she carried a small, well wrapped package.

*I'm sure he's going to enjoy the food. Falafel is one of his favorites.*

The dish the Arab refugees had brought with them had also become the favorite food of the neighborhood as well. The smell of the ground and spiced chickpea balls, deep fried in olive oil often encouraged one or two neighbors to call around, bringing with them their own dishes to a shared meal. Today, she managed to save a few pieces for her father, left Salma with the women having their after-dinner mint tea and set off for the goldsmith's shop.

The crisp autumn air caressed her face. She looked up and there were hundreds of migrant birds gliding high in the sky, almost effortlessly.

*They are flying south ... to Syria.* She blew them a kiss. *Take this with you.*

She stood still and gazed up as the flock passed over her, wishing she had wings. She didn't want to think what her home country looked like now. The last glance she taken of Aleppo had been of a heap of ruins.

*I should better get going before the falafels get cold.*

She looked down again attempting to go on her way only to see John standing a few feet away, staring at her intently, a wide grin on his face. She was so startled she jerked back a little. Her heart started racing.

He looked so handsome, wearing a new military costume that fit him like a glove, his gaze reaching deep inside her soul.

"Hello, Mariam. How have you been?" he asked softly as he walked towards her.

"Good." She nodded then took a deep breath. Butterflies fluttered inside her stomach. "When did you arrive?"

"Just now. I left the men at the camp and came straight to see you.

265

I've missed you," he said to her and touched the back of her hand. Chills cascaded inside her.

*What would it feel like to be in his arms again?*

But it wasn't dark and they weren't on some secluded terrace. Instead, they were in the middle of the street and in broad daylight, albeit with too few by-passers. She hadn't expected to see him then and there, and once the initial surprise had subsided, it was replaced by a pleasant feeling of happiness.

She heard herself say: "I've missed you too, John," then sucked in a deep breath, not quite believing what she had just uttered. So strong were the emotions rushing inside her that she couldn't keep them restrained.

His eyes glinted.

"Really?" He sought her confirmation to the words he just heard in disbelief. But her expression repeated her words more clearly.

"More than you could imagine, more than I ever imagined."

John stood there, clearly overwhelmed with joy, his grin got even wider, but somehow he managed to regain his senses. "We're in the middle of the street. Let's go somewhere where we can talk."

"I'm going to father's shop to bring him lunch." A beautiful smile finally blossomed on her face. "Come along. He'll be happy to see you."

***

He walked beside her the remaining few hundred feet to the shop, as if walking on air, glancing at her, his heart beating fast.

*Even my wildest dreams didn't come close to this.* The person who at the same time had been the most invincible walled city he had ever encountered was finally lifting up her gates and allowing him his own triumphal procession into her heart. How miraculously and dramatically she had had such a change of heart, he had no idea, but it was real and he couldn't have been happier about anything else in the world.

A moment later they were stepping inside the goldsmith's shop. Jabra had been working on some jewelry. He raised his head and saw two faces shining with joy. Seeing John in his shop had been enough of a surprise yet even that grew small beside seeing genuine happiness on Mariam's face. It had been a long time since he had seen his daughter smile heartily.

She looked at her father as she put the lunch package on his table and said with the same beautiful smile.

"John's come back, father."

He smiled back, tears gathering in his eyes.

"It's you who has come back, my dear. I've missed you, the sweet you. I thought you'd never come back. You're welcome home, Mariam, and you too, John," then advanced to embrace the person who had brought such joy with him.

Her father's tears and his words made tears quickly spring and fall on her cheeks.

John extended a hand and softly rubbed away her tears.

"No more crying for you, my darling. From now on, you'll only shed happy tears. I will be beside you to make sure of that."

# ABOUT THE AUTHOR

Although Basheer has worked for the past fifteen years as a civil engineer, his life experience, literary and historical inclinations have inspired him to write this novel. He was born and raised in Bethlehem, a town that belongs to a region with a rich past, a turbulent present, and an uncertain future. He has seen firsthand what it is like to live on a disputed territory, and to grow up as a member of a minority. His ethnic, religious, national and linguistic affiliations have placed him on the crossroads of cultures and civilizations. For the past ten years, he has been living with his wife Amira and three children in Greece, something which has enriched and completed his knowledge cycle of this novel's background.